THE SHANGHAI TUNNEL

THE SHANGHAI TUNNEL

SHARAN NEWMAN

A TOM DOHERTY ASSOCIATES BOOK
NEW YORK

This is a work of fiction. All of the characters, organizations, and events portrayed in this novel are either products of the author's imagination or are used fictitiously.

THE SHANGHAI TUNNEL

Copyright © 2008 by Sharan Newman

Quotes from the T. L. Eliot Papers, the diary of Ned Chambreau, and the Simeon Reed Papers courtesy of Special Collections & Archives, The Eric V. Hauser Memorial Library, Reed College.

Map art by David Cain
Map template courtesy of the Portland, Oregon, City Archives.

Book design by Spring Hoteling

A Forge Book
Published by Tom Doherty Associates, LLC
175 Fifth Avenue
New York, NY 10010

www.tor-forge.com

Forge® is a registered trademark of Tom Doherty Associates, LLC.

Library of Congress Cataloging-in-Publication Data

Newman, Sharan.
    The Shanghai Tunnel / Sharan Newman. — 1st hardcover ed.
      p. cm.
    "A Tom Doherty Associates Book."
    ISBN-13: 978-0-7653-1300-3
    ISBN-10: 0-7653-1300-6
  1. Portland (Or.)—Fiction.   I. Title.
    PS3564.E926S53 2008
    813'.54—dc22

                        2007038741

First Edition: February 2008

Printed in the United States of America

0 9 8 7 6 5 4 3 2 1

For Steve and Lucy, my second-favorite couple

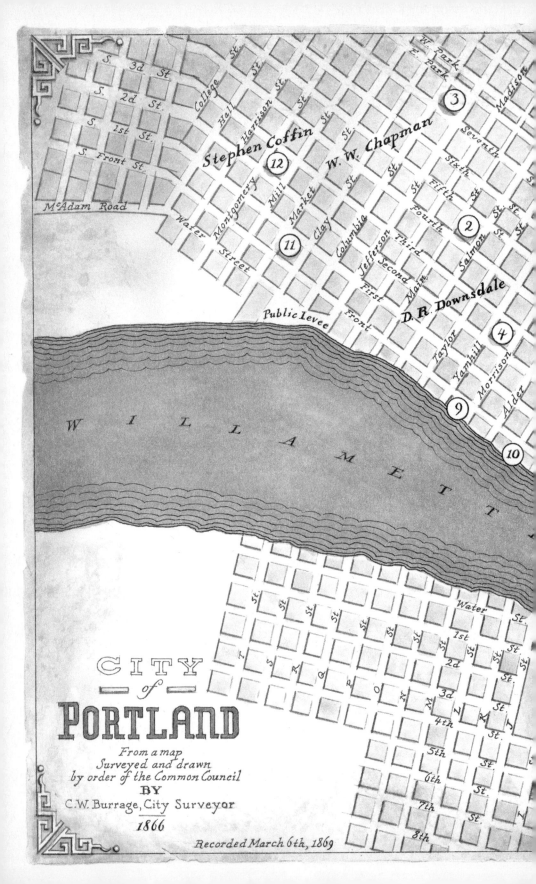

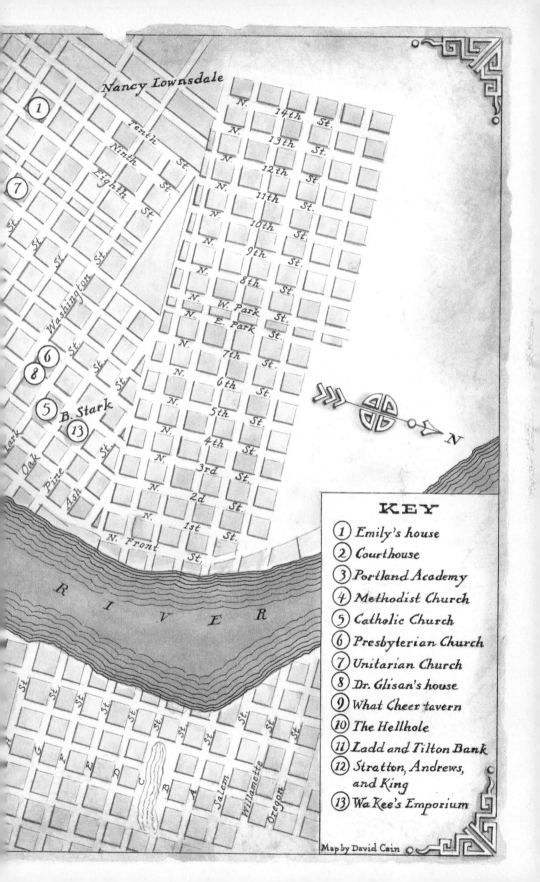

Nancy Lownsdale

N. 14th St.
N. 13th St.
N. 12th St.
N. 11th St.
N. 10th St.
N. 9th St.
N. 8th St.
N. W. Park St.
N. E. Park St.
N. 7th St.
N. 6th St.
N. 5th St.
N. 4th St.
N. 3rd St.
N. 2d St.
N. 1st St.
N. Front St.

Tenth St.
Ninth St.
Eighth St.
Washington St.
B. Stark
Stark
Oak
Pine
Ash

R I V E R

St.
G
E
D
C
B
A
Salem
Willamette
Oregon

N

KEY

① Emily's house
② Courthouse
③ Portland Academy
④ Methodist Church
⑤ Catholic Church
⑥ Presbyterian Church
⑦ Unitarian Church
⑧ Dr. Glisan's house
⑨ What Cheer tavern
⑩ The Hellhole
⑪ Ladd and Tilton Bank
⑫ Stratton, Andrews, and King
⑬ Wa Kee's Emporium

Map by David Cain

ACKNOWLEDGMENTS

Although Portland is my hometown, its history was a discovery for me. Many people helped in my explorations. Mistakes, of course, I made all on my own.

Lori Shea Kuechler, Executive Director, Portland Police Museum, for letting me look at early police reports.

Harry Stein, Portland historian *par excellence,* for advice on where to find information.

Dr. Joanne Wakeland, for giving me some transliterations of Mandarin Chinese.

Gay Walker and Mark Kuestner of Reed College Special Collections, for letting me camp out in their work space and rifle through the letters and diaries of the early citizens of Portland.

Miriam Yoshioka of Northwest Natural Gas Company, for sending me information on the early gasworks.

All the helpful staff at the Portland City Archives.

And Jon Biemer, Christine Drier, Carl Hay, Linda Neale, and Jude Siegel, for reading early chapters and making great suggestions for improvements.

The Shanghai Tunnel

PROLOGUE

PORTLAND, OREGON, NOVEMBER 1867

The second street saloon was full that evening. A boatload of prospectors had just landed, coming downriver from the Idaho mines. Most had found nothing; the mines were about played out. But that was all the more reason to pour raw whiskey down their throats and search their pockets for enough change to have some feminine company.

Alex Peterson had spent six months digging and panning and had only found enough gold dust to buy his passage this far. He told himself that tomorrow he'd see if anyone needed a day laborer. Maybe he could make enough to get another stake and head up north to try his luck in the British Columbia gold fields. He knew that somewhere there was a vein that would make him rich.

"Hey, Ned!" he called to the barkeep. "Fill it again, will ya?"

He lurched through the press of humanity to the bar, his glass held high to catch Ned's attention.

Alex swayed as the barman refilled his drink. He blinked several times, trying to focus on which of the three he saw was the real glass. Ned poured the whiskey to the rim.

"You'd best sit over there," he told Alex. "You don't want it all spilled before you can take a swallow."

He pointed to a small table in one corner. A woman was seated at it. In the light of the oil lamps, she might almost be young, almost be pretty. She smiled at Alex and held out her hand to guide him over.

"I've been saving this seat all night, just for you," she said when he'd made his way to her. "Just sit down and enjoy your drink. Maybe afterwards, we could go somewhere quieter and get acquainted."

"I'd sure like that, ma'am." Alex gulped half the glass. "I haven't been in spitting distance of a woman in the past six months."

The woman smiled, repressing a shudder. "How sweet. No, don't get up now. You can finish first. There's no hurry. We've got all night."

"Mmmmm," Alex answered. He managed to get his hand around the glass on the second try and most of the liquid down his throat. The rest dribbled down his beard until it puddled on the table. He studied it a moment, considering whether to lick it up. He'd paid for it, hadn't he? It'd be a shame to waste.

Alex lowered his head to the table and missed. He landed on the floor, sliding off the chair. The woman grabbed it as he toppled so that it remained upright. She moved it slightly away from him. After nudging Alex with her toe a few times with no response, she caught Ned's attention and nodded. The barman reached under the counter as if going for another bottle. He pulled a lever.

A trap door opened in the floor. Alex dropped through without making a sound. A moment later, the woman was again sitting alone.

Chapter One

❧

[In San Francisco] the men seem of a higher quality than the women. . . . Nor is this inconsistent with reason; the men, dealing with great practical necessities and duties, are less harmed, on the whole, by the dominant materialism of life here than the women, whose pressing responsibilities are lower and fewer; . . . Extravagance is lamented as a common weakness among them. . . . Their point lace is deeper, their moiré antique stiffer, their skirts a trifle longer, their corsage an inch lower, their diamonds more brilliant, . . . than the cosmopolite is likely to find elsewhere.

—Samuel Bowles, *The New West*

San Francisco, Friday, January 10, 1868

The stench of embalming fluid rose from the open coffin and struck Emily with the force of a tidal wave. She put a scented handkerchief to her nose and pushed her tongue against the roof of her mouth to keep from gagging.

"Really, Mrs. Stratton," Mr. Phipps was at her side in a moment. "It wasn't at all necessary for you to do this. It's better if you could remember your husband as he was."

"I had to see him," Emily said through the handkerchief. "I had to be sure."

Phipps averted his eyes from the corpse. The embalmers hadn't got to it soon enough.

"There was no need," he repeated. "Can we please shut that now?"

Emily nodded. The poor man seemed on the edge of hysteria. One would think he'd never looked on death before. Emily did feel ill, but for a different reason. The man in the coffin was certainly Horace, her husband for the past eighteen years.

The lid slammed down. Phipps exhaled gratefully.

"There was never any doubt that it was Captain Stratton," he told Emily with reproach. "I identified him myself and there were many at the hotel who knew him. You should have spared yourself this ordeal."

"I'm sorry, Mr. Phipps," Emily said. "If I hadn't seen him, there would always have been a doubt in my mind. Some part of me would have refused to believe he was gone and continued to expect him to return."

Phipps nodded in sympathy. "I understand. At least he wasn't lost at sea. Then you might have continued to hope forever."

Hope? Emily almost laughed. *Dread* was the word she would have used. The thud of the coffin lid over Horace's body was like a bell of freedom. She hadn't realized until that moment how much she feared the possibility that his death had been a ruse.

Now he could never hurt anyone again.

The feeling was followed by a sense of shame. Whatever else Horace had done, he had provided for her and their son. Perhaps she had been the one who had failed. Her husband had believed that the young daughter of an unworldly missionary could be dutifully trained to suit his requirements. Emily knew she hadn't lived up to expectations.

Emily sighed as she turned away from the coffin. Now neither of them would have the chance to change.

Phipps took her arm and led her out of the funeral parlor. He wished the woman hadn't been so insistent on seeing her husband's remains. But it was hard to reason with a grief-stricken widow. Inwardly, he shook his head in amazement that any woman could have been so blind as not to have known the kind of man Horace Stratton was. But perhaps the merchant had behaved differently during his brief stays at his home in Shanghai. Many men showed one face to their families and another to the world.

It didn't occur to him that the private face might be worse.

Emily returned to her hotel room. She left Mr. Phipps in the lobby after assuring him that she would dine at the hotel. He didn't press his invitation to join him and his wife at their home.

"Of course you need time to recover from all this." He patted her hand. "To have come all the way from China and then have Captain Stratton die so suddenly while you were visiting in Monterey, you must feel devastated. Please feel free to call upon me at any time if I can assist you."

Emily climbed the thickly carpeted stairs of the elegant hotel. Crystal chandeliers on each level glittered against mirrors, making the hallways seem infinite. The gaslight flickered in such a way that each reflection was slightly distorted, as if a hundred different faces looked back at her. She wondered if any of them were real.

In her room she was greeted by her maid, Mary Kate Kyne. Mary Kate was newly hired. Horace had insisted that his wife not bring any of the Chinese servants from Shanghai. He had been determined to make her adapt as quickly as possible to their new life in America. But at least it had been Emily and not Horace who had chosen the young Irishwoman, almost as new to the country as she. Mary Kate had been a chambermaid at the hotel in Monterey, where Horace had left Emily while he went up to San Francisco. She had proved so helpful and level-headed when word had come of his death that Emily had decided to take her on.

"There is no doubt," she told Mary Kate, as the maid helped her off with boots and coat. "My husband is dead. Mr. Phipps assures me that I am now a wealthy widow."

"Well, that's something to be grateful for, isn't it?" Mary Kate's deep blue eyes showed her concern.

"It is," Emily admitted. "My son shall want for nothing." Her voice trembled. "My poor Robert! How can I tell him that his father has died? If only the ship would arrive. I can't bear the fear that something might happen to him, too."

Mary Kate made soothing noises. "It should only be a few more days before the lad is here with you. Didn't you say he was taking the train across Panama instead of going all the way around South America like I did? Why, that journey should be nothing to a boy who's traveled from China to Boston for his schooling."

Emily smiled sadly. "I have no doubt that he's enjoying the journey mightily. Robert always did love adventure. It seems odd that my husband was so insistent on our son studying law. You'd think he'd want Robert to become a merchant captain as he was."

Mary Kate had quickly become used to her mistress speculating aloud and knew that she wasn't required to comment. She took a clothes brush and began smoothing Emily's crumpled wool skirt.

"Will you be taking Captain Stratton's coffin up to Oregon?" she asked instead. Emily had said nothing of her plans. Mary Kate fretted that they might not include her, especially if Mrs. Stratton decided to return to China.

Emily nodded. "His sister telegraphed that she wanted him buried in the family plot. I replied that we would come as soon as Robert had some time to recover from the shock of such news on top of his long journey."

She was quiet a moment, allowing the soft sound of the brush to calm her jangled nerves.

"Mr. Phipps seems to think that I should return to Shanghai," she said at last, "but Horace wanted us to live in his old home in Portland. Even though it will be strange to me, I think that's what we should do. There is nothing for me to return to. The house we lived in is let, the furniture all in boxes here at the wharf. I have no family there since my parents passed away."

She closed her eyes as unwanted memories rushed in. She resolutely pushed them back, took a deep breath, and concentrated on the problems of the present. As Mr. Longfellow said, she would "let the dead past bury its dead." It was enough to cope with the living.

But how was she to cope? Emily was truly grateful that she could live comfortably. She knew that she had no skills with which to support herself. In Shanghai the servants had been horrified at the idea that she should do anything but give orders and attend social functions.

She hadn't been very good at that, either.

Suddenly she was the master of her fate. It terrified her.

The next morning Mr. Phipps arrived at the hotel immediately after breakfast. He was armed with a portmanteau stuffed with documents for her to sign.

"What is all this?" Emily looked up at him in bewilderment.

"Nothing for you to worry about," he smiled. "Just business papers, things to do with the estate. Unfortunately, Captain Stratton didn't leave his affairs in the best of order. There was a will, of course. It leaves everything to you as guardian for your son, with provisions for your support once he comes of age. It will be formally read when you reach Portland. But there are a number of matters that can't wait. If you'll just sign these, I can take care of everything."

He smiled again. Perhaps it was the light, but Emily had the oddest impression that his canine teeth were longer and sharper than normal.

"Thank you," she said.

He gestured for her to sit at the writing desk.

Emily remained in her chair by the window.

"I know very little about my husband's business," she explained. "But I think it's time I learned. Please leave everything with me for now. I'll read it all and ask you if there's anything I don't understand."

"But . . . but, Mrs. Stratton," he sputtered. "It will take you days to go through all of this. Many of these matters require immediate attention."

"I see." Emily walked over to the desk and leafed through the pile. "In that case, perhaps you could put the most pressing business on top."

Phipps was both amazed and infuriated that such a small woman could be so adamant. First the ghoulish need to see the body, now her stubborn unwillingness to leave financial affairs in his hands.

He wondered if she was as ignorant about Horace's business as she pretended. What if Emily Stratton had even helped in some of the more unsavory aspects of the import trade? Her parents may have been missionaries, but that didn't mean their daughter was a holy innocent.

Grudgingly, Phipps relented and agreed to leave the papers for Emily to study. He was glad that she would soon be the problem of the surviving partners in the captain's firm up in Portland.

———————

Emily spent the evening going through the stack of paperwork, stopping now and then to take a bite from the tray of sandwiches that the hotel had sent up. At first the documents seemed tediously straightforward, one lading bill after another, lists of shipments of tea, spices, porcelain, silk, opium, all the things that made the dangerous Pacific crossing worthwhile.

But as she laid the papers out in neat piles, trying to arrange them by date instead of subject, Emily began to realize that the figures didn't match. How could more have been delivered than had been put on the ship in the first place? She ruffled through the papers, hunting for a second lading bill. Perhaps Horace had added a consignment of fruit and sugar in the Sandwich Islands.

Emily rubbed her eyes and began again. She would not own that Mr. Phipps had been right about her ability to understand business. She would simply have to learn. It was either that or continue to allow her life to be controlled by others.

No. Never again.

With cold fingers, she picked up her abacus and tried to make the sums come out.

As she felt the familiar click of the beads sliding across the metal rods, Emily's mind wandered back to her childhood. She had learned to do sums on an abacus. The Chinese children in the classroom had laughed at her at first, but soon they forgot she was a foreign devil and made her one of their own. Her parents had wanted her to understand Chinese ways so that she could one day preach the Gospel to the natives in terms they understood. What they had not realized was that their Methodist daughter was being converted herself.

Although marriage to Horace had meant moving away from the poorer quarter where the missionaries worked into the world of European traders and soldiers, Emily had still felt that, however bad it was, she knew the rules of the world she lived in.

Then her parents had been killed in Nanking, and Shanghai itself had come under siege from the Taiping revolutionaries. Horace had been at sea at the time, and she and Robert had faced the terror without him. Somehow, they had survived, although the horrors she had witnessed would be with Emily forever.

The events in Shanghai had convinced Horace that, as soon as the Civil War in America ended, Robert should return there with him to attend a preparatory academy in Boston. Two years later he had unexpectedly decided to move the family back to America and settle in his hometown of Portland, Oregon. There he planned on living well and impressing his friends with the wealth he had amassed in the Far East. He even spoke of entering politics.

Emily had not been consulted about any of this. She had been told to pack their things. A month later, they were at sea. Horace had arranged everything. Her only duty was to obey. Then he had died, leaving her to cope on her own.

Mr. Phipps had made it clear that Horace had expected her to continue to obey, to be a secluded widow, in mourning the rest of her life. What else was she good for?

Emily didn't know, but she was determined to find out.

San Francisco was as alien to her as the moon. Portland might have been the land of Cockaigne for all she knew of it. How was she to navigate in this strange world? The only ray of hope was in knowing that Robert would be with her soon. Emily was resolved to be strong for him, to prove that she could care for them both. More than anything, she wanted to keep Robert from the influence of the sort of men that Horace had associated with. The only way to do that was to deal with them herself.

She gave a sharp breath of frustration. Why wouldn't these stupid numbers add up?

The abacus slipped from her fingers and bounced on the carpet, beads spinning.

Mary Kate found her the next morning, slumped over the desk, her cheek stuck to a customs form.

"Gracious, ma'am!" She exhaled sharply. "You gave me a terrible turn, all crumpled over. I was that glad to find you still breathing!"

Emily groaned as she got up from the chair. "I'm sorry, Mary Kate." The paper she had drooled on in the night detached from her face and fluttered to the floor. The maid picked it up.

"All those chicken scratchings!" she said. "Don't tell me you spent the whole night winkling out the sense of them?"

Emily looked ruefully at the scattered papers. "I'm afraid not." She sighed and stretched. "All I'm sure of is that Mr. Phipps was right when he said that Robert and I are provided for."

She stopped, her arms still in the air, and looked down at her severe black dress. A month in America had made her aware that it was ten years behind the fashion.

"Mary Kate," she decided. "It would be a shameful thing if you and I were to appear in Portland to meet my husband's family dressed like paupers, don't you think?"

Mary Kate put her hand down to cover the patch she had put on the one dress she owned that she thought good enough for a lady's maid. "You don't want them thinking you're looking for charity," she agreed.

Emily looked at the papers again, then at Mary Kate. An expression of wicked delight spread across her face. "You're right," she said firmly. "Help me gather these up and put them in the safe. You and I are going shopping. The wife of an English diplomat in Shanghai once told me that there was nothing like a new wardrobe to give a woman confidence. I am feeling very lacking in confidence at the moment. I'm going to test her theory. Put on your cloak, Mary Kate; we are going to be the most fashionable pair in the entire city."

When Mr. Phipps arrived to pick up the signed papers, he found an entirely new Emily waiting for him. She was head to toe in black mourning, as was proper. But instead of the plain-cut wool with the severe collar she had worn the day before, this costume was almost sumptuous.

The dressmaker had informed Emily that this was the finest in mourning wear. The dress was in the Gabrielle style and made of black gabardine that shimmered in the gaslight. It was buttoned down the front with jet beads and trimmed with black Cluny lace and floss tassels. At the back was a deep flounce. The woman had pieced it together that day from bits already in the shop. More clothing would arrive over the next week.

Mr. Phipps's only perception was that this elegant figure was not the woman he had parted from two days previously. She was more composed, more assured. She even seemed taller. The transformation unsettled him greatly.

"Good afternoon, Mr. Phipps," Emily greeted him. "Please sit down. Would you like some tea? No?"

She went over to the desk and selected a small pile of papers.

"I believe that these are the only ones that need my signature at the moment," she said as she handed them to him. "I appreciate the work you did to allow me to access immediate funds. The rest of the documents will require further study, I'm afraid. I shall take them to Portland with me so that I can compare them with the records kept by Captain Stratton's partners there."

Phipps rose as if pulled at the end of a rope.

"Now, now, Mrs. Stratton," he pleaded. "That isn't at all the thing to do!"

"I believe I am now in charge of my husband's business affairs, am I not?" There was the merest hint of a knife in her tone.

"According to his will, yes," Phipps admitted. "But he never intended for you to sully yourself with the mundane details. It's not fitting."

She appeared to consider this. "It is true that I have allowed myself to be left in ignorance of the source of that which provides my daily bread," she said. "My husband was of your belief that such matters were not a woman's provenance."

Mr. Phipps started to relax.

"And yet . . . ," Emily added.

Phipps could feel his stomach tighten.

Emily smiled. "And yet he did leave the responsibility to me. I must at least try to fulfill his trust."

"But, Mrs. Stratton. . . ."

"I am grateful for all you have done. Of course you must continue as agent to the company here in San Francisco." Emily moved to open the door. "I shall take the steamer for Portland as soon as my son arrives. When we have settled in and buried Captain Stratton, I shall consult with his partners as to the future of the company."

She glanced out the hotel window. "I see that the fog is clearing at last. Do enjoy the rest of the day."

There was nothing the man could do but take his hat and go.

He went immediately to the telegraph office to warn Stratton's partners just what was about to descend on them.

Emily hobbled back to the chair and eased into it. These high heels might be the latest style, and they did put her a bit closer to being able to look Mr. Phipps right in the eye, but they were horribly uncomfortable to balance in.

The little man had made a good point. It was very strange that Horace had left his business interests to her without appointing someone to manage them for her. Certainly, he had never given any indication that he thought her capable of understanding commerce. He had told her more than once that she was a great disappointment to him, in all respects. Perhaps he had believed he would live long enough to pass everything directly to his son. Or it may simply never have occurred to him that she would actually try to manage things rather than turn business matters over to Mr. Phipps.

No, it wasn't like Horace at all. Emily felt there was something she was missing.

There was a knock at the door.

"It's the porter, ma'am." Mary Kate was bubbling with excitement. "The ship from Boston has come in. Your son is here at last!"

Emily's face lit. Robert! She fairly flew down the hotel stairs and into the waiting cab. In a few moments she would be able to hold her son in her arms again.

All the other worries were chased out by overwhelming joy.

CHAPTER TWO

Meetings have already been held in this city with a view of having an expres-
sion of public sentiment upon the Railroad question. Reports have also been pub-
lished by communities upon the same subject. The City Council, too, have taken on
the matter in hand and propose to give the subject a thorough investigation, but as
yet no definite plans have been made.

—PORTLAND CITY DIRECTORY, 1868

TUESDAY AFTERNOON, FEBRUARY 25, 1868

Thick fog rolled up against the second-floor window of the weathered clapboard building, but the men inside didn't notice, being enveloped in a haze of smoke from their own cigars. It said something about the character of these men that they always preferred to create their own environment. In large part, they had been successful. But today they had gathered to discuss a possible threat to their carefully crafted existence.

"Why is this woman coming here?" The man with the biggest cheroot shook his head in disgust. "She doesn't know anyone in Portland."

"I thought she'd go back to China after Horace died," Matthew King complained. "Widows always want to minister to the heathen, don't they? And she's already trained for it."

"Can't see why Horace Stratton took it into his head to marry a missionary's daughter in the first place." Norton Andrews, a small, pale man with a gift for creative accounting, stared at the stub of his cigar, as if looking for the answer.

"Probably had to go that far to find parents who'd never heard of him," the first man laughed. "Would you have let your daughter marry Stratton?"

"Good God, no!" King shook so at the thought that the spill he was using to relight the cigar slipped and singed his long whiskers.

"Gentlemen!" The man sitting behind the desk hadn't spoken before. The other three instantly stopped their banter and gave him their full attention.

"Mrs. Stratton is unlikely to remain in Portland for long," he assured them. "She has no family here and her background doesn't indicate that she would have any interest in her husband's business. I'm sure we can convince her to sell us his shares in the company in return for some sort of annuity."

"I don't know." The man with the smoking beard shook his head. "Phipps in San Francisco wrote that we should watch out for her. I don't know what she did to spook him, but he sounded shocked."

"Really?" The man at the desk smiled. "Then perhaps Emily Stratton isn't as spotless as we assumed. If so, it will be even easier to get her to sign her shares over to us. Our wives certainly shouldn't be mixing socially with someone of tarnished character. A little pressure on that front might be all we need."

"What about the business that Stratton was doing for us in San Francisco?" the man with the cheroot asked. "Phipps said that he couldn't find anything about it in his papers."

The man at the desk pursed his lips. The movement made his thick moustache weave into his beard. "It may be that Stratton didn't have anything incriminating with him. Or he may have put the information among his private papers. In that case, his widow may well have what we need and not even know it."

He paused to think the matter over.

"I suggest that we do nothing until Mrs. Stratton arrives," he told the others. "It may be that the problem will resolve itself without resorting to unpleasantness. Thank you for coming, gentlemen."

The men instantly reached for their hats.

After they had left, the proprietor of the office opened the windows to let the smoke out. Outside, the fog clung to the roofs of the wharf houses nearby. They blocked the sight of the Willamette River, but not the smell. The man inhaled the moist air with satisfaction. Fools had gone west to find gold in the mountains and rivers. He had made his own out of land, steel, and steam. The businessmen of Portland jumped when he gave the order. The politicians and judges were at his disposal.

With that kind of power, he had no worries about his ability to handle a little Methodist missionary widow.

At that moment Emily was gripping the rail of the steamship *Cincinnati*, praying that the pilot didn't run them aground as they approached the dock reaching out over the Willamette River. She didn't feel dangerous, just cold and fearful.

Emily had endured several crossings of the Pacific. At the age of four-teen, she had sailed through the Strait of Magellan on her way to the Methodist school in Boston, and three years later she returned the same way to China. She had survived storms, pirate attacks, and the unwanted atten-tions of any number of male fellow travelers. But crossing the bar at the en-trance to the Columbia River had been the most terrifying experience of her life. Fierce waves had battered the ship back and forth, shoving it first out to sea and then pulling it inexorably to the rocks where the skeletons of earlier wrecks lay in pathetic, jagged heaps.

Once through that gate to Hell, the ship had steamed its way upriver with more tranquility to land at the port town of Astoria. But they had been given barely enough time to go ashore for a bite to eat before they continued on to Portland. The river was still iced over at the banks, and she overheard one of the other passengers say that it was frozen solid farther up. As she watched the land roll past on either side, Emily considered again that she might have made a rash decision in insisting that she would take up res-idence in her late husband's home, a place she had never been and which he had rarely mentioned.

From her vantage point on the deck she had seen only a few small villages on the riverbanks with wind-beaten buildings and no sign of roads leading in or out. In between them was nothing but an unbroken dark forest of enormous fir and cedar trees, taller than any she had ever imagined, heavy with melting snow. The scent of them filled the air with a wild spice that called to her in a way that was both exciting and terrifying. What monsters and wonders might hide in that dense wood?

At last the ship entered the mouth of the Willamette River. It was winter twilight, and Emily had expected to see the city lights at once. Instead there were nothing but farms and occasional storage sheds. All the docks they went by were too small to service the steamer. Would they have to change boats yet again to reach the shore? Emily sighed, worn out with travel and apprehension.

After a while the farmhouses started to be placed closer and closer together. Then brick buildings began to appear with shop signs lit up by oil lamps over the doors. The city must be just around the next bend in the river.

Emily waited for Portland to appear. But it seemed that they were making their landing in this little town. The steamer was heading for a wharf on the western bank. It was the tallest building on the waterfront, able to discharge passengers on the upper level and freight on the lower. Most of the other buildings were wooden, backing onto the river. They seemed to be shops and businesses, but of what sort, Emily couldn't tell. Was this the city that Horace had been so proud of? She peered into the dark, trying to discover some sign of a thriving metropolis.

From one of the waterfront buildings there came a crash of breaking glass, accompanied by shouts of anger. Emily leaned over the railing to see what was happening.

"Well, Mother, what do you think of our new home?" The voice at her ear made her jump. She turned her head to smile at her son, Robert.

From the moment he had stepped off the gangway in San Francisco, Emily had rejoiced in the reunion with Robert. She had been so afraid that his years at school would have made him less attached to her, but from his first hug, her fears had vanished. Even though, at sixteen, he was now several inches taller than she, he was still the little boy she loved and who loved her. Even more, he had grown into someone she felt she could lean on.

"I see now why Father preferred that we stay in Shanghai." Robert laughed at her expression. His arm swept out. "Mud huts, hardly any signs of civilization. I'll wager that there isn't a theater or a bath house in the place."

"But this can't be the city!" Emily exclaimed more loudly than she'd intended. In the darkness of late winter, she could only make out lights from windows and a few scattered streetlamps.

A man near her turned. He removed his hat, exposing his thinning dark hair to the wind. "I assure you, Mrs. Stratton," he said. "This is indeed our fair city. In the brightness of morning, you'll be able to appreciate it much better. And I assure you, young man, that we have all the amenities, including two theaters and a lecture hall."

"Of course, Mr. Carmichael." Emily gave a nervous smile. "I was only surprised at how quickly we had arrived." She turned to gaze back to the town, adjusting her expression into what she hoped was eager approval.

But no matter where she looked, to Emily's eyes, the city of Portland was extremely rustic, not like any of the cities she had seen: Shanghai, Peking, Yokohama, New York, and Boston. Half the buildings she could see were constructed from fresh timber. Beyond what appeared to be a tiny commercial area she could discern few lights. In the street, there were cows wandering about, to the apparent unconcern of the citizens.

"Wait," Robert whispered. "I was mistaken. There seem to be an amazing number of public establishments here. And, I do believe, a brewery. At least the natives have some sort of entertainment."

"I'm certain there are other attractions," Emily told her son firmly. "I have been assured that there is a Methodist church. And a Catholic one," she added as Mary Kate joined them at the rail.

"Don't be worrying about that, ma'am," Mary Kate said. "I have my rosary. I'll not be needing a Mass very often."

Robert snorted. "In that case, I suppose we have all that a civilized society craves."

Emily took her son's arm. He seemed to have acquired so much more sophistication than her finishing school had given her. He was remarkably poised for a boy of sixteen. It gave her such comfort.

"Don't make fun of your father's home," she chided gently. "He wanted us all to live here, you know. I think we owe it to his memory to do so. And, of course, you have an aunt and cousins that you've never met."

Robert yawned. "I look forward to embracing the entire family." He bent to kiss her cheek. "But I can't imagine that they will be half as sweet as you."

Emily looked up at him fondly. "You are prejudiced," she said. "But I'm very glad of it."

There was a jolt as the boat reached the bank. Emily turned her attention to the collection of people waiting on the dock. None of them was familiar.

"My husband's partners sent word that they would have someone meet us and take us to the house," she explained to Mr. Carmichael. "But I have no idea how to identify them. I see no one I have met before."

Carmichael scanned the faces at the bottom of the gangway. "I don't believe that any of Captain Stratton's partners are here. Perhaps they mistook the date."

"Perhaps." It didn't seem likely to Emily, since Mr. King and Mr. Andrews had sent her the steamship schedule. "In any case, I must arrange for a carriage to the house and a wagon to follow with our boxes. And the coffin! I had almost forgotten that. I must take care of my husband's remains."

"Certainly you must not!" Mr. Carmichael looked horrified. "I shall see to it at once. Andrews and King have been most thoughtless. The idea that you should have to worry yourself with such things during these days of sorrow is appalling!"

"Thank you, Mr. Carmichael, but you have been too kind already," Emily began, but he brushed that aside.

"I well remember the months after my own sweet wife passed on," he said. "It's not a time to be troubled with trifles."

Emily felt tears starting. She wiped them away, knowing that Mr. Carmichael would assume they were caused by grief. If only she could have had a husband worth grieving over! It was the tenderness in Mr. Carmichael's face when he spoke of his wife that caused her to weep. Horace had never looked at her tenderly. She chastised herself for being envious of the late Mrs. Carmichael, who had been loved.

Mr. Carmichael looked away, pretending not to notice. "There's

Hogan of Portland Dray and Hack!" He pointed out a man in a black coat and gray trousers standing next to a one-horse carriage. "I'll wager that he was hired to fetch you. Hogan!"

Mr. Carmichael went bounding down the gangplank with an energy that surprised Emily. She had thought him rather elderly for such speed. He went up to the man and spoke for a few moments. Then he hurried back.

"Just as I thought," he said in triumph. "He's to take you and your hand luggage up now and return with the cart for the rest. The, um, coffin will go directly to the undertakers. That's all arranged. Robert, would you help me get your mother's things?"

The young man had not noticed his mother's attempts to pick up all her hand luggage. He had been leaning over the rail, staring at the row of buildings that lined the street next to the river.

"Look, Mother," he said, pointing. "There are as many Chinese here as in San Francisco!"

Emily gave a brief glance. "Yes, that's interesting," she murmured. "But I would guess that they are mostly from Guandong, poor things. They won't speak our dialect."

She sighed. Even though the past few years in Shanghai had been harrowing, she still felt more comfortable with the Chinese people and customs she had grown up with. It would have been nice to have people that she could talk to.

"Robert?" Mr. Carmichael smiled and nodded at the bags at Emily's feet.

"Oh, of course, sir." Robert scooped up two of the bags.

Mr. Carmichael took the other two bags and led the party to the carriage. Mary Kate followed, clutching the satchel containing everything she owned in the world. She had passed the three-day boat journey listening to the tales of the crew. They said this Portland place was a wild town, half savage, and that the forests were full of enormous bears that came down into the gardens of the settlers, looking for fresh meat. That hadn't worried her until she saw how close the trees were to the town. Wisps of evening fog caught the branches, slithering around them as if alive. Not since she had left Ireland had she seen a place where the *sidh* would be so much at home.

———

Mr. Carmichael insisted on accompanying them, despite Emily's mild protests and Robert's glowers.

"Since the welcome committee hasn't appeared, I feel it's my duty to see you safely to your home," he told them. "A fine impression you must have formed of the hospitality of Portland society!"

The house was only a few blocks west of the river, but as the carriage headed away from the dock the area quickly became rural. Emily could hear the sounds of pigs snorting from somewhere close to the road. She hoped that they were securely penned. Not far from that, she spotted a weathered log cabin next to a cow pen. A few feet away, at the end of a worn path, was an outhouse. She reminded herself that she was going to be brave.

But soon their route began to pass stately homes, as fine as anything in Boston, surrounded by landscaped gardens. In some of the lit windows, Emily could glimpse fine furnishings and the sparkle of crystal chandeliers. She wondered if one of them belonged to Horace's sister. He had once mentioned that Alice had married well.

The carriage drew up in front of one of the largest of these estates, entering through a gate flanked by stone pillars leading to a long drive to the portico over the front entry.

"This is Captain Stratton's house?" Emily asked as the carriage came to a halt. It hadn't occurred to her that Horace would have spent his money on anything this fine for them.

"It is indeed." Mr. Carmichael handed her down. "His parents built it fifteen years ago, just before they died, but he had it enlarged and modernized in the last year when he decided to return home. I understand that there is gas lighting and even an indoor pump and water heater."

"Gracious!" Emily couldn't stop gaping. The slender iron key in her reticule gave no indication that it unlocked anything this grand. And it was now hers and Robert's. The furniture she had brought from Shanghai wouldn't begin to fill so much space!

The house was three stories tall, with a mansard roof and long dormer windows. There was a balcony on the second floor and windows in the attic that indicated a large area for servants. It was painted a startling yellow, with white trim. There was a stable a few yards from the main house. Emily wondered if Horace had bought a carriage and horses for them. She wished he had told her more of the place he had intended to become their home.

"Mary Kate!" She turned to the maid in sudden panic. "How shall we ever maintain a place so large?"

Mr. Carmichael seemed puzzled by her reaction. "I'm sure you can find servants. As you must know, the Chinese are excellent, especially at cooking and garden jobs. You could ask your sister-in-law to help you, if you don't trust your own judgment."

Her sister-in-law! Emily wasn't sure. Alice had written to her when she heard about her brother's death, offering to arrange for the sale of the house and asking that Horace's remains be sent home. Emily wrote back, thanking her and explaining that she and Robert planned to take up residence in Portland. Alice had not replied.

"Mother, could we at least see what's inside?" Robert prompted. "It's deuced cold out here."

Emily was brought back with a start. They were standing on the front path like unwanted guests. She reached into her bag and took out the key. Aiming it at the door like a general leading a charge, she thrust the key into the hole and turned it.

Robert gave a push and the door swung open.

They stared into a murky foyer. Emily's first impression was of overwhelming gloom. The floors were of dark wood. Cedar paneling went three quarters of the way up the walls. They faced an imposing wooden staircase, leading up into darkness. There were bulky forms in the entry, furniture covered in sheets, ghosts of chairs and bureaus.

"Mother." Robert gave her his arm and escorted her into their new home.

All up and down the street, curtains twitched back into place.

By morning the whole town would know that the widow Stratton had arrived.

CHAPTER THREE

The Chinese are a very important element in our social life on this coast—I believe in them and in their future here. Their inhumane treatment is a phase of our vulgar and cruel hate, not yet melted into toleration and good will.

—LETTER FROM REV. STEBBINS OF SAN FRANCISCO TO REV. THOMAS ELIOT OF PORTLAND, 1868

Emily had, with difficulty, convinced Mr. Carmichael that they could manage for one night without the amenities.

"Tomorrow morning I'll go to my husband's office, if his partners don't come to see me," she told him. "I can order everything then."

"May I at least see to having your boxes brought up?" he asked. "There must be things you'll need at once."

"Hardly," she smiled. "I packed months ago in China and have been surviving on the contents of my steamer trunk ever since. We have all that is necessary for one more night. We are very tired and only want to explore our new home and start to settle in."

That was as obvious a dismissal as Emily dared to give. She felt a pang of guilt. Carmichael was the only person who seemed to have the slightest interest in them, and she was turning him out.

"But really, Mary Kate," she explained later, when the gentleman had finally departed. "I could hardly ask him in for a cup of tea. Even if it had been proper, I have no idea if we even have tea, or a kettle to boil water."

Mary Kate sighed. "I'll admit I've been thinking all afternoon of a nice hot cup of tea."

"As have I. And that is the first thing we're going to find," Emily told her fervently. "That is, right after we locate the coal scuttle. I only hope there's coal in it. Robert, would you please take our bags upstairs? Thank goodness there is furniture, at least. Choose the room you like best for your own. Mary Kate and I shall seek out the kitchen."

It could have been worse, Mary Kate admitted to herself. There was coal and kindling in the scuttle next to the stove. The kitchen seemed fitted out with the latest improvements, even to the pump and sink. There was an array of pots and bowls in the cupboards. Although Mary Kate had no concept of cooking, she could make a fire and boil water, and it was with a cry of triumph that she held up a kettle. Emily cheered her discovery.

"Now all we need is tea." The maid looked at the kettle wistfully.

"I have some in my valise," Emily said proudly. "I'll run up and get it."

"Is it real tea or that bitter green stuff you like?" Mary Kate was suspicious. Although at this point even the brew that Emily preferred sounded good.

A bit of milk to put in it was beyond hope. She wondered where they could buy food. They had passed any number of public houses on their way but not one vegetable stand. Perhaps one of the farms nearby would sell her milk, eggs, and bread, enough to make a meal tonight.

It surprised her that no one had come round with a pie or a loaf as soon as they arrived. Even if Captain Stratton's sister hadn't got word they were coming, some one of the neighbors should have seen them and realized there would be not so much as a crumb in the house. A strange place. They'd had little enough to eat when she was a child in Connemara, but people shared what there was. When her mother lay dying, there was always a dish in the pantry brought by someone from the parish. But here not even a wave of welcome. Mary Kate's mouth curled in scorn. What else would you expect from a bunch of Protties?

She tied her shawl over her head and went out in search of food.

Upstairs, Emily moved through the twilight rooms. The long windows that were meant to let in every bit of sun in this cloudy land had all been shuttered. Long curtains covered them on the inside, making the house feel as close and as cold as a mausoleum.

"Be careful, Mother!" Robert appeared at her side, an oil lamp in his hand. "You could trip in this Stygian dark. Come see! I found the perfect room for you. It's in the back and overlooks the garden, at least I think so. There's even a little balcony, just like in Shanghai."

Emily followed but didn't take in most of what the boy was saying. Nothing here was like Shanghai. The people, the streets, the very sounds and smells of the place were foreign. How had she ever imagined that they could make themselves a home here?

Perhaps the best thing would be to bury her husband, sell the house, and return . . . where? Not Shanghai. There were too many sad memories there. Boston? She barely remembered the place. Back to San Francisco? Emily leaned her face against the windowpane, feeling like a puppy left behind with not even a familiar scent to guide it home.

She shook herself. This was weakness. Her mother would have been ashamed of her.

Tea. What she needed was a good dish of tea. And a good night's sleep in a bed that didn't rock with the waves. And windows open to let in the light, if light ever came to this gray corner of the world.

Emily came downstairs to find that Mary Kate and Robert had managed to start a fire in the stove. The warmth cheered her a little. She chided herself for feeling so bleak when she had her son next to her, a warm bed, and food on the table. So many women she had seen in China would have been grateful for even one of these.

The three of them ate a supper of eggs and bread. Mary Kate had discovered that most of the homes nearby were still farmhouses, with chickens and other small livestock. She had simply knocked on doors until she found someone with food to spare.

In the scuttle in the kitchen she had found enough coal to light the stove and in a cupboard, an ironstone skillet to cook in.

"It's not much," she apologized. "I told the woman at the farm who we were and why I was running about after dark scavenging a meal. She acted as if I were making up a story and naught but a beggar. She told me she'd never heard of Captain Stratton having a wife. Seemed put out about it, like she'd just learned her old auntie was a whisky smuggler or something."

Emily shook her head. "My husband wasn't often in Portland," she explained. "It's likely that many of the neighbors didn't know him well at all."

"That's no reason for her to be calling me a liar," Mary Kate fumed.

Emily agreed. She sighed. Perhaps Horace had preferred to let the woman assume he was a bachelor. She wondered how many other women in town would be chagrined to learn he had had a wife.

They had finished eating and were preparing to go up to bed when they were startled by a loud banging that echoed through the house. It was a moment before Emily realized that the sound was the pounding of the heavy brass knocker on their front door.

Robert took out his pocket watch. "It's after nine," he told his mother. "Who could it be?"

"Perhaps Mr. King or Mr. Andrews just learned of our arrival," Emily suggested, but her voice was doubtful. "Mary Kate, would you see who it is?"

As the maid went to open the door, a deep masculine voice on the other side started shouting.

"Horace, you old sea rat! Why didn't you stop by on your way up, like always?" he boomed. "I didn't know you was back 'til I saw the lights. Here, I brung a bottle to show I forgive ya."

Mary Kate looked back at Emily.

Emily took Robert's arm. "What should we do?" she whispered.

"Might as well open up," he said. "Otherwise he'll wake the whole town."

"Just a minute," Mary Kate ran back to the kitchen and returned clutching the handle of the ironstone pan. "All right, then."

She opened the door.

The man on the porch was clearly the worse for liquor; Emily realized that at once. His tie was under one ear and his collar crumpled. He wore a greatcoat of rough leather and his trousers were stuffed into the tops of his boots. He grinned at Mary Kate.

"Well now," he said. "I can see why Horace was too rushed to see an old friend. You're a pretty colleen, I'd say."

He spotted Emily's face in the glow of the candle she carried.

"Two of you!" he exclaimed. "You could share the wealth, you horny coot! Horace! Come on out and introduce me to your lady friends."

Mary Kate raised the pan. "You put one foot in this house, you spalpeen, and I'll flatten your ugly face!"

The man laughed. "Horace does like 'em feisty!"

Emily had had enough. She stepped forward. Robert appeared from the shadows to stand beside her. He was holding a poker he had found in the parlor.

"Hey now!" the drunk took a step back. "What's goin' on here? What have you done with Horace?"

"I don't know who you are, sir," Emily said. "But obviously no one has informed you that my husband died six months ago in San Francisco. We were just about to retire so I must ask you to leave."

Their visitor stared at her, the grin still on his face but doubt in his eyes. He took in the black dress and widow's cap Emily was wearing and the black band on Robert's sleeve.

"You can't be Horace's wife," he insisted. "He married some little Chinee girl in Shanghai. He told me so."

"How dare you slander my mother like that!" Robert rushed at the man, the poker raised.

Emily caught his arm. "Never mind, my dear. Your father seems not to have explained matters very well to his friends."

Or to his son and me, she added to herself.

The grin was now gone. The man put down the bottle and removed his hat.

"I'm sorry, ma'am." The news had sobered him enough to remember his manners. "Horace dead? I can't believe it. How did he go?"

"They say it was his heart," Emily replied, tight-lipped.

"He had a . . . ?" The man realized what he was saying and stopped at once, but Emily knew what the last word would have been.

It appeared that the man really *had* known her husband.

It finally penetrated his muddled brain that he was not making a positive impression on Mrs. Stratton. He bowed carefully.

"Forgive me, ma'am," he said. "My name is Daniel Smith. I worked for Captain Stratton, managing the loading and unloading of the cargo here in town. I'm most sorry for your loss and, when I'm more myself, I'll be happy to provide you with any service you might need."

Emily inclined her head. "Thank you, Mr. Smith. Now, as I said, we were just about to retire, so, if you will excuse us?"

"What? Oh, of course." Mr. Smith put his hat back on and picked up the bottle. "I bid you welcome to our fair community and a good night."

He tottered back down the drive.

Emily shut the door, bolted it, and then leaned against it, as if Mr. Smith might change his mind and decide to invade the house.

"Well!" was all she could think of to say.

"This place may prove more interesting than I thought." Robert grinned. "If this sort of thing happens often."

Emily looked from her son to her maid.

"I can only pray that the rest of our callers won't be like the first," she told them. "Now, let's take our candles and find our beds before anyone else decides to pay us a visit."

Emily woke early the next morning. The crowing of a rooster just under her window reminded her that she was no longer at sea. The gray sky outside gave her no hint of the time, only that dawn had arrived. Somehow her fear had left her in the night. This is an adventure, she told herself. A new life, and I can make it anything I wish, if only I have the courage.

She fumbled on the nightstand for her watch pin and discovered that it was past seven.

Hurriedly, she put on her dressing gown and slippers and ran downstairs. Half the morning gone already and so much to be done!

Mary Kate was standing in the middle of the kitchen when Emily entered.

"I hope you're not counting on me to do the cooking, Mrs. Stratton," she said. "Unless you plan to live on eggs, rashers, and spuds."

"Don't worry, Mary Kate," Emily laughed. "You're a lady's maid now, remember? I'm sure they don't cook. I shall have to hire someone."

"Well, I can at least boil water, ma'am," Mary Kate said. "So if you'll go back to your room I'll bring some wash water and help you into them corsets."

On her way back to her room, Emily looked in on Robert. To her surprise, he was already up and dressed. He was putting something in a drawer when she wished him good morning. He shut it quickly when he heard her step and looked up with a smile.

"Feeling better today, Mother?" he asked. "You know, this is really a splendid house! Do you know if the outbuildings are ours, as well? I thought I heard someone shutting the stable door in the middle of the night, but perhaps it was a neighbor coming home late. I'd like to have my own horse again."

He kissed her. Emily beamed. She had been so afraid that the time in boarding school would have changed her son, but he was as dear and affectionate as ever and seemed to have missed her as much as she had missed him.

"I confess that I have no idea how far our property extends," she told him. "I intend to ask Mr. King and Mr. Andrews that along with many other things as soon as I am dressed to go out."

"Why don't I run down to their office and leave a note telling them we've arrived and asking them to call on you at the first opportunity?" Robert suggested. "I want to get out and explore the town."

"That's an excellent idea," Emily said. "In that case, I'll spend the morning seeing about getting us provisions and someone to cook them for us."

She heard Robert thumping down the stairs a few moments later and smiled, glad that he, at least, seemed excited about living in Portland.

After she and Mary Kate had wrestled her into her widow's clothing, unrelieved black from head to toe, including jet earrings and bracelets and a cap with a veil that could be turned down over her face, Emily went to the kitchen to prepare a list of things they would need.

"Flour, sugar, salt, molasses . . . I don't suppose we can get any bean curd," she sighed.

"Didn't you buy some of that in San Francisco?" Mary Kate asked. She was hoping they wouldn't be able to find any more of the foul stuff. How Mrs. Stratton and her son could eat it so eagerly was more than she could grasp.

They were interrupted by the sound of someone knocking at the door.

"Goodness!" Emily exclaimed. "It's barely eight. Who could that be? Mary Kate, can you see who it is? Give me a moment to get to the parlor to receive them."

Hoping that it wasn't another of Horace's reprobate friends, Emily smoothed her dress and adjusted her cap as she hurried from the kitchen to the parlor. As she entered, she realized that the furniture was thick with dust and the hearth cold. Not the best way to greet a caller. Perhaps Robert had convinced Mr. Andrews or Mr. King to come. There were so many things she needed to discuss with them.

But when Mary Kate returned, she wasn't leading a man of business. Just behind her was a woman with graying blond hair and the most upright posture Emily had ever seen. She pulled her shoulders back, conscious that she had slumped.

The other thing that struck Emily was that the woman was dressed in mourning just as severe as her own. Even the handkerchief she held in her black glove was black lace.

"Dear sister Emily," she cried. "How dreadful that we should finally meet in such heartbreaking circumstances! I am Alice, dear Horace's only sister!"

CHAPTER FOUR

The ordinance referred to seems to your committee to be defective, in as much as it did not provide for any particular time by which said road should be commenced or completed and while it placed the bonds at once into the hands of a trustee for the purpose of selling them, it did not guard the city of Portland against any loss liable to be sustained by the city, in case said company should fail to build the road.

—REPORT OF THE SPECIAL COMMITTEE ON CITY IMPROVEMENTS
TO THE PORTLAND CITY COUNCIL, FEBRUARY 5, 1868

WEDNESDAY, FEBRUARY 26, 1868

Unlike his mother, Robert had no qualms about Portland. Some of his friends at school had scoffed when he said he was going to live out west, but he knew they were secretly jealous. They had all read dime novels about trappers and Indian fighters, gold miners and daring desperadoes. Despite his veneer of Eastern condescension, Robert was thrilled to be in this land of adventure.

Mr. Carmichael had told him that the city was less than twenty years old. To Robert's eyes, it looked newer. Shacks and crude cabins stood in farm lots. Here and there were a few other mansions, most still built recently enough that the lawn was only a muddy promise. Almost every plot was studded with tree stumps. So were many of the roads. Behind him to the west, the great forest loomed over this small attempt at civilization, dark firs that gripped the earth and climbed into the hills until lost in the morning fog. He wondered what mysteries and monsters lived there.

He inhaled deeply. The scent of cedar, fish, and wood smoke was intoxicating.

Making his way into the business district, Robert also realized that Portland was booming before his eyes. New and half-built shops were everywhere. He saw shops of every sort: jewelers, dry goods, shoemakers, clothiers, bookstores, druggists, even a candy factory. Most of them were constructed of wood, but there were a few of brick, including the banks: First National, Ladd and Tilton, and the Bank of British Columbia, where his father had kept his accounts.

Although he had the address, Robert wasn't sure of the location of his father's office. After walking a few minutes, he stopped a man driving by on a cart loaded with sacks of potatoes.

"Can you tell me how to get to the offices of Andrews, Stratton, and King?" he shouted.

The man reined in his team.

"Down on First Street somewhere," he said, pointing in the direction Robert was already headed. "Andrews lives above, if it's important. Don't know about the others."

Robert thanked him and went on. As he neared the river he saw more wagons and men. Most of the wagons were empty, their loads having been transferred before dawn into the holds of waiting ships. Some Chinese workers were still loading boxes, but the greater part of the men had finished for the day and were heading to the public houses for breakfast and a beer.

Robert caught one of them as he was entering the What Cheer tavern.

"Sure, I know the place," he replied to the boy's question. "You've gone down too far. Up a block to First then over another five blocks or so to C Street. But there'll be no one there before nine."

"I understand that Mr. Andrews lives above the office," Robert said.

The man laughed. "He does indeed, most times. But it'd be more'n your life's worth to get him up unless the vault was on fire."

He looked Robert up and down, noticing the tailor-made trousers and jacket and silk tie.

"If you're looking for a clerking job," he advised, "there are better masters to work for. Andrews, Stratton, and King can get blood from a turnip; they squeeze their help just as tight."

Robert opened his mouth to give a biting retort, then reflected that the man was twice his size and probably had friends around. He contented himself with a haughty bow. There was some Boston in him, still.

"Thank you for the information," he said. "I'm delighted to know that my finances are being handled with such prudence."

The man let out a guffaw that sprayed tobacco juice, so that Robert had to hop back to avoid being covered in it.

"Well ain't you the la-dee-da!" he exclaimed. "I guess we won't be seeing you at the What Cheer come payday."

Robert suddenly grinned.

"Or I might be in there buying drinks for the house," he said. "Thanks for your assistance, sir."

He wheeled about before the man could respond.

He found the office with no further adventures. As predicted, the shutters were closed, but he thought he could hear someone moving about inside.

He knocked loudly. The noise stopped, but no one came to the door.

"Mr. Andrews!" he called. "It's Robert Stratton, Captain Stratton's son. Mother and I arrived last evening. She sent me to inform you."

There was no sound from inside. Robert wondered if he had been mistaken. He looked around for an outside staircase to Andrews's apartment.

He found it at the side of the building. The wooden steps took up practically all the space between Andrews, Stratton, and King and the dry goods store next to it. Robert hurried up and pounded on the door at the top.

"Mr. Andrews!" he shouted again. He wondered if the man was deaf not to have heard the knocking down below. He paused to listen.

Was that a sound or just the creaking of the timber stairs? Robert put his ear to the door.

"Help." The word was no more than a squeak.

Robert rattled the door; it was locked. "Mr. Andrews, are you in there? Are you all right?"

Something shuffled on the other side of the door, like a python or, Robert reflected more practically, like a man trying to crawl across the floor.

Robert threw himself against the door but it wouldn't give. There wasn't enough space for him to put his full weight behind it.

"Mr. Andrews, I'm going for help," he called. "I'll return at once."

He leapt down the stairs, three at a time. There was no one on First Street. The shops were all still closed. Robert raced back up the street to the tavern. He burst in and stood panting in the entry as thirty men turned to stare.

"It's Mr. Andrews," Robert said. "I think he's ill. Please, someone come help me."

Three men got up at once, among them the one Robert had spoken with earlier.

"You'd better not be playing tricks, boy," he warned. "Where is he?"

Robert led the way back and the men, working together, managed to break down the door. Crashing into the room, it barely missed a man lying on the floor, his right arm outstretched. Robert started to enter and stepped back. The room reeked of acrid vomit.

"Andrews!" The men clustered around him.

"Is he alive, Jake?" one of the men asked.

Robert's acquaintance bent over the prostrate man and nodded.

"But it sure looks like something didn't agree with him," he commented. "Ned, run for the doctor."

Ned nodded and left.

Jake and the remaining man lifted Mr. Andrews back to the bed. They found a washbasin and towel to mop up the mess.

"Oysters," Jake pronounced after looking around. A pile of shells was still on the table. "He probably thought they'd stay cold all day on the windowsill. You'd think he'd 'a known better."

Robert stood in the doorway, wondering what he should do. The men seemed to have the messy situation in hand. He knew for a fact that his mother had enough cash money to take care of them for the moment. A good thing, since it didn't seem that Mr. Andrews would be able to get her more anytime soon. Perhaps he should try to find the remaining member of the company, Matthew King. He turned and started back down the steps.

He met the doctor hurrying up with Ned.

"Are you the one who found him?" the man asked Robert.

The boy nodded. "My mother sent me to tell him we were here," he explained.

"And who are you?" The doctor pulled him along, back into the sick-room.

"My name is Robert Stratton," Robert said. "My father was the part-ner of Mr. Andrews."

Everyone but the man on the bed stopped and gaped at him.

"My god!" Ned exclaimed. "The fat's in the fire now."

Emily was feeling overwhelmed. Her sister-in-law was a good head taller than she and much more sure of herself. Alice Bracewell was the sort of blonde that poets wrote sonnets to. Even in her forties the golden locks were only lightly highlighted by silver threads. Her skin was flawless and her nose seemed designed for looking down at lesser mortals. Emily was reminded of the wife of the English consul.

"I am shocked!" Alice repeated. "Someone might have sent word that you were coming. To think that you had to show up on your own doorstep like uninvited guests. It's inexcusable."

"We managed quite well," Emily assured her. She had the odd feeling that she should be apologizing for having been inconvenienced. "I telegraphed from San Francisco before we left," she added in her own defense.

"Oh, you should never trust that contraption," Alice waved the tele-graph away. "The lines are always down and the men who take the messages drunk half the time."

Emily decided not to argue the matter.

"We do have tea," she said. "May I offer you some? There's even fresh milk."

"Thank you, my dear, perhaps another time," Alice told her. "I just came by on my way to the Presbyterian ladies' meeting to introduce myself and inform you of the plans for Horace's interment."

She emphasized the denomination.

"Yes, of course," Emily said. "I'm sure that Horace would want his own minister to perform the funeral service."

"Naturally," Alice answered. "I've arranged everything. My poor brother will be buried next to our parents at Riverside Cemetery. The ser-vice is at ten o'clock Friday morning."

"That will be fine," Emily cringed. "Should I go or stay home to re-ceive callers?"

Alice seemed surprised by the question. "You are expected to attend the service. You and my nephew will join us in the family pew."

She rose to go. As she was putting on her gloves she looked around the room, noticing the dust.

"Is there anything you need?" she asked. "Your housemaid doesn't seem to be very efficient."

"Thank you," Emily said. "I don't have a housemaid yet, only a per-sonal maid. I've sent my son to Horace's partners' office. I'm sure Mr. Andrews or Mr. King will be able to advise me further."

"On what, my dear?" Alice inquired. "They are men, after all. What do they know of running a household? You'll need someone to do the heavy cleaning once a week. Mrs. McCarthy will do. I'll send her round. Now, you can get an excellent Chinese cook and gardener. They have a hiring agency on Front Street. It's amazing how well those people have learned to cook proper American. You just need to keep an eye on them, of course, or they'll serve up rats and puppies and such like."

She paused. "But of course you know all about that."

Emily was puzzled by her expression. Then she realized that Alice thought that Emily might have picked up a taste for puppies during her life in China.

"I am familiar with some Chinese customs," Emily explained. "And quite accustomed to the food. My parents preferred Western meals when we could get them, but that was rarely. However, I understand that most of the Chinese here are from the southern provinces. The food and customs are different there. Even the language isn't the same as the one spoken in Shanghai. I won't be able to speak with them."

"Really?" Alice was uninterested in diversity within China. "That's no problem. The domestics speak English after a fashion. Well enough, anyway. I can have a selection of cooks sent up for you to choose from, and garden workers, too, when it gets a little warmer. You don't have to converse with them. No one else does. What about your carriage?"

"I have a carriage?"

"Of course," Alice said. "Horace boarded the horses with Hogan. But you should get a driver. The Irish are quite good with horses. I'm sure we can find someone sober if we look hard enough."

That taken care of to her satisfaction, Alice made Emily promise to call on her the next week.

"We have a little social improvement society that meets in my home once a month," she explained. "All the women in it are very much worth knowing."

"I'm sure that will be delightful," Emily said, privately dreading the event.

"Fine." Alice smiled slightly. She patted Emily's hand. "I'll leave you now to become accustomed to your new home. I just wanted you to know that all dear Horace's family and friends are ready to welcome you into our community."

"Thank you," Emily smiled back, remembering their visitor of the previous night.

"I'll just take my leave, then." Alice seemed to want to say or do something more, but Emily had no idea what it was. She later admitted to herself that she didn't try very hard to find out. Her sister-in-law made her nervous.

"It was very kind of you to come," she said instead, leading Alice to the door. "I know that Robert will be sorry to have missed you."

"I'll send the carriage for you on Friday," Alice announced. "It will take you directly to the church. Horace rarely visited in the past few years but he has many friends from his youth. I expect a large attendance."

Emily wasn't sure if that was meant as a boast or a threat or simply a statement. Forcing another smile, she led Alice out.

When she opened the door, she noticed that there was a phaeton sitting outside the house, the driver shivering in the open seat. As he got down to assist Mrs. Bracewell, Emily saw a flash of silver as a flask disappeared into his pocket.

Alice gave Emily a stiff embrace before she left. As she did, she whispered one last thing, in a rapid flow, as if she didn't want the words to be associated with her.

"They gossip about Horace here, you know," she hissed. "But don't listen. It's all lies, jealous, spiteful lies!"

She let Emily go, turned, and got into her carriage. The driver remounted and they drove off.

Emily watched from the doorway until they turned into the road. She wondered what sort of gossip there might be and how close it came to the unpleasant truth. How much did Alice know of her brother's activities? Both the Chinese and Western women in Shanghai had told her that it wasn't a woman's business to know what men did, as long as it wasn't done to them. But that Mr. Smith last night, he hadn't been surprised to find two unknown women in the Stratton home. And he had no doubt what they were there for.

Emily felt her face grow hot. If only she could have remained ignorant. Her father hadn't been like that. Was it because he was a man of God? She believed he would never have let her marry Horace if he had known how his only child would be treated. For years she had puzzled it over in her head. Horace had told her there was something wrong with her, that she was a frigid, hymn-singing prude.

All this time and she still didn't know if he was right.

The doctor was the first to recover from Robert's statement. He looked the boy up and down.

"Not much of Stratton about you," he commented. "Must favor your mother. Well, Andrews won't care whether you're here or not for some time, if ever."

He glanced at the moaning figure on the bed.

"Ned," he continued. "You'd better go find Matthew King and tell him what's happened. Andrews looks to have gotten rid of most of whatever sickened him but he's going to need care. Somewhere else, for preference. Jake, why don't you get some of the coolies from the laundry down the block to come up here and clean this mess?"

Ned and Jake wasted no time in getting out of the fetid room. Their friend had already made his escape. Robert tried to follow, but the doctor called him back.

"Get over here," he ordered as he bent over Mr. Andrews. "I may need your help."

"I don't know anything about taking care of sick people," Robert said as he edged toward the bed.

"You don't need to; I do," the doctor snapped. "Just hold him up while I get this down him."

Robert cringed but obeyed. Mr. Andrews's nightshirt was gooey with vomit, and there was no way to keep it from staining Robert's expensive Scottish wool jacket. He shuddered and tried not to gag. The doctor took a small bottle from his bag, poured a bit into a large spoon and tipped it into Andrews's mouth. Some of the liquid ran down into the sick man's already encrusted beard.

"Looks like we got to you just in time," he told his half-conscious patient. "Anything left of them oysters, this ipecac will bring up."

Robert tried to get out of the way as this prophecy proved true, but some bile still spattered on his good trousers. Unable to stand it any longer, he ran for the doorway just in time to bend over the railing and deposit his breakfast on the mud below.

He was wiping his mouth when Ned and Jake returned.

"King says he'll send the carriage to bring Mr. Andrews to his place," Ned told them. "His wife is none too happy about it, but he told her it was their duty as Christians and that shut her up."

Jake made a noise in the back of his throat. The doctor gave him a sharp glance.

"You two help me get him ready then," he ordered. He looked at Robert. "Why don't you run on home now, young Stratton? Tell your mother what's happened and clean yourself up. You did well."

Robert's first reaction was anger at being dismissed like an errand boy. Then relief asserted itself and he ran back down the stairs, away from the mess and the stench. So far, his first day in Portland had not lived up to expectations.

When he arrived back at the house, Robert found a wagon in the drive, with boxes, trunks, and barrels being unloaded. His mother was running back and forth, telling the men where each one went. She greeted him with a smile, the first genuine one he had had from her since the morning she had met him at the dock in San Francisco and told him his father was dead.

"Darling! Look! Now we can make this our real home!" she cried.

Then she sniffed and noticed the stains on his clothing.

"I'll explain everything, Mother," he promised. "Just as soon as I've changed."

He went through the hallway and up the stairs. Around him the air smelled of his childhood, incense and camphor wood and the pungent aroma of the patchouli used to pad the packing barrels. For a moment he was transported back to Shanghai where he had been a little god in the household, adored by all. He took a deep breath and the stench from his clothing rose to his nostrils. Abruptly, he was jolted back to the present. He shook himself and continued to his room.

As she ran back and forth, Emily noticed that small clusters of people had gathered along the roadway to watch her possessions being taken in. She waved to them politely and then bowed as she saw a clutch of Chinese men standing to one side, blue pants sticking out from under rough winter greatcoats. They started in confusion. One made a quick bow in return before they all scurried away.

Emily turned her attention back to supervising the unloading. She was eager to see how many of her porcelain dishes had survived. It would be terrible if they made it all the way from Shanghai only to be dropped on her doorstep and smashed. Even more, she longed to unpack her own things, to put some mark of her existence on this home that Horace had furnished without her knowledge or desire.

When Robert came back down and explained what had happened, Emily was sorry for poor Mr. Andrews but not concerned about their situation.

"Your Aunt Alice paid me a visit this morning," she told him over the stomping of the carters. "She has kindly offered to help us get settled."

Robert raised his eyebrows. "Your voice sounds just the same as when Bishop White used to come by."

Emily colored. "I confess she had much the same effect on me. A good woman, I'm sure, but rather daunting. When we become better acquainted, I'll no doubt feel differently."

Robert grinned. "As you did with the bishop? In that case, we should start scouting out cupboards for you to hide in when she calls."

Emily gave a laugh. Then she sighed, looking at the chaos around her. She wanted nothing more than to spend the rest of the day putting her home in order.

"I suppose I should go and pay my respects to Mr. and Mrs. King," she sighed. "And inquire as to the health of Mr. Andrews. Can you find out where they live, Robert?"

"Next block over," said a man who had overheard her. "Not more'n a step, ma'am."

"Thank you." Emily was surprised by the informality among the classes in America. She knew that Horace had always demanded respect and instant obedience from his workers, just as he did the sailors on his ships. Her Chinese servants had known better than to imply they had overheard one of her conversations, much less respond to it. But she had seen that things were different here in the West and, although it frightened her a bit, she rather liked the assumption of fellowship.

The man winked at her before vanishing into the basement with his load.

"As soon as these men are gone, I'll clean up and change into a walking dress," she told Robert. "Will you escort me there, my dear?"

"Of course, Mother darling," he said. "But I hope you'll excuse me from getting at all near Mr. Andrews. Until the boxes are opened, this is my last clean pair of trousers."

CHAPTER FIVE

[I]t takes 80 tons per mile with 4 tons extra for tracks and switches, say total, 84 tons per mile. 2½ tons spikes per mile 2 tons chains per mile. Iron costs in San Francisco from $75 to $80 per ton, spikes cost $150 per ton, chains $400 per mile Switch and frog irons $200 per sett [sic].

—Simeon Reed's account book, 1868

LATER THAT DAY

In a plush upper room at the Ladd and Tilton bank, four men sat around a table piled high with reports and accounts from the Oregon Steam and Navigation Company. The men regarded the paperwork with satisfaction.

"We'll be able to build the twenty miles of railroad we need for less than one hundred thousand dollars," Simeon Reed told his partners. "I've calculated the costs of the iron, wood for the ties, and labor."

"But can we do it in time?" his partner John Ainsworth asked. He was older than the other three, the only one clean shaven, and he always wore a skullcap to keep the drafts off his balding head. He looked like a New

England parson but had actually spent most of his life on the river as a steamboat captain.

"No reason why not," R. R. Thompson concluded, admiring the predicted profit margin. "We drive the first spike sometime the middle of April. We'll have all summer to finish. Then we get the government rights of way, sell the land, and recoup any initial outlay."

The fourth member of the group, William Ladd, was also their banker. He was less confident.

"They say Ben Holladay is planning on challenging us," he fretted. "He's going to throw in with the Eastsiders and get the twenty miles laid no matter what the cost. He's got investors all over the country. Our pockets aren't that deep."

"I've been in contact with the people in Salt Lake," Reed assured him. "They say they've made no agreement with Holladay. They're eager to support our bid. A line from Portland to Salt Lake will be beneficial to us both. It's time that OSN expanded into railroads." He stroked his dark beard protectively. "We need to be in position to send goods east when they finish the transcontinental tracks."

"Just think," Ainsworth said. "No more going round the Horn or across the Isthmus of Panama to get to New York. It's a new world."

Ladd raised his eyebrows. "I never said I wasn't all for the railway. I simply don't like depending on other people's whims. And I don't like anything in connection with Ben Holladay. The man's an unmitigated scoundrel."

"We can handle him." Thompson grinned. "We unloaded that steamship on him with no trouble."

Ladd permitted himself a smile. "And he thought he'd made a bargain. Never knew we'd intended to sell it all along."

Ainsworth shivered. There was a draft coming from one of the windows.

"There's been some grumbling from the old stockholders," he commented. "I felt bad about not letting Henry Corbett in on our plans."

"He's a senator," Ladd reminded him. "It wouldn't have looked right. And the others are all men of business. They know the rules. No one forced them to sell OSN stock at a loss."

The others agreed. Business was not for the fainthearted or the overscrupulous. They had broken no laws by driving the stock price down. If they had sold their own shares to a third party working on their behalf and then bought them back at a profit, so what? The company had become too unwieldy with so many men having a voice in the decisions. Now that it was just the four of them, things could be done in good time without debate. They would need every edge if they were going to go up against the California tycoon, Ben Holladay.

Reed gave his brown beard one last tug. "I just wish I knew what Horace Stratton was doing in San Francisco when he died."

"I think we all know what he was doing." Thompson chuckled.

Ladd gave him a disapproving look.

"There's no reason to think that Stratton was planning to make any outside deals with Holladay," he said, but his tone was more of a question.

Reed shook his head. "I don't see how. Horace was at sea or in China most of last year. It does seem strange, though, that after all this time he should have suddenly decided to pack up his home in Shanghai and bring his wife and son to Portland."

"He once told me that China was the best place to keep a wife," Thompson added. "I half thought he'd invented her to keep any of his lady friends from getting ideas."

Ladd snorted. "None of his friends were ladies."

Reed was sure of that. He'd never invited Stratton to dine at his home for that reason. Not the sort of man you want your wife having to entertain.

"However," he continued the thought aloud. "The widow is among us now. I'll ask Amanda to pay a call on her, at least leave a card. My wife is an astute judge of character. She'll know if this woman was in league with Horace's schemes or just another innocent whom he deluded."

"My wife will go with her," Ladd said. "Carrie will feel it her duty to welcome the woman. Might even take the pastor along. He'll soon know if she really was a missionary. That's the most unbelievable part of Horace's whole story."

"I'd like to know the truth of that, too," Ainsworth added. "If it's so, she certainly wasn't able to convert Horace."

On that, all the men could agree.

———

Emily stood in the middle of her room, looking longingly at the boxes yet to be opened. She stepped into the hoops so that Mary Kate could tie them in place.

"Why do we do this to ourselves?" she moaned. "Hoops *and* a pannier! As if corsets weren't bad enough. And people think that Chinese foot-binding is barbaric! With all this weight I can hardly move!"

Mary Kate had become accustomed to these complaints and paid them little mind. As a working woman, she never bothered with such con-stricting clothing. Her leather stomacher was enough for fashion. She was curious, though, about the silk pyjamas that were supposed to be in the trunks from China. Emily had threatened to start wearing them, at least in private, as soon as they came. Mary Kate wondering if she would wear high wooden sandals as well and tie her hair in a long braid down her back.

That would be interesting.

Eventually Emily was suitably attired to pay a call. Her skirt was black wool with velvet and jet trim. There was a matching shirtwaist. She wore another pair of jet earrings and her widow's cap, a silk concoction with black rosettes and ribbons that perched unsteadily on the top of her chignon and had to be held in place with a pearl hatpin.

When they came down to the hall where Robert was waiting impa-tiently, Mary Kate had to lace up Emily's overshoes because Emily couldn't see her feet, much less bend to put on shoes. Emily sighed again at the in-sanity of Western clothing.

Robert helped her into her hooded cloak. "I've found out which house is Mr. King's," he said. "You can see it from the street. But I don't know how you're going to get there without picking up a bucketful of mud on the hem of your dress. The day is clear but the streets look like a pig run."

"You'll just have to try to guide me around the worst of it," Emily said. "I understand now why Alice brought her phaeton. I thought that she was just trying to impress me."

"If she's anything like Father," Robert commented, "she has more than one reason for doing anything." He grinned. "Do you remember how he used to let me scramble up the trellis on the side of the house to pick flow-ers for you? I thought it was because he was too heavy. It wasn't until he

took me back to the States that I realized he was training me to climb rig-
ging, just like the sailors."

Emily repressed a shudder at the memory of her little boy halfway up
the second story. Robert spoke with such affection and pride. She tried
to remember that, whatever Horace's faults, he had doted on his son. If
Robert had fallen, Horace would have caught him. Probably.

Robert needed to believe that. Emily held her tongue.

The fog had lifted, leaving the day chilly, the air crisp and clear. Robert
guided his mother down the gravel drive of their property to the street,
which looked, as he had said, as if a herd of pigs had been let loose to root
in it. Here and there amidst waves of mud a tree stump stuck out, making
even wheeled traffic dangerous.

Emily tried to avoid the worst of it, but she resigned herself to the fact
that the weight of her walking dress would soon be greater by the addition
of a rim of earth sticking to the hem.

Still, the walk was a short one. Mr. King's home was only two blocks
down from theirs. It was a solid frame building with a grove of apple trees
behind and a small lawn in front, nothing as ostentatious as the Stratton place.

As they neared the house, they saw a man come down the walk from
the front door and head toward them. He was wearing a beaver top hat that
seemed far too dignified for his youth. His cheeks were red with the cold
and he sported a neat, reddish-brown goatee. In his arms he carried a bundle of cloth that seemed to be trying to escape his hold.

"Good day!" he called to them.

He lifted his hand to tip his hat, but a jerk from the bundle caused him
to grasp it again with both arms. The hat flew into the street.

Robert ran to fetch it.

"Thank you, young man!" The gentleman took his hat with a smile.
"I'd have chased the thing myself but for my burden here." He regarded
it tenderly.

The blankets shuddered and suddenly a face peeked out. Emily realized
that beneath all the scarves was a baby of about a year or so. The man introduced himself.

"Tom Eliot, ma'am." He had an accent that she couldn't place. "And this is my son, William. We were just paying a call on Mr. King, to see how Mr. Andrews is faring."

Emily smiled. Eliot was fairly bursting with pride in his chubby off-spring. She wondered if it was common in Portland for gentlemen to take their infants when they went visiting. It was not a custom she had ever noticed in Boston or Shanghai, but one she approved of.

"My name is Emily Stratton," she said. "I was also going to see the Kings. And this is my son, Robert."

Robert bowed and handed Mr. Eliot his hat back with a flourish.

"Delighted to meet you!" Eliot said. "Do you live nearby? I don't think I've seen you in town."

"We arrived just last night," Emily explained. "But we plan to take up residence here. My late husband was a native of Portland."

"I've only been here two months, myself," Eliot admitted. "But I find the country wonderful. Willie is thriving here in the clean air. He loves it, too. My wife, Etta, is a bit under the weather, today. She'll be sorry not to have met you."

He paused, his brow creased as he chased a thought.

"Stratton," he said. "You wouldn't be any relation to Caroll Stratton, the Methodist minister?"

"If so, my husband never mentioned it," Emily answered in surprise. "How odd! I was raised Methodist. I had planned to attend services there next Sunday."

"He gives a fine sermon," Eliot said.

"Then perhaps we shall see you at the church," Emily said with plea-sure. She was liking this enthusiastic young man very much.

"Not this Sunday." He gave an impish grin. "I'm afraid my congrega-tion likes me to be with them most Sabbath days. I'm the new Unitarian minister."

With that, he took his leave, bounding down the road with baby Willie laughing in his arms.

"Interesting," she said to Robert as they continued on their way. "Your grandfather always insisted that Unitarians were worse than pagans. They don't even think dancing is a sin."

"Nor do I, Mother," Robert said. "I learned to dance at school and my teacher said I was quite graceful. Shall I give you a spin?" He held out his arms with a roguish chuckle.

"Mercy, no!" Emily stepped away from him, hurrying to the door.

They were admitted by a girl about Robert's age, with blond pigtails and hands damp with dishwater. She showed them to the parlor.

"Mrs. Stratton," she announced. "And . . . oh dear." She looked at Robert. "I forgot to ask your name."

"That will do, Myra." The woman seated on the horsehair sofa shook her head at this lack of training. "You may return to your work."

The girl bobbed a curtsey and backed toward the doorway, nearly running into Robert, who gave her a wink. She blushed scarlet as she stumbled out.

The woman sighed. "You see what we have to work with here, Mrs. Stratton. I am Dorothea King. Please accept my condolences on the loss of your husband."

"Thank you," Emily answered. "Robert and I were most grieved to learn of Mr. Andrews's indisposition. I hope he is doing better."

"The doctor says he should recover shortly," Mrs. King said. "I believe he is still sleeping. Oysters, they say. You can't be too careful with shellfish."

She gestured toward a pair of armchairs. "Please, do sit down. I'll ring Myra to make tea. Let me have your cloaks. The stupid girl should have taken them at once."

Emily and Robert waited while Myra was given their wraps, the order for tea, and a sharp rebuke. The girl seemed to take all of these in stride.

"We really can't stay long," Emily explained when they were all seated. "We haven't unpacked yet. I did want to make some arrangement for Mr. King to come by the house so that we could go over financial matters."

"Oh, I'm sure he could, if you like." Mrs. King added a lump of sugar to her tea. "But really, you don't need to concern yourself about that. Just send Matthew the bills to be paid. He's assured me that you have quite enough funds to take care of both of you. He'll see to everything."

She offered them the cream.

"No, thank you," Emily said, both to the cream and Mrs. King's suggestion. "I prefer to examine Horace's accounts, myself. There are some holdings that I would like to sell. And I have some thoughts about investments."

Mrs. King's cup shook in the porcelain saucer.

"Well! I don't know how Matthew will feel about that," she said. "He might not want you to take risks. Really, it would be better if you let him manage things. He's quite good at it."

Emily finished her tea.

"I'm sure he is," she said as she stood up to go. "But I feel obligated to take care of some matters that my husband left undone. I spent several weeks in San Francisco studying his accounts, so Mr. King needn't worry about having to waste time explaining them to me. Please give him the message and ask him to call on me, perhaps early next week? And I hope that soon after that I'll be prepared to entertain social calls. I do hope you'll visit."

She smiled brightly at the dumbfounded woman. "Excellent tea, Mrs. King. Thank you so much."

"Really quite good," Robert agreed. "Please compliment your maid on her skill."

Mrs. King accepted their appreciation with a nod. But the look in her eyes did not bode well for them or for the serving girl, Myra.

"Mother," Robert waited until they were back on the street to speak. "You told Mrs. King a fib."

"I? What do you mean?"

"You told me that Father's accounts made no sense at all to you," Robert said. "Perhaps before we face the partners, you and I should go over them together."

Emily bit her lip. She knew how much Robert had admired his father. There were notations in the account books that worried her greatly. Horace, it appeared, had been trafficking in people as well as goods. And some of the goods had not been entirely legal. Robert's loss was still too keen. She couldn't upset him.

"I'm sure I can make the numbers agree, if I work at it," she said.

"Watch out for that tree root!" Robert steered her around the obstacle. "Mother, I shall have to handle our money one day. Don't you agree that the earlier I learn the better?"

"Yes, but . . ." Emily groped for something to say that wouldn't hurt him.

He stopped and placed his hands on her shoulders. His blue eyes were sincere but amused.

"You're afraid I'll find out that Father wasn't always completely upright in his business dealings, aren't you?" He laughed. "You should have heard the boys at school bragging about the methods their fathers used to cut costs. And the money they made by tricking the competition. He can't have been any worse than they."

Emily's eyes grew round with shock. It suddenly hit her that it might be better if he understood the magnitude of Horace's business. And yet, what if he treated her with condescension, telling her that it was the way of the world and she was an idiot to expect otherwise?

What if he agreed with Horace?

"Robert," Emily became aware that there were other people in the street. "This isn't something to discuss here. But you are right. You are almost a man now and you deserve to know where our wealth comes from."

Robert released her and put her arm through his. He gave her a fond smile.

"That's my good little mother." He patted her hand. "Don't fret. Whatever we discover, we can resolve it together."

Emily gave his arm a squeeze. Fervently, she hoped he was right.

When they got home, they found that Mary Kate had company. A Chinese man of about forty was in the kitchen with her. He was taking parcels out of a large basket. When Emily entered he jumped up, bowing deeply to her.

"My name Ah Sung," he said. "Missee Blacewell tell me come here chop chop. I cookee for you good good loast beet."

Emily blinked. "What? I'm sorry, *Wo bu mingbai. Ni hui shuo Zhongguo hua ma?*"

"Mother," Robert laughed. "He *is* speaking English, or pidgin, at least. Do you speak Mandarin?" he asked in that language.

Ah Sung looked puzzled. He bowed again. "*Ngoh hng mihng.*"

"Well I understand him right enough," Mary Kate announced. "That's how the Chinese in San Francisco talked. That Mrs. Bracewell sent him up to cook for you. I say you should let him. If he can make roast beef fit to eat, it'll save you from another night of bread and eggs, for it's all I can give you."

"Ah Sung, can you read Chinese?" Emily asked. "I have never learned to use pidgin. I hate the sound of it."

She found a pencil and paper and hastily scribbled a note. When she handed it to the man, his eyes widened. He bowed again.

"Yes, Missee Stratton," he said. "I makee you good good food."

"Thank you," Emily went to her purse and took out some coins. "Go buy as many of the things on that list as you can. And a proper rice pot."

She almost moaned in anticipation. The man took his basket and hurried out.

Emily at once began prying open one of the barrels in the kitchen.

"Come help me, Robert. We need to find the bowls and chopsticks. If Mr. Ah can cook as well as he says, we'll feast on real food tonight!"

"Um, Mrs. Stratton," Mary Kate interrupted nervously. "I was totally forgetting that today is Ash Wednesday. If you'll allow it, I should be going to a Mass this evening, just to see if there are any other Irish about. I won't be needing any supper, I'm thinking."

Emily looked up from her rummage through the china barrels. "Of course, Mary Kate, if you wish. Don't you want any of Ah Sung's dinner?"

Mary Kate thought of the scribbles Emily had written on the paper. She thought of rats and puppies and strange shapes she'd seen hanging in shops in San Francisco.

"Well, you know now," she said, "I'm sure it'll be delicious and all, but this is a fast day. I'll just have to make do with eggs."

She wondered how many such meals she'd have to make do with. And she'd been so looking forward to a plate of roast beef and spuds!

CHAPTER SIX

PORTLAND ACADEMY

AND

FEMALE SEMINARY

EXECUTIVE COMMITTEE

DR. W. H. WATKINS, HON. M. P. DEADY

HON. E. D. SHATTUCK

------------0------------

This school begins its second year, under present management, Sept. 2, 1867. The course of study is thorough and practical. Native teachers of French and German are employed. We use every appropriate means to impart life and interest to the school and secure the health, good discipline and advancement of the pupils.

For catalogues containing a list of students for past year, full information concerning boarding facilities &c., address

T. M. GATCH

Principal

—PORTLAND *OREGONIAN*, ALMOST EVERY WEEK 1867–1868

FRIDAY, FEBRUARY 28, 1868

The funeral service was mercifully brief. Emily sat next to Alice in the family pew, both women heavily veiled. Robert was on Emily's other side, holding her hand. She was vaguely aware of Alice's husband shepherding them up and down the aisle, but the rest of the day was a jumble of confused thoughts and impressions.

The coffin lay in state in front of the pulpit. Remembering the imperfect state of the embalming, Emily couldn't help but stare at it, fearing that it would begin to drip essence of Horace. The horror of it made her shake. Robert put his arm around her and handed her his handkerchief.

"It will be over soon," he whispered. "I'll take you home before I go to the cemetery."

"I need to go with your aunt, to receive," she whispered back. "I'm all right. It's just that, being here, it seems like it all happened yesterday."

He gave her a comforting squeeze.

Emily closed her eyes. She felt again the shock of learning that her husband had died suddenly. The terror of being left alone in a strange town, of not knowing what she was to do next. Even worse was the rush of anger at Horace, for leaving her in this predicament. She knew from the way the men had avoided her eyes what had brought on his heart attack. She only prayed that the poor girl had not been hurt, that he had not used her as he had abused their maids, as he had treated his own wife.

These were not the thoughts that should be weighing on a woman at her husband's funeral. Emily loathed herself for being such a hypocrite. All these people were friends and family of Horace. They were here to give her sympathy and support. Her tears were of grief for the things she had not been strong enough to put a stop to, not for the loss of a loving husband. How could she face their solicitude?

As they left the church, someone pressed close to her and whispered.

"Don't think that because he's dead the bastard will get away with it."

Emily twisted to see who it was but the speaker could have been any of half a dozen people.

She grasped Robert's arm more tightly.

"Tell your Aunt Alice I am unwell," she told him. "I want to go home."

———

When she got back, Emily found she couldn't rest. Instead she worked feverishly unpacking the last of the boxes. The familiarity of her possessions calmed her so that by the time Robert came home, she had composed herself enough to listen to the details of the burial.

But at the back of her mind she wondered how many of the mourners had hated her husband. Who else was relieved that he was now safely below ground? And who might have carried resentment against him even beyond the grave?

By that evening, Emily had things put away. With help from Robert and Mary Kate, she had replaced the lugubrious landscapes hanging in the parlor with light Chinese watercolors. The stuffed birds under glass had been banished to the attic along with the cast bronze figures of various generals. In their place were cloisonné vases and porcelain statues. Emily had covered her bedroom furniture with embroidered silk, brightening it considerably. The shutters and curtains were now wide open to catch the weak winter sun.

The house was beginning to feel like home.

"Here's another pile of cards," Mary Kate told Emily the next morning. "A lot of people have come calling on you. I'm thinking that you'll need to be buying some rubber boots and start returning the visits."

Emily sighed over her noodle soup and tea. She reluctantly picked up the top cards from the salver.

"Mrs. Simeon Reed, Mrs. William Ladd, Rev. C. C. Stratton, Mrs. Charles Burrage, Mrs. Ira Goodnough, Mrs. Rodney Glison, Mrs. J. L. Atkinson," she read. "So many! Perhaps I shouldn't have said I was indisposed."

Mary Kate made no comment although her expression announced that it was better to be indisposed than to greet one's guests clad only in a loose pair of embroidered silk trousers and jacket. She still didn't know what to make of her mistress's at home costume, although she had to admit that it looked tremendously comfortable.

Emily picked up another pair of cards. "Oh, that nice minister came! Dr. Eliot. I wonder if he brought the baby. And Mr. Carmichael came by twice. I know it's not proper for me to visit him on my own, but I suppose I must send him a note."

There was one more paper on the salver. Instead of a small calling card, this was an envelope ostentatiously sealed with a signet ring in wax. Emily opened it.

"Dear Mrs. Stratton," she read. "I regret that I was unable to be present when you called upon us the other day. I should be much obliged if you and your son would come to the office at your earliest convenience to discuss the disposal of your share in the company. Mr. Andrews and I would be happy to offer you either an interest in the profits or, more appropriately in your situation, to purchase Captain Stratton's partnership from you outright. Please bring any business papers Captain Stratton may have left in your care. Your obedient servant, Matthew King."

Emily stared at the paper, her lips tightening in anger. He had given her no welcome to the community, she noticed. But she already had guessed that Horace's surviving partners didn't want her here.

She finished slurping her noodles, drank the remaining broth from the bowl, and sucked thoughtfully on a chicken foot, while deciding what to do next.

Her reverie was broken by the entrance of her son. Robert was wearing a worsted work shirt and woolen trousers. He had a blue bandanna tied around his neck in place of the silk tie he customarily sported.

"Good morning, dearest Mother," he greeted her with a kiss. "Is that *tangmiàn* with chicken feet? Is there any more?"

"Of course, darling," Emily smiled. "Ah Sung, more soup, please. You look dressed for mucking out stables," she told Robert. "What are you planning to do today?"

"I want to go exploring up into the woods with a couple of fellows I met," he answered. "They're going to show me some trails back there. Maybe we'll do a bit of hunting. Ah Sung, can you cook bear meat?" he added as the cook came in with his soup.

"I cook anything," he answered. "You shoot bear, I make stew. Missee Stratton, write please what for dinner."

"Not bear, I think," Emily answered. "I'll make a list. Thank you, Ah Sung."

"You'd better lay in a bushel of potatoes for Mary Kate," Robert laughed. "I don't think she appreciates chicken feet."

"She's more adventurous than you think," Emily told him. "It's not the meat but the spices that she's not used to."

Robert shrugged. He remembered the first time he'd eaten a potato. It was months before he got used to the texture. He couldn't imagine living on nothing else, as the Irish seemed to do.

"Will you be gone all day?" Emily asked. "I really must start returning all these calls and I need an escort."

"I'd be happy to do it, Mother, but I did promise these fellows I'd go with them," Robert apologized. "Why don't I drop by and ask Aunt Alice to go with you? She knows everyone in town."

Emily's heart sank, but she had to admit that the suggestion had merit. It might make up for leaving Alice alone to receive the guests after the funeral. And she could probably give Emily good advice. There were rules in every town concerning social visiting that were every bit as arcane and convoluted as that of the imperial court in China. There was no point in starting out by offending people. She was sure there would be enough op- portunity for that later.

Robert got up from the table. "Oh, I might not return until late. We thought we'd stop on the way back and visit with Jack's uncle. He has a farm just north of town."

Emily's head came up. "You won't wander the woods after dark, will you, my dear?" she entreated. "There are not just bears, they say, but moun- tain lions and maybe red Indians."

Robert laughed. "Never fear, my poor nervous mama. We'll be safe in- doors long before dark."

"And these 'fellows,'" she persisted. "What are their full names?"

"Just Jack and Hank," he answered. "I met them up at the Portland Academy on Thursday when I went to inquire about enrolling."

"Robert! How wonderful!" Emily clapped her hands in delight. "I didn't want to bring it up so soon, but I do believe that another term of study will prepare you to take your exams for Harvard much more than if you just read at home. You must bring your friends by the house soon." She looked down at her pyjamas. "Although not without telling me in advance."

Robert left on his errand and Emily went upstairs so that Mary Kate could encase her in attire appropriate for calls. She was just pinning on her watch when her son returned with the news that Aunt Alice was paying calls all day and would be happy to have her come along.

"Don't look so gloomy," he chided her. "She's coming in the carriage so you'll be in style. By the look of the clouds, you'll be glad of it. And, before you say a word, I have my slicker and a waterproof cap."

Her maternal worry at rest, Emily prepared herself for the day. Deep breathing was out of the question with the corset, but she did try to clear her mind. She imagined a candle flame and tried to keep it from flickering, tried to see nothing but the flame. Her teacher in Shanghai had started her on this meditation and it was still the hardest for her to accomplish. Peace . . . quiet . . . calm.

A furious shriek sliced the air.

"You wicked spalpeen! Get out of here! Out! Right now!"

Ah Sung came running down the back stairs, followed by Mary Kate, wielding a broom. The man flung himself at Emily, speaking in excited Cantonese.

"What is going on here?" she demanded. "Mary Kate, put down that broom."

"I found him up in your room!" Mary Kate told her. "He was going through your wardrobe. Dirty-minded heathen thief!"

"I no thief!" Ah Sung shouted from behind Emily's skirts. Beyond that, his English seemed to have deserted him.

"Mary Kate, bring me pen and paper," Emily sighed. She motioned for Ah Sung to sit at the kitchen table.

Why were you in my room? she wrote when the maid had brought writing material.

I beg your forgiveness, he wrote back. *I thought you had left and I remembered that you said you had a spice box from China. I was looking for it to begin preparations for the evening meal.*

Emily nodded and scribbled another line. *I shall bring you the spice box. It is not proper for you to be upstairs. Please ask me if you need something else.*

Ah Sung bowed over the paper. Then he stood and bowed again. "*Wo ming pai,*" he said in accented Mandarin.

Mary Kate had been watching the proceedings with dark suspicion.

"Did you give him the boot?" she asked.

"It was a misunderstanding," Emily explained. She told Mary Kate where the spice box was and sent her to get it.

While they waited, Emily tried to find out more about Ah Sung. To her scribbled questions, he only answered that he came from a poor farming family. He had come to America to get rich in the gold mountain of California. When he had found no gold, he had come north, cooking at the railroad camps. His only desire was to earn enough to keep his father and mother, wife and children and other assorted relatives from starvation.

Mary Kate brought down the wooden box containing the herbs and spices Emily had packed in Shanghai. She gave it to Ah Sung.

"Now you have no need to go upstairs," she told him firmly.

He bowed deeply, his long braid swinging to the floor. "Thank you, thank you," he said as he backed through the kitchen door. "Very sorry, Missee Stratton."

They both heard the jingle of harness as Mrs. Bracewell's carriage came up the drive. Emily pulled on her gloves.

"Am I properly dressed for the occasion?" she asked Mary Kate.

"You look positively splendid," Mary Kate assured her.

"Don't worry about Mr. Ah," Emily said. "I think you terrified him enough that he won't leave the kitchen today."

"Then I'll stay upstairs and get on with the dusting," Mary Kate said. "Just in case he should take it into his head to hunt for something else."

She opened the door to see Emily out.

Emily squared her shoulders and prepared for an afternoon of social pleasantries, interspersed by a flow of gossip from her knowledgeable sister-in-law.

Alice didn't disappoint. If Emily could believe her, Portland consisted of a large number of reprobates, heathens, and thieves with a few radicals and suffragists thrown in for good measure. Against these was ranged a thin line of right-thinking, well-bred Presbyterians and Episcopalians who fought the good fight to preserve civilization on the wild frontier. And that was just among the people one had to associate with.

"The real problem, of course," Alice complained, "is that hardly any of the common people know their place. Shop boys and clerks speak to us as if we were equals. I know how to handle them, of course, but my daughters haven't learned the art of preserving a frosty reserve when approached by that sort or person."

"I had hoped that I would meet your daughters today," Emily commented, trying to find a safe subject.

Unfortunately, this seemed to touch a sore spot with Alice. "They begged to be excused from making calls as they had to prepare for the cotillion this evening."

"That's quite excusable," Emily laughed. "I don't dance, but I know how excited the ladies of the merchant quarter in Shanghai would get when someone organized a musical evening."

"I'm sure that was quite different," Alice sniffed. "Privately arranged with an exclusive guest list. This is some grubby dancing school party. Mr. McCann used to hold his school over the newspaper offices and, of course, I'd never allow Sarah and Felicity to attend there. But now he's moved to a hall over Randall's music store. I don't see that it makes much difference. He still allows anyone in who has sixty cents in his pocket. But the girls pleaded and George gave in. He's far too indulgent."

"George?"

"Mr. Bracewell, of course," Alice said. She brushed a leaf from her skirt. "Here we are. This is Dr. Glisan's house. He's very important, used to be an army surgeon. She's quite nice, although she has no sense of style and is *much* younger than he. They are quite well-connected in town."

Emily alit from the carriage, her head a whirl of jumbled information about the private lives of the people she was likely to meet. The one thing that remained in her head was that she had never before heard the name of Alice's husband. Horace had rarely mentioned his sister, much less her family. Until she met George Bracewell at the church, Emily had assumed that Alice was a widow.

They were admitted to the Glisans' by a young maid who led them into the drawing room, where three other women were seated, holding teacups. One of them put down her cup and rose as the maid announced them.

"Mrs. Stratton." She came to Emily with outstretched hands. "I'm so delighted to meet you. I'm Elizabeth Glisan. Please do sit down and have some tea. This is Mrs. Burrage and Dr. Thompson."

Mrs. Burrage proved to be a woman of about Emily's own age, slightly plump, with a kindly expression. To Emily's bewilderment, Dr. Thompson was the other woman, an attractive lady in her early forties, with dark hair and amused eyes. Alice hadn't mentioned her.

"How do you do?" Emily said. "I'm very pleased to meet you. I'm sorry I haven't been able to make proper calls before. There's so little that I know about my new home. I hope you'll educate me."

"Sarah Burrage." The other woman held out her hand. "We are so sorry for your loss. It must be very strange coming here without your dear husband."

"I intend to take care of her," Alice told her decidedly. "But of course she won't be doing much socializing until she's out of mourning."

The other ladies murmured sympathetic agreement. At that moment, the young maid returned with a tray holding more teacups and a pot of hot water. She was followed by an even younger girl with a plate of cakes. Emily and Alice each accepted the offerings.

"I would like to become involved in something useful though," Emily announced. "There must be some sort of women's charity that needs a volunteer, don't you think?"

Young Mrs. Glisan put down her cup. "How interesting! We were just discussing that very subject."

"In the course of my work I have come across several families that need help of various sorts," Dr. Thompson explained. "We have a number of women in town who are trying to support their children by their own efforts. Their husbands have either died or gone to the gold fields in Idaho to make their fortune. Some are in desperate circumstances."

"I would, of course, be happy to donate something to aid them," Emily said. "But I was hoping for something a little more active. It has never been my nature to sit in my house all day."

"Perhaps you should ask Reverend Stratton about the Methodist ladies' organization," Mrs. Burrage suggested. "They have a very active missionary society. Wouldn't that be more natural to you?"

Emily suppressed a shudder. "I have already received a note from them, asking if I would come and speak on the progress of the faith in China."

"I am a bit confused," Mrs. Glisan said. "I understood that you were brought up in China, but Reverend Stratton told me that the Methodist mission only began there about twenty years ago."

"That's correct," Emily agreed. "My parents were not from an American mission but a British one. They went first to Macao in 1838, when I was four. I was immediately set to learning the language so that I could help interpret my father's sermons. Unfortunately, he never became very adept at Chinese, although many of the other missionaries did. When Shanghai was opened to Westerners in 1842, we moved there. I have seen many men from the southern part of China here in Portland. They must feel dreadfully alone in this country. Is anything being done for them and their families?"

There was a heavy silence.

"More tea, Mrs. Stratton?" Mrs. Glisan lifted the pot.

Dr. Thompson smiled. "The general opinion here is that the Chinese workers are transient and that they take care of their own sufficiently."

"George says that they are useless to the economy," Alice added. "They hardly buy a thing and send all their money back to China."

Emily nodded. "You know that most of them come from a region that has been heavily struck by war and famine," she commented, taking another piece of cake. "The money they send back from America is all that keeps their families from starvation. Excellent tea, Mrs. Glisan."

She could feel a cold breeze as Alice stiffened beside her. The other three women exchanged glances. Dr. Thompson smiled.

"I hadn't known that, Mrs. Stratton," she said. "Thank you for explaining." She stood. "I must leave now. I have a few patients to visit this afternoon." She turned to Emily. "I should very much like to see you again. Perhaps I could call upon you next week?"

"Certainly." Emily wasn't sure if the invitation was sincere, but she hoped so. She liked the sparkle of intelligence and good nature in the woman.

Alice also rose to leave. "We mustn't take up more of your time," she told Mrs. Glisan. "I promised to make a few other calls with Emily today."

"Yes, of course." Mrs. Glisan signaled to the maid to bring their coats. "Thank you so much for coming."

They settled themselves into the carriage and the driver shut the door.

"*Well,*" said Alice. "It is clear that your upbringing has not included suitable subjects for conversation among ladies of refinement. The welfare of our Chinese visitors is not our concern."

"Oh my," Emily spoke softly. "Did I embarrass you, Alice dear? I'm so sorry."

Alice continued her diatribe all the way to the next stop. She watched nervously throughout the next visits, ready to leap upon any more *faux pas.* To her relief, Emily remained docile.

They rode home in the late afternoon, in a cloudy twilight. Alice kept up a stream of information about the better families of Portland. Idly, Emily looked out the window, wondering why the cook had really been in her room. His history was a common one, typical enough to be true, but he had been vague about it. Of course, there were many reasons he might have had to come to America, some that he might not want her to know. But it did seem odd that he should have been searching her possessions. Could he possibly have something to do with Horace?

Next to her, Alice rambled on.

It was after dark when they returned home. Mary Kate met Emily at the door.

"That Chinese man is in cooking something for you that smells like laundry day at the poor farm," Mary Kate said. "But he also put in a nice roast chicken, spuds, and onions, so I guess I won't starve tonight. He hasn't left the kitchen since he came back from the market."

"Thank you, Mary Kate." Emily gave the maid her coat and cape. "I don't want to judge hastily, but I think we should keep an eye on Ah Sung. He may have just been in my room hunting for spices, but I have the feeling that he is much more educated than he pretends to be. His writing is very good, better than mine. I'm almost sure he understands Mandarin, and we can't neglect the possibility that his English is good, too."

"If he can do all that, ma'am," Mary Kate asked, "then why would he be working here?"

"I don't know," Emily said. "That's why he needs to be watched."

She sat down to have Mary Kate remove her boots.

"Is Robert upstairs?" She wondered why he hadn't come down to greet her.

"He's not back yet from his hunting trip," Mary Kate told her. "It could be the boys stopped at one of the other houses to warm up first."

Emily glanced out the window. The night was dark. A sharp wind was whistling through the fir trees by the road. She had a vision of her son lying in the snow, mauled by a bear or scalped by Indians. Robert had said he would be late, but she hadn't thought he'd meant to miss supper. She should have asked the full names of the boys he had gone with.

"Perhaps you could bring me some tea." She spoke softly so as not to miss the sound of his step in the drive. "We'll wait supper for him."

But the night wore on and Robert didn't return. Mary Kate and Ah Sung ate their respective meals and Emily continued to wait in the parlor, imagining horrors.

CHAPTER SEVEN

In the beginning woman consisted of a single rib. Now she is all ribs, from her belt to the rim of her petticoat.

—*HARPER'S WEEKLY*, SEPTEMBER 7, 1867

MUCH LATER, THAT SAME NIGHT

The hall clock had just struck eleven when Emily heard a scuffling on the front porch. She rushed to the door, getting there just before Mary Kate, who had not gone to bed as ordered. In the low gaslight she saw her son, fumbling with the key. He gave her a puzzled smile.

"Robert, darling!" Emily threw her arms around him. "Are you all right? What happened? I was so worried."

Robert gently disengaged her. "I'm sorry, Mother. I did tell you that we were stopping at Jack's uncle's. He gave us supper and then drove us home in his carriage. I didn't expect you to wait up."

"Yes, of course," Emily admitted. "I just didn't think it would be this late."

She examined his face in the light.

"You're so flushed, my dear," she fretted. "Do you think you might have caught a chill? You should have an herbal tea and go right up to bed."

Robert laughed. "I'm fine, Mother, just rosy with the cold. But I am ready for bed, and you should go up, too. Aren't you braving the Methodist congregation tomorrow morning?"

"Not without you on my arm," she responded. "You promised, Robert. I can't go alone."

"I'll be bright and bonny." He yawned mightily.

Mary Kate, still waiting to take his greatcoat, caught a whiff of his breath.

"Your coat, Master Robert," she said frostily, holding her arm out for it.

Robert tried to unbutton the coat, but his fingers slipped.

"My poor boy!" Emily undid the buttons for him. "You must be frozen! Hurry on up and get right in bed. I'll bring you the tea."

"Don't bother yourself, Mrs. Stratton," Mary Kate told her. "I've a kettle just off the boil. I'll make the tea. Young Robert may be glad of a bit of bread and cheese, as well."

"Thank you, Mary Kate." Emily suppressed a yawn. "I confess that now that I've no cause for worry, I'm very tired."

She went up the stairs. Mary Kate hurried to the kitchen, shaking her head. "If that boy hasn't spent the evening tipping the jar, then I'm a Chinese princess."

In his room off the kitchen, Ah Sung listened to the clatter of the cups and plates, along with Mary Kate's worried muttering. Finally, the door swung shut and her footsteps stomped to the second floor. He waited a bit longer to be certain that she had gone on to her own room under the roof; then he hid his queue under a knit cap, wrapped himself in a long cloak, and pulled the hood over his face. Taking a dark lantern to light the ground before him, he slipped out the back door.

Emily was dreaming that she was back on the ship, rocking back and forth, back and forth. Suddenly a wave crashed against the side, knocking her to the deck.

"Mrs. Stratton! Do wake up!"

Emily opened her eyes. Mary Kate was shaking her in a way that no well-trained lady's maid would dare.

"What is it?" she mumbled. "Are we on fire?"

"I thought maybe he'd poisoned you." Mary Kate exhaled in relief. "So he could come in and steal your jewels."

"What? Who?" Emily sat bolt upright, looking around for her assailant.

"That Ah Sung man," Mary Kate said. "I came down this morning to find the kitchen cold, the door unbolted, and Mr. Ah Sung gone."

"Mary Kate, there's no reason to assume he's run off." Emily collected herself. "He probably just went out early to shop."

"He'd have lit the fire before," Mary Kate insisted. "You mark me, ma'am. He came here to steal from you. He knew I was watching him and now he's gone to earth. We'll not be seeing him again."

Emily got out of bed and went over to her jewelry box. It was still locked. Nothing appeared to have been disturbed.

"Is anything downstairs missing?" she asked.

"I couldn't say for sure," Mary Kate admitted. "I didn't look carefully. But I remembered you said there was something odd about the man. I thought I'd better find out first if you hadn't been cruelly murdered in your bed."

Emily put a hand on her arm. "That was a kind impulse. Thank you."

She reached for her dressing gown. "Let's go inspect the rest of the house. Did you wake Robert?"

"I could hear the snoring through the door," Mary Kate told her. "So I knew he was alive. I thought I'd let him sleep it off."

"He was out quite late yesterday," Emily agreed. "I do hope he hasn't caught cold."

Mary Kate bit her lips and said no more on that subject. She wished it were her place to warn Emily about the friends her son was making.

They found nothing missing anywhere, except Ah Sung.

"But he must be planning to return," Emily pointed out. "You see, he's left his things."

"Well, I suppose," Mary Kate conceded with reluctance. "But where is he then?"

Emily had no idea but was sure the cook would be back soon. In the meantime they made do with tea and toast. Emily took a cup up to Robert, reminding him that he was to accompany her to church.

His red and bleary eyes gave her concern.

"Are you sure you're not ill, my dear?" she asked.

"Just a touch, mother," he said bravely. "Not enough to keep me from taking my best girl out today. Give me a few minutes to wash, run a comb through my hair, and find a clean collar."

"You may have a whole hour." She kissed him. "Drink your tea down. I've put in a few of Dr. Chung's herbs that should make you feel better."

Ah Sung had still not come back when they were ready to leave. The day was gray but dry and the church only a few blocks away so they decided to walk. Emily kept an eye out, expecting at any moment to see the cook hurrying toward them, laden with groceries. But she saw no Chinese at all.

She was unprepared for the curious stares that greeted them from everyone who passed. Some people smiled and bowed, others looked away quickly without meeting her eye. Emily wondered if it was just that she was a stranger or if they had known her husband and didn't want to meet her.

The church, on Third and Taylor, was newly built in the New England style, with an elegant spire. The bell started ringing as they approached. Emily felt Robert wince.

"Are you sure you're quite well, my dear?" she asked.

"Please stop asking me, Mother," he snapped. "I'm fine!"

"Of course, dear," she answered quietly. "I'm sorry."

They were on the steps of the church now. He squeezed her hand in apology as they entered.

Emily was pleasantly surprised to find that the choir was quite good and the sermon mercifully short. Reverend Stratton was not as concerned about hellfire as her father had been, at least not this morning.

As they were waiting to introduce themselves after the service, Emily found herself standing next to Mr. Carmichael.

"Good morning, Mrs. Stratton." He tipped his hat. "I've been wondering how you're settling in."

"Quite well, thank you," she answered. "I saw your cards on the hall table. I should have sent a note round to thank you for your concern and for your care of us when we arrived."

"No need, no need at all," he beamed at her. "It was little enough to do. I understand that Mr. Andrews has been ill. I hope that his indisposition hasn't affected your ability to access funds."

Robert answered for her. "We are in no danger of the poorhouse, Mr. Carmichael," he said with a glare.

"Of course not." Carmichael backed away a step. "I apologize for prying."

He turned to leave.

Emily stopped him with a hand on his arm. His hurt expression melted under the sympathy in her brown eyes.

"I'm sorry," she said quietly. "My son is perhaps too protective of me."

"No man, Mrs. Stratton," he answered, "could protect you too much."

Unaccountably, Emily felt herself blushing. *How ridiculous!* she chided herself. *He's just a nice older man with a fatherly interest.*

Quickly, Mr. Carmichael replaced his hat and walked briskly away.

"Robert, you shouldn't have said that," Emily spoke mildly. "Mr. Carmichael has been kind to us and he won't understand that you were just joking."

Robert shook his head slowly. "Mother, you don't know much about the world. It's my duty to see that no one takes advantage of you."

"I promise, my darling boy," Emily laughed, "that I'll consult you before buying any shares of mining stock or recipes for patent medicine."

He didn't smile. "I'm serious, Mother. You think the world is a loving place, and I love you for it. But you are far too trusting. There are those who would take everything you have and leave you to starve."

"Robert!" Emily shook her head. "Where do you get such ideas? It's so dear of you to want to protect me, but I'm not as simple as you seem to think. I won't let anyone take advantage of us."

Her voice changed with these last words. Robert looked at her sharply. For a fleeting moment, he wondered if his mother was hiding a side of herself from him, just as he was from her. Then it was their turn to meet Reverend Stratton, and it was all he could do to keep from throwing up on the man's shoes as he bowed. Confounded home brew! From now on he would stick to proper whiskey and brandy.

————

The drizzle began as they started home. By the time they reached the house it had settled into a light cold rain that penetrated the layers of Emily's clothing and chilled her to the bone. Mary Kate met them with hot tea and the news that Ah Sung was still absent.

"I don't understand it," Emily fretted. "He didn't seem the type to go without notice. Perhaps I should find out from Alice where she hired him. Although I hate to imply that her judgment is poor." She sighed. "I suppose I should go now, while I'm still dressed for making calls."

"You don't need to be going to Mrs. Bracewell," Mary Kate said. "I know where he came from. There's a Chinaman who speaks English down on Second Street who gets Chinese workers for people. He's a Mr. Wa."

Emily and Robert looked at her in surprise.

"I asked Bessie, Mrs. Bracewell's washwoman," Mary Kate told them. "She said that Mrs. Bracewell didn't interview him herself, just sent a boy down with a note to have a cook at your place right away."

"Then it's Mr. Wa I'll have to go see." Emily picked up her damp cloak and looked about for an umbrella.

"Not alone," Mary Kate said.

"I'll be fine," Emily assured her. "Robert, you go straight up to bed. I don't want that chill to turn into an ague. Mary Kate, if I don't return in an hour, you have my permission to call out the watch."

Emily enjoyed her stroll down to Second Street. The drizzle seemed to soften the rough edges of the town. It was like seeing the world through a silver curtain. There was a tang in the air that made her feel as if she were waking from a long and confusing dream. This was a new day and a new life. She couldn't reclaim the years she had lost, but she could make the next ones worth living.

It didn't take her long to find "Wa Kee's Emporium." The name was written in large letters in both English and Chinese characters over the door. The music of wind chimes and the pungent aroma of incense and opium greeted her as she entered.

Inside the air was thick and warm and familiar. The front room was a small shop, with tea, rice, pots, small lanterns, incense sticks, and canned goods stacked on shelves. A red curtain hid the room behind. Emily guessed that it was a combination shrine and meeting place where the men would talk, smoke, and pray. She knew that even a Chinese woman would not be welcome there. A small brass dinner bell sat on the counter. She picked it up and shook it gently.

A man came out from the back. He was dressed in Western clothing: woolen pants, boots, shirt, jacket, and vest. But he hadn't cropped his hair and he wore a Chinese blue cloth cap embroidered in gold thread.

"Go way, missee," he said. "We closed today."

"I don't want to buy anything," Emily answered. "I'm looking for Ah Sung."

"Ah Sung, he work in a big house for rich lady," the man told her. "Go way."

"Yes, I know. He works for me, but he's gone and I'm worried about him," Emily said. In desperation, she switched to Mandarin. "He went out last night and didn't come back. Have you seen him?"

She could tell from his expression that the man understood her, but he just shook his head in bewilderment. Emily wondered how many pipes he had smoked today.

"I'd like to speak to Wa Kee," she said. "I'll wait."

The man vanished behind the curtain. A few moments later, another man came out. He was wearing the robe of a military official, with a high-ranking insignia square on the front.

"*Wo xing Wa.*" He bowed to her but only a fraction. His speech was educated Mandarin, much more so than hers. "We do not give refunds if the men we send run away. If I see Ah Sung, I shall insist he return to you at once."

"Thank you, honorable sir," she answered. "Ah Sung is a fine cook. I do not wish to lose his services. I am only concerned for his well-being. If he has not come back here, where else would he go?"

Wa Kee opened his silk-clad arms as if encompassing the world. "To try his luck in the mines; or get a job in the woolen mill or the salmon plant," he suggested. "Or perhaps he went in search of a boat that would take him back to Nanking."

He bowed to her again. This time it was a dismissal.

"Come back tomorrow and I will find you another cook," he told

Emily. "I'm afraid that he won't speak Mandarin, but I think you might understand Cantonese better than you pretend, *Missee* Stratton."

He folded his arms and waited in silence for Emily to retreat.

Instead, she took a step closer. "I do not want another cook, Wa Kee. I want Ah Sung, who also understands better than he pretends."

With that she turned and swept out, somewhat hampered by her hoop skirts and the narrowness of the door.

She walked home at a much brisker pace than she had coming. Wa Kee's words had both angered and frightened her. What did he mean about Ah Sung going back to Nanking? He couldn't have come from there. Of course not. The Taiping rebellion had been crushed four years ago. Almost everyone in Nanking had been brutally slaughtered. Wa Kee knew that, certainly. But why did he suggest that she understood the language of the rebels? What did he know?

She wished there were someone she could run to for help, for advice. But in this, as in everything else now, she was on her own. Why had she always been so submissive? She wanted to curse her parents for all the naïve, self-sacrificing mistakes they had made that had led her here. But all she could feel was a dull pity and a deep, deep grief.

It was several minutes before she realized that she had made a wrong turn somewhere. Instead of being in front of her house, she was across from a lot full of tree stumps. In the center was a small white building. There were lanterns in the windows. With a stab of alarm, Emily realized that it was almost dark.

As she crossed over to ask the way, the door opened and people came streaming out. Evening service, she realized. How early the darkness fell here! Some of the men carried lanterns. Surely someone would be going her way.

"Mrs. Stratton, good evening!" The minister stood on the step. Emily's face brightened. It was the same young man she had run into at the Kings'.

"Reverend Eliot." She held out her hand. "I'm so glad to see you. I've lost my way."

He nodded solemnly. "And you've come here to find it again. Well, hallelujah!"

"Oh, no! I meant, I mean . . ." Emily was terribly flustered. Then she saw that the young man's lips were twitching.

Someone behind her started to laugh. Emily joined in. Reverend Eliot threw his head back and whooped like a boy. "I'm so sorry, Mrs. Stratton. I couldn't resist."

"I quite understand," Emily said. "I should have put it better. Now, is there any one of your congregation who might guide me back to my house?"

"Of course," Eliot said. "Mr. and Mrs. Reed, you know Mrs. Stratton, don't you? You live quite near her. Could you show her the way?"

"Certainly." A lovely woman with dark hair and small wire-rim glasses came over. "Sim and I will be delighted. I'm sorry you were indisposed when I called. Now we can have a chance to become acquainted."

The walk back was more pleasant than Emily had expected. Mrs. Reed's quiet manner soothed her jangled nerves. She didn't ask any prying questions but chatted about the town of Portland, the people, new books at the lending library. The gold glow of the lantern in Mr. Reed's hand made the mist glitter magically, a globe of safety circling them.

The couple took Emily to her door. She thanked them sincerely and promised to call on them soon.

Robert was waiting for her in the parlor. Seated next to him was a strange man. He was around thirty, in an ill-fitting suit. He jumped up as soon as she entered.

"Mrs. Stratton." He spoke with a soft drawl. "My name is Seth More-land. I'm from the city police. I'm sorry to have to tell you that your servant, Ah Sung, was found floating in the river this afternoon. I'm afraid he's dead."

"Oh, how terrible!" Emily cried. "The poor man! What a dreadful accident. I'll see to it that his body is returned to his family in China. How did it happen?"

"Well, ma'am." Moreland wriggled, as if his collar was too tight. "I don't know as I should tell you, but the doctor don't think it was an accident. It seems he had a pretty big shotgun hole in his chest."

Chapter Eight

I hear the sad news that Chinamen are to be taxed *fifteen dollars a month. This I call robbing by law . . . You pretend to love God, yet you make this law which is very dangerous to the Chinamen. I hope some wise men and honest judges will take this danger from Chinamen who will never forget the kindness.*

—Letter to the *Oregonian* from Dr. Jim, a Chinese resident of Portland, 1868

Sunday evening, March 1, 1868

Emily stared at him for a moment.

"Shot?" She couldn't take it in. "But why?"

Mr. Moreland shrugged. "Who knows? Some feud that started back in China, maybe. Or a fight over a woman or a wager. Those moon-eyes gamble about anything. Of course no one down there is talking."

This last was said with a bitter twist. Emily wasn't surprised that the Chinese wouldn't answer his questions. They probably wanted to handle the matter themselves.

"Will you investigate?" she asked.

"Not me." Moreland seemed relieved. "Somebody higher up gets to do that. They just sent me to tell you and to get his things."

"His things? For what reason?"

"Evidence, I guess." He scratched his head. "Looking for a threatening letter or something. I don't know. But the boss wants them."

"I see." Emily didn't like handing over Ah Sung's belongings. At least, not until she had had a chance to go through them herself.

"I'm sure you must be cold, Mr. Moreland," she said. "You wait here by the fire and I'll have Mary Kate bring you some tea while I collect Ah Sung's things and put them in a box for you."

The policeman seemed to have no suspicions. He grinned. "That would be most kind, ma'am. This country drives the cold in like nothing I ever felt in Tennessee."

Emily hurried to the kitchen.

"Mary Kate," she ordered. "Make a nice pot of tea, please, as slowly as you can, and serve it with anything sweet we have. I need about fifteen minutes."

"Of course, Mrs. Stratton," Mary Kate answered calmly. "I let the man in. A fine-looking fellow. I wouldn't mind keeping him long enough to learn if he's spoken for."

Emily hugged her. "Thank you, Mary Kate!"

It didn't take fifteen minutes to go through Ah Sung's few possessions: two changes of clothing in the cupboard, a pair of soft slippers under the bed, a comb, and hair pomade on the dresser next to a small brass figure of the goddess Kuan Yin, a burnt joss stick at its feet. She opened the dresser drawer. There were a few undergarments, neatly folded. And at the very bottom, a book.

Emily knew at once what it was, a Chinese Bible. Folded in the Gospel of Luke were several sheets of paper, badly printed in woodblocks. She recognized those as well, Methodist tracts.

This didn't automatically mean that Ah Sung had been a Christian, just as the statue didn't mean that he wasn't. Many Chinese read the Bible as a novel for amusement, much to the chagrin of the missionaries. Some who had converted still prayed to their family gods. But why had a man with tracts written at the Shanghai mission come to her door? And what did he have to do with Nanking?

Emily could no longer believe that Ah Sung was merely a cook. He had planned to be hired into her household. Or someone else had sent him. But why? And what had he done that had brought about his murder?

Her hand trembled. The sheets of cheap paper fluttered to the floor. She had to hold onto them until she discovered the answers.

The kitchen was still crowded with empty packing boxes. Emily got one and put the clothes and other items in it. She had searched the drawers and shelves in Ah Sung's room for a letter from home, something to say where he had come from and who would mourn, but there was nothing more. The Bible she slipped into the knife drawer. She told herself that she'd give it to the police after she'd had a chance to examine it.

When she returned to the parlor, Mary Kate was pouring tea for Mr. Moreland. She watched him add five lumps of sugar with a look that said she had discovered he was still a bachelor. Robert was watching with open amusement.

"I'd be adding a bit of whiskey to that, if this weren't a dry house," Mary Kate whispered to the policeman.

Emily suppressed a smile. She set the box on the floor.

"Do finish your tea first," she told Mr. Moreland. "Will you have to patrol the streets all night?"

"Just another four hours," he said. "But a warm drink is welcome any-time."

He spoke to her but his eyes were on Mary Kate, who beamed at him and offered some plum cake. He ignored the plate and ate it with his fingers. After a second of hesitation, Robert took a slice and did the same.

Moreland finished the tea and cake, wiped his mouth with his sleeve, and stood to go. He picked up the box and looked surprised at how little was in it.

"Not much for a life, is it?" he said. "Poor thing. It makes me want to go home and write my mother."

"It is sad," Emily agreed, surprised and shamed by his depth of feeling. "I hope there is someone from his family here to be sure his people know what happened."

"Pity we'll probably never know who did it," he sighed. "The Chinese never let us mess in their private business."

"I'm sure you'll do your best," Emily said. "Mary Kate, would you show Mr. Moreland out?"

"Thank you for the tea, ma'am." Moreland started to put his hand out, then reflected that it wasn't quite proper. He contented himself with tipping his hat, which he had forgotten to remove.

As soon as they left, Robert turned to his mother.

"Ah Sung didn't strike me as a man who would be killed for a gambling debt," he told her. "Or in a brawl."

"Nor me," Emily said. "But you never know how people may change under the influence of liquor. In any case, it's not our business."

She spoke so sharply that Robert looked at her in alarm.

"Of course not," he agreed. "I really wanted to speak with you about getting properly enrolled at the Portland Academy tomorrow morning."

Mary Kate returned.

"Well, ma'am, Master Robert," she sighed. "Until we find another cook, I'm afraid it's back to eggs and toast for breakfast and supper, with a plate of boiled spuds on the side.

"It could be worse, Mary Kate," Emily said. "There might be nothing but chicken feet in the house." Mary Kate blanched at the thought.

Monday morning Norton Andrews entered his shop at the usual time. It would be another hour before King, his remaining partner, normally arrived.

Their clerk, Garrick, a boy of seventeen who had already starting looking for other employment, greeted him with some surprise.

"Good morning, sir. How are you feeling?"

"How would you feel if you'd been poisoned and some damn doctor had dosed you with ipecac?" Andrews snarled back.

"Fairly miserable, sir," the boy replied. "Are you sure you're well enough to work?"

"Rather that let things go to hell, yes." Andrews went into his office and slammed the door.

Garrick was a great fan of Charles Dickens, currently on a lecture tour of America. He wondered if Mr. Andrews had ever read *A Christmas Carol*. Garrick sighed. It was doubtful that even a visit from ghosts could make his employer a better person.

A few minutes later, Matthew King came in. He greeted Garrick in a more civilized manner, then also vanished into the office. Garrick casually rose from his desk and went over to dust the shelves next to the door.

"Keep your voice down," Garrick heard Andrews say. "I know that boy listens at doors."

Garrick hurried back to his desk.

Inside the office, King lit a cheroot. He inhaled deeply and exhaled, sending a blast of smoke directly at his colleague.

Andrews winced. He waved his hand in front of his face, dispelling the fumes.

"Don't do that," he whined. "My stomach is still dicey enough as it is."

King had endured this for long enough. "That's what you get for leaving fresh oysters out all day."

"I tell you, it wasn't the oysters!" Andrews slapped his hand on the desk. "I was poisoned!"

"So you keep saying." King exhaled again, this time toward the window. "But who would want to poison you, and why?"

"Any number of people we've done business with." Andrews looked at his partner in disgust. "And, as for why . . ." He scratched his chin. "Well, it could have been just out of spite or to keep me out of the way so they could rifle the safe. Everyone knows it's up in my rooms."

"But the safe wasn't tampered with," King pointed out.

"Perhaps because the Stratton boy got there in time," Andrews said. "I suppose I should thank him."

"I think we should avoid both the Strattons for the present." King ground out his cheroot. "I sent her a note telling her to bring all the accounts so that we could buy her out. She wrote back that she wanted to see us so that she could examine our records! My wife told me that Horace's widow wants to have a part in running things. We'll soon disabuse her of that idea. Her little Methodist toes would curl if she knew where her living came from."

Andrews wasn't so sure. "I keep remembering what Phipps told us after Horace died. He said she was slick and we should watch out for her."

"Well, we can always use the boy to keep her in line, if we have to." King turned to stare out the window. It only looked out on another whitewashed frame building, but the view seemed to satisfy him. "I hear that young Robert is a chip off the old block. He was down at the Hellhole on Saturday, buying drinks for the house and putting away a few himself."

"Do you think his mother knows?"

King snorted. "Did your mother ever see your peccadilloes, Norton? They're all blind to such things, bless 'em."

Andrews coughed. "I think that, now that I've recovered, we should agree to see her. We've got to find some way around her obstinacy if we want to continue the firm. We can't be running to her every time a decision needs making. She may own more than she realizes. Did you know that Horace was buying up any shares of the company that came on the market, using Johnson in San Francisco as a front?"

King had started to light another cheroot. The news made him drop the spill on the carpet. He stamped at it with his foot. "The devil you say! Of course I didn't know! That old bastard had more twists than the Snake River. Bad enough he kept evidence to blackmail us with. At least Phipps found that. Good thing he's also in it up to his chin."

"How do we know that was all?" Andrews asked gloomily, "What if Horace also found out about the railroad deal?"

King lost patience entirely. "There's no way he could have! You're searching for reasons to panic, man! I'm beginning to wish you *had* been poisoned."

On the other side of the door, Garrick smiled.

That morning Emily took Robert over for his first day at the Portland Academy. Although the school had been founded by Methodists in the early days of the town, students of all faiths attended. Alice had assured her that it was the best school in Portland. When Dr. Thompson and Mrs.

Glisan agreed, Emily was convinced. She was pleased when Robert's friend, Hank, waved at him as they entered. It was a comfort to see her son settling into his new home so quickly.

She had just returned to the house and was tackling the problem of finding another cook, as well as a coachman, when Mrs. Bracewell's driver showed up at the kitchen door, with a note asking if she and Robert would like to dine with them that evening.

"It would solve the problem of what to eat tonight," she said to Mary Kate. "Can you manage to find something for yourself?"

"And didn't I grow up eating spuds for breakfast, dinner, and tea every day?" Mary Kate said. "You go on. It's time your son met those cousins of his."

There being no other excuse, Emily went into the sitting room to scribble an acceptance while Mary Kate gave the coachman a cup of tea. Emily wondered if he'd bring out his silver flask but resolved not to ask.

At this point, what she wanted most was to go up to her room, get out of her corset and examine Ah Sung's Bible and the tracts inside it. She couldn't believe that he had been murdered because of a private feud. Had he been in Nanking? Was he a secret Christian? If so, why hide it now that he was in America? Or perhaps the Bible had nothing to do with Ah Sung's death. What if he had been in her home solely as an agent for someone who wanted to find the papers Horace had left? If so, then he might have been murdered because of her.

In any case, it was her responsibility to find out all she could.

Robert hadn't thought to bring a lunch to school. At his boarding school in Massachusetts, meals had all been provided. He was considering what to do when Jack and Hank sidled over to him.

"Did your mother buy the story?" Hank asked.

"Of course," Robert answered. "Why shouldn't she? What about your parents?"

"No problem," Hank grinned.

"What about you, Jack?" Robert asked.

The other boy looked away. "They didn't even ask,"

Hank stuck an elbow in Robert's side. "Tell you later," he whispered. "Where's your lunch?"

"Forgot it," Robert said. "Thought I'd just stop at a restaurant. Anything near here?"

"This ain't New York City, you dumb toff!" Jack sneered. "Maybe you should send the butler down to the What Cheer for some oysters."

Along with the rest of the town, they had heard about Mr. Andrews's misadventure.

"Here, my mother gave me a ham and cheese sandwich and pickles," Hank said. "I'll split 'em with you."

"Sure," Jack added. "I've got cold fried chicken and apple cake."

"Thanks." Robert accepted a drumstick. "I owe you. Say, I was talking to Ned Chambreau on Saturday. He says all the good fun is on the east side of the river. What if we planned a camping trip there next weekend?"

"Are you insane?" Hank's jaw dropped. "If my dad found out he'd skin me alive and nail my hide to the barn door!"

"And how's he going to find out?" Robert said. "Unless he sees you coming out while he's going in? What about you, Jack?"

"Naw," Jack answered, his mouth full of cake. "I got better things to do."

He shook out his lunch pail and headed over to the pump for some water.

"What's wrong with him?" Robert asked Hank.

Hank watched until he was sure Jack was out of earshot.

"Jack's father spends most Saturday nights on the East side," he explained. "Everyone knows he's got a lady friend over there. His mother knows, too, but she just takes another spoonful of laudanum. She never knows if Jack's home or not. I overheard my mother and your aunt talking about it one day."

"That's okay," Robert said cheerfully. "We'll find something else fun to do."

Hank handed him another sandwich. "Sure. We can go up on the courthouse roof with slingshots and take potshots at the coolies. Last month we used snowballs. It was a real hoot. We'll have to find something else to shoot now that the snow's most gone. Pinecones are hard to aim and the constables get after us if we use stones."

"Right," Robert said absently. It didn't sound like fun to him. He shook himself. "What else is there to do here? Got any baseball?"

Hank grinned. "We sure do! Jack! Come over and tell Robert about the Pioneers!"

The subject slid into smoother waters.

Emily wished that she didn't have to wear black for her interview with her late husband's partners. There was something about mourning that made one seem pathetic. She wanted to appear competent and businesslike. The current fashions didn't aid her. After much consideration she put on a severely tailored waist and the skirt with the least embroidery and no fringe. Her only jewelry was a jet and gold brooch at her throat with matching earrings.

She took her umbrella—black, of course—and set out.

She found the office without difficulty, a two-story clapboard building squeezed in between a harness shop on one side and a dry goods store on the other. The door opened into a waiting room with only a few straight-back chairs and a desk at which sat a young man not much older than her son. He was trying to balance a pencil on the end of his rather wide nose. When he saw Emily, he jumped up, the pencil tumbling to the floor.

"Good morning," Emily smiled reassuringly. "I have an appointment with Mr. Andrews and Mr. King. Would you please tell them that Mrs. Stratton is here?"

"Mrs. Stratton?" His eyes widened. "Yes, ma'am. Right away, ma'am. You just sit down here and I'll get them."

He pushed his chair back so abruptly that it fell over with a clatter. "Sorry," he said to her as he righted it. "Sorry, ma'am."

He opened the door behind his desk and vanished. A moment later, a man emerged. He was in his forties, of middle height, with a slight paunch. His beard was nearly gray and of the untrimmed weeping willow variety so popular at the moment. Emily rose to greet him.

"Mr. King?" she asked, holding out her hand.

"Yes, indeed." He gave a broad smile. "I'm sorry I wasn't in when you called the other day. I hope my wife received you hospitably."

"She was very gracious," Emily said. "I hope you have some time for me this morning. I've been going over the account books left by my husband and I have several questions for you."

The smile wavered then recovered. "Of course you do!" he said heartily, ushering her into the office. "You must be curious to know what your income will be. I can assure you that Captain Stratton left you very well provided for. You really needn't bother about finances, but Mr. Andrews and I will be happy to explain anything that you may not understand. Garrick," he added to the clerk. "Will you see if you can find a cup of tea for Mrs. Stratton?"

The inner office was much more richly furnished than the reception area. The tables were mahogany, the carpet a fine Chinese weave. Oriental vases and figurines were displayed on shelves against one wall. Glancing at the opposite wall, Emily gasped and swayed.

King was at her side at once.

"An amazing likeness, isn't it," he said.

Emily nodded, unable to speak. It was a painting of Horace Stratton. Just a painting, she repeated to herself. The artist had captured him perfectly, standing on a deck, the wild ocean and stormy sky behind him. For one horrible moment, Emily had felt his sharp blue eyes upon her, as if he knew what she had in mind and would do anything to stop her.

Quickly she composed herself and turned to greet Mr. Andrews, thin and pale from his recent illness. Deliberately, she seated herself with her back to the painting.

"Well, gentlemen," she said firmly. "As you know, Captain Stratton's business affairs were many and complicated. It's taken me several weeks to sort them out. In doing so, I have noticed several irregularities."

She took a sheet of paper from her reticule and smoothed it out on her lap. It was covered with writing. Both men stared at it as they might a rattlesnake about to strike.

She picked up the sheet and studied it.

"Now then," she began. "I think we should begin with the disparity between the profits listed on the ledger for 1866 and the actual income the company derived from the shipping and sale of opium."

Both men knew they were in for a long hard morning.

Mr. Andrews started wondering how the woman could be convinced to go back to Shanghai.

Mr. King was deciding the best way to eliminate her entirely.

CHAPTER NINE

As a horse that requires punishment is unsuitable for a lady, she holds the whip butt upwards, the lash pointing toward the flank . . . . Spurs should be worn only by very experienced horsewomen: their misuse has occasioned most serious accidents.

—PETERSON'S MAGAZINE, APRIL 1868

MONDAY, MARCH 2, 1868

Emily progressed slowly down her list, concentrating on the page in front of her. The paper shook so in her hands that she didn't dare look up to see what reaction her words were having. As she went through her questions, she could feel the air in the room thickening, as if a localized storm were brewing.

Finally, she raised her eyes and looked steadily at the two men with an air of innocence intended to assure them that she believed they could explain everything.

Mr. Andrews's pale face had turned a vivid shade of mauve. In his temple a vein stood out, pulsing with anger. Next to him, Mr. King seemed mildly amused. But his hand trembled as he lit his cigar.

"My dear Mrs. Stratton," he said with paternal patience. "You have certainly studied the books diligently. But you must realize that you do not have a solid understanding of the complexities of the China trade. Of course, with your religious background, you might find the importation of opium objectionable, but it is not illegal. We feel that we are bringing a measure of comfort to the poor coolies who have come so far to work. It's not as if Americans are harmed by it."

"I do know that, sir," Emily answered. "I am well aware of the arguments in favor of the trade. My personal distaste for it is not the question. What interests me is what happened to the receipts for the import duties."

"That is none of your concern!" Andrews snapped, his face glowing ever brighter.

Emily began to fear he was about to have an apoplectic fit.

"I'm sorry," she said softly. "But I'm afraid it *is* my concern. My son and I are the heirs of Captain Stratton's estate. That means that much of our income is derived from this trade."

Mr. King leaned forward, tapping cigar ash into a fine Ming porcelain dish. Emily winced.

"All the more reason for you to let us handle matters," he told her. "You should not have to soil yourself with the mundane aspects of business. A woman like you is far too well bred. Horace would want us to take care of all that for you."

Emily tried to look grateful.

"It is very kind of you to be willing to add so much extra work to your already increased load now that my husband is gone," she said. "But it's not at all necessary. I have a responsibility to handle Horace's affairs, as best I can. Of course, I do not intend to captain my own ship."

She gave a self-deprecating laugh.

"Although," she continued thoughtfully. "Perhaps after all, I do. I regret not knowing more about the business that provides for my home, clothing, and comfort. It's time I did, don't you think?"

Putting the paper back into her bag, Emily stood up.

"I would like to see all the record books for the past ten years," she told them. "Paying special attention to the areas in which I found irregularities in Captain Stratton's accounts. I'm sure that we can find a way to reconcile them."

She held out her hand somewhat timidly.

"I don't wish to trouble you gentlemen with overseeing my education," she said. "I'm sure that if I go slowly though the books, all will become clear to me. And perhaps my knowledge of China will be of some help to you. For instance, it's very difficult to get decent bean curd here. Every Chinese person in America would line up to buy as much of that as we can import. Perhaps we could let others provide them with opium."

Andrews's guffaw was more of a choke. Mr. King stood and took her hand, bowing over it.

"An interesting suggestion, Mrs. Stratton," he murmured. "Norton and I will give it due consideration."

"Thank you so much for your time. Please have the ledgers sent to my house. I hope to meet with you again, perhaps on Wednesday?" Emily picked up her gloves and reticule. "Good day, Mr. King, Mr. Andrews."

Andrews only gave a grunt and a curt nod. King extinguished his cigar and showed her to the door to the street.

When he returned to the office, King found Andrews pouring a glass of whiskey.

"A large one for me, Norton," he said.

Andrews filled two glasses almost to the rim. He handed one to King and took a deep draught from the other.

"Where the hell did she get those numbers?" he demanded. "What was Horace doing, leaving her that information?"

King sipped his whiskey. "I don't think he intended to die just yet, Norton. But, unless he had a brain seizure, Horace wouldn't have left anything in a place he thought she could find. She must have found the accounts where he had stashed them for temporary safekeeping."

"Phipps said he hunted everywhere," Andrews said.

"Prying little bitch." King waited as Andrews poured another glass. "The question before us now is, what do we do about Mrs. Emily Stratton, with her demure mourning garb and those very un-Methodist brown eyes?"

"Well, we can't give her the excise receipts she wants," Andrews stated. "They don't exist."

"She knows that perfectly well," King said. "Did you vomit up your wits with those oysters? She only asked for them to make us aware of the fact. I just wish I could figure out what she's after."

"I tell you it wasn't the oysters," Andrews shouted. "I was poisoned!"

"Lower your voice," King ordered. "For the last time, no one wants to poison you, Norton."

"Why not?" Andrews bristled. "I'm important enough. They might have wanted my money."

"Perhaps," King conceded doubtfully. He was thinking of something else. "Matthew, you aren't married. If you did die, what would happen to your shares in the company?"

"I specified that they be sold and the proceeds sent to my sister in Indiana, why?"

"Just wondering," King answered. "You own a third, right?"

Andrews looked embarrassed. "Well, more like twenty percent. I found myself in a ticklish situation a few years ago and sold a bit. But together, you and I still have more than half, right?"

"Oh yes," King said absently. "Yes, of course. Nothing to worry about."

Andrews studied his glass for several moments.

"I suppose we could cut back on the opium imports for now," he sighed. "As long as that woman doesn't get wind of the railway project, everything will be fine."

"I told you that there was no way she could know," King said. "We've played it close to the chest all along."

"Right," his partner agreed. "But who knows what else that bastard Stratton left for her to use against us?"

King swirled the liquid in his glass, watching the way it tried to form a vortex.

"It doesn't matter," he said. "She already knows too much."

He finished his whiskey in one long gulp.

On the walk home, it occurred to Emily that it hadn't been very wise to confront her late husband's partners head on like that. But she didn't know of any way to be subtle about it. And, although they were both clearly up-set, it seemed that King, at least, was relieved by the areas of her questions. Either he was more honest than Horace had been, or there was something else he had feared she would discover. But what could be worse than such trade in human misery?

It would have been nice to hire a third party to find out how deeply Mr. Andrews and Mr. King were involved in Horace's illegal businesses, someone who knew the ins and outs of finance. But whom could she trust?

The murder of Ah Sung had shaken her greatly. She was certain now that he had been sent to spy on her. Horace's partners were the most likely suspects, but until she got to know more about the life her husband had led in Portland, she couldn't be sure. There was that strange man who had been their first caller, Daniel Smith. He had seemed an amiable, if coarse, drunk. But he might have been pretending. He could have known that Horace was dead and that she had come to town. But why would anyone hire and then kill a spy? Unless he had found what he had been told to look for. Had Ah Sung found something she had missed?

Emily rubbed her forehead. She was developing a headache.

Perhaps the answers lay in Ah Sung's Bible. It seemed strange that he should have had those Methodist tracts. Most of the missionaries in South-ern China were Baptist. She needed to look though everything carefully. Perhaps he had made notes in them or at least written down the name of his next of kin.

Not for the first time, Emily began to feel in over her depth. She had never thought that the threads of her life here would still be tangled up with events in Shanghai. She had hoped she would never have to face them again.

"Good day, Mrs. Stratton," a cheerful voice greeted her.

Emily looked up from her brown study to see Mr. Carmichael. He was standing in front of a solid two-story house. It was plain, like the ones she remembered from New England, with no furbelows to blow off in a storm. He was wearing worn buckskin pants and a thick woolen sweater and hold-ing a pair of pruning shears.

"Good day, Mr. Carmichael," she smiled. "A cold day for gardening, isn't it?"

"We had an ice storm a few weeks past," he explained. "I wanted to trim some of the branches here that had been damaged. And you? Getting your constitutional in before the rains come again?"

"Yes, and hurrying back to a warm fire and a cup of tea," she answered.

He looked up at the sky. "Then I mustn't delay you," he said. "Shall I see you at Sunday services?"

"Of course," Emily said. "Do be careful with your pruning."

What a ridiculous thing to say, she thought. *As if the man doesn't know how to tend his own garden.*

It was odd how Mr. Carmichael's gentlemanly courtesy could disconcert her so. And he seemed quite comfortable, even standing there in old clothes. She wondered if he couldn't afford to hire a gardener. Strange that of all the people Alice gossiped about, she hadn't mentioned him once.

Thinking of Alice reminded her that they were to dine with the Bracewells that evening. While the thought of spending more time with her in-laws was daunting, she was curious to meet her nieces and get to know George Bracewell. Perhaps he could be the father that poor Robert needed now. Emily was all too aware that she was ill equipped to send a young man out to face the world, even a son as dutiful and loving as hers.

Mary Kate was out when Emily returned home, but the kettle was still warm and the tea things set out, along with a slice of plum cake. Emily poured herself a steaming cup and settled in near the fire to drink it. The hot drink took the chill out of her bones. She poured a second cup and opened the kitchen drawer where she had put the Bible.

Emily's breath caught. There was nothing in the drawer but a stack of dishcloths and a rusty tin opener.

Mary Kate had no explanation.

"There was no one in the house while you were gone," she insisted. "And I locked the door before I left. It couldn't have been five minutes before you got back."

She looked around the kitchen nervously.

"Are you sure that's where you put it?" she asked.

Emily nodded. "I've looked through all the other drawers, too," she added. "Where could it have gone? I don't suppose Robert felt the need to use it."

Even maternal devotion didn't stretch that far.

"He didn't know where it was," Mary Kate pointed out. "Nor did I, for that matter."

"Then someone else has come in and searched the house," Emily concluded.

They stared at each other. No doors had been forced, no windows broken. Someone else must have a key. Emily felt a sudden cold, as if someone were walking over her grave.

"Mary Kate, there must be a locksmith in Portland," she said. "Do you think you could get him to come over at once?"

"I'll not be sleeping another wink in this house until he does." Mary Kate reached for her coat and shawl.

Mary Kate must have been persuasive, for she was back in less than half an hour with the locksmith and his assistant.

"This is Mr. Wolff, from the dry goods store," Mary Kate explained. "He and Mr. Myers, here, have offered to put in the locks for us. They closed up the shop and everything."

"Not a problem, Mrs. Stratton." Mr. Wolff was a burly young man with dark hair and a pronounced German accent. "We had some very strong locks in stock. When Miss Kyne here told us what had happened, Charles and I, we couldn't rest until we had you nice and safe again."

"Thank you," Emily was moved by their concern. "There are two doors. I'll need keys for myself, my son, and Mary Kate, of course."

She retreated upstairs to let them work. The two men seemed most eager to be of assistance. It was very generous of them to stop their work to take care of strangers. She wondered what Mary Kate had told them. Of course, if she had explained that they were two women and a boy alone in the house, that might have been enough.

It suddenly occurred to her that the maid might not have had to say much of anything. Mary Kate was barely twenty-five, with rich brown hair, porcelain skin, and a wicked Irish smile. Emily remembered hearing that Portland was a town full of bachelors. Perhaps Mr. Wolff and Mr. Myers were among them.

The men were through quickly, although they took a moment to take Mary Kate up on her offer of tea and cake. They enjoyed the cake so much that Mary Kate wished she had baked it. Maybe a course in cooking wouldn't come amiss. That Mr. Wolff was a fine set up man and handy, too.

With the house secured, Emily had no reason to put off their dinner with the Bracewells. At seven, Alice's phaeton appeared at the door to transport them.

"Now, you'll be quite safe, won't you?" Emily asked Mary Kate.

"It's sure and I'll be," Mary Kate said. "I've the frying pan and the dinner bell to scare off anyone who tries to get in. And it will be a great surprise when they find they can't just turn the key any longer."

"We won't be late," Emily promised. "Perhaps you should come with us."

"I don't think I'd be welcome at Mrs. Alice's dinner table," Mary Kate laughed. "Don't be worrying yourself about me."

But she knew Emily would, bless her.

The Bracewell home was lit as if for a royal visit. Lanterns lined the drive and the gas-lit chandelier in the entry sparkled through the window as they approached. Emily and Robert were admitted by a man in a black suit. For a moment, Emily thought she was at the wrong house, but she was spared making a fool of herself by Alice's entrance.

"My dears!" she cried. "I'm so glad you've come! Lewis, take their coats. Robert, come kiss your Aunt Alice!"

CHAPTER TEN

The history of every country should have as much to record of woman as of man; but this can never be until women's field of Employment is extended. She must go out and work. She must do her own business, execute her own intentions, act nobly her part in life wherever she can be the best rewarded for her industry and judgment. I would not make woman unwomanly, but would crown her with all the grace and dignity of true Female worth.

—Aims and Aids for Girls and Young Women, on the Various
Duties of Life, G. S. Weaver, 1856

I'm enchanted to meet you properly, Aunt." Robert planted a loud kiss on her cheek. "I own I was too occupied at the funeral to see you clearly. Father never mentioned how much younger you were than he."

Alice beamed. "What a delightful young man! Welcome to the family. Come in and see your Uncle George and meet your cousins."

She led them into a brightly lit parlor. It was a large room but so full of sofas, chairs, occasional tables, lamps, curio cabinets, and a piano that it was difficult to move without bumping into something. There were also three people in the room: George Bracewell, hiding behind a newspaper, a young girl seated at the piano, and a slightly older one seated near the fire working some embroidery. Emily paused in the doorway, trying to plot a course through it all. Alice took her hesitation for shyness.

"Don't worry, my dear," she said. "It's just the family tonight. No fuss. George, you remember poor Horace's wife."

The newspaper came down to reveal a handsome man of about forty-five, his blond hair touched with silver. Like almost every other man in town, he had a full and untrimmed beard. He rose to greet her.

"Welcome!" he said heartily. "Welcome to Portland. I know we met at the service, but that wasn't a time for a proper greeting. I'm glad you've decided to settle here. I told Horace for years that it wasn't right to leave the two of you alone in Shanghai, especially after your parents passed away."

"Thank you." Emily's hand was enveloped in his. The man loomed over her like a great golden bear. "Robert and I are pleased to be here. Portland seems a lovely place."

"But nothing like what you're used to, I imagine." The sewer got up from the sofa with a smile. "I'm Sarah."

She was also blond but of a slightly darker shade than her father. Her features were pretty and delicate, but Emily sensed an underlying strength in her young niece.

The girl at the piano didn't get up but began to play a triumphal march.

"Felicity," Alice chided her daughter over the laughter of the others. "Don't be rude. Come greet your aunt and your cousin."

Felicity was so pale that Emily thought she would be almost invisible in the gray world outside. Her skin was but lightly tinged with ivory and her hair and eyebrows were nearly white. Her nose was a little large for her face but Emily trusted that she would soon grow into it.

The girl got up reluctantly. As she came toward them, Emily realized that she had a slight twist to her spine that caused one shoulder to be a bit higher than the other.

"I'm happy to meet you, Aunt Emily, Cousin Robert." She gave a curtsey and scurried back to the piano.

"Now sit down, please." Alice gestured toward the chairs. "We'll dine shortly. I'll have Lewis bring us some sherry to warm us up."

"None for me, thank you," Emily said at once. "But a glass of water would be lovely."

Alice blinked. "Of course. I forgot that Methodists don't partake of wine."

"Then I thank God I'm not Methodist!" George laughed. "You know that there's nothing in the Bible that condemns liquor."

Emily was about to mention Noah's little problem but decided it wouldn't be polite. The butler brought in a tray with a decanter of sherry and one of whiskey. George poured himself a glass of the latter. Alice waited for Lewis to give her the sherry in a small crystal wine glass. He then poured some for the girls, cutting it with water.

Robert looked with longing at the drinks, but accepted his water with a smile at Emily.

"Now," George said when they had settled. "How are you liking our city? Not the bustle of Shanghai, of course, but up and coming, never you doubt it."

"It's very different from any place I've ever lived," Emily admitted. "But it's beautiful and so fresh. It feels as if you could spread out forever."

"You should have been here twenty years ago," George said. "When I arrived, the town was nothing but a few tiny cabins and a lot of big dreams."

Alice shuddered. "Really, I'd never want to return to those pioneer days. Life was too primitive for words."

She looked around the room as if taking inventory of the comforts she now possessed.

George ignored his wife's comment. "Robert, I hear you've started at the Academy. If Professor Gatch gives you a hard time, you just send him to me."

"Thank you, Uncle." Robert grinned. "I think you could take him out in one round."

George roared at this immoderately. "My girls are both sweet as peach blossoms and I wouldn't trade 'em for anything, but I've missed the rough and tumble of having a boy around."

"Robert has never given me a moment's worry," Emily started to stand up for her son.

Alice cut her off. "There are more than enough rough boys in this town," she announced. "I hope Robert knows how to behave around innocent young girls."

Sarah rolled her eyes at this but said nothing.

"I consider it my duty to shelter my cousins from any coarse influences," Robert told her. "Just as I would their mother."

This time there was a strangled cough from Sarah's corner. Even Emily thought that Robert was spreading it a bit thick. Alice, however, seemed charmed.

"You remind me so much of dear Horace," she sighed. "What a good brother he was to me."

Emily expected another sardonic gesture from Sarah but the girl gave a firm nod of agreement.

"Uncle Horace was wonderful." She smiled at the memory. "He always had time to play with us."

"And he brought wonderful presents," Felicity chimed in. "Beautiful dolls from China and Japan."

"And a shrunken head from Borneo or some such place," Sarah interrupted. "We used to hang it out the window to scare Mama's visitors."

"Sarah!" Alice was shocked. "That was not amusing. You might have given poor Eutheria heart failure."

"Now, now," George laughed. "Eutheria was younger then. It probably did her heart good to give it a start."

Alice shook her head but the rest of them joined in the laughter.

"Did you girls enjoy the dance last Saturday?" Emily asked.

"Dance?" Sarah asked.

"She means Mr. McCann's cotillion," Alice explained. "Really just an opportunity for the young people to practice their steps. All the important balls are in the spring."

Emily was about to ask another question but Lewis came in to announce dinner. Her brother-in-law gave her his arm to escort her in and Robert offered his to Alice.

The dinner was excellent, although somewhat more than Emily was used to eating at once. She was unusually grateful for her son's adolescent appetite as he stuffed himself with onion soup, salmon, roast venison, potatoes, two kinds of tinned vegetables, and slaw. The meal was served by a silent Chinese man whom Emily assumed to be the cook.

She wanted to ask him about Ah Sung but saw no way to do so. She did notice that every time he offered her the serving platter, his hands shook. Perhaps he was subject to palsy, but Emily doubted it. Alice would not have hired anyone with an affliction, so Emily had to suppose that she was the cause of his nervousness.

Alice noticed her watching the cook.

"Have you found anyone to replace the man I sent you?" she asked. "Imagine him getting himself killed like that! If I'd known he was connected with the more unsavory Chinese element, I never would have let Wa Kee hire him."

"I haven't really had time yet," Emily said. "Perhaps I should put an advertisement in the paper."

"Nonsense!" Alice said. "I dare say that Ah Ling, here, has a cousin who would do. They all seem to be related, you know."

Emily thought of explaining the Chinese naming system, how few family names there were and how, in foreign lands, those from one area would come together as a clan to care for each other. But she was too full to attempt education. She merely nodded.

"Ah Ling, any of your family as good a cook as you?" George asked.

The cook put down the meat platter. "I couldn't say, Mr. Bracewell," he answered. "But I shall ask tomorrow when I go to the market."

Emily's jaw dropped. They had been talking about the man as if he couldn't understand a word. Instead, his English was flawless. He even managed George's last name with only a hint of accent.

"My goodness," she exclaimed. "You speak so well, Ah Ling. Where did you learn English?"

"In Hong Kong, madam." He bowed to her. "I worked for the family of an English naval officer."

"Isn't he just a gem?" Alice said. "Ah Ling knows everything about British customs and manners."

"Taught me a thing or two," George chuckled.

His wife's lips tightened but she didn't respond.

"I'll ring when we're ready for dessert," she told Ah Ling.

"Very good, madam." He bowed and left the room.

"I'm amazed that someone so educated would consider working as a cook," Emily said when the kitchen door had swung shut.

"What else would he do?" George asked. "Run a laundry? Peddle vegetables? Level ground for the railway tracks? I pay him three times what he could get in those jobs, and give him a bed to himself."

"I've often wondered about why he stays with us, too," Sarah said. "Ah Ling knows a lot of things besides cooking. He even helps me with my geography lessons."

"Anyone who's been farther south than Eugene City knows more than you about geography," Felicity teased.

The conversation passed on to the topic of schooling. Both girls went to the female seminary attached to the Portland Academy that Robert now attended. Felicity also studied music, both piano and violin.

"Perhaps you'll play for us after dinner," Emily smiled.

"Of course, Aunt Emily," Felicity agreed at once. "I know lots of religious pieces."

"That will be most edifying, I'm sure," Emily said soberly.

They declined the carriage in favor of a walk home. The night was misty, but Alice had given them a lantern and clear instructions.

"I need to walk," Robert confided to his mother. "If I don't move that dinner around I'm sure to get dyspepsia."

Emily squeezed his free hand. "Your aunt seemed to think we'd be preyed upon by bandits and wild animals, but the town is quite tranquil tonight."

It wasn't much past ten and there were a few people still on the roads. Some, like them, were dressed for dinner engagements. Others were men coming home from the saloons, where they had eaten their evening meal. None of them appeared more than slightly inebriated and each one tipped his hat as he passed.

"I hope Ah Ling finds us a new cook soon," Robert said.

"You can't be hungry again already!" Emily half-thought he might be.

"No, but a man should always think ahead," he replied.

They walked in silence for a time. Emily inhaled the spicy scent of fir trees, mixed with the smoke of wood fires. There was a breeze from the east that brought with it the faint sound of music. A much more bouncy tune than the hymns Felicity had played for her.

"I'm not sure we should get another Chinese cook," Emily announced as they neared their home.

"Whyever not?" Robert asked. "You can't want to live on venison and blancmange and stewed tomatoes."

"Of course not." Emily found the new key and inserted it into the front door lock. "I'm just not sure we should risk it after what happened to Ah Sung."

"Mother, that had nothing to do with us." Robert pushed the door open. "Hello! Mary Kate, what are you doing up?"

Emily looked over his shoulder.

Mary Kate was sitting on the steps in front of them, wide awake, a shotgun across her lap.

"I heard them first at the back, just after I'd turned down the lamp." Mary Kate took a sip of heavily sugared tea from a mug beside her on the steps.

"Whoever it was had a key, just like you feared," she went on. "They tried the front door when the back didn't work and after that the windows. I was shivering and quaking all the while, thinking to myself that they'd smash their way in!"

"You should have gone up to your room and locked yourself in," Emily said.

"And let them devils rob you! Never!"

"Better that than murder you, you silly girl!"

Mary Kate gave a grateful smile. "You're a good, kind woman, Mrs. Stratton. I'm making too much of this. After listening to them scrabbling away like that, I started to feel more angry than afraid. And I was right. Once I shouted through the door that I had a gun, they went away fast enough, cowards that they were."

"You didn't!" Robert exclaimed in awe.

"Good thing, too," she added. "I don't know where your late husband hid the shot."

"This is intolerable," Emily declared. "The first thing tomorrow, we are going to report this to the police. Then I am hiring a new cook as well as a coachman. Perhaps even a butler, like Alice has. I promise that we'll never leave you alone in the house again."

Emily lay awake that night, listening for the thieves to return.

No one had mentioned that Portland was a lawless town, at least west of the saloons. So she had to assume that there was something special about her or about her house.

She had given Mr. King and Mr. Andrews all the information from Horace's papers, but they must think that there was something else. What could they believe she was hiding?

Or, what if the intruders had been sent not by King and Andrews but in search of something Ah Sung had left behind? But what? She had given everything but the Bible to the policeman. And someone had stolen that. Unless the cook had hidden something more. In the morning she would search the kitchen again.

If anyone had wanted to simply rob the house, they could have done it much more easily before she had come to live there. These men must be looking for something in particular, something that hadn't been there before. But what? And did it have to do with Horace or with something Ah Sung was up to?

It was useless. There were no answers in her mind. Emily slid out of bed, wincing at the coldness of the floor. She found her slippers and put them on, then she went into the closet and pushed aside a row of black gowns. Behind them was a little alcove, built for no purpose she could imagine. In it she had placed a little carved teak table. There stood her statue of Kwan Yin, goddess of harmony and peace. Next to it was a box of matches and a pile of joss sticks.

Emily lit one of the sticks and placed it in a holder in front of the statue. On her knees, she made her obeisance.

"Please, gentle lady," she whispered. "Show me the path. Bring me from this darkness to the light of understanding. I am all alone and confused. And I'm trying not to be afraid. If it's not too much to ask, could you make me a little more brave?"

She then took out another box. In it were a small book and a set of coins. Reverently, Emily cast the coins on the table. She studied the result and threw again. Sometimes she stopped to consult the book. When she was finished, she bowed again to the statue.

"Thank you, gentle lady," she said. "I shall continue on the path, although I still fear where it will lead."

Of course, Emily considered over the next few days, the problem with the *I Ching* was that it offered general guidance rather than exact directions. Experience had taught her that it was useless to try for precision. So she tried to concentrate on immediate problems, trusting that at some point the way would become clear.

Mary Kate gave her burnt toast and tea for breakfast.

"I'm that sorry," she said. "I only turned away for a minute and the bread started smoking. I wouldn't blame you if you gave me the sack. No kind of cook and not trained up as a lady's maid."

Emily took her hand. "Never mind, Mary Kate. Yours was the first kind face I found when I came to America. You're courageous and honest and loyal. You are a fine lady's maid. You shouldn't be asked to do anything more."

Mary Kate took her hand away. She fumbled for her handkerchief, wiped her eyes, and blew her nose.

"As if you weren't the first person I ever worked for who treated me like a person," she choked. "The first real lady I ever met."

She turned away and busied herself with the dishes. Emily wiped her own eyes. "You know," she said in a more businesslike tone. "It might be better if you were the one to choose the people you'll have to work with."

Mary Kate's jaw dropped. "Mrs. Stratton!" she exclaimed. "Even *I* know that just isn't done."

"Yes, that's true," Emily answered. "But Portland seems to be a place where one can try out new ideas. I'll make the final decision, but I'd appreciate it if you would see if you could ask around for a reliable cook and someone to drive and care for the horses. Will you?"

A smile spread slowly across Mary Kate's face as the implications of the request struck her.

"That I will, ma'am." She dried her hands energetically on a dish towel. "And if they don't please you, then you can give us all the boot."

Emily didn't think that would happen.

By the end of the day Mary Kate had found a widow from Germany, Mrs. Bechner, who cooked according to her tastes, and a coachman, John Mahoney, whose appearance pleased her. She swore, though, that John was a fine man from Mayo who was better with horses than with people and rarely, if ever, drank. With Alice's Mrs. McCarthy to come in once a week for the heavy cleaning and the laundry sent down to one of the many places on Second Street, Emily felt that domestic matters were well in hand.

It wasn't by accident that now there would always be at least two people in the house.

Wednesday came and went with no sign of the account books Emily had requested from Horace's partners. She wasn't surprised. Perhaps she should write a polite note reminding them. It wouldn't do to let them think she had forgotten. Of course they had never paid duty on the opium they imported. The drug was never declared but stashed inside fine porcelain vases and cheap wooden dolls. But let them think her only worry was that they would be indicted for smuggling. She knew that Mr. King and Mr. Andrews sneered at her disgust toward the trade. They hadn't seen how it destroyed lives, not just the poor addicts but also their families. They didn't know how it was eating away the dignity of China.

Or perhaps they did, and didn't care.

Emily dipped her pen and began her letter.

CHAPTER ELEVEN

On the 4th of March the Senate notified the House that they were ready to re-ceive the Managers of Impeachment. They appeared, and the articles were formally read. . . . Chief Justice Chase sent a communication to the Senate to the effect that this body, when acting upon an impeachment, was a Court presided over by the Chief Justice . . .

—HARPER'S NEW MONTHLY MAGAZINE, MAY 1868

THURSDAY, MARCH 5, 1868

M ary Kate, did you know that the president was being impeached?" Emily had taken to eating breakfast in the kitchen with her maid and Mrs. Bechner. She preferred it to the cold dining room. No one but Alice seemed to think it odd.

Mary Kate reached for another piece of bread.

"Isn't this a grand country?" she said. "If only we could do that with the English. What did the poor man do?"

"I'm not certain yet." Emily went back to the paper she was reading. "Apparently all the articles of impeachment were in an earlier edition."

"I don't know why they bother, with the election coming up this fall," Mrs. Bechner commented. "My money's on General Grant to win."

"Well, since I'll be voting for him, there's no doubt that he will." John Mahoney grinned at the cook and held up his plate for more bacon. "Will you be needing the carriage today, Mrs. Stratton?"

"No, thank you, John," Emily answered. "It's so lovely out I think I'll walk into town. I've been invited to a candy pulling tonight. Does anyone know what that is?"

"I don't think it's something you'd be wearing your best gown for," Mary Kate opined.

"I suspected as much." Emily looked at the kitchen clock. "Goodness! Nearly seven and not a sound from Robert's room."

She put down the paper with a sigh. "I'd better go up and see that he isn't late for school again. He must have been studying far into the night."

The other three exchanged glances. They waited until they heard Emily's footsteps on the floor above.

"Shouldn't someone tell her?" Mrs. Bechner shook her head as she collected the breakfast plates.

"And what would we say?" John countered. " 'Your son's a wastrel who climbs out his window most every night and goes down to the tavern.' I don't think we'd be working here long if we did."

"I'm only fearing that he'll come to harm in those places," Mary Kate said.

"Don't you be fussing about that, Mary Kate Kyne." John reached out to pat her hand, but she pulled it away with a laugh. "They know who he is down there and whose son he is. There's many there who did business with Captain Stratton. And I hear young Robert is a cheerful sort, always buying rounds. They may cheat him blind but no one will dare to lay a hand on him."

"All the same." Mrs. Bechner slammed the fry pan into the sink. "She shouldn't be kept in the dark. The boy has no father to advise him."

"From what I hear," John interrupted, "he's following in his father's tradition."

"Hush," Mary Kate warned. "They're coming down."

Robert certainly didn't look the worse for wear. He greeted them all cheerily, grabbed a slice of bacon from the platter for breakfast, and picked up the lunch pail Mrs. Bechner had packed for him.

"I hope you've put some of your apple strussel in today," he told her. "The other fellows line up for a taste of that. Sorry to be so late. See you this afternoon, Mother."

He kissed her cheek and went to the hall to put on his jacket and scarf. A moment later, the door slammed behind him.

Emily went to the window to wave at him as he passed. John, Mary Kate, and Mrs. Bechner looked at each other and shrugged. Emily turned back to them with a smile.

"I thought I'd go to the printer's," she announced. "To have calling cards made up. And then I'll just explore the town a bit. All on my own."

"Very good, ma'am," Mrs. Bechner said. "Will you be home for luncheon?"

"I'll spend the day getting the carriage house in order, then," John decided. "If that meets with your approval."

"And I have mending to do," Mary Kate added. "But I'd like to drop by for a visit with that nice Mrs. O'Shea, who does for the priests."

They all looked at Emily.

It was a moment before she realized that they were waiting for her approval of their plans.

"That sounds fine," she told them. "I'll have something to eat in town, Mrs. Bechner. If you'd care to go out for a time when Mary Kate comes back, you may."

They all settled back contentedly.

Emily felt a thrill of amazement. They had looked to her for direction! In Shanghai the servants had followed her orders, within limits. When she had attempted to make any changes, she had been politely but firmly told that it was not the way things were done. Even the idea of going out of the house by herself would have been met with shock. Of course, well-bred Chinese women rarely left their own homes, and certainly not unaccompanied.

As Mary Kate had said, this was a grand country.

But freedom had limits and responsibility. As a woman of her class,

Emily knew that there were still rules as to where she could go and what she could do and not lose her respectability.

Emily had spent more than one sleepless night coming to terms with her new situation. She had spent so many years feeling trapped, bound to Horace for better or worse. Now she knew that she had been so full of her own misery that she had not believed she could make things better for anyone, especially herself. The one time she had tried. . . .

She had been sound asleep that night, grateful that Horace hadn't come to her bed. The screaming wakened her, high, terrified and full of pain. She had run down through the kitchen to the servants' quarters. The shrieks grew louder but no one else seemed to have heard them. All the doors were shut and the hall was empty. How could that be? Someone in the room at the end of the corridor was being murdered. Emily flung it open.

There stood Horace. One of the newest maids, a girl of twelve, was bent naked over a bedframe. Blood was running down the back of her thighs.

Horace was so involved that it was a few seconds before he saw his wife, standing frozen in horror. He didn't even have the grace to appear ashamed.

He struck the little maid. "I warned you what would happen if you made any noise. Get out!"

Emily couldn't find her voice.

"You look like a dead fish!" Horace snorted. "That's about what you are in bed, too. Get back upstairs where you belong. What I do down here is none of your business."

She had fled, but the next morning Emily had faced him down. "You have said that I am in charge of the servants. I won't let them be abused by you."

He had been amused. "And what do you think you can do about it?"

That had been difficult. There was nothing legal that she could do, and he knew it.

"I shall, very privately, mention to a few of the women at the next embassy dinner that you haven't been well lately. I'll ask if they can recommend a physician expert at mysterious rashes and other personal problems. By the next day everyone in town will know."

It had worked. He had not molested any of the maids again. But he had taken his revenge out on her. The first nights after he came home from a journey were terrible ordeals that left her numb with shame.

She had never told anyone, and she never would. The mortification was too great.

But she wasn't going to allow Horace to continue controlling her life from beyond the grave. And she had to do what she could to undo some of the suffering he had brought to others.

In order to do this, Emily realized that she would have to go places no proper lady should. It made her uncomfortable, but there was no other way. She knew no one in town she could trust.

Her interview with Mr. Andrews and Mr. King had convinced her of that.

While Horace's partners had seemed annoyed by her questions about finances and the opium trade, Emily sensed that they were relieved to have that be her only issue. There was something else the men were involved in that they didn't want her to know about, but what?

Now, she had found evidence in his private account books that for some time Horace had been investing large sums of money at an amazing return. But nothing told her what the business had been. It could be that Mr. Andrews and Mr. King were part of this. But it was just as likely that her husband had more than one enterprise going and had kept them in the dark.

There had to be more records. If Horace had left them in the house, neither she nor the various intruders had been able to find them. If they had, she reasoned, they wouldn't have bothered to try again after the lock had been changed.

The only answer she could come up with was that Horace had another office. It may have been only a room, or even just a safe at someone else's place of business. Emily had a strong suspicion that it wouldn't be at the sort of place a lady normally frequented.

She had made up her mind to search out the one person who might be willing to help her. He hadn't inspired trust on their first meeting, but perhaps that had been due to his condition. Emily was willing to give him another chance. She couldn't see any other choice.

But where to find him?

Emily considered this as she went through her daily lacing-up. The first place to search for evidence would logically be Andrews, Stratton, and King, but if this were an enterprise that Horace was conducting on his own, it didn't seem likely that he'd hide the evidence under the noses of his partners. Although, she considered, it wasn't impossible. No, she would have to begin at the dock. Emily sighed. It would be so much easier if she were a man and could just stroll into one of the saloons.

Suitably attired for strolling in a simple black silk walking dress, the skirt trimmed at the bottom with four bias ruffles, the jacket trimmed with gimp and accentuated with large black buttons and a black velvet hat that left her neck exposed to the cold, Emily set out.

Fortunately, the day was mild for March. On her way downtown, Emily encountered a number of vaguely familiar faces. They all smiled and bowed. Some stopped to chat a moment. It amazed her how many people she had managed to meet in such a short time.

"Will you and your son be at the candy pull, tonight?" plump Mrs. Burrage asked. "It's sticky but fun. The children love it but we older folk do even more. It's a chance to make work into play."

Emily assured her that they would. The delight the woman showed was so unexpected that Emily almost cried. After being lonely so many years, it was wondrous to meet so many people willing to be her friends. She prayed that she would do nothing to change that.

She knew there was a shipping house on Front Street somewhere. That seemed a good place to start her inquiries. However, she found herself dawdling along the street, first browsing in the McCormick Franklin book and music store after ordering her calling cards and then seeing about a new suit for Robert at the clothiers next door.

Finally she arrived at the shipping house. McCraken, Merrill, & Co. was the local branch of a San Francisco firm. It was possible that Horace, with his interests in California, would have done business with them.

If the clerk was surprised at her request, he didn't show it.

"No, your husband didn't have any contracts with us, Mrs. Stratton," he told her. "Yes, I know Dan Smith. He sometimes does odd jobs for us when we have to send out a large shipment. This time of year there isn't much work. Haven't seen him in a while. I don't know where he lives. You might try asking at the wharf."

Emily thanked him and retraced her steps back along the river. The water was high, lapping against the posts holding up the wooden buildings that lined the bank. Seagulls scavenged amidst refuse bins outside the taverns. Their raucous calls reminded her of home. She stopped at the thought. A surge of joy ran through her. That wasn't right. *This* was home.

A ship had just docked at the wharf when she arrived. Men with handcarts crossed her path, some laden with boxes, some on their way for more. It was several minutes before she found someone who would stop long enough to help her.

"Daniel Smith?" The man looked around. "Over there." He pointed. "Checking off the lading bill for Corbett and Failing."

Emily dodged the carts and mules and men across the cavernous unloading area. As she approached Mr. Smith, her courage began to ebb. He seemed much more forbidding than the amiable drunk who had shown up at her front door. She wondered if he would even remember her.

He was totally absorbed in his work. Ringed by stacks of packing barrels, he was marking each one with chalk and then crossing it off his list.

"Raisins!" he shouted. "We're still missing two boxes of raisins. Jim, go see if they got mixed up with all that stuff for the Reeds' new house."

Smith caught sight of her then. He remembered her.

"Mrs. Stratton!" He yanked his hat off. "What in h . . . tarnation are you doing here?"

Emily smiled. "Good day, Mr. Smith. I'm sorry to interrupt your work, but I was wondering if I might speak with you about the work you did for my husband."

His eyes moved back and forth like a trapped rabbit.

"Well, I'm mighty busy just at the moment," he began.

"Of course," she agreed. "Perhaps we could meet after you finish? I could come to your office."

"Well, I don't really have an office. Hey! Dutch, be careful with that," he yelled suddenly. "Can't you read? It says 'glass.' "

He turned back to Emily. "Probably can't read," he confided. "I got to watch these men all the time."

"I don't wish to keep you." Emily stepped back to avoid being run over by a load of railroad ties. "Could you come by the house this evening? I can have our cook give you some supper."

"Sure. That would be fine." Smith was eager to be rid of her. "We should have this lot in the warehouse by four or so."

"Thank you," Emily said "Of course you know the house."

He had the grace to look uncomfortable, but only nodded.

As she was leaving, Emily heard her name.

"Mrs. Stratton!" Matthew King was staring at her in outrage. "I know you said that you wanted to have a part in running the company, but this is totally uncalled for."

Emily steeled herself. She put her hand out. "Good morning, Mr. King," she said pleasantly. "I hope you are well. And Mrs. King, how is she?"

"We are both in excellent health," he snapped. "Now, would you mind explaining why you are wandering about the dock, getting in everyone's way?"

Emily looked up at him. She considered a moment. "Yes, Mr. King, I think I would mind. I'm here on a private matter. However, since we've met, I should like to remind you that I still haven't received the information to enable me to reconcile my husband's account balances with those you gave me. I even wrote you a note about it."

He seemed affronted. "I didn't realize that you seriously wanted them."

"Why else should I have asked to see them?" Emily replied.

"I have no idea," he answered. "I have no experience with women such as you. I shall instruct Garrick to make copies and bring them to your house as soon as he can."

"Thank you, Mr. King." Emily made herself smile at him. "I'm very grateful. I'm sure I'll soon understand enough to be of help to you."

King snorted. "As you can see, Mrs. Stratton, neither your understanding nor your presence are at all necessary. Horace left provision for your support. I suggest that you accept the income and find a more suitable occupation. This is no place for a woman of your stature."

Thankfully for Emily's temper she noticed that they were being watched. There was another woman at the wharf that morning, despite Mr. King's last statement. She was in her forties, by the look of her, although hard work and worry may have added years to her face. She had been standing meekly just on the edge of the loading area, waiting. Emily went over to her.

"Good day," she said. "Did you wish to speak to Mr. King?"

"Yes, ma'am." Her voice was hoarse. "I don't like to bother you, but I have to know."

"What is it?" King asked, not really interested.

"I'm Clarissa Peterson," the woman said. "I've asked everywhere I can think of, and someone said you might be able to help me."

"I honestly doubt it," King answered and started to move away.

Emily reproached herself for putting him in such a bad mood. Poor Mrs. Peterson was shaking with fright. She put an arm around the woman and drew her toward Mr. King.

"Tell us the problem," she spoke quietly. "We'll help if we can."

"Oh, bless you!" Mrs. Peterson fought back tears. "It's my son, Alexander. He went upriver to the mines. He wrote me he'd be home by the New Year, but he never came. I know he got as far as Portland. One of his friends told me he'd seen him here. I came to find him. But no one knows where he is. A man over there said you might have hired him. He's a big, strong boy."

Something flickered in King's eyes, then vanished. "I have no idea what happened to your son, madam," he told her. "I don't hire the day laborers. Perhaps he took ship for British Columbia. The mines there aren't played out, they say."

"But he wouldn't have gone without coming to see me!" Mrs. Peterson clawed at his sleeve. "Please at least look at his picture."

She held up a small pocket case with the photograph of a young man of about twenty. He was posed stiffly in his best suit, but his face still had a good-natured expression. Emily didn't think he looked like a man who would go away without telling his mother good-bye.

King glanced at it.

"No one I know," he said curtly. "I'm sorry I can't help you. Good day, Mrs. Stratton, Mrs. Peterson."

The woman closed her eyes, swaying a little. She was wearing home-spun wool, a dress based on a pattern from before the war. Her hair was almost completely gray, her face lined from working outside in all conditions. Emily's heart went out to her.

"Mrs. Peterson, come with me, please," she said. "You're all done in. It's nearly time for luncheon. I was going to eat alone, but I'd much rather have your company."

"Oh, I couldn't." Mrs. Peterson's glance took in Emily's silk dress, jet jewelry, and fur wrap.

"You need to keep your strength up," Emily insisted. "I've been told that the Columbia Hotel serves an excellent luncheon. I'd be grateful if you'd be my guest there. You can tell me more about Alexander. I have a son of my own."

She pulled out the small gold locket with Robert's face on one side and one of his baby curls on the other.

"Younger than yours," she said, comparing the two faces. "But I know how I'd feel if he were missing."

Mrs. Peterson saw the way Emily looked at the picture of Robert. The fact that the fine clothing was all black finally struck her. Gently, she took back her photo and tucked it in her bag.

"Thank you," she said. "I'd be pleased to take luncheon with you."

Emily's walk home was thoughtful. Clarissa Peterson had showed her a world she knew nothing about. The woman had come out to Oregon in the early fifties as a bride, to homestead in the Tuality Valley. She had borne eight children and buried five, along with her husband, killed in a fall during a barnraising. The young man in the photo was her only surviving son.

How could anyone endure so much heartbreak and still get up in the morning?

Emily returned home in a chastened frame of mind. She told Mary Kate she would stay in her room for a while. Amidst the swirl of incense, she prayed to Kwan Yin and Jesus for the safe return of Alex Peterson.

There was a clatter out front, but Emily ignored it. However, a few moments later she heard a knock at her door. Mary Kate apologized as she came in.

"It's that Mrs. Bracewell," she said. "I told her you were resting but she'd have nothing of it. She's in a fair moither and won't go until she sees you."

"It's all right," Emily sighed. "Tell her I'll be right down."

She threw a dressing gown over her Chinese blouse and trousers and descended the stairs quickly. Something dreadful must have happened.

"Alice, what a surprise!" She came toward her sister-in-law to embrace her, but Alice moved away. "Whatever is the matter?"

"I came over as soon as I heard." Alice paced back and forth in the small parlor. "Please just tell me it wasn't you."

"I don't know what you mean," Emily answered, her heart sinking. Alice must know she had gone hunting for Daniel Smith. How could she explain?

"Of course you do," Alice said. "You were seen. If you wanted to consort with some uncouth farmer's wife, did you have to do it at the nicest restaurant in town? I thought you understood about being careful in your friendships."

"Widow," Emily corrected.

Alice stared at her blankly, stopped in mid-diatribe. "What?"

"Mrs. Peterson is a widow like me. Her son is missing. She is terribly distraught about it. I thought she needed a good warm meal before she returned home."

That brought Alice up short.

"Well, of course, your charitableness does you credit, my dear," she admitted. "But your method of showing it was perhaps ill-advised. You could have just given her a few dollars and directed her to the police."

"She wouldn't have taken money and she'd already been to the police." Emily was wearying of the conversation. "Besides, I like her and I wanted to get to know her better."

Alice shook her head at such unworldliness but was mollified. She agreed to sit down and have a cup of tea before going.

"Actually, I'm glad you stopped by," Emily said, trying to remember not to let the trousers show beneath the dressing gown. "I so rely on you to guide me in social matters. Do you happen to know exactly what one wears to a candy pulling?"

CHAPTER TWELVE

Lemon Gingerbread—*Grate the rinds of two or three lemons, and add the juice to a glass of brandy, then mix the grated lemon in one pound of flour; make a hole in the flour, pour in half a pound of molasses, half a pound of butter, melted, the lemon-juice and brandy, and mix all up together with half an ounce of ground ginger, and quarter of an ounce of Cayenne pepper.*

—*PETERSON'S MAGAZINE*, JANUARY 1868

FRIDAY, MARCH 6, 1868

Emily looked at the thick griddle cakes and decided to have an apple for breakfast.

"How can you eat after so many sweets last night?" she asked Robert, who was shoveling food into his mouth with barely a pause to breathe.

"That was hours ago," Robert said. "I'm starving. May I have more, Mrs. Bechner?"

Emily had never indulged in spirits, but she wondered if this was what a hangover felt like. From the amount of candy she had consumed at the taffy pull, her stomach was decidedly sour, and she felt sluggish and out of sorts.

She was also worried. Mr. Smith had not come to the house as he had promised the day before. He might have been detained elsewhere or he might have only agreed to come in order to get her to leave. Whatever the case, it meant that she would have to brave the wharf again.

The rain beat against the kitchen window. In the garden beyond, a few patches of snow lingered, but they were a dirty brown and would soon melt. It was cold and blustery, the sort of day she would rather spend by a warm fire with a book. Perhaps she should give Mr. Smith more time before accosting him again.

Robert pushed himself away from the table and picked up his lunch pail.

"Now, you're sure you're going to be warm enough?" Emily fretted. "Perhaps John should take you to school in the carriage."

Robert was horrified. "Mother! I'd be the laughingstock of the school. Only girls are that soft!"

"Well, then, at least bundle up," his mother insisted.

"Of course," he laughed as he kissed her good-bye.

A few moments later, John came in from his room over the carriage house. Mrs. Bechner started to dish up a plate for him, but he shook his head.

"Mrs. Stratton, ma'am," he said, "I'd be obliged if you could come out to the stable with me. There's something I think you should see to."

Emily got up. "Certainly, John, but can't it wait until you've had your breakfast?"

"I don't think so," the coachman answered. "But I'd be grateful if you'd save some for me."

"Let me get my coat and umbrella." Emily went to the hall.

"What's all this about?" Mary Kate demanded of him as soon as she had gone.

"Never you mind," John told her. "If the missus wants you to know, she'll tell you. It's not my place to be spreading tales."

Mary Kate sprang up. "If you've uncovered a body in there, it's the police you should be calling, not Mrs. Stratton."

"Calm yourself, woman," John laughed. "I've found nary a bone. But this concerns her and not you."

Emily returned then and forestalled the cutting retort that Mary Kate was trying to think up. John left the kitchen first, opening the umbrella over Emily's head.

"Why all the mystery, John?" Emily teased. "Did you find a treasure in the carriage house?"

It suddenly occurred to her that he might have done. She should have thought of looking there herself. There must be lots of places there to cache papers or valuables. Hadn't Robert mentioned hearing someone there the night they had arrived?

"No, ma'am, although you can be sure I'd tell you if I did," John said. "It's only that he didn't want anyone to see him with you."

He pushed open the stable door. There was a smell of leather and horse, although the latter was faint. John had done serious cleaning. He pointed to a chair over by the coal stove where a man sat holding a coffee mug.

"Mr. Smith! What are you doing here?" Emily was taken aback. "Why didn't you come to the house?"

"He's been here since last night, ma'am," John said. "Dan and me, we go back a ways. I let him stay until I could get you."

Mr. Smith rose. "Thanks, John," he said. "You're a pal and no mistake. Why don't you go get your breakfast while I talk to Mrs. Stratton? We won't be long."

"Is that all right?" John asked. "It doesn't seem proper."

Emily nodded. With a worried glance over his shoulder, John went back to the house.

Mr. Smith's expression toward Emily was less friendly. "What were you thinking of, coming down to the dock looking for me?" he demanded. "Do you want to get me killed?"

"I . . . I don't understand," Emily sputtered.

He shook his head. "Of course you don't," he admitted. "Old Horace wouldn't have told you a thing. But there are those who won't believe that. You must be more careful."

Emily sat on a pile of tack. "Why don't you tell me, then, so I don't endanger you further?"

"That's why I'm here." He sat down again and drank the last of his coffee, if that's what it was. "What do you know about the railroad here in town?"

"Railroad?" Emily was confused. "There isn't one, is there?"

"Not yet," Smith said. "But two different companies are trying to get the concession from the government to build one."

"Yes? And you and Horace invested in one of them?" It still didn't mean anything to her.

"Let's just say we had a stake in it." Mr. Smith seemed unsure about how to proceed.

Emily didn't have time for niceties.

"Mr. Smith, I was married to Horace Stratton for eighteen years," she said. "I am well aware that his morals were not what he represented them to be to my parents. If you and he had some scheme to defraud, I shall not be surprised or shocked."

He blinked. "Well, in that case—"

She held up her hand. "I should warn you that I have no intention of permitting any such activity to continue, however."

"That's fine, ma'am." Smith leaned forward, speaking earnestly. "As long as you don't start poking around in what's already been done. I'm through with the business, myself. But there are those who might not want to forgive or forget."

"And what was the business?" she asked with diminishing patience.

Now he tipped the chair back, balancing it on two legs. "Ah, that. Well, part of it was the coolies. Horace got them in Hong Kong and shipped them up here to grade the road and lay the track."

"Sad for them," Emily said. "And reprehensible, considering how they are treated. But it's done all the time with no protest from officials. That isn't enough to cause you to be so fearful. And, before you confess further, I already know that the men are kept docile with the opium Horace also shipped. What else? I presume you also provided prostitutes."

The chair came down with a clatter. "Mrs. Stratton!" Smith was honestly shocked. "You shouldn't know such words."

"Being a missionary means seeking out the lowly and the outcast," Emily reminded him. "I don't know why people assume I know nothing of the sordid side of the world. And my life with Captain Stratton taught me everything that my parents' ministry didn't."

He ruminated on that a while, looking at his empty cup.

"I suppose that's so," he agreed at last. "Yes, we brought girls in, too."

"So far, Mr. Smith, all the distasteful business you've told me about is handled more by a bribe to the right official than through murder." Emily rose. "Why do you fear for your life?"

"Have you heard of a man named Ben Holladay?" Smith asked abruptly.

Emily sat down again. "I did. In San Francisco. Horace had some dealings with him, but I don't know what they were."

"Well, Holladay is moving up into Oregon," Smith explained. "It's his money that's behind the East Side railroad company. Horace promised to deliver some congressmen and state senators to vote for the East Side."

"And did he?"

Smith avoided her eyes. "Well, he set out to. But then he got the idea of using the money for other things."

"So he took funds for bribes and then embezzled it." Emily felt a bit sick. Was there nothing she owned that wasn't tainted? "But Mr. Holladay can hardly bring Horace to court for this, even if he were still alive."

"That isn't his style. He's a man who takes care of things on his own," Smith said. "So far, ma'am, he doesn't know those men haven't been bought. And no one knows that I was in on it. But if you come nosing around the wharf wanting to talk business with me, what are Holladay's agents going to think?"

"You could return your share to him," Emily suggested. "As I should."

"My share went to a nice little ranch near John Day, where I'm going to retire pretty darn soon," Smith said. "And how can you return money you're supposed to know nothing about?"

He got up and put the mug on the chair. "So I'd be obliged if you just pretend we never met, ma'am. No offense."

"Wait a moment." Emily followed him. "That doesn't explain anything. What about Ah Sung?"

"Who?"

"My cook," she said. "He was found shot and floating in the river last week. What did he have to do with this?"

"Nothing!" Smith insisted. "I never heard of him. He was probably killed for a gambling debt. Those Chinese are always betting on something. It was just a coincidence."

"I don't believe that, Mr. Smith." Emily blocked his way to the door. "And I don't believe that you're telling me everything. What did my husband leave with you? If there are more records, I must have them."

Smith tried to edge past her. "Truly, ma'am, I've told you all I know. More'n I meant to, for a fact. I got a nice pile of cash from a man who can afford to lose it and I didn't meddle with the legislature. All I want is to live long enough to settle down on my ranch."

Emily realized that she was going to get no more from him. She stepped aside.

"Just one thing more," she said. "Did Horace have another office in town? A room he paid rent on, perhaps in one of the saloons, or the establishments upstairs from them?"

"Mrs. Stratton, you are a one!" Smith put his hat on. "Horace spent enough time in those places to pay rent but I never heard of him doing it officially. And that's all. Good day, ma'am."

He bent his head and ducked into the downpour.

Emily stood at the door. She wished she could stand out in the rain until all the scum from Horace's life washed off. Was there nothing despicable that he wasn't involved in? If only she could find one honestly earned dollar that she could use to support herself and her son. Her only choice at the moment seemed to be between poverty and living off the misery of others.

Could she do that to Robert? Emily hoped she wouldn't have to face that decision. It was so much easier when she had been a child and poor. She knew what her parents would have wanted her to do. They had never placed any value on worldly possessions. But they had also believed that faith would protect them from harm. And so they had died. And yet they had encouraged their only child to marry Horace Stratton so that she would never know poverty again.

Emily felt totally confused. Now she was back where she had started.

John had thoughtfully left her the umbrella. She walked slowly back to the house, wondering what to do next.

Perhaps there was nothing more to find. Horace had been involved in

enough corruption to damn him a hundred times over. Emily found no satisfaction over the idea of him burning in Hell, but she could feel no pity, either. It wasn't enough that he had forced her into a moral dilemma. From
what Mr. Smith had told her, Horace had left behind enough intrigue to
endanger her life and, even worse, that of his son.

John was just finishing his griddle cakes, bacon, and eggs when she got
back.

"I think I will need the carriage today," she told him. "I must start paying calls on all those who have come to see me, although I had hoped to
wait for less inclement weather."

"That might be a dreadful long wait," Mary Kate said. "I asked someone when they thought the rain would stop and he answered, 'Sometime
before Independence Day, usually.' "

Emily stared out the window at the sodden world. Patches of snow lay
in sheltered corners, pitted by the rain. Streams of water poured off the roof
and fell on either side of the portico. But in the garden shoots of jonquils
were poking up and the oak tree alongside the drive had shiny red buds.
Spring was coming. She only wondered if there would ever be sun again.

She must have said something aloud, for John answered.

"Sure enough, Mrs. Stratton. The sunshine will come when you least
expect it," he laughed. "You'll not believe it now, but there'll be days in
August when you wonder if it will ever rain."

"I look forward to that," Emily sighed. "Could you have the carriage
ready at ten, please?"

Before she paid formal calls, Emily had one errand to make. On her way
downtown the day before, she had noticed a sign on a building on Washington Street, SEE FAN, PHYSICIAN. If he was a genuine doctor, Emily was
sure he would be able to speak with her. She needed more medicines to
ward off the grippe. And perhaps he could also tell her something about
Ah Sung.

She told John to wait near the corner of First and Washington.

"I'll only be a few minutes," she promised.

The office of See Fan also sold herbal medicines. Emily felt a welcome
sense of order and calm as she entered. The mingled odor of a hundred

herbs scented the air of the dimly lit room. The walls were lined with shelves containing little wooden drawers, each one marked with the name of the medicine inside. There was a long counter on which stood a set of scales, mortar and pestle, a flat stone for grinding and chopping, and an abacus. The only bright spot in the place was the red curtain leading to the examining room at the back.

The curtain opened at once. The man seemed not at all surprised to see a Western woman. He bowed formally.

"I am See Fan," he said. His voice was deep and musical; his English was clear.

Emily put her hands together and returned the bow. His eyes widened, either in astonishment or amusement.

"Honorable Dr. See, do you have the herbs I need for a winter tonic?" she asked. "I am in good health and wish to remain so."

"Very wise," he told her. "Let me feel your pulse."

Obediently, she held out her hand. He closed his eyes and measured the beating in her wrist.

"Yes, a good balance at present," he agreed. "I can give you a mixture of *jin yin hua, ju hua* and *long yan rou*. Boil it in four teacups of water until it becomes two cups. Then drink it hot two or three times a day. You may add sugar if the taste is bitter to you."

"Thank you," Emily said. "Do you have any fresh *gan jiang*? I can only find it here as a powder."

The doctor smiled. "I had heard there was a Chinese-speaking *gai jin* in town. Yes, I have some ginger root. With spring onions, it also makes an effective tonic, although one must sweeten the breath after drinking it."

He got out the ginger and wrapped it for her.

"I also wanted to ask you about Ah Sung, the man who was shot recently," she told him.

His hands continued folding the package. "Yes, you went to Wa Kee about him," See Fan said without looking up. "He was not of my clan," he said. "Ah Ning is the head of his family group."

"And where can I find Ah Ning?" she asked. "I wish to be sure that Ah Sung's bones will be sent home for burial, and I would like to give something to his family."

He finished tying the package and handed it to her.

"I will have to make the other tonic to the right proportions for your body," he explained. "Can you return for it tomorrow?"

"Yes." Emily understood. "Thank you for your help."

As she hurried back through the rain to where John was waiting, she wondered if it had been wise to be so direct. She hoped Dr. See understood that it was important to find out why Ah Sung died. His calm, warm fingers on her wrist had brought back memories. He was a real doctor who had passed examinations and was certified in China, she was sure. Now if only he could also be someone who would help her.

Now that she had taken care of a winter tonic, visiting Alice was the next duty. Emily half hoped that her sister-in-law would be out, but it appeared that this was Alice's day in. Even worse, her friend Eutheria was also in attendance.

"My dear!" Alice got up to kiss her. "How noble of you to brave the showers to come see me! Eutheria and I were just lamenting that the rains seem to be lasting longer this year."

Eutheria echoed her. "Fewer clear days every year, I'm certain. It's a judgment, I'm sure of it."

"You'll stay to luncheon, of course," Alice said. It wasn't a request. "Mrs. King is coming and Dr. and Mrs. Glisan and Mr. Carmichael. George will be home. You'll make the even number."

With an inner groan, Emily realized that it was nearly eleven-thirty.

Emily resigned herself to a meal with the Bracewells. She liked the Glisans and Mr. Carmichael. George Bracewell had already won her heart by offering to take Robert out for a day of fishing on the Columbia when the weather was better. It would even be useful to see Dorothea King again.

"Thank you," she said. "I'll need to tell John to return for me."

"Oh, just send him home." Alice waved her hand like a wand. "Eutheria will be happy to take you back, won't you, dear?"

"Of course." Eutheria smiled dimly.

The luncheon turned out to be nicer than Emily anticipated. She was seated next to Mr. Carmichael, whose old-fashioned courtesy pleased her very much. George was in good form as host, telling amusing stories and drawing out interesting information from his guests. To her astonishment, Alice said very little, beyond asking if anyone wanted more of the superb soup, salmon, and fig pudding.

"Are you becoming more comfortable living in Portland?" Mr. Carmichael asked her during a lull in the conversation.

"Yes, thank you," she answered. "The people I've met have mostly been very kind. All that I knew of the United States was from my years in boarding school near Boston. It's different here, more . . ." She searched for a word. "More unexpected," she finished, although that wasn't exactly what she meant.

But Mr. Carmichael seemed to think it a good answer.

"That's what I found also. Endlessly surprising and full of possibility." He lifted his wineglass. "Here's to a long stay in the unexpected Portland."

She clinked her water glass against it.

"A long and peaceful stay," she amended.

But she feared that this wish would not be fulfilled.

CHAPTER THIRTEEN

The moon-eyed gentry are about as thick as rats in Portland now-a-days.

—HARVEY SCOTT, *THE OREGONIAN*, MAY 14, 1866

SATURDAY, MARCH 7, 1868

Dr. See Fan delivered the message to his friend Ah Ning when they met for their weekly Mah-Jong game.

"Mrs. Stratton seems a kind woman, for a Westerner," the doctor observed. "How much she understands of our customs, I can't be sure. She spent most of her life in Shanghai, but you know how the Europeans hide in their enclaves."

"Ah Sung told me that she spoke the Shanghai dialect well," Ah Ning said. "And that although her writing has no artistic style it is clear and correct."

"But she was shown China through Christian eyes." Dr. See shook his head. "Those missionaries are as much a curse as opium."

"So, why do you think she wants to meet me?" Ah Ning asked. "She should at least know that the clan will see that Sung's ashes are sent back to his village. We don't need her money."

"I think his death bothers her," See Fan said. "I'm not sure why. Do you know who killed him?"

"The police came and asked questions about his gambling habits." Ah Ning shrugged. "He gambled little and had no great debts that I know of. They then wanted to know if he was an addict. I told them that he did not indulge in opium. They didn't believe me. They wanted a Chinese to arrest. So they told their masters that he was killed in a fight by 'an unknown assailant.' The matter has been closed."

The two men were seated at a low table in Ah Ning's room over his import shop. They were sipping tea from thin porcelain cups. Dr. See set his gently on the tray.

"You think that Ah Sung was involved in the crimes of the white demons?" he asked.

The merchant thought this over.

"No," he said at last. "At least, not knowingly. He may have seen something he shouldn't. Or he may have taken a job without knowing it was dangerous. Sung was not a bad man, or a brave one. He wanted only to earn enough to return to his family and pay for his sons' education."

"I think that if he is to have justice, our best hope is with this woman," Dr. See answered.

Ah Ning gave a short laugh. "Justice for us in this country is as random as a throw of the dice. If he must depend on the benevolence of a Christian widow to find his killer, poor Sung's spirit will never be avenged."

Emily was busy compiling the questions she wanted to ask Ah Ning when Robert came bounding into her room.

"Uncle George just sent a note asking if I'd go riding with him this afternoon," he told her. "He and some friends are going across the river and up into the hills, maybe do some hunting. May I go, Mother?"

"Of course," Emily beamed. "How kind of him to think of you! Just bundle up. I'm having a preventative tonic made up today for us. But I have ginger and onion now. Just have a cup before you go, please."

Robert made a face, but agreed.

Once she had seen him off, Emily prepared to return to Dr. See's. She had written down the questions, in case Ah Ning spoke neither English nor a dialect she knew. The most delicate of the queries involved the possibility that the cook had been a Christian convert or, more dangerous, one of the followers of the Taiping leader, Hong. Ah Sung had worn the queue and shaved the front of this head as all subjects of the Manchu Emperor should, but that didn't mean he hadn't been part of the rebellion.

If that was true, his death might have had nothing to do with her. Or, even worse, it might have nothing to do with Horace and everything to do with the actions of her parents. What if the cook's death was linked to theirs?

She had to know.

As the day was indeterminate with only a chance of serious rain, Emily decided not to take the carriage. It seemed so ostentatious to her to ride just a few blocks, although she had to admit that it was much more comfortable than the curtained sedan chairs used by ladies in China. But in Portland almost everyone walked.

She passed a number of people she didn't know, all of whom greeted her with a polite "good day" or a comment on the weather. The streets were full of the Saturday bustle of shopping and paying calls. Children swooped in and out, some playing, some intent on errands.

Amidst the hurrying, Emily noticed one pair who seemed not to be heading anywhere in particular. The woman would walk a few steps and then pause to wait for her companion to investigate a pinecone or a pebble that had caught his eye. As she neared them Emily recognized little Willie Eliot and his mother, whom she had met at the candy pull.

"Good morning, Mrs. Eliot," Emily greeted her. "How are you? I trust the Reverend Eliot is well."

"Please, call me Etta," she replied. "Every time someone calls me 'Mrs. Eliot,' I look around for my mother-in-law. Tom is working on his sermon for tomorrow, so Willie and I thought we'd go out and give him some quiet time to write."

"Then you must call me Emily. I understand from your husband that you also write?"

Etta stooped to keep Willie from tasting a worm he had picked up.

"No worms, precious; you'll spoil your dinner. Yes, I write an essay now and then. And I dabble in poetry the way some women play at watercolors. I have no grand ambitions."

"You may underestimate your talent," Emily said. "If it isn't too personal, I'd like to read some of your work."

Etta Eliot gave Emily a long appraising look. Then she smiled. "Yes, I'd be happy to show you a few things. Please come to call, if you don't mind disorder, that is. We are still camping in a place provided by the congregation while we hunt for a house and wait for our furniture to arrive. It's coming by ship around the horn. I'm hoping to see my things again by May."

Emily laughed and promised not to pass judgment on the house. She bade them both good-bye and hurried on to the doctor's office.

Dr. See was waiting for her with the herb mixture. There was no one else with him.

"Ah Ning is not sure that he can help you, Mrs. Eliot," the doctor said. "But he is willing to meet with you. He should be here shortly. Would you care to wait in my examining room?"

He gestured toward the curtain.

The room was dimly lit and redolent of patchouli. Emily sat on a dark wooden bench to wait. A moment later she was startled by a slight cough. What she had taken to be a statue in the corner was actually a man.

"Good day, Mrs. Stratton," he said in English as he bowed. "I am Ah Ning."

Emily recovered herself enough to observe the proper formalities. When these were finished, Ah Ning came directly to the subject.

"I understand you want to know who shot my lamented clansman, Ah Sung, and why," he said. "I can answer neither question. He was a quiet man who had no enemies that I know of in the community."

Emily leaned forward, inviting confidence.

"Can you at least tell me more about him?" she begged. "Wa Kee told me he was from Nanking, is that so? He didn't speak with that dialect."

"Wa Kee was mistaken," Ah answered. "He came from a village near Canton, Lianhua. He was never in Nanking."

"Forgive me"—Emily moved a bit closer—"after Ah Sung died, I found a Bible in his room. It was the translation used by the Heavenly Army. Do you know if Ah Sung was a follower of the Younger Brother?"

"No!" Ah Ning spoke sharply. "I am certain of that. He and his family suffered terribly because of the Taiping. I don't know why he had that book, but it was not for worship."

Emily exhaled in relief. "Thank you. One more question, please. Do you know who hired Ah Sung to work for me?"

"You should ask Wa Kee." Ah Ning seemed nervous.

"I don't think he would tell me," Emily said. "I thought it was Mrs. Bracewell, my husband's sister, but she says not. Who chose him to come to my house?"

Ah Ning considered. "You believe he was sent to spy on you?"

"Yes," Emily answered.

"He wasn't inclined to intrigue," Ah Ning said. "But he wanted very much to go home. I'll see what I can find out."

"Oh, thank you!" Emily clasped her hands in gratitude. She hadn't realized until that moment how alone she had felt in her search for the truth.

Ah Ning rose and ushered her into Dr. See's main office.

"I'll send word for you to meet me here if I discover anything," he promised. With that, he vanished behind the curtain.

Emily thought of one more question. "Mr. Ah?" She pushed the curtain back to ask him.

The room was empty.

On her return Emily was astonished to find an invitation from the Kings. It was written by Mr. King, an even stranger puzzle. *My dear Mrs. Stratton*— his flowery hand was elegant—*Mr. Andrews and I feel that we have begun our relationship with you on a bad footing. Please forgive our hasty response to your most reasonable request for company records and allow my wife and me to welcome you officially to the city with a dinner party tomorrow night at eight o'clock. If you could send your acceptance by messenger, we would be delighted.*

Emily read it through several times. Whatever was his intention? Did he mean to lull her into compliance or was he really ashamed of his behavior? The thought of an evening with the Kings and their friends was about as appealing as the prospect of facing the death of ten thousand cuts.

"Mrs. Stratton, I didn't hear you come in." Mary Kate came down the front stairs. "There was also a package that came with the note. I left it in the sitting room. Do you want tea now?"

"Yes, thank you." Emily went in and found a large box, wrapped in brown paper. She opened it to find a stack of account books, all freshly copied.

It appeared that Mr. King was really trying to mend fences. She wrote out a note thanking him and agreeing to attend the dinner. Then she settled in to compare the accounts with those that Horace had left.

Several hours later, the gas had been lit and the tea had gone cold on the table beside her. Emily shut the last book in frustration. Everything matched. Oh, there were a few small discrepancies in the arithmetic but nothing that substantially changed the results. They hadn't even tried to pretend that duty had been paid on the opium shipments.

It didn't make sense.

For one thing, she knew that Horace's accounts in the bank in San Francisco showed a great deal more money than he had taken in through the company. How had he made the rest? Were there still more account books detailing other ventures with Andrews and King, or was Horace investing on his own?

It wasn't just the knowledge that the money that supported her was tainted. She was coming to terms with that and what she must do. What she was afraid of now was that someone thought that she knew more than she really did about its source.

And that someone had killed Ah Sung.

The next morning after church, the Reverend Stratton asked Emily if he could schedule a time when she might give a lecture on her experiences in China.

"Just a bit about life and customs there, you know," he said. "And the state of missionary work. You might bring a few small items to show. Would you be willing?"

"I don't feel comfortable speaking in public," Emily equivocated. "Perhaps in a few months, when I know the people here better."

He seemed so disappointed that she felt a stab of guilt. After all, it was part of the duty of a missionary to report on progress in the field. She didn't feel right reminding him that it had been her parents who had signed on for the labor, not she.

"Of course," he replied. "I understand. Perhaps later in the spring."

As Emily turned to go, she found Mr. Carmichael at her elbow.

"I see that your son hasn't accompanied you today," he began.

"Robert was out late riding with his uncle yesterday," Emily explained. "I thought he should sleep a bit longer this morning."

"I see." He seemed pleased. "In that case, may I escort you back to your home?"

"That would be very kind," Emily said.

"I should warn you," he continued as they started on their way, "that I will have the honor of dining with you again this evening. Mrs. King sent me an invitation yesterday afternoon. I hope you aren't becoming bored with my company."

"Not at all," Emily answered sincerely. "I shall be grateful for a friendly face."

He looked down at her in confusion. "Have people been unkind?"

"I mean, I feel I know you better than the others," she stumbled. "After all, you were my first friend in Portland."

"I'm glad to hear it," he said. "And I look forward to this evening."

They walked a while in silence, Emily admiring the homes along the way.

"How long have you lived here, sir?" she asked when he pointed out a fine building on a lot that he remembered as nothing but forest.

He winced at her use of the term. He must seem ancient to her!

"Nearly twenty years," he replied. "My wife and I were among the first settlers in town. I set up as a lawyer but I also speculated a bit in land. Now I just speculate."

"And you have no children?"

"We had a stillborn daughter." His voice caught. "After that, there were no more."

"I'm so sorry." Impulsively, she laid a hand on his arm. "I didn't mean to bring back old sorrows. Tell me about your business. Do you just trade in land?"

"That's my major investment," he told her. "But I also have a share in some mining stock and the iron foundry down in Oswego. I keep enough to live on and play a bit with this and that. I'm really a very timid investor. Not at all a financier like Reed and Ladd."

"You mentioned the railroad." Emily was thinking. "Are you supporting the Eastsiders or the Westsiders?"

He laughed. "I see you're learning about local politics. I've put my stake on the West Side party. The others are supported by a Californian named Ben Holladay. He's been up here a few times and I agree with my friend Ladd that the man is a thorough reprobate. I think he's either duped the investors or they are as crooked as he."

Emily was silent, trying to remember what else she had heard about the Oregon railroad lines. It had been mentioned in the paper several times, and even the ladies she called upon had commented on it.

"Mrs. Stratton?" Mr. Carmichael broke into her thoughts. "You seem worried. Have you invested in the East Side company?"

"To be honest, I'm not sure," she told him. "Until Horace died, I never thought about where his money came from. I thought it was all in shipping. I'm finding out that it's much more complicated than that. Dorothea King thinks I shouldn't bother myself with it but just let her husband manage everything. Do you agree?"

"No I don't," he answered decidedly. "I think it's criminal to keep women from knowing the state of their husbands' business. When I was practicing law I saw too many widows cheated out of everything they had by unscrupulous advisors, sometimes even their own relatives. I could name you any number of women who run their own businesses with great competence. There's no reason to keep our wives and daughters in such ignorance!"

"Why, Mr. Carmichael," Emily laughed in delight. "I believe you are a supporter of the suffragists!"

"Well, perhaps." He seemed discomfited by his outburst. "I do sometimes think that if women had had the vote, the late war might have been avoided."

He looked around with a sheepish expression.

"But I'd rather not have it generally known." He bent down to whisper. "I'm not ready to march with a banner or take to wearing a Bloomer."

The image of this tall, distinguished gentleman in a shirtwaist, bonnet, and Bloomer trousers was too much for Emily. She laughed so hard that she had to stop at the gate to catch her breath.

"Thank you for a most entertaining walk home," she said, giving him her hand. "But please don't say anything like that at dinner or I shall surely disgrace myself."

"I promise." He bowed. "Until tonight."

For the rest of the afternoon, Emily found her work distracted by that absurd image. Mary Kate wondered if her mistress was quite all right, because for no apparent reason, she would suddenly start chuckling.

At the Bracewell home, Alice was preparing for the dinner.

"I should have been the one to give her the first party," she complained to her husband. "That Dorothea King should know better than doing anything so frivolous before our year of mourning is over."

George bent to kiss her but instead patted her hand. She was layered in creams from neck to hairline. Her friend, Eutheria, sat nearby, embroidering a cover for her sewing scissors from a pattern she had found in *Peterson's Magazine*.

"Not everyone is as careful of the proprieties as you, Alice," she said. "You might decline."

"No, it would be churlish to refuse the invitation," Alice admitted.

"The Kings have a good cook," George reminded her. "And an excellent wine cellar."

"As if that were of any consequence to me," Alice sniffed. "But for your sake, I'm glad of it. I suppose poor Emily could use some exposure to a better class of people than she spends her time with now. I can't imagine why Horace would have married her. No money and so plain."

"Oh, I don't think she's plain," Eutheria commented. "It's just that black is a dreadful color for her."

Privately, George agreed. There was no doubt that his wife was still a fine-looking woman, tall and blond like a Nordic princess. But there was something to be said for Emily's more delicate frame and soft brown hair. Actually, once a man had looked into her eyes, it was hard to notice anything more.

Twenty-odd years of marriage had taught him to keep thoughts like that to himself. He made his escape down to the smoking room.

Alice wiped off the cream and began to apply some discreet enhancement to her cheeks.

"Eutheria," she said, not looking at her friend. "Now that you've met her, don't you wonder why my brother chose to marry that drab woman? He could have had his pick here."

Eutheria concentrated on a knot in her thread. "It was quite a surprise, I'll admit. For a time I thought he was joking. Then he brought back the photo of his son." Her voice broke.

"Exactly." Alice ignored the emotion. "I can't imagine that he would have given up the wonderful opportunities he had here if someone in Shanghai hadn't put pressure on him. But what sort of pressure is a conundrum."

"I suppose they really were married?" Eutheria asked.

"Oh, yes, I saw all the papers." Alice dusted her face with powder. "But I know there was something else going on, and I'm going to find it out. Mrs. Emily is not the sort of woman I want living in my poor brother's home."

Dutifully, Eutheria agreed.

Chapter Fourteen

About this time, I got verry hugly and desparat, drink verry hard, and getting into fights every day. One night I came home verry late and my dear Wife, as useal, meet me with a smile.

—Ned Chambreau, "Memoir"

SATURDAY EVENING, MARCH 7, 1868

Emily was seated at Mr. King's right, an honor she would rather have passed on. Alice was opposite her, and Mr. Andrews sat to Emily's right. Mr. Carmichael was far down the other side of the table, partnering another widow, a Mrs. Snyder, who had progressed to half-mourning and was wearing a silvery gray evening gown that very much suited her. Across from Mrs. Snyder was Mrs. Ladd, wearing a deep green gown with black velvet ribbons. She was seated next to George Bracewell. Across from Emily, next to Alice, sat Mr. Ladd, the banker. Alice had admonished her to say nothing *outré* in front of him.

"He's an important man in finance," she told Emily before dinner. "Both George and Norton King want to stay in his good esteem."

Emily felt the contrast between the two ends of the table. She and Alice looked like gloomy black ravens while the other women reminded her of bright tropical birds, rare and lovely.

Mr. Ladd smiled at her. He was in his early forties, with a neatly trimmed graying beard. "I understand from my wife that you are going to deny us the pleasure of a lecture on your life in the Celestial Kingdom," he said.

"Oh, Emily, dear, you really must reconsider," Alice exclaimed. "I'm sure that more than just the Methodist members of the community would come hear you. Reverend Stratton must be so disappointed by your refusal."

"I didn't refuse," Emily defended herself. "I only asked if I might wait a few months, until I feel more at ease in the community. I also would need to gather together the materials and prepare a talk."

"I'm so glad," Mrs. Ladd leaned forward over her plate to speak to her. "I've always been fascinated by the Orient. Your life there must have been so interesting."

"To me, it was normal," Emily said. "I didn't know until I went to boarding school that there was anything unusual about my childhood."

"They say you speak the language," Mr. Ladd said. "I'd have liked to learn it, but wouldn't know where to begin. It sounds to me like a badly tuned violin."

Emily took a sip of her water. "It is very different from English and, of course, many dialects are incomprehensible to one another. I speak the Mandarin dialect of Shanghai and a bit of some others. My parents came to the study too late to ever master the language, so they often took me with them to translate their exhortations."

"Well, I think you would give a fascinating lecture," Mrs. Ladd said. "I do hope you decide to do it soon."

Emily gave a sigh of relief as the topic turned to the Baptist Ladies' festival, to be held later that week. Perhaps if she wrote it out beforehand she could present an image of China and the missions that wouldn't shock the people of Portland. But she didn't believe she had enough tact and discretion to answer spontaneous questions.

From his corner of the table, Mr. Carmichael gave her a smile of reassurance. Emily thought of him in the suffragists' parade and cheered up immediately. Such a nice older man, so sensitive to her moods! She wished her father had been like him. But poor Benjamin Hoar had given all his attention to his savior, and there hadn't been much left for his child.

The meal was good and the wine the others drank made the conversation lively. Emily was happy to listen and make an occasional comment. Next to her, Mr. Andrews was extremely attentive, filling her in on the background of some of the topics and teasing her for her teetotal habit. She could hardly believe it was the same man she had met earlier. Was it the wine, or did he really intend to mend fences?

She was sorry when the ladies adjourned for coffee, leaving the men to their cigars and brandy. Mr. King had apologized for his rudeness, but Mrs. King had not. Beyond a frosty greeting, she had not said a word to Emily all evening. So it came as a shock when they were seated, each with her coffee and a thin lemon biscuit, that Dorothea addressed her first.

"Norton Andrews is such nice man, don't you think, Emily?" she asked archly. "It seems odd that he should still be single."

"I had the impression that he gave all his time to business," Emily answered.

"Well, not tonight." Alice emphasized the last word. "I've never seen the man so animated. You must bring out the best in him."

"Perhaps he has taken a little too much wine," Emily suggested. It was the only reason she could imagine for Mr. Andrews expansiveness.

The ladies all chuckled at her naïveté.

"My dear," Dorothea said. "I believe that he was inebriated by something other than wine."

"What?" Emily asked.

"Ah, well." Alice patted her hand. "I can see that you are still too wrapped in your grief to notice such things, and very proper, too."

"He's quite well off," Mrs. Snyder observed, pushing a stray curl into submission. "I've always thought that he'd be so much happier if he had a home and a good woman to take him in hand. Imagine, not knowing that oysters had gone bad! He might have died."

Emily was finally getting the drift of the conversation.

"Perhaps he can be encouraged to hire a cook," she suggested. "Our new cook, Mrs. Bechner, is wonderful, if a bit more inclined to use lard than I would like. And I'm not used to so much meat in my meals."

"I once read that in the siege of Shanghai, all the pet dogs vanished from the foreign quarter." Mrs. Ladd caught Emily's thought and helped to steer the subject from Mr. Andrews. "Were you there then, Mrs. Stratton?"

"Yes," Emily said. "It was a worrisome time. My husband had just left on another voyage. I was alone in the house with only my son and the servants. The streets were barricaded and soldiers patrolled day and night. In the Chinese part of the city the number of refugees overtaxed the food supplies. Many of the pets belonging to the Westerners disappeared. I fear they did go into soup pots."

The ladies shuddered.

"But you must remember that people were starving." Emily felt that she had landed in the fire with this topic, too. "Wouldn't you rather give up a pet than watch your children die of hunger?"

"Yes, of course I would," Mrs. Ladd's calm voice cut through Emily's rising defense. "The way my four eat, I'm glad we live in such a land of plenty. It breaks my heart to think of how those poor people have suffered."

"I agree," Mrs. Snyder chimed in. "We none of us understand life in the Orient the way you do. That's why you should reconsider telling us of your experiences."

"Yes, do, Emily dear," Alice said. "Sarah and Felicity should learn how fortunate they are. And your sad tales might increase the donations to the missionary fund."

"Well," Emily gave up. "When we're more settled in. I suppose I'll tell Reverend Stratton that I'll be happy to speak."

The gentlemen soon returned with the offer of a few rubbers of whist. Emily begged to be excused. "I never learned card games," she explained. "And I should be getting home. I told my coachman to return for me at ten, and it's past that now."

"He's out in front," George said. "Talking with the Ladds' driver."

"Then we must go, too," Mr. Ladd said. "Can't leave the horses standing long in this weather."

"It's been a lovely evening," Emily said. "Thank you so much for asking me. Mrs. King, I plan to be at home next Thursday afternoon, if you'd care to call. Mr. King, I shall visit you and Mr. Andrews at your office at your earliest convenience."

"What the hell did she mean by that?" Andrews demanded.

He and King were in his study finishing up the brandy. Andrews was pacing the carpet. His partner wondered that Norton didn't have heart problems. The man could never sit still.

"Well, she might want to get to know you better, Norton," King snorted. "The way you were laying it on tonight, I thought you'd be proposing to her before dessert."

"You told me to be nice to her," Andrews fumed. "Coldest little bitch I ever met."

"She may have just been too overwhelmed by your charm to respond," King said. "Try again. I'd do it myself, but they frown on bigamy in this country. Think about it. Marrying her would solve all our problems. We'd have control of Stratton's share in the company and we wouldn't have to worry about his widow asking for inconvenient accountings."

"What about the boy?" Andrews asked. "He'll be of age in five years."

"He's going back east to college soon." King leaned back and lit a cheroot. "If we make his allowance big enough, he'll never return."

"I don't suppose we could train him to join us." Andrews stopped pacing for a minute. "He seems bright enough and not overly fastidious. After all, he's Horace's son."

"Why don't we wait and see how he turns out?" King gave a huge yawn. "She's had the raising of him, mostly. Once he sows a few wild oats, he may turn into a disgusting prig. I've seen it before." He opened the door for Andrews. "You'd better be toddling back to your rooms, just in case Mrs. Emily decides to visit again at the crack of dawn. I'll ring for Hong Ju. He can accompany you with the lantern."

"Thanks." Andrews put on his coat. "When are you going to get streetlights up here?"

"Probably not until the city council decides whether to go with gas or oil," King grumbled. "They've tried both and still can't make up their minds."

"I've got some money in the gasworks," Andrews said. "I'm betting it's the coming thing."

"Good, good." King ushered him out. "The question is, how long before it arrives?"

The night was clearing when Andrews left the Kings. He could see his way well enough in the moonlight but was glad of someone with him. The rougher element in town didn't always stay by the river.

They were passing the Stratton house when he noticed someone prowling around in the bushes.

"Hong," he whispered. "Cover the lantern. I'm going to investigate."

Drawing his revolver from his coat pocket, Andrews crept to the side of the house. If he caught a burglar on her property, Emily might look more favorably on his suit.

The rustling in the bushes grew louder. It occurred to Andrews that bear sometimes came this far into the city this time of year. Just out of hibernation and really hungry. He stopped a safe distance away.

"You!" he called. "Come out of there. I warn you, I'm armed."

The rustling stopped. Andrews raised the revolver, praying that the intruder wasn't even now pointing a gun at him.

"Wait! Don't shoot!" the burglar said softly. "I'm coming out."

The moonlight glinted on the barrel of the gun, shaking in Andrews's hand. A shape came out of the undergrowth. He didn't look too dangerous, and he had his hands up.

"Now, then," Andrews said, his courage restored by the slight form in front of him. "I'm taking you down to the city jail. You can explain to them what you were doing here."

"I was trying to get in without my mother finding out, Mr. Andrews," the burglar said calmly.

Andrews lowered the gun. He should have guessed that it was Horace's son. There'd been enough talk about how he'd been frequenting the saloons and brothels by the river almost every night.

"Well, that's a damn fool thing to do, boy," he said. "You could have got yourself killed."

Robert agreed. "I didn't know that Portland had such public-spirited citizens. I'll have to be more careful in future."

Andrews shook his head. "I won't ask where you were, but I'd air out that suit. It reeks of cheap perfume. You're a Stratton, all right."

Robert laughed softly. "I hear that a lot. Wish I'd known my father better. I always thought he was a stodgy old fellow, except on our trip back to Boston. I learned then that he was a different man away from home."

"You can say that again." Andrews put the gun back in his pocket. "Now get back to your room and don't let your mother catch you."

"She never has yet." With a mock salute, Robert vanished again into the shrubbery. A moment later Andrews heard the crack of branches and the creak of a swinging shutter.

The remainder of his walk home was uneventful. But a row of elephants could have passed by unnoticed. His encounter with Robert had sent Andrews into a whole new realm of speculation. There was more than one way to tame a widow.

When Emily woke the next morning, the day was clear and bright, a day dropped out of spring to tantalize a winter-weary world. She was washing her face in the basin when she happened to look out the eastern window.

"Gracious!" she said. "Who put that there?"

A few moments later she was running down the stairs in her dressing gown and slippers. She burst into the kitchen.

"Do you know there's an enormous mountain just across the river?" she asked Mary Kate and the cook.

Mary Kate ran outside to look. She was back in a moment, eyes round as saucers.

"There's two of them!" she exclaimed. "One in the north and one in the east. And I think there are more. We've been here more than two weeks and never a whisper about enormous piles of rock and snow almost at our doorstep."

Mrs. Bechner calmly continued stirring the oatmeal.

"It's always a treat when the mountains are out," she said. "The one in the east is Hood and the northern one is St. Helens. Nice, aren't they?"

Emily thought this was an understatement. She'd never seen anything like them. Their isolation and grandeur gave her a queer feeling in her stomach. She couldn't define it, but it unsettled her.

After breakfast, Emily dressed and went into the garden. Crocuses were already in bloom alongside the pathways, and sharp green shoots of other bulbs were pushing their way up. The young oak trees and the lilac bush had soft new leaves, and even the firs lining the road shone fresh in the sunlight. It was a sudden explosion of nature. On a morning like this, anything seemed possible.

Perhaps she could learn to love this country.

She had planned to spend the day going over the accounts again, but it was impossible to imagine staying indoors on such a morning.

"I'm going exploring," she announced to Mary Kate. "I may not be back until teatime."

"Very good, ma'am," Mary Kate said. "I've some sewing to do and the sheets to wrap up for the laundryman. Then, if it's all the same to you, I might do a bit of exploring, myself."

"Mrs. Bechner?" Emily asked. "Are you feeling adventurous today?"

"Only enough to do the shopping," the cook answered. "I've been in Oregon eight years now. I know what spring looks like."

Emily started off with the intention of seeing how far the town went before the forest and West Hills took over the landscape. But she soon realized that the terrain was too rough for her fashionable walking dress and high-heeled boots. As she started back, this was proved true as she skidded on a muddy incline and landed firmly on her bustle.

She sat for a moment to compose herself. From her vantage point, Mt. Hood filled the view to the east. The city on the riverbank seemed so flimsy beneath it. How could human beings attempt to build anything lasting with that monument ever before them? All those men with their plans for railroads and industry, couldn't they see how impossible it was to match the glory of that single natural edifice?

"Mrs. Stratton!"

The call came from above and to her right. For a second, Emily expected to see a divine messenger in keeping with her celestial musings. Instead she found herself looking up at a fine bay horse. The rider was staring at her in consternation.

"Mr. Smith?" She tried to pick herself up, but the ground she sat on was too slick for rapid movement.

He was at her side in a moment.

"What are you doing up here?" he demanded. "You could've been breakfast for a bear, sitting there like that. Are you hurt?"

He helped her up. She examined her dress and adjusted her bonnet.

"I believe I've cracked a couple of hoops," she told him. "But otherwise I'm fine. Thank you for stopping for me. I take it that you are still working in town?"

"Not for long," Smith said. "As soon as the ice breaks up on the upper river, I'm heading out. I hope you've given up poking around in old Horace's business."

"No, but you can rest assured that he didn't leave any evidence of your partnership," she told him. "At least, none that I can find."

"That does relieve my mind," he admitted. "But I'd rather you stopped looking. Can you walk on your own now?"

Emily tried a few steps. On the fifth she wobbled and had to grab hold of Smith to keep from landing on the ground again.

"Perhaps if you could just give me your arm until we reach drier ground?" she asked.

"Here," he said. "I'll hoist you up on Juniper and you can ride down. I'll lead him. Can you manage to stay on?"

"I think so." She let him lift her onto the horse. The western saddle allowed her to sit sideways and grip the pommel to keep from sliding down.

"You can see that this isn't your kind of place, Mrs. Stratton." Daniel was amused at her undignified position. "You should go back to China, or maybe San Francisco. The more you find out about Horace, the less happy you'll be. Just be glad he left you taken care of."

Emily only nodded. She was tired of being told where she should be. The more people told her to leave, the more determined she was to stay.

It was galling to hear Mr. Smith defend Horace in any respect. Yes, he had taken care of her. She had to admit that, whatever his other faults, he had never left her short of funds. Perhaps the payment he had exacted for that was no different from other men. She had always pretended everything was fine. How many of the women she met had been doing the same?

Horace had uncharacteristically left her in charge of his money. Why? He knew that his partners could get access to any business records and possibly even personal ones under the guise of relieving her of the worry. They might even be able to take documents legally, without her permission, as company property.

Company property. Of course! She sat up straight, staring at the mountain as if it had just given her the answer to a riddle. How stupid she had been! Anything to do with the partnership was the concern of Andrews and King. But they couldn't touch anything that had been left in her name alone. Was that what Horace had intended?

"Mr. Smith!" she called. "You can let me down now. Thank you. I can make it from here."

She had to get home and change. This was something she must investigate at once.

CHAPTER FIFTEEN

[T]he bank of Ladd and Tilton has grown steadily and rapidly, until it stands in the front rank, if not at the head of all others in the northwestern states.

—HUBERT HOWE BANCROFT, *HISTORY OF THE LIFE OF WILLIAM S. LADD*
(SAN FRANCISCO, 1900)

MONDAY, MARCH 9, 1868

The next time I go exploring, I'm going to wear buckskin and home-spun," Emily vowed as Mary Kate clucked over the wreckage of her walking dress.

"Mrs. Bracewell would have something to say about that, I'm sure," Mary Kate said.

"That's true," Emily sighed. "I sometimes wonder if the world wouldn't be a happier place without bishops and Mrs. Bracewells."

"You might add British landlords," Mary Kate agreed. "I know Ireland could live without them."

"I think China could, too," Emily said. "Let's be glad we don't have all three of them after us at the same time."

She and Mary Kate got her into another presentable costume. Then she went out at once to discover if her new theory were true. Had Horace left something in her name alone?

It seemed that everyone in town was out enjoying the sunshine. Emily was so intent on her mission that she barely nodded to people she knew. It did surprise her that so many of the faces were familiar.

The business accounts that Horace had left were at the Bank of British Columbia on Front Street. No one there had said anything about her having one of her own, but she stopped to ask, just in case.

"No, Mrs. Stratton," the cashier said, after checking the list of depositors. "Captain Stratton had only the accounts with us that we've shown you. If you'd care to open a new one . . . ?"

Emily declined and went down the street to the Bank of Oregon. It was an imposing brick structure decorated with stone ornaments and curlicues that rivaled anything in San Francisco. A small plaque on the wall read LADD AND TILTON, PROPRIETORS. She wondered if it was the same Ladd that Mr. King had been trying so hard to impress the night before.

She announced herself to the clerk and asked to see the manager. The boy vanished into the back. A moment later he emerged, followed by Mr. Ladd.

"My dear Mrs. Stratton!" He held out his hands to her. "I was hoping you'd come by. Carrie and I enjoyed our conversation with you last evening. Please, come into my office. Gerald, have some tea brought in for my guest."

The office was as sumptuous as the rest of the building, with thick carpet and solid mahogany furniture. Some fine pictures hung on the walls, including a portrait of Mrs. Ladd.

When they were seated and Emily had sipped her tea, Mr. Ladd went over to his massive desk.

"I suppose you've come for the box your husband left for you," he said.

A box! Emily's heart leapt.

"Yes, at least to examine the contents," she answered, trying to appear calm. "I don't have a safe in the house and would prefer that anything valuable be left here for the present."

"Certainly. I'm honored that you place your trust in us." Ladd rang for the clerk.

"Take Mrs. Stratton to the corner room upstairs," he ordered. "I'll get your box from the safe. You can stay as long as you like. Ring for Gerald if you need anything."

Emily's heart was pounding as Mr. Ladd returned with a long metal box under his arm. He set it on the table in front of her. She reached for it and then realized that she'd forgotten one thing.

"How silly of me," she exclaimed. "I didn't bring the key!"

"Oh dear, I'm afraid he didn't leave a second one with us," Ladd apologized. "We could have it broken open, if you wish. It is your property."

"Yes, I'm afraid we'll have to," Emily said. "So many things are still unpacked. It might be days before I found it. I'd assumed that Horace would have had faith in your security."

"Your confidence is most appreciated," Ladd said. "But not many people share it, especially with family heirlooms."

"Yes, I suppose they don't," Emily said. *Heirlooms? What is he talking about?*

Mr. Ladd sent Gerald for tools to remove the lock.

Emily cast about for a topic of conversation. Anything to keep her mind from pointless speculation.

"There were surveyors in the street when I was coming here," she commented. "Someone said they were setting out the route for the railroad."

"Yes, we hope to start grading the road for the track by the middle of April," Ladd said proudly.

"Then I take it you support the West Side company?" Emily asked.

He drew himself up proudly. "Mrs. Stratton, my partners and I *are* the West Side company. The Eastsiders are nothing but a bunch of charlatans and crooks. I hope you weren't considering investing in them."

"It was the farthest thing from my mind," she said with all honesty. "I still don't know what investments I have. But I don't anticipate putting any money into transportation."

"You shouldn't be quite so certain," Ladd told her. "The railroad is the coming thing. Imagine, from one coast to the other in less than two weeks!

It will revolutionize commerce like nothing since the telegraph. It's only the speculators that should be avoided. You can put your money safely in a solid, well-run company."

His enthusiasm was so contagious that Emily was about to ask for a prospectus when Gerald returned with a bag of tools. He had the box open in a minute, which made Emily wonder why Horace had bothered locking it at all. The men left her in private to examine the contents.

The box contained two more boxes, a wooden one, of the sort used by the Chinese for jewelry, and a smaller, more flimsy one. She took out the larger and opened it.

"Ohhhhh!" she gasped.

Inside lay a necklace and earrings. Each earring had a large sapphire surrounded by diamonds. The necklace held three sapphires of a size that made the diamonds around them seem insignificant. There was a card under the jewelry. *These were my mother's and are for Robert to give to his bride.* Horace's florid script was unmistakable, as were the next words. *And don't let my greedy bitch of a sister near them.*

Emily wondered where such a piece had come from originally and what kind of family curse it held.

There was another level to the box. Emily carefully lifted the necklace out and set it on the table. Underneath it was another piece of jewelry, an ivory miniature of a young woman wearing the dress of forty years previous. She was haughtily pretty, with blond curls. Around her neck was the necklace in the upper box.

Emily stared at it for a long time. She had never seen a picture of Horace's mother. Alice looked much like her. This explained a lot. It wasn't fair of Horace to leave her in this quandary. Of course Alice would want these pieces for herself and her daughters. But for the moment it was just as well that she didn't know that Emily had them.

Emily paused. Could this have been what the burglars were looking for? Who besides Alice would know they existed? And if the jewels had belonged to her mother, then why hadn't Alice asked about them? Although Emily's family had possessed nothing like this, Emily knew that normally it was the daughter who got any family jewelry, while the rest of the property went to sons.

There was still the other parcel. This was a cigar box wrapped and tied with string. The knots were impossible. Emily was ready to scream in exasperation when she noticed a letter opener on a cabinet against the wall. Assiduous sawing finally snapped the string. The box flew open and papers spilled out.

Most of them seemed to be letters, in a dozen different hands. Emily picked one up and started reading.

My dearest Horsy Horace; Your last visit was the highlight of my season . . .

Emily put it down.

The next one was from another writer but in much the same vein. . . . *Remember, my dear, the gates of San Francisco will always be open to you!!*

Emily felt nauseated. It didn't surprise her that Horace had made conquests. He could be a very charming man, especially when he wanted something. It was only when he got it that his interest turned to apathy and, eventually, contempt. He had probably not even considered how she might feel upon finding these letters. They were like hunting trophies to him. He hadn't cared enough to want to hurt her.

What did upset her was that she *was* hurt. She had had no illusions about her husband, but it was a shock to realize that some part of her still hoped that she had meant something to him.

Her response angered her. She felt like a whipped dog, still hanging about, hoping to be taken back in by its master. Why couldn't she simply accept the fact that Horace had thought her the worst mistake he had ever made? He had told her so often enough.

With shaking hands, Emily put the rest of the letters aside, praying that it wouldn't be necessary to go through them. There were also several sheets of notepaper, filled with Horace's meticulous captain's script, so different from the hand he used for personal correspondence.

They seemed to be a sort of diary.

Oct. 7. 1866. Reed still obdurate. Ainsworth just as bad. Told D. to go ahead anyway.

Oct. 10. $23,000 from H. That should cover a lot of tracks. King getting suspicious. Thinks he won't get his cut.

Oct. 29. The proof is in the pudding. Ready to bring E. & R.
home. Watch out for Carmichael. He knows too much.

Emily stared at the last entry. Carmichael? No, she wouldn't believe it.
Was he involved in this? How could it be? He had made her laugh! He
couldn't have been part of Horace's schemes. But here it was. Carmichael
knew too much about something, perhaps the bribery scheme. "H" must
be the financier, Ben Holladay. Was Carmichael involved with him, too?
Was all his kindness to her only a ploy to learn more about Horace's
schemes?

She sank into the plush armchair and leaned back, eyes shut tight to
stop the tears. It served her right for letting her guard down. She had even
thought of going to Carmichael for advice.

After a few moments she sat up straight, wiped her eyes, and went back
to work. This was no time for weakness, she told herself sternly, even
though her insides felt scooped out and put back any which way.

There were a few more sheets in the box, even more enigmatic than
the first. Horace had filled them with notes to himself, figures and people
named only with initials. She put these in her reticule to read over at home.
The necklace and the affectionate letters she returned to the box, which she
took back to Mr. Ladd.

"Is it possible to put this in a safe until I can get the lock repaired?" she
asked.

"Of course," Ladd told her. "But, in order for you to be completely
at ease, I'll send Gerald down to Failing's to buy a new strongbox. Then
you'll still have the only keys."

Emily started to say that it wasn't necessary; she trusted Mr. Ladd. But
could she? She didn't know enough about these people and their relationship to Horace. Who had he been in partnership with? Who had he
cheated? And what did Mr. Carmichael know too much about?

Her head was spinning. All she wanted was to go home, get her stiff
corset off, and lie down with a cup of herbal tea.

"Thank you, Mr. Ladd," she said weakly. "That's very kind."

———

Across town, Alice Bracewell and her dear friend Eutheria Totenham were paying a call on Dorothea King, Alice to thank her for the lovely dinner and Eutheria in the hope of being invited to the next one.

"It was so generous of you to have us," Alice said. "It wouldn't have been proper for us to host a party while we're still in mourning, but it seems so uncivil not to welcome Emily to Portland."

"I was happy to do it," Dorothea said. "Captain Stratton was Matthew's partner, after all. And he felt that he had been too harsh with her on their first meeting. She is, after all, newly widowed, in a strange place. He thinks that once she knows us better, she'll not worry so much about all those boring business matters."

"Wait until she's out of black," Eutheria interjected. "She'll have her hands too full with suitors to bother with anything else."

"Do you think so?" Dorothea asked. "I suppose her wealth will draw a few fortune hunters. We must make it our duty to protect her from them."

She sipped her tea thoughtfully.

"I understand that Mr. Bracewell is quite taken with Captain Stratton's son," she said. "What's the boy like?"

"Robert reminds me a bit of my dear brother at that age." Alice smiled. "Charming, kind, full of energy."

"A boy that age needs a strong hand and a man's guidance," Eutheria said. "Otherwise he'll fall in with the wrong company."

"How very true." Dorothea nodded. "Myra," she said to the maid. "This pot has gone cold. Fetch another at once."

The girl bobbed a curtsey, took the teapot, and left the room.

"I know she listens at doors," Dorothea told the other two. "I should tell you that I have heard rumors that young Robert Stratton has been seen in some less than respectable establishments in the past few nights. There was some sort of commotion near one of them on Saturday. I hope he wasn't part of it."

"Of course not," Alice said primly. "He and George went riding out on the east side, up beyond Mt. Tabor. They had nothing to do with that nasty incident."

"What happened?" Eutheria asked.

"Oh, a bunch of unreconstructed drunks were harassing a colored man," Alice said. "Someone named Johnson, a cook at the Lafayette. The police arrested some of the men but of course they were out on bond the next day."

"Some people don't seem to know that the war is over," Dorothea sniffed. "As if half the Southerners in Oregon aren't here because they were running away from conscription into the Rebel Army."

"It's all those saloons down on Front Street." Eutheria shook her head. "The police will never do anything about them."

"They are rather lax about keeping dangerous persons off the streets," Alice said. "Do you remember that man, Ager, who was running about a week or two ago, exposing himself? I refused to let Sarah and Jessica leave the house until he was caught. And just when I thought I could breathe easily for them, I heard that idiot Porter had paid his bond and he was out again, probably terrorizing more women."

"Any man who hangs his privates out in February ought to be in the asylum, not jail," Eutheria said decidedly.

"The point is," Alice interrupted her, "that my brother's son should be kept away from such people. That's why George is taking an interest in Robert. We owe it to Horace to see that his mother doesn't spoil him entirely. The woman has no idea of how to raise a child."

Having found perfect agreement, the three women concluded their visit.

Emily arrived home with a headache that seemed also to have settled in her heart.

"I'm going to rest until Robert gets home from school," she told Mary Kate. "If there are any callers, tell them I'm indisposed. And ask Mrs. Bechner to send up a luncheon on a tray, with a pot of hot water, please."

Mary Kate took the message down to the kitchen.

"Something upset her while she was out," she told the cook. "The poor thing looked like she'd been crying."

"Them cats in the big houses can scratch awful fierce," said Mrs. Bechner, giving the chicken she was jointing for dinner a vicious chop.

Mary Kate began putting the tea things on a tray.

"It's not right she should be so alone," she sighed. "She needs a friend to confide in. If she were Catholic, now, she could tell the priest. I don't care to, myself; it's no man's business what I've been up to. But I think it would do Mrs. Stratton good."

Mrs. Bechner gave the fowl another chop and held her tongue. She was a good Lutheran and only tolerated Papists if they kept their candles and beads to themselves.

Mary Kate took the tray up to Emily and found her struggling to get the corset off.

"I hate this thing!" she said passionately.

"No more than any other woman." Mary Kate put down the tray and came to help. "I don't bother with 'em myself, just a nice old-style stomacher I can lace up the front."

"I don't want any of it!" Emily was still pulling at the leather. "I want nice soft silk robes and trousers that I can move in and feel the chair under me when I sit. I can't do this!"

"No more should you," Mary Kate said, trying to soothe her. "Here, I've got the bloody thing undone, if you'll pardon my language. Now, make up your nasty-smelling tea and have a good cry. I'm thinking you've been needing one for quite a time now."

"Thank you, Mary Kate," Emily gulped, ashamed of her outburst. "I'm just tired, I think. Ask Robert to come up and wake me when he gets home. I need to talk with him."

"I'll do that, ma'am," Mary Kate said. "Now you just rest and I'll not let a soul disturb you."

Emily drank her calming tea and lay on the bed. But even that plus her meditation exercises couldn't relax her enough to rest. Her mind spinning with new shock and fear, she stared at the ceiling with dry eyes that hurt worse than tears.

Chapter Sixteen

The following new books have been added to the Portland Library: The
Guardian Angel *by O. W. Holmes;* Fingal, an Epic Poem, *by Lossing;* The Lost
Galleon, *by Harte,* Lila: or Spain Fifty Years Ago, *by Caballero;* Love in Let-
ters, *by Allan Grant;* Three English Statesmen, *by Smith;* Opportunity, *by the
Author of* Emily Chester.

—*Oregonian*, February 22, 1868

Monday afternoon, March 9, 1868

Immediately upon arriving in Portland, Emily had joined the lending library, which was a room above a store at 66 First Street. She encouraged
Robert to use it to supplement his school books. He was happy to oblige
her, as he could stop in there for a few minutes and then pass the rest of the
afternoon in a more agreeable establishment. Today he came in to return a
book on the life of Napoleon. In exchange, he picked up the first thing he
saw, a philosophy treatise by the heft of it, and was about to leave when he saw
that annoying Mr. Carmichael.

The man had been reading one of the newspapers from other cities that the library subscribed to, but he put it down when he saw Robert come in.

Robert groaned inwardly. Now he'd not only have to talk with the man but stay long enough to make his excuse for coming home late plausible. Carmichael was bound to tell his mother of their meeting.

"Good afternoon, sir," he said. "I trust you are well."

"Very much so, thank you," Carmichael answered. "I'm delighted to see you here. I come by every week to keep up on the news from the rest of the country. Can't rely on just what the *Oregonian* and the *Herald* think we should know, right?"

"I suppose not, sir." Robert didn't really care. "I only came in for something to help with my schoolwork."

"Excellent." Mr. Carmichael cocked his head to read the title that Robert had picked up. "Rousseau? That's a bit radical for the Portland Academy, don't you think?"

"I don't know, sir; I haven't read it, yet," Robert answered, looking at him steadily.

"Well, you seem a sensible young man," Mr. Carmichael conceded. "I'm sure you'll evaluate his theories intelligently. When you've finished, I'd be interested in your opinion on him."

Robert searched the man's face for a hint of mockery but found none. Did Carmichael really believe that he intended to spend his evenings poring over some dusty French philosophy book?

"I'll be happy to give it," he answered. Damn the man! Carmichael wouldn't forget. Robert knew he was doomed to at least skim the book. He wished now he'd chosen something lighter.

After a few more moments of polite conversation, Mr. Carmichael picked up his hat and gloves to go. Robert nearly cheered. There might still be time to meet Hank.

"Please give my regards to your mother," Carmichael said as he put on his greatcoat. "There's a literary evening at Saverio's on Wednesday, do you know if she plans to attend?"

"No, sir," Robert answered.

"Ah, well, you might mention that I hope to see her there. It should be quite interesting."

With that he finally took his leave. Robert waited a few moments to be sure he was out of sight, then stuffed the book in his bag and raced to meet Hank at the Hellhole.

The bartender, Ned Chambreau, a usually cheerful drunk, was what Robert thought of as a real Westerner. A native French Canadian, he'd come to Oregon early on. He'd been a miner, homesteader, and, if he was to be believed, Indian fighter. Now he dispensed drinks, broke up fights, and provided entertainment for "gentlemen of all tastes." As an old friend of Robert's father, he was happy to see that Robert was provided for as well.

"Your friend got tired of waiting and went up." He winked at Robert. "Lily's up there, too, waiting for you. She's learned a couple of new tricks she's really eager to show you. Want a glass to get your courage up?"

The men at the bar laughed uproariously at this. Robert gave a snort of disdain. "That's for all you old married men," he jeered.

The laughter followed him as he took the steps two at a time. Robert ignored it. He figured he could spend an hour with Lily and be home in time to change for dinner with his mother. Hank would have to look out for himself. He knocked at the scuffed door. It opened a crack and a young Chinese face looked out, then brightened when she saw who it was.

"Mr. Robert." She bowed. "What would you like me to do for you?"

It was past five when Robert let himself in the front door, hoping to get up to his room to wash before his mother could smell the cheap perfume on his skin. He was in luck. He could hear the rattle of dishes as Mary Kate, John, and Mrs. Bechner had their tea in the kitchen. He made it safely to the top of the stairs and was just heaving a sigh of relief when he felt a draft behind him.

"Robert, darling!" His mother was standing in the doorway to her room. "You're very late. What kept you?"

She was wrapped in a brightly embroidered robe that Robert remembered from his childhood. She had let down her hair, and it tumbled around her shoulders. In the twilight, she looked no more than eighteen. It made him feel uncomfortable.

"I went to the library, Mother," he said, holding up his book bag. "I saw Mr. Carmichael there. He sends his regards."

"Does he now?"

Robert had never heard a tone like that from her.

"Mother?" he asked, his voice small. "Are you all right?"

She seemed to suddenly wake up. "I'm sorry, dear." She smiled reassuringly. "I just have a bit of a headache. It's nearly gone. Did you have a good day?"

"It was fine," he told her. As he backed into his room. "And as soon as I get changed and washed up I'll tell you all about it."

Well, almost.

Emily went back to her room to get ready for the evening. She must have slept after all, for she remembered a confused nightmare with people shouting and the streets full of smoke. It left her with a sense of foreboding although the shouts were in Chinese and the streets those of Shanghai.

So, Mr. Carmichael sent his regards. A few hours ago, that would have pleased her. Now he had moved from the world she was trying to create to the one Horace had left behind. She told herself that she shouldn't have been so trusting. Just because the man was courtly and well-spoken didn't mean he wasn't as ruthless as any pirate. He had even told her that now he just speculated. In what? Silk, tea, grain, opium, human souls?

Stupid girl!

She jabbed hair pins in recklessly, grazing her scalp more than once. Was there anyone now whom she could trust?

It was so tempting to simply give up and let Mr. King and Mr. Andrews continue as usual, managing her share in the company. She could close her eyes as she had for so many years, ignoring the suffering that purchased her comfort.

She thought of the little shrine in the corner of her room to the goddess of mercy. Kwan Yin wouldn't approve of such behavior. Emily suspected that Jesus wouldn't think much of it, either.

Her early training chose the most inconvenient times to assert itself.

But what more could she do? She had found nothing that could bring down Andrews and King. If they were taken to court for failing to pay import duties on their opium, the likelihood was that they would be given no more than a fine. And her goal wasn't to destroy the company but divert it to her own ends.

If only she could be sure that neither they nor Mr. Carmichael had anything to do with the death of Ah Sung. Especially Mr. Carmichael.

There was a tap on the door.

"Mrs. Bechner says to tell you dinner will be ready at seven," Mary Kate said when she saw that Emily was up. "I polished up the silver today. We thought you might like to eat in the dining room."

Well, that was a gentle reminder of her place.

"Thank you, Mary Kate," Emily said. "Tell Mrs. Bechner I'll be down then. And ask John to bring in some wood for the parlor fireplace. Robert and I are staying in tonight."

After dinner Emily went through the mail. There was a letter from a friend in China, the wife of a British merchant. It was full of gossip about people they knew, with very little information on what was happening outside the foreign corner of Shanghai. There were the usual cards from people who had called while she was out or resting. She wondered if one was supposed to keep score of how many callers one received against how many calls one made. One hand-delivered note made her smile.

"Robert, Mrs. Eliot says that she and her husband are going to a concert tomorrow night. They want to know if we would care to join them. What do you think?"

Robert looked up briefly from Rousseau. The book wasn't as dry as he had assumed.

"I may have too much studying to do," he said. "But I think you should go. It would be good for you."

"She doesn't say what kind of concert." Emily reread the letter.

"If a minister is going, it can't be anything awful," Robert teased. "No chorus girls in tights or anything like that."

"And what do you know of chorus girls?" she teased back.

He reddened slightly. "Well, I went to a few shows in New York, some with school friends. Father took me to a couple when he visited, too. He said they weren't refined enough for you, but we thought them jolly fun."

Emily bit her lip. She tried not to think of where else Horace might have taken his son. But, no, the boy's face was so full of innocent amusement.

"Is that so?" was all she said. "Well, I suppose I should broaden my horizon more. I'll write and accept the invitation. Happy?"

For answer Robert got up and gave her a big hug and kiss.

Emily met the Eliots in front of the Oro Fino Hall. It was strange to see them both without the baby. They stood outside during a pause in the rain.

"Where's Willie tonight?" she asked them.

"Our friends the Burrages took him," Tom explained. "They have several children of their own, and he fits right in among them. He's probably asleep by now."

"We love him dearly, of course," Etta added. "But it is nice to have an evening without him once in a while."

"I understand that the concert is upstairs," Emily said, noting that the Oro Fino had a lively saloon at street level. "I fear that my parents would have been horrified to see me even this close to a place that sold liquor."

They all laughed for no reason other than that it was a pleasant night and they were enjoying each other's company. Farther down the street Emily noticed a young Chinese man coming out of one of the laundries with a large package. As he made his way toward them he stepped off the sidewalk into the street to avoid bumping into anyone. A moment later a party of men rode up from the direction of the river. They spotted the laundry man.

"You, Chinaman!" one of them shouted. "Out of the way!"

As he came alongside, the rider leaned from his horse and knocked the package out of the laundryman's hands. The paper wrapping split, sending clean linen flying over the muddy road.

With a cry of despair, the man scrambled after the laundry. Tom Eliot turned in time to see it.

"Excuse me, ladies," he said.

He went over to the man and helped him pick up the linen, now crumpled and dirty. Emily saw the glint of a gold dollar piece folded in with the pile he handed over.

"He's ruined those trousers," Etta commented. "We'll have to send them down to be cleaned, as well."

Emily looked at her. Instead of being embarrassed or annoyed by her husband's behavior, Mrs. Eliot was watching him tenderly.

"Does he often do this sort of thing?" Emily asked.

"Very often," she laughed. "If he sees something wrong, he doesn't think about it. He just goes and does what he can to put it right. I should warn you that he speaks his mind, as well."

Emily thought about this as Tom Eliot finished his task and suddenly became aware that he was about to go into the concert with mud all over his trousers. The man he had helped had vanished back into the laundry. In a moment the laundryman was back with a brush, which he used with such energy that most of the muck rubbed off. Tom thanked him and returned to the ladies.

"Nice man," he said. "Wish I could talk with him more."

"If only you'd known we were coming here, you could have studied Chinese instead of Latin and Greek," Etta teased.

Emily stared at them both. There was no trace of mockery in their faces. They seemed to have no hidden scandals. They weren't interested in those of others. And they so obviously loved and respected each other.

She took a deep breath. There was still a corner of sanity in the world, and in it lived these two young people. She wondered what kind of upbringing they could have had to embrace everyone and everything so freely.

"It's time to go in," Tom said, looking at his pocket watch. "What is it we're listening to again?"

"Mr. Everest's benefit concert," Etta said. "Songs, instrumentals, the Mechanics Band, a mixture of local talent. Mrs. Stratton—Emily, that is— were you serious about wanting to see some of my work? I've been writing a piece on originality for a magazine back east, and I'd like your opinion on it before I send it in."

"I was quite serious," Emily said. "I'd love to see it. May I call upon you tomorrow?"

"If you don't mind talking around Willie, I'd be delighted," Etta answered.

"I'll come around ten," Emily promised.

Despite the fact that the piano was out of tune and one of the sopranos shrill in the upper range, it was the nicest evening out that Emily had ever had.

The next morning Emily attacked her griddle cakes with enthusiasm. She was looking forward to reading Etta's work and intended to praise it to the skies no matter how insipid it might be.

"Mrs. Stratton." John came to the door. "I'm sorry ma'am, but I'm afraid there's something in the coach house that needs seeing to again."

"Again?" Emily was surprised. "I thought that matter was completely finished with."

"So did I, missus." John was apologetic. "But it's come back on us. Could you have a look at it now?"

"Let the poor woman eat first," Mary Kate remonstrated.

"No, I should take care of this." Emily rose, setting her napkin on the table. "Mrs. Bechner, could you keep these warm for me?" She followed John out.

"Mr. Smith has come back?" she asked. "What does he want?"

"Didn't tell me, ma'am," John said, annoyed. "Only that he had to talk to you at once. Thinks he's the bleeding Prince of Wales, he does."

Emily overlooked the language. She couldn't imagine what Daniel Smith would want to tell her. He'd made it clear on their last meeting that he wasn't going to help her.

"Go have your breakfast, John," she told the groom. "I don't think I'll be long."

Smith was seated in his customary chair by the stove. He sprang up when she entered.

"Mrs. Stratton, I don't know what you've been doing," he began. "But it's got me into a peck of trouble. I'm not waiting for spring. I'm leaving tomorrow morning."

"I'm sorry, Mr. Smith," Emily said. "I certainly didn't mean to cause you any difficulties. Who are you in trouble with? Mr. Holladay?"

"Not him yet, but others," Smith said. "I just came to tell you to watch yourself. Word is you got something out of a box at Ladd and Tilton. There are those who want to know what it was."

"How did anyone find out about that?" Emily knew the answer as she asked. Half a dozen people had been in the back when Ladd went to get the box. Why should he assume it was a secret? But she didn't remember seeing anyone she knew.

"I hear you've also been asking about charities in town," Smith continued. "Setting up to be Lady Bountiful, are you? If you want to start giving back all the money old Horace swindled out of people, you go ahead, but first you'd better be sure they didn't deserve swindling in the first place. Sometimes doing what you think is right just makes everything worse."

Emily was becoming both annoyed and alarmed. "Could you be a little more specific?"

"No I can't!" he exploded. "It's more'n my life to be here now. But you're Horace's widow and I figured I owed you. Just stop poking around in the past. Leave it be. There's too many who don't want things brought up."

"What things, Mr. Smith?" Emily demanded. "I can't very well be careful unless I know more."

"Don'cha hear me?" he shouted. "The more you know, the less safe you'll be! Go back to your mission. Take the boy, too. This isn't the place for either of you."

He wrapped his thick scarf around his mouth and refused to say more, only stuck his head out the door, looked quickly right and left, and then slithered out.

Emily shook her head. "What a strange man!" she observed.

Back in the kitchen, she finished her griddle cakes slowly, thinking over the vague warnings that Mr. Smith had felt obliged to give her. Was he really concerned, or had someone sent him to try to scare her? It didn't matter. It was too late to stop. She had set her hand to the plow and wasn't going to turn back.

CHAPTER SEVENTEEN

Mr. John Everest's benefit concert was attended last evening by a very good audience, considering the bad state of the weather. The performances, as was anticipated, were generally excellent, and many of them were heartily encored.

—*OREGONIAN*, MARCH 11, 1868

WEDNESDAY, MARCH 11, 1868

It's still a bit rough." Etta Elliot handed the pages to Emily. "No one but Tom has read it, and he's too kind to make corrections."

"I don't know how good a critic I am, but I'm happy to help," Emily said.

They were sitting in a parlor that did indeed look as if the Eliots were camping out. There were several pieces of mismatched furniture, a couple of braided rugs, and some scuffed occasional tables that Etta had draped with bright scarves to cheer up the room.

The two women were sipping coffee and nibbling on ginger biscuits. The baby was playing on the floor but interrupted them every few moments to show his mother something he had found or to ask for attention.

"I have a congregation full of mothers who are happy to advise me on child rearing," Etta confided to Emily. "But he's such a dear little thing that I can't find it in my heart to discipline him much."

"I agree," Emily said. "There will be time enough for that when he's older. And I understand he won't be the king of the castle for long."

"Yes," Etta laughed. "I wanted to wait to announce it, but Tom is so delighted that I believe he's told everyone in town. Even Willie knows he'll soon have a little 'brothersister.' I hope our things come before then. The poor lamb is sleeping in a travel trunk now, and we don't have another to use as a cradle."

From what Emily had seen, the Eliots had only to ask to be inundated with baby gifts. The night before, they had been greeted by name by almost everyone attending the concert. And the couple had been in Portland only two months longer than she.

"Etta," Emily began nervously. "I don't know if anyone has told you about my late husband. . . ."

"I know he was a sea captain and importer," Etta answered carefully. "Of course I've met his sister. Mrs. Bracewell speaks of him often."

"Yes, well," Emily said. "I'm embarrassed to say that I didn't know much about his trade, even after eighteen years of marriage. He was away a great deal and didn't often speak of business matters."

"A lot of men are like that," Etta said. "A minister's wife doesn't have that complaint. Tom's work is all around us."

She indicated a pile of books and papers on a desk in the next room.

"I help with his sermons, especially when his eyes are bothering him," she said. "And of course I have a Sunday school class and participate in most of the church activities. I suppose your mother did much the same."

"Yes, my parents worked together in all aspects of their missionary work," Emily said. She didn't elaborate.

Etta sensed that the subject was not one Emily wanted to pursue. "You were speaking of Captain Stratton?" she asked. "Yes, Willie, that's a red ball. Very good!" Etta hugged the boy. Willie went back to his toys.

Emily watched him, remembering the days when Robert was never far from her skirts. She pulled herself back to the present.

"Yes, as I was saying," she continued. "After his death, I discovered that my husband had not acquired all his money in ways that I consider moral."

Etta nodded. "I knew a woman in St. Louis who was a strong abolitionist. She was devastated to find out that her father had made his fortune in the slave trade."

"What did she do about it?" Emily asked.

"She worked all the harder at ending the practice," Etta told her. "When the war ended, she used his money to set up schools for the freedmen. She's still running them, I believe."

Emily nodded. "That was something on the order of what I had in mind. So much of my comfort has been purchased by the misery of the Chinese people. You can't imagine how the opium trade has destroyed the country. And we encourage it, even when the Emperor has forbidden the use of the drug."

Etta looked grave. "I didn't know that," she admitted. "I thought it was long established in the Orient."

"Not at all," Emily said. "It was introduced by the British, but Americans have taken advantage of the addiction of the Chinese, and I'm ashamed to say that my husband was one of them. Therefore, I should like to do something to help the Chinese living here. Last night was the first time I saw anyone in town treat one of them as a human being. That's why I thought I'd ask you and your husband to help advise me."

"I can't answer for Tom," Etta said. "But I'll do whatever I can. What did you have in mind? I was under the impression that they were very clannish and resisted any outside efforts to improve their lot."

"Not exactly," Emily tried to explain. "But very few of them intend to stay here long, so they put up with dreadful living conditions in order to save every cent to send home or to put aside for their passage back and a better life there."

"And that's why they don't adopt American dress and customs?" Etta seemed genuinely interested.

"For the most part, yes," Emily said. "At least I think so. Of course, the queue and shaven forehead are signs of allegiance to the Manchu Emperor. But why should that cause people to torment them so?"

She spoke with more passion than she had intended. The way the Chinese were treated in Portland reminded her too much of the way she and her parents had been received in China. Their clothes, customs, even their language weren't what made them despised. It was their light skin, light hair, and big noses. They would always be different and resented.

Emily knew that no matter how she dressed or how flawlessly she spoke Chinese, she would always be a barbarian to the natives of Shanghai. Every slur, every clot of mud thrown at a Chinese man in the streets of Portland made her see again her father, with his badly printed pamphlets, the target of derision by the villagers he wanted to convert. She had loathed the Chinese arrogance toward foreigners even while she wanted desperately to be accepted by them.

Now she was sickened to realize that the Americans were just the same.

"I don't know where to start," she ended. "I don't want to convert the Chinese. I don't want to make them American. I just want to stop the abuse."

Etta sighed. "You've set yourself a huge task, Emily," she said. "It's not one that can be solved with money. Although money is always needed. Tom's family has been working for years to make some small dent in the injustices of the world. They have started soup kitchens and homes for newsboys. They spoke out for abolition and even rights for women. One friend of theirs, and mine, is Dorothea Dix, do you know her?"

Emily shook her head.

"She has been speaking out for better treatment of the insane for the past twenty years and more," Etta said. "Her weapons in this battle have been words. She publicized the horrors that these unfortunate people have suffered. Her articles and reports woke people up. She made the states set up asylums that were hospitals instead of prisons. Dr. Hawthorne's asylum in East Portland is an example of her beliefs put into practice."

Emily felt as if caught in an unexpected sunrise. This young woman sitting across from her in a put-together room with jelly stains on her dress was throwing open a window and letting in a world that Emily had never known existed.

"One woman did all that?" she asked.

"Pretty much," Etta said. "She's indefatigable. She travels constantly, inspecting institutions and writing to lawmakers. We're hoping she'll come out here when the railroad is completed."

Emily was both fascinated and intimidated by the thought of meeting such a woman. "I don't know if I could speak out like that, for the Chinese here," she admitted. "Or if they would want me to."

"There are very few people like Miss Dix," Etta told her. "And many are glad of it. Most of us just have to start small and not expect to find much success. Perhaps while you are deciding how to proceed, you'd be interested in joining the local Ladies Aid Society. It's for women of all faiths. They even let me join!"

"Yes, thank you," Emily said. "That would be a place to start. I've been so caught up in all my new responsibilities that I've felt at sea without a compass. Thank you for giving me one."

Etta clapped her hands in delight. "How kind of you to say that! But I'm sure you would have found your way soon enough. Shall I put your name forward at the next Ladies Aid meeting?"

"Please," Emily said as she rose. "I've taken far too much of your time. Thank you for your wonderful hospitality."

Etta scooped up the baby and escorted Emily to the door.

"Good-bye, Etta," she said. "And thank you."

Halfway down the path, Emily looked back to enjoy a little longer the image of the mother and son waving at her from the threshold.

Despite Etta's claim to have been of no help, talking with the minister's wife had made Emily realize that her plans weren't as well thought out as she had imagined. She had hoped to find some untainted source of income so that she and Robert could continue living as they always had. That was not only unrealistic, it was arrogant. Just giving back the money made from the suffering of others would do little toward ending that suffering.

She thought of Miss Dix, devoting all her time and energy to obtaining better treatment for the insane. All her time! Emily didn't know if she had the moral strength to do that. She didn't want to end up as her parents had, disillusioned and defeated. They had devoted their lives to a cause that their only child no longer believed in.

And what of Horace's partners? If she sold them her share of the company, they would simply continue the trade she abhorred. Yet, if she asserted herself and tried to change the direction of the business, what chance did she have of success?

And yet. . . . And yet, there were people like Tom and Etta Eliot, so sure they could make the world a better place by their example. Emily wondered if her parents had ever been so young and full of hope. She couldn't remember them like that. Would the blows of life beat down the Eliots? If she took the next step, would she be crushed under the reality of modern business?

No one would fault her if she behaved like other wealthy widows. She could give benefit galas for charity, visit orphanages, and donate to civic projects. When she died, someone would put a plaque up to remember her generosity.

Kwan Yin had told her to move forward with courage. Perhaps she should throw the coins again to see if the goddess had changed her mind.

Over in the Hellhole saloon, Ned Chambreau was taking down the chairs and setting up the tables for the day when his boss came in.

"Morning, Ned," he said. "Looks like we had a good take last night."

He surveyed the clutter of empty bottles and the pile of broken glass and chair parts.

"Only had to throw out a couple of drunks and break up a fight or two." Ned shrugged. "It was kind of quiet."

He continued his work, waiting for the man to explain his presence at a place he preferred not to have people know he owned.

"I hear that Ben Holladay is sending up another three hundred coolies to work on his railroad," the boss commented.

"He'd better send up some girls, too," Ned said. "The ones we got can't handle all that extra trade, especially with the locals taking such a shine to them."

"I'll find out." The boss grimaced as his boots stuck to a spot on the floor. "I understand that Robert Stratton has been visiting our Lily with some regularity."

Ned looked up nervously. "It didn't seem no harm. Lily says he knows his way around. She's not his first."

The other man snorted. "Of course not. Horace took him to a house in Honolulu on his way to Boston to get the boy initiated properly. I just want you to keep an eye on him. See that he gets whatever he wants. Tell Lily to treat him extra nice. After all, it was his father who paid to set her up in this fine establishment."

He turned to go. Ned started to relax. Then the boss stopped and shook his head.

"And throw a couple buckets of soap and water on the floor, Ned," he said. "The muck in here is worse than in the street."

Mary Kate put down her teacup with a sigh of satisfaction. She was seated in the kitchen of the Catholic rectory and having a good chat with the housekeeper.

"Thank you, Mrs. O'Shea," she said. "That German lady of Mrs. Stratton's isn't a bad cook, but she can't do a proper cup of tea and I never learned the trick of it."

"Nothing to it, me girl," Mrs. O'Shea said. "I'll show you gladly. The real trick for me has been getting them Belgian priests to drink anything but coffee. But now that Father Delaharty has joined them, he's been helping me."

"Does he preach in the Irish?" Mary Kate asked wistfully. "I might start going to Mass again myself, just to hear it."

"I've no doubt that he can," Mrs. O'Shea answered. "But I'm thinking that the others wouldn't like it. They'd want to know what he was telling us. And how's your Mrs. Stratton settling in here? Any better? No more prowlers, I hope?"

Mary Kate shook her head. "It's been quiet since John Mahoney moved in. I'm still worrying about Mrs. Stratton, though. Sometimes I think she's more Chinese than Christian. She's got a little shrine in her room to some heathen goddess and she burns incense to it."

"And don't you light a candle to the Virgin every day, Mary Kate Kyne?" Mrs. O'Shea asked. "How do you know that isn't the poor lady's way of praying to her? It breaks my heart to think of how she was brought up, foreign idols on one side and sour-faced Protestants on the other! You stick by her, Mary Kate. That's a woman who needs a friend."

Mary Kate promised. "I only wish I could tell her about Master Robert's shenanigans. The boy has a kind heart, I believe, but he tips the jar too much for a lad his age and there's been talk of him getting into other scrapes, too."

"She'll find out, soon enough," Mrs. O'Shea said. "And then she'll need you there for support. And it may all come right in the end. He's sowing wild oats enough, I'll grant you, but they might not all come up tares."

"For all that, I've landed on my feet for sure," Mary Kate reflected. "I never thought I'd be a proper upstairs lady's maid. Back at home, I'd've been allowed in a grand house like that only to scrub the floors."

Mrs. O'Shea dropped a second lump of sugar in her tea. "Not even that, Mary Kate, not even that."

Emily returned home feeling much less alone in the world than when she had left. It upset her to think how she had counted on Mr. Carmichael to be someone she could talk with openly. When she realized that he was also involved in Horace's business, it seemed that the floor had vanished beneath her. She scolded herself for being so naïve. Why else would the gentleman have been paying her so much attention?

She let herself in, remembering that Mary Kate was down at the rectory getting local gossip from Mrs. O'Shea. There was a thump from the kitchen and she called out to Mrs. Bechner to let her know she was home. Then she went up to her sitting room to do some sewing and decide what her next step should be.

She was working on a particularly intricate arrangement of tucks for a camisole when she thought she heard the kitchen door shut. A glance at the clock told her it was close to teatime. Perhaps Mary Kate had learned something interesting that she could share over cake. She put down her work and started downstairs.

She was halfway down when a screech like a steam whistle pierced the house. Grabbing hold of the railing, Emily hurried down and into the kitchen.

The cook, still wearing her coat and hat, was standing in the midst of a puddle of broken eggs and spilt milk. Her mouth was open, leaving no doubt as to where the noise was coming from.

"Whatever is the matter?" Emily shouted over the screaming. "Are you hurt, Mrs. Bechner?"

Then she saw what the woman was staring at.

Emily inhaled and then choked.

On the floor of her kitchen, his head smashed like a melon, lay Daniel Smith.

Chapter Eighteen

❧

Mrs. M. A. Thompson
Electrician, Accoucher, and Electric Physician
Chronic Diarrhea, Ague and Paralysis
Rheumatism, Glandular Enlargement, Deafness and
Neuralgia treated successfully.
Special attention given to Female Diseases.
Examinations made by Electric battery connecting the nerve forces.
Board with Pleasant Home for a limited number of patients.
Calls will be attended to in any part of the city.
Batteries for sale and instruction given upon the scientific use of
Electricity as a Remedial agent

—*Oregonian* advertisement, February 1868

Upon hearing the shriek, John came running from the carriage house, reaching the kitchen a moment after Emily. His eyes bulged at the sight that greeted him.

"Jesus, Mary and Joseph," he breathed as he crossed himself. "What happened?"

He looked at Mrs. Bechner howling amidst the ruins of her shopping. "What did you do to him, woman?" he shouted.

Emily had overcome the shock of finding the body. "Don't be stupid, John. Mrs. Bechner must have come home and found him like this."

She took the woman's arm and tried to get her to sit down and cease her screaming.

"Please, try to calm yourself, Mrs. Bechner," she said. "John, run for the doctor, please, and then the police."

John was still staring at the remains of Daniel Smith. "You poor bugger, what had you got yourself into?" he said softly.

Slowly, Emily's order penetrated. "Yes, ma'am. Right away!" He left the house at a gallop.

A few moments later a carriage rolled into the drive and Dr. Thompson hopped out. She stood in the doorway long enough to take in the situation.

"There's nothing to be done for him, I'm afraid," she said after a quick survey of the corpse. "However, I do have something for hysterics."

She knelt down by the chair where Mrs. Bechner had subsided into long high-pitched moans. Then she took the lid off the sugar bowl and stuck a lump of sugar into the woman's mouth.

The noise stopped at once as Mrs. Bechner shut her mouth in surprise.

"Now," Dr. Thompson said. "Can you put the kettle on, Mrs. Stratton? I have a homeopathic powder that should quiet her and let her sleep a while. Do you need one, as well?"

"No, thank you," Emily told her. "I need to be alert enough to deal with the police. How did you get here so quickly?"

"Your man stopped me on my rounds and told me what had happened." The doctor took a twist of paper from her bag and poured it into a teacup, adding more sugar to it. "You don't happen to have any brandy in the house? No? Well, this should be effective anyway."

Emily tried to stop her shivering as she lifted the kettle from the stove and poured the water.

"Are you sure you wouldn't like something to take later?" Dr. Thompson asked, looking at her with concern. "Shock sometimes hits one several hours after the event. I'll leave a few of these with you just in case."

Once they had made Mrs. Bechner take the drink and lie down in her room, Dr. Thompson turned her attention to the body.

"He was hit more than once," she said. "From behind first, probably. Then, as he swung around, the attacker hit again. Caught him both at the crown of the skull and the forehead. Then maybe another few blows to the face to be certain he was dead. It took a great deal of force. I doubt you'll be a suspect unless the city marshal is unbelievably stupid."

She sounded as though that wasn't impossible.

"He must have been here all the time," Emily said from far away. "I went upstairs and took out my sewing box and mended clothes while he was lying here dying just below my feet."

Dr. Thompson got up and maneuvered Emily into a chair.

"Why don't I make up some good strong tea and you and I can have it in the parlor," she said firmly. "There's no reason for you to stay here. He's not going anywhere."

"I'll go when the police come," Emily said. "The body shouldn't be left alone."

Dr. Thompson regarded her strangely.

"This isn't the first violent death you've seen." It was a statement.

"No," Emily answered. "I've seen worse than this."

She didn't elaborate, and the doctor didn't ask.

There was a clatter of hooves in the courtyard, and the marshal, Daniel Jacobi, came in, followed by two deputies. He stopped and knelt by the corpse.

"Jim," the marshal said over his shoulder. "Run down to Brelsford and tell him we need a body removed. Then go to Mr. Samson on Yamhill and say that we need a coffin put together. Nothing fancy, the city will likely have to pay for it."

One of the deputies left.

"Ladies." Jacobi tipped his hat. "Would one of you like to tell me why Dan Smith is lying in your kitchen with his face bashed in?"

"I'm Dr. Mary Anna Thompson." The doctor stood. "I was summoned here about twenty minutes ago by Mrs. Stratton's driver. When I arrived, she was trying to calm her cook, who apparently was the first to discover the body. I gave the woman a sedative, so you'll have to wait to question her."

"I see." Jacobi was a tough man in his late thirties, who still spoke with a slight German accent. He didn't appear to be the kind of person who sympathized with hysterics.

"Mr. Jacobi." Emily also stood. "I'll tell you what little I know. Could we possibly take our conversation to the parlor?"

Dr. Thompson was putting her medicines back in her bag. "There's nothing more I can do for you at the moment," she told Emily. "I have patients who are expecting me."

"Of course." Emily put out her hand. "Thank you so much for your care of Mrs. Bechner. I'm very grateful."

"I'll be back when I've finished to see how she's doing," the doctor promised.

Emily led the woman to the front door and thanked her again before she left.

After giving instructions to the second deputy, Marshal Jacobi followed Emily, meeting her in the chilly parlor.

"My maid, Mary Kate, should be back soon," Emily began. "Could you please have someone meet her and bring her in the front way? I don't want her to have to see the body."

"Was she close to Dan?" Jacobi asked.

"Close? Of course not. She only met him once," Emily answered. "But Mrs. Bechner never met him at all, and look what the sight did to her. It isn't one I'd want anyone to come across unawares."

"Very well." He stepped back into the kitchen and issued an order to the deputy. "Now, I'll need some information from you, if you don't mind."

"Of course not." Emily wished she'd had her cup of tea before being questioned, though. "I'll tell you anything I can."

She's a cool one, Jacobi thought. *Either she knows who did it, or the reality of what's happened hasn't come to her yet. I wonder which?*

"Now," he said. "You said you were upstairs when the murder occurred."

"No," Emily corrected him. "I was coming downstairs when Mrs. Bechner found the body. I don't know when the murder occurred."

"From the pool of blood around his head, I'd say not long ago," the marshal said. "I forgot to ask that lady doctor her opinion, but it didn't seem to me to have even started congealing."

"I didn't look that closely." Emily felt slightly queasy. Then a worse thought struck. "But that would mean that the person who killed Mr. Smith must have still been in the house when I arrived home!"

Jacobi fixed her with a piercing look. "Is that so? And yet you didn't hear any cries, any sound of a fight? Not even a thud?"

"No, at least I don't think so." Emily tried to remember. "Certainly no shouts. But maybe a thump. Yes, I'd forgotten. There was a sound from the kitchen just after I got home. I thought Mrs. Bechner had dropped something, but there was nothing else, so I didn't go in to check."

"Lucky thing you didn't," the marshal observed. "Or you might be dead, too."

"Yes, that's true," Emily answered. "But I don't understand why Mr. Smith was killed in my kitchen! He shouldn't have been here at all."

Very cool one! Jacobi thought. *She didn't do more than wince at the idea of being in the house with a murderer.*

"Perhaps he arranged to meet someone here," he suggested. "Dan Smith wasn't always on the right side of the law. He and a confederate could have come to rob you."

"In the middle of the day?" Emily said. "With people coming and going all the time? It doesn't seem very smart."

"Maybe," Jacobi agreed. "But they may have thought everyone was gone. You could have surprised them by coming home unexpectedly."

"Then why didn't they just leave?" Emily objected. "It makes no sense for a burglar to hear me come in, panic, and kill his partner."

Jacobi leaned back in his chair with a sigh. "No, it doesn't. Forget I suggested it. I'll have to ask around to discover if any of the neighbors saw anything, find out what old Dan was up to, who he'd been working with." He shook his head. "A lot of investigation. The city council isn't going to like this. It may mean adding on another constable."

Emily remained silent. The problems of the city council were of no interest to her.

Jacobi got up. "I'll set my deputy to work on it, Mrs. Stratton," he told her. "We'll start by questioning your other servants. In my experience, you usually don't need to look far from the site of a crime to find the criminal."

"None of them had anything to do with this," Emily said as she led him back to the kitchen. "Mary Kate was down at the rectory and Mrs. Bechner was shopping."

"What about John Mahoney?" Jacobi asked. "Doesn't he live over the coach house? You sent him to find me so I guess he was here."

"Why would he want to kill Mr. Smith?" Emily asked. "They were friends."

His eyebrows went up. "Were they? That's interesting. You might have mentioned that first thing."

Emily bit her tongue. Of course the marshal would have found that out sooner or later, but there was no reason for her to have told him.

Was there?

Mercifully the deputy had thrown a blanket over the body by the time they reentered the kitchen. At the moment he was blocking Mary Kate from coming in.

"Mrs. Stratton says you're to go round to the front," he was telling her again.

"Don't be a fool," she said. "I've never been through a front door in my life. What's going on? Someone came running down to the rectory saying there'd been a murder up here. I raced all the way home with my heart hammering like a steam engine fearing it was Mrs. Stratton. You let me in now to tend to her!"

"Mary Kate." Emily gently pushed the deputy aside. "Robert and Mrs. Bechner and I are all fine. It's Mr. Smith who's been killed."

"Smith? That drunk who came to the door? Whatever for?" Mary Kate was poleaxed. She managed to get past the deputy to see the covered shape on the floor and the blood-stained blanket. She let out a scream.

"Look at all that blood! Mrs. Bechner just scrubbed that floor! She'll be fair moithered about this."

"She already knows," Emily told her. "Do you have any idea why Mr. Smith would have come here today?"

"Not a one." Mary Kate shook her head, still staring at the shape under the blanket.

Emily turned back to the marshal. "I hope you can find out who did this soon. I won't feel safe in my own home until you do."

"We'll do our best, ma'am," Marshal Jacobi told her. "But unless someone can tell me more than you, it won't be easy."

The undertaker came and took the body back to his establishment, after Jacobi assured him that the city would pay for the burial. Mary Kate was itching to get the floor scrubbed before Mrs. Bechner awoke, but the marshal stopped her.

"We haven't finished examining the room yet," he said. "You get out that mop and I'll think you want to get rid of evidence."

"It's a puddle of blood!" Mary Kate protested. "What do you think you'd be learning from that? And look at all the muddy tracks from your boots. We have a scraper right by the door, you know."

But Jacobi was firm. He sent her out of the kitchen while he and his deputies went over it thoroughly.

"What do they think they'll find?" Mary Kate complained to Emily. "A letter from the poor man's killer saying, 'I did it'?"

Emily was spared having to speculate by a pounding at the front door.

"Would you get that, please?" she asked the maid. "I'll be in the parlor."

Mary Kate came back a moment later, followed by George Bracewell. He was panting as though he had run all the way to her house.

"Sister Emily!" he began. "I heard there'd been a break-in here and someone killed. Alice sent me at once to be sure you and Robert were all right."

"Thank you." She held out her hand to him. "I'm fine, as you can see, and Robert is still at school. Mary Kate, would you take Mr. Bracewell's coat and bring him some tea, please?"

"Now, tell me what has happened." George seated himself across from her and took out his handkerchief to wipe his face. "I confess the report I got was most alarming."

Emily explained what she knew. "I understand that Mr. Smith worked for Horace but I have no idea why he was in my home. Mr. Jacobi thinks that he and an accomplice might have been trying to rob me. But, if so, who stopped them, and where is the accomplice?"

Her brother-in-law listened to her with a growing expression of horror.

"I can't believe such a thing could happen here in broad daylight!" He shook his head in consternation. "You and Robert must come and stay with us until the murderer is captured. Neither Alice nor I will have a moment's peace thinking of you here alone."

"That's kind of you, George," Emily said. "Oh, here's Mary Kate with the tea. How do you take it?"

The pause gave her time enough to frame her answer. She poured a cup, added milk, and handed it to him. Mary Kate had also brought the last of Mrs. Bechner's ginger cake. George accepted a large slice.

Emily put the plate back on the tray. She smiled at George.

"Robert and I aren't alone," she said. "Mary Kate and Mrs. Bechner are here, although I don't know how long Mrs. Bechner will want to stay after this. And John is just across the way."

"That's hardly what I'd call protection!" George objected. "You'd both be much safer at our place. We have lots of room for guests, and Alice would love to be able to see you more. I can pay off your servants and close this house until you decide what to do."

Emily tried not to be annoyed. He was being perfectly reasonable, she told herself.

"I have decided what to do," she told him. "I'll be sure to lock and bar the doors in the daytime as well as at night, and I'll get us all school bells to keep beside our beds in case of more intruders. But I do not wish to leave my home, and I believe that my son will agree with me."

George mopped his face again. He was turning red with the effort of keeping his patience. He leaned forward and took her hand.

"My dear Emily," he said. "You aren't thinking clearly at the moment. Who could, with such a horrible event in their own home? Why don't you finish your tea and lie down for a while? I'll wait for Robert and tell him what's happened. When you've had a rest and a chance to think, I know you'll agree that remaining here is foolhardy."

Emily withdrew her hand. "I do appreciate your concern," she said.

"I'd rather wait for Robert myself. If he thinks we should accept your invitation, then I'll agree. But only for a few days. I'm sure they'll soon discover who killed Mr. Smith and why it happened here. Shutting down the house is really not necessary."

George sighed then smiled. "I told Alice that you were tougher than she supposed. Horace would be proud of you, I know. He told me you didn't leave Shanghai, even when the Taiping were attacking."

"That's true," Emily said shortly.

It was also true that there had been no place *to* go. The international enclave was surrounded. Her parents had left, not for safety, but to venture into the heart of the rebellion. There was no way bluff, good-natured George could be made to realize what she had gone through. She had been terrified the whole time.

"But I do think it would be wise to stay somewhere else for now," he continued. "Robert will understand, I'm sure. He's a smart boy. Doesn't look much like Horace, except for his grin. When we were out shooting last week and he brought down his first bird, I'd have sworn his father was there beside me. He's a good shot. Did he and Horace hunt much in China?"

"No," Emily said. "He must have learned at boarding school. I haven't thanked you for your interest in him. He very much enjoyed your outing."

"So did I," George told her. "It's great to have a nephew to take with me. Other men bring their sons, and I've always been a trifle jealous. I hope you'll allow me to continue standing in for Horace."

Emily was beginning to relax. George was not as obtuse as he appeared. It had been wise of him to distract her with talk about Robert.

"I'd be very grateful if you did," she said. "A boy his age needs a man to look to for guidance. Robert has never given me a moment's worry, but it's so easy at this time in his life to be led astray without a father's care."

There was a knock at the parlor door. Emily looked up. Marshal Jacobi was standing in the doorway as if undecided whether or not his authority allowed him to come in uninvited.

"Have you finished your search?" Emily asked.

"Yes, ma'am, for now," he answered. "We think we found the murder weapon."

He held up a heavy iron meat grinder, the kind that was fastened to a table by a vise at the bottom. It was covered with blood. Emily gasped.

George leapt to his feet. "What's wrong with you, Jacobi?" he shouted. "Bringing that thing in here?"

"Pardon, but I need to know if it's yours and if it looked like this the last time you saw it." The marshal held it up. "Could be beef blood, I suppose."

Emily stood. "I'm afraid I'm not that familiar with the contents of the kitchen," she apologized. "But I am absolutely certain that Mrs. Bechner would never have ground meat so sloppily, nor would she have left the grinder in that state. You'll have to ask her tomorrow, but I think you can assume that you now have the instrument that bludgeoned poor Mr. Smith to death."

It was at that moment that Robert came home from school.

CHAPTER NINETEEN

◈

We have been the favored ones of the Republic. Neither War, nor Famine, nor Pestilence, have come within our borders. Peace, and Health, and Plenty, have held undisturbed dominion over us. And it gives me pleasure to say that the people of Oregon have not been unmindful of these blessings. Everywhere within our borders the hand of industry has wrought diligently, and a rapid development of all the material resources of our State has been the result.

—Governor George L. Woods to the Oregon State Assembly, 1868

Robert was whistling a lively tune as he entered the house. He dropped his book bag and lunch pail with a clatter.

"Mother!" he called. "You'll never guess what happened today."

He stopped upon seeing Marshal Jacobi, still standing in the doorway, the meat grinder upraised in his hand.

"What's going on?" he asked, taking a step back, as if preparing to flee. "Marshal Jacobi, what are you doing here? And what's that?"

Emily hurried to him, barely giving Jacobi time to get out of the way.

"Something dreadful has happened, my dearest," she said. "But you are not to worry about it."

Robert gave her an odd look. "Mother, that doesn't make sense."

He looked over her shoulder. "Uncle George! What's wrong? Is something wrong with Aunt Alice or my cousins?"

"No, no, nothing like that," George said. "Come in and sit down. I'll explain everything. "Jacobi," he added sharply. "Do you think you could put that thing away now?"

"I'll have to take it as evidence," the marshal told him, looking embarrassed to be still holding the meat grinder.

"Please do," Emily said. "I don't think we'll be using it again."

The marshal nodded and vanished back into the kitchen.

Robert looked from one to the other as he came in and sat down. "Uncle George," he said carefully. "I'm ready for the explanation now. And please, don't leave anything out."

Emily fled while George told Robert about the murder. She didn't want to hear it from her brother-in-law's perspective. Another recital would be more than she could take. She had survived the horrors of the war in China by closing down her feelings and concentrating on the task at hand. But memories are insidious, and the death of Mr. Smith was causing them to rise again, without the carefully constructed emotional shields.

She wanted to go to her room and lock the door. She needed time to meditate, to restore balance. Failing that, she wished there were a place where she could at least scream herself empty.

Instead she went back to the kitchen. The undertaker was loading the body into his cart, and Mr. Jacobi had finally given Mary Kate permission to get out her mop. The maid was wringing the red water into a bucket with grim determination.

"A good thing the floor is that linoleum," she commented. "We'd never get the stains out of wood."

Emily agreed, but she was already thinking about replacing the floor covering. No matter how much they scrubbed it, she would always see the blood. She tiptoed into Mrs. Bechner's room. The cook was still asleep, snoring softly. Marshal Jacobi would have to wait a while longer to question her.

A few moments later Robert and his uncle came to find her. Robert hugged her tightly.

"Poor little Mother," he said. "To have to see that! You've suffered so much already."

He patted her shoulder as if he were her senior. Emily was surprised once again by how much he had grown. But she would not turn over responsibility to her son, for all his compassion touched her. She bent his head down and kissed his cheek.

"Thank you, my dear, but it was far worse for Mrs. Bechner," she said. "Did your uncle tell you that he has invited us to stay with him until the investigation is over?"

"Yes, and I'll go if you'd rather," Robert answered. "But I see no reason to leave our home."

"You need to get out because it's not safe for you here," George interrupted. "We don't know who killed Smith or why. They could come for you two next."

"If that is true, why is it only unsafe in our home?" Emily asked. "If we are in danger, we could be attacked anywhere. Do you propose that we remain cloistered in your house? What of the security of Alice and the girls? I should feel dreadful if we were the cause of harm coming to them."

"I have a better idea." Robert's face lit up and suddenly he became a boy again. "We need a dog. A good large watchdog to chase away intruders."

Emily clapped her hands. "That's a wonderful idea! Why didn't I think of it? Do you know where we can get one?"

"Jack's uncle has half a dozen roaming about his property; he'd sell us one, I'm sure," Robert said. "Shall I go out there now and ask?"

"Yes," Emily decided. "Take John with you. Do you need any money?"

"No, he'll trust me for it." Robert went to get his wraps.

George shook his head. "A guard dog can alert you," he pointed out. "But then what?"

"Then we come down and confront these villains." Emily stuck out her chin. "We find out who they are and why they are persecuting us."

"Villains? What do you mean?" George said in confusion. "Have you been bothered before? Why didn't you say anything?"

"I did," Emily told him. "I said we thought someone had broken in. I told Mr. Ladd and you that I believe Ah Sung was killed because he worked for me. My suspicions were not considered worthy of examination."

"I don't remember your telling me this," George said. "At least not so forcefully. But if true, it can't have anything to do with you personally. You're a stranger here. It must be the result of some business deal that Horace was involved in."

"I do appreciate that fact." Emily sat down wearily at the kitchen table. "I have asked Mr. Andrews and Mr. King, and neither one seems to know what it could be. Of course, Mr. Andrews still insists that someone tried to poison him, which would indicate that someone is angry with the company. Do you have any idea?"

George thought a moment, chewing his long moustache intently.

"No," he said at last. "I never knew much about their arrangements. My company imported tea and silk, before I sold it. I shipped through Stratton, Andrews, and King, but that was all."

Emily sighed, rubbing her forehead. "Perhaps Marshal Jacobi will be able to discover something. I've done all I can."

"Horace didn't leave any documents that might explain things?" George asked.

"Not with me," she said firmly. "Everything I have has been shown to Mr. Andrews and Mr. King. There are discrepancies between Horace's accounting and theirs, but I hardly think it's worth killing over, and particularly not killing Mr. Smith."

"Why not?" George asked. "We don't know what Smith was up to. The fact that he broke into your house just before he died shows that he wasn't one hundred percent."

"None of this makes any sense," Emily said wearily.

"Mrs. Stratton?"

Emily looked up. Mrs. Bechner was standing unsteadily in the doorway of her room. She was wearing her coat and hat and had her carpetbag in her hand.

"I don't know what kind of house this is," she told Emily, "but I'm not staying another minute in it. I'll live with my sister on Oak Street until I find another situation. You can send my wages there."

"Mrs. Bechner, please." Emily tried to bar the way out. "I know you've had a terrible shock, but you mustn't leave us. We need you."

"You'll have to do without me, all the same," the woman insisted. "This place is evil. Dead men in the kitchen, heathen idols in the parlor, rustling in the bushes at night when there's no wind to cause it. . . . This is no place for a Christian woman, and nothing you can say will make a difference."

Emily pleaded with her, offered to double her salary, but Mrs. Bechner was adamant. She refused even to stay until a new cook could be found.

"Who knows when that would be, once people hear of this?" she explained.

Emily watched her go with a sinking heart. Her dinners might have been heavy and the vegetables boiled to mush, but they were better than a constant diet of eggs and bread. She remembered that George and Alice had a Chinese cook. His invitation was becoming more appealing.

He must have thought so, too.

"There now," he said with a ring of triumph. "You'd better come with us unless you want to live on what that Irish woman can make. Potatoes and poteen, I'd imagine."

This was all too close to the truth.

"Give me some time to consider," she begged him. "This has been such a shock. I don't want to decide anything until I've had time to think."

George was at once solicitous. "Of course, my dear. I only wanted you to know that you had a refuge if you needed one."

"And I'm grateful," Emily assured him. "If I decide to accept your offer, I'll send John over to let you know."

"If he hasn't been arrested," George muttered.

He stared at the patch on the kitchen floor that now gleamed in the weak winter sun. Mary Kate had mopped and then scrubbed, and he noted to himself that no trace of death remained. That hadn't impressed Mrs. Bechner. George agreed completely with the cook. Who would want to continue to live in a house where a violent murder had occurred? Perhaps Alice could convince Emily to come to them. He'd done his best.

"I'll be going then," he said more loudly. "I left my coat in the entry-way. I can let myself out."

"Of course not." Emily remembered her duties to a guest. "I'll come with you."

She showed him out, then shut the door behind him and leaned against it, glad to finally be alone.

The moment of solitude was short. She had just started up the stairs when there was another knock at the door. Emily stopped. She knew that Mary Kate was at that moment washing her bloody apron in cold water. Mrs. Bechner was probably already at her sister's, having a cup of coffee and regaling the family with the gruesome tale. There was no one else to answer.

With a sigh, Emily came back down and opened the door. She gasped. Mr. Carmichael stood in front of her.

At the sight of her expression, his timid smile vanished.

"I beg your pardon, Mrs. Stratton." He raised his hat. "I don't mean to intrude. I heard there was . . . an accident here. I came to offer my services."

Quickly Emily composed herself. A short time before, she would have welcomed him. Now, remembering Horace's cryptic note, she was instantly suspicious.

"Thank you, Mr. Carmichael," she said coldly. "I really can't think of anything that you might do for me at the moment."

He reacted as though she had slapped him.

"I . . . I . . . apologize," he stammered. "Of course . . . I just thought there might be something. . . ."

He put his hat back firmly on his head, bowed, and started back down the drive.

"Wait," Emily called after him.

He turned.

"Did you know Daniel Smith?" she asked.

"Yes," he said. "He did some work for me when things were slow at the wharf. He's lived in Portland since the early days." He came back to the doorway. "Was he the person who died here?" he asked her. "My house-keeper only said that a body had been found in your kitchen."

Emily was again amazed at how quickly news traveled in this town. It was as if every house had its own telegraph machine.

"Yes," she admitted. "He was bludgeoned to death. I don't know by whom or why. And I definitely don't know why in my home. If you have any information, I would appreciate knowing it."

"I?" He seemed confounded. "I can't imagine why anyone would want to harm Dan. He was a likeable chap. His only failing was a weakness for the bottle but even then, he wasn't the type to start a drunken row. It's totally incomprehensible to me."

"I see," Emily nodded. "Then there isn't anything more you can help with. If you should think of something, perhaps you could let Marshal Jacobi know. Thank you, Mr. Carmichael."

"My pleasure, Mrs. Stratton." His expression was pleasant, but Emily saw the hurt and confusion in his eyes. It smote her heart. It was as if she had kicked a puppy who had come to her to have its head patted. What if she were mistaken? If only she could be sure. How she wished she could trust him again!

But for now she let him go, watching at the doorway until he turned onto the road and vanished behind the hedge.

Mary Kate had changed her clothes from head to toe and washed her hands with all the fervor of Lady Macbeth. She met Emily on the upstairs landing.

"What shall we do now, ma'am?" she asked. "I'm ready for anything you say."

Emily could have hugged her.

"You don't want to look for another situation, do you?" she asked. "I would give you excellent references."

"And what kind of a person do you take me for?" the maid asked indignantly. "That I'd be leaving now when you need me?"

"Oh, Mary Kate!" Emily did hug her. "I'm so glad! I don't know how I'd manage without you."

"No more do I," Mary Kate grinned. "So, spuds and bacon for supper again?"

"Let's leave the kitchen for a bit," Emily decided. "I wonder if the Arrigoni restaurant will send a meal over."

"I wouldn't say no to a pot of macaroni," Mary Kate said. "I'll go down now and ask them."

At last Emily was alone. After being certain that both doors to the outside were locked and bolted, she went up to her room and knelt before the shrine. She lit a stick of incense and bowed to the statue of Kwan Yin.

"Dear Mother of Peace," she prayed. "Help me find the answers to this horrible crime and give me the courage to face the truth, whatever it may be."

She thought of throwing the coins, but she wasn't ready to know the future. Whatever lay in store would have to wait until she had rested.

For a wonder, she was able to have an hour of fitful sleep before she was wakened by the sound of someone struggling with the locked door.

Taking a poker from the hearth in her room, she crept down to find that Mary Kate had been unable to get the new key to turn the bolt. Weak with relief, Emily let her in.

"We'd best be oiling that," she told Emily. "It's wicked hard to turn. Mr. Arrigoni says he'll be pleased to send up a pot of macaroni and bread. And something he calls aunti pasty."

"I wonder what that is," Emily said.

"Well, it can't be worse than that Chinese food you like," Mary Kate opined.

"Did he say what time?"

"About seven," Mary Kate answered. "Will that do?"

"Yes, fine," Emily said.

She realized that they were carefully keeping to the very banal subject at hand. Any deviation from immediate needs would lead to analysis of what had happened and then speculation. Neither woman was ready to go down that path yet.

They were spared the possibility by the sound of a deep baying that resounded through the house.

"Saint Paddy's Purgatory!" Mary Kate exclaimed. "What *is* that noise?"

The front door burst open, letting in a monstrous animal, as big as a pony and as shaggy as a bear. It was followed by Robert and John, the latter hanging on to a leash for dear life.

Emily gaped at the apparition.

"What kind of animal is that?" she asked her son. "I thought you were going to get a dog, not a wolf."

Robert laughed. "Isn't he magnificent?" He patted the animal's head with an amazing lack of concern. "Jake's uncle thinks he may have a bit of wolf in his family tree, but he's really a very friendly dog, aren't you, boy?"

Emily wished Robert would move farther away from it.

"Well, he should certainly make any burglars think twice," she conceded. "Does he have a name?"

"Cerberus, isn't that amusing?" Robert said.

"Hilarious," Emily agreed. "Is there someplace we can keep him outside?"

"There's a shed next to the carriage house that can be a kennel," John told her. "I'll put in some straw. But it might be best to let him sleep in the house. The grounds aren't fenced, so we can't let him roam free at night."

"I'll make him a bed in the kitchen," Robert offered. He knelt by the dog and rubbed its ears. "And then I'll go down to the butcher shop and get you a beef shin to chew on. You'd like that, wouldn't you, Cerberus?"

Emily could have sworn that the dog understood him. He stopped pulling on the leash, sat in front of Robert, and whined ingratiatingly.

"In the house," Emily shivered. "Well, I can't see any intruder getting past him. I just hope he doesn't eat all of us instead."

And so Cerberus became part of the household.

Chapter Twenty

When complaint is made to a magistrate, of the commission of a crime, he must examine the informant on oath, and reduce his statement to writing, and cause the same to be submitted by him, and also take the depositions of any witnesses that the informant may produce in support thereof.

—Law of Arrest, Sec. 343 (Portland, 1864)

Thursday, March 12, 1868

City Marshal Daniel Jacobi was not happy about the murder of Dan Smith. It wasn't that he and Dan had been particular friends; Dan had been a harmless enough fellow, by all accounts, but no one special. It was that this was a crime he'd be expected to do something about. And he'd be willing to bet that the city council would have no sympathy for the extra work it made or give him the funds needed.

Jacobi was used to violent death in town. There were brawls and street fights enough down by the wharves. Men hit their wives one time too hard. Wives got fed up and shot their husbands. There'd been that Chinaman dredged from the Willamette a couple of weeks before with a bullet in him. And just the other day they'd found a body in a ravine west of town that nobody had missed and nobody had claimed.

But this was different. Mrs. Stratton was a wealthy woman with connections. She wouldn't be satisfied with a "death by misadventure" conclusion. Unless . . . A hopeful thought crossed his mind: unless she was involved. No, he decided sadly. Although he was sure she was hiding something, it probably wasn't the murder of Dan Smith.

He had hoped to find out more from Mrs. Bechner. However, when he interviewed her at her sister's house, the cook had been able to tell him nothing but that it was a cursed house full of papists and heathens and nothing would induce her to set foot in it again. Even when he had questioned her in German, she could give him no concrete information.

Jacobi sighed. The council would never pay enough overtime for him to do a proper investigation.

Still, he brightened; they might be able to pin it on John Mahoney. An Irishman and his friend having a few drinks, an argument that leads to a fight. Smith tries to get away by running to the house. Mahoney follows him, hits him a few times with the meat grinder, and then goes back to his room over the carriage house to clean up the evidence and pretend he'd not seen Smith in days.

It fit so beautifully that Jacobi knew it was most likely not the answer. For one thing, if Mrs. Stratton had really been upstairs the whole time, she would have heard a fight. Unless she was covering for Mahoney.

Jacobi stumbled on the uneven surface of the road. The mud was freezing up again. He turned up the collar of his coat. Damn! He'd thought winter was finally over, but the clouds were coming in, low and dark. It seemed they were in for another blow before spring finally came.

Matthew King ran all the way down to his office, jumping over tree stumps, rocks, and other obstacles in the roads. He was panting hard by the time he got there and had to lean on his clerk's desk for a few minutes before he could compose himself enough to make the climb to Andrews's apartment.

"Is everything all right, sir?" The clerk bent to see if Mr. King's face was distorted by anger or anguish. He saw only exhaustion.

"Nothing that concerns you!" King snapped. He took one last long breath and stood upright again. He straightened his cravat, then entered his office, shut and locked the door, and finally pressed the latch that opened a panel hiding a secret staircase up to Andrews's place.

"Norton!" he called as he came up. "You'll never guess what Horace's widow had dumped in her kitchen this afternoon. Norton! Norton?"

He had reached the top. Andrews was nowhere to be seen. The sparsely furnished room was unnaturally neat. No shaving gear by the water pitcher, no blankets on the daybed. King went over to the curtained corner that hid the clothes hooks and pulled it aside. All Andrews's suits and jackets were gone. There were no clothes in the chest of drawers either.

In a panic, King ran down to the office to check the safe. His fingers were trembling so much that he misdialed the combination twice. When it finally swung open, he breathed a sigh of relief. The sacks of gold coins and envelopes of notes seemed to all be there. At least . . . he counted the bags. Twelve. There had been twenty-four yesterday.

King fought down the rush of panic. What had Andrews done?

As he raked through the envelopes, opening each and checking the contents, he found one with his name on it in Andrews's unmistakable minute hand. He pulled out a thin sheet of paper on which only one line was written:

Matthew, I flee for my life!

King stared down at the sentence. What kind of melodramatic nonsense was this? Had Norton Andrews gone loco?

He felt a chill slither across his neck and down his spine. This couldn't have anything to do with the murder of Dan Smith, could it? He had been thrilled to hear Smith was dead. The man had been too much a crony of Horace's to be completely trustworthy. And to have him die in such a way as to cause embarrassment to Emily was an added piece of luck.

Or was it?

King went back into the receiving room.

"Garrick," he said to the clerk. "Have you seen Mr. Andrews today?"

"Yes, sir," Garrick answered. "He was here this morning, working very hard. He told me not to interrupt him. He went up to his room for lunch and told me then he wouldn't be back the rest of the day."

"Did he say where he was going?"

"No, sir," the clerk said. "I thought he was going to rest. He hasn't been looking too well since he ate those oysters."

"No, he hasn't," King agreed absently. "Thank you, Garrick. Anybody else call in today?"

The clerk thumbed through his notes. "The captain of the *Columbia* wanted you to know that the shipment was loaded and ready to go out. A couple of men looking for work. Oh yes, Mr. Carmichael stopped by. He said he wanted to talk with you about something but that it was of no great importance and could wait."

"Really?" King pursed his lips. "Well, it doesn't sound pressing. I'm going down to double-check on that shipment. Anyone else comes, tell them they can find me at the wharf."

"Mr. King?" Garrick asked nervously. "Is it true that Dan Smith is dead?"

"I'm afraid so," King replied.

"Well, I know it sounds rather cold." Garrick cleared his throat. "But Dan was supposed to be supervising work tonight. Who should I put in his place?"

That brought King up short.

"I'll look around when I get down there and see if I can get someone for now," he told Garrick. "Although I can't think of anyone smart enough to do the job. Where are those job applications?"

Garrick handed him couple of sheets of paper. "I took down the information from Mr. Lumm. He can't read or write."

"That might be an advantage if he's just loading boxes," King commented. "But not if he needs to read the labels. I'll go down there and see what turns up. Do the job myself if I have to. It won't be the first time."

He walked down to the wharf, passing first the better shops: the jewelers, confectioners, dry goods and clothing, McCormick's books, and Gross's drugstore. He went on down the street until the saloons, chandleries, and "ladies' boarding houses" began to predominate. He paid no attention, not even when an unruly drunk flew out of the Hellhole, followed by an irate

Ned Chambreau, shouting at him never to attempt to enter the establishment again.

What had spooked Norton Andrews? He'd taken time to pack his things as well as half the gold in the safe. That smelled more of a getaway than a flight. Was he running from an assassin or absconding? And where had he gone? No steamship had left between noon and now. Could he have gone on horseback? King doubted it. The weather was chancy this time of year. No one set out on a long journey, especially not alone. No, of course not. The man was burdened with cases of clothing, along with twelve bags of company cash!

Then another thought struck him, so forcefully that he stopped dead in the street, causing an old woman with a basket to run into him.

What if Andrews had killed Smith? Then he would certainly have to run for his life. On the face of it, it seemed unlikely. Smith was younger and in better shape, but if he had been caught unawares, he might have succumbed to a steady rain of blows. It wasn't impossible. Andrews had been behaving oddly lately. What if Smith had been blackmailing him? That made sense. Who knew what the man had learned from Horace Stratton?

He turned this over in his mind. The loss of the money was bad, but Norton had taken no more than his share. King could absorb the loss. It would be just as if he'd bought out his partner. He started walking again, this time with a brisk assured stride. Smith dead, Andrews vanished, matters might be looking up.

All he had to do now was take care of Emily Stratton.

Emily endured a stream of callers that afternoon. Some came to offer sympathy but most were clearly titillated by the shocking and apparently inexplicable murder. Everyone wanted to "see how she was taking it." Then they could feed their reports directly into the eternally grinding rumor mill.

"My dear, you must have been terrified," said a woman who sniffed her smelling salts as if even the thought made her faint. "I don't see how you can stay a minute longer in this house."

"It's my home," Emily answered pleasantly. "Would you like another rock cake?"

"And you have no idea why the man was here," another said in a tone that indicated otherwise.

"None at all," Emily smiled. "Do you need more tea?"

"Well, I can't say how much I admire your amazing *sang-froid*," mispronounced the first woman. "To continue living here after such an awful experience. And without a man in the house to protect you!"

"John is just across the courtyard," Emily said. "And, of course, now we have Cerberus. You may have heard him as you drove up. He doesn't let anyone approach the house unnoticed."

"Gracious! Was that howling from your dog?" The smelling salts went again to the woman's nose. "I hope you keep him chained."

"During the day," Emily said pointedly. "At night he's allowed to wander freely through the house. I feel most secure now."

"I should think so." The ladies soon took their leave, riding off to relay their impressions of the terrible misfortune at Mrs. Stratton's to the rest of their acquaintances.

Emily flopped on the sofa, as much as her corsets would allow. These visitations taxed her body and soul. But Mary Kate had pointed out that if she didn't receive, then the word would go out that she was prostrate over the death of a "stranger."

"Them biddies will cluck no matter what you do," she said sagely. "But it's better if you can tell them a few things first, to keep the tales from growing even more."

Emily saw the sense in this, but she would rather have walked across red hot coals.

The clock chimed five. Surely no one else would bother them today. Emily yearned to get into her soft silk pajamas. She gathered up the tea things and put them on the tray.

"Mrs. Stratton, that policeman is back." Mary Kate spit out the words as if announcing another murder. "He's in the kitchen and wants to see you."

"Yes, I thought he'd return." Emily handed her the tea tray. "Have him come in here, please."

Marshal Jacobi had remembered to remove his hat. He came in with Mary Kate and stood until she invited him to sit.

"How can I help you?" she asked.

"You could go to city council meetings for me," he answered with feeling. "Sorry, madam, I've just spent most of the day arguing that I can't hunt down stray dogs, keep order in the streets, see that the gaslights stay on, and find out who killed Dan Smith without more men."

"I gather that they didn't agree with you?" she said.

"No, they seem to think that I'm overpaid and have ample help." Jacobi shook his head. "They also think that the most likely suspect is your coachman."

"John? But why?" Emily asked.

"Opportunity," the marshal explained. "He was on the property when Dan died and says he didn't hear or see a thing. They knew each other. That's enough."

"I don't believe it," Emily said. "They were friends. And if John had done it, don't you think he would have made up a story about hearing shouts or seeing someone running away?"

"I don't know," Jacobi said frankly. "I don't have much experience with sober murderers. I had a man tell me once that the giant snakes had killed his wife, but we had witnesses that said he had his hands around her throat. I'd like very much to have a witness in this case."

He looked at her pleadingly.

"I wish I could help you," Emily said. "All I heard was one thump, no cries nor sounds of a fight. Nothing more until Mrs. Bechner began to scream."

She looked down at her hands. The sound still echoed through her head. The reality of what had happened was beginning to penetrate.

"Forgive me, Mrs. Stratton." Jacobi shifted uncomfortably. "But that doesn't sound very likely. The murder was so brutal; there must have been more than a thump."

"I know. That's been bothering me, too," she admitted. She tried to remember the muffled noise she had heard. "Perhaps what I heard wasn't the body falling, but the shutting of the door behind the killer or . . ." She looked up at the marshal, struck by an idea. "Or perhaps Mr. Smith was already dead when he landed on my kitchen floor."

"What? With all that blood?" Jacobi didn't think much of her theory. "Head wounds bleed like crazy. There would have been a trail of it."

"Not if he'd been wrapped in something. I'm sure you noticed that the blood was all in a pool surrounding his head." Emily ignored the start Jacobi gave. "There was none on the chairs or table, no sign that Mr. Smith had grabbed for anything to catch his fall."

"No, but—" Jacobi began.

"And there was almost nothing under his head," Emily continued. "What if he had been hit on the back of the head somewhere else, hard enough to knock him out? He could have been dragged to the house and dropped on the floor. Then the murderer could have taken the meat grinder and finished the job on his face. If he were still alive there would have been the same effusion."

"How do you know that?" Jacobi asked in genuine interest.

"Shanghai is not a city for the weak," Emily answered. "I suspect Portland isn't, either."

Jacobi decided it wouldn't be worth his while to follow that line of questioning, but it did make him wonder just how strong delicate Mrs. Stratton really was. He couldn't see her dragging a body, but did she have the strength to bash a man's face in?

"Very well," he considered. "That might explain why you heard nothing, but it only makes everything else more complicated. I saw no sign of anyone being dragged to your door. It would have needed a very powerful man to carry him. Also, it would be taking a huge risk to haul a body around in the middle of the day."

"I suppose so." Emily was reluctant to give up her theory. "Apart from John, do you have any suspects?"

"Either none or too many," the marshal sighed, not mentioning that she was one of them. "Dan was not always straight in his business deals. Work at the docks is too tempting for many men. His associates weren't the most upstanding."

Emily thought of his friendship with Horace, but said nothing.

"On the other hand," Jacobi continued, "I haven't found anything on John Mahoney. He takes a beer now and then but no more and seems to be well liked by everyone I spoke to. He worked for Hogan as a driver for five years before he came to work for you. No complaints."

"So you plan on looking elsewhere for the killer," Emily exhaled in relief.

"I don't see how, if the council won't pay for another detective," Jacobi said. "I'm not saying that we will arrest him. But unless someone else confesses, he's as good a suspect as I have."

Emily couldn't believe it.

"Are you saying that catching stray dogs is more important than catching a cold-blooded murderer?"

"They pay me two dollars a dog," Jacobi shrugged.

"And nothing to catch a murderer?" Emily was appalled.

"You don't understand," the marshal explained. "Portland doesn't have a regular police force. I'm a political appointee. I have two detectives and four part-time watchmen. None of us have any idea of how to investigate a murder. I'll do the best I can: ask down at the wharf where he worked, find out who his associates were, if he owed anyone money, had his life threatened recently. But if we don't find out in a week or two, we probably never will."

"Does that mean you'll return and arrest John, just to have a culprit?" Emily couldn't keep the sarcasm out of her voice.

"Some might," Jacobi said. "Where I came from in Bavaria, it would have been normal. I, however, don't work that way. I won't make an arrest unless I believe the person is guilty. I'm just telling you honestly what the chances are of ever finding that person."

Emily felt her anger ebb, to be replaced by despair.

"Marshal Jacobi, we must find out why Mr. Smith died." She looked at him pleadingly, her large brown eyes trapping him in their depths. He remembered with effort that he was a happily married man with children.

"Do you have any suggestions as to how to go about it?" he asked with difficulty.

Emily sighed and looked away. "Not at the moment," she admitted. "But I think that it's possible Mr. Smith was coming to tell me something, to warn me perhaps."

"Of what?" Jacobi was skeptical.

"I don't know; he didn't reach me," she said sharply. "But I think"—she paused, then made up her mind—"I think that an investigation into my late husband's business connections, all of them, might be profitable to you."

"Mrs. Stratton, you amaze me!" Jacobi gave her a look of respect. "I knew Captain Stratton slightly. I know more of him by hearsay. You realize, don't you, that we may find things that won't reflect well on his memory."

"Yes," Emily said. "But my son and I will never be completely safe until the entire truth is known. You mustn't let concern for me have any part in your inquiry. If Mr. Smith died because of something my husband did, then I am prepared to take the consequences."

Jacobi stared at her for a long moment. Did she have any idea of what kind of things he might turn up? She could be ruined, both financially and socially. He noticed how her hands were gripping the embroidered silk of her skirt. She likely didn't even realize that she was holding on so tightly that her knuckles were white.

She understood.

Jacobi regarded her with even greater respect. If Mrs. Stratton was willing to risk everything in the name of justice, how could he let her down?

CHAPTER TWENTY-ONE

Fri. Mar. 13. snow. Home all day. Began sermon over again.

—THOMAS LAMB ELIOT, DIARY, 1868

FRIDAY, MARCH 13, 1868

Emily woke in the pale dawn. Her sleep had been unsettled, full of enigmatic dreams.

Wearily, she swung her legs to the floor. Outside her bedroom window a gentle snow was falling. Emily stared in disbelief. What had happened to spring? The mountains had vanished again. She could see no farther than the next house. Oddly, she found it comforting to have the world reduced to such a small area. It gave the illusion of providing a respite from her problems.

Outside she heard the scrape of a shovel as John worked to clear the drive. It occurred to Emily that she should arrange to have their horses stabled in the coach house. Now, every time she wanted the carriage, John had to walk down to Hogan's to get the horses. If they were going to stay in the house, they needed to have transportation close by.

And they were going to stay. Emily had decided. This house was the first thing that was all hers, hers alone. She wouldn't let anyone chase her from it. Nor was she about to be intimidated from finding out who was responsible for the things that had happened here.

The smell of burning bacon rose to the bedroom. Emily remembered that there was no longer a Mrs. Bechner to provide them with cooked food.

She quickly revised her plans for the day. She had to find a murderer, but first she had to hire a new cook. She wondered if it was this sort of distraction that kept women from running the world. She would have to ask Mr. Carmichael's opinion on that—if, she sighed, she was ever able to trust him again.

The kitchen door was wide open when she entered, bringing in a cold draft that was not doing much to get rid of the smell. Through the acrid smoke she made out the form of John in the act of throwing a lid onto the flaming pan of bacon. Mary Kate stood by the doorway, fanning the fumes out into the snow.

"I'm so sorry, Mrs. Stratton!" she moaned. "I put too much coal on the fire or something and then some grease spilled and the next thing I knew . . ." She gestured sadly at the wreckage of their breakfast.

"It's not your fault, Mary Kate," Emily said. "You were trying to help."

Yes, she concluded, a new cook was the most important task this morning.

John found a pair of dishcloths, which he wrapped around his hands. He picked up the covered pan and carried it outside.

"Good morning, missus," he greeted her cheerfully on his return. "Whoever marries herself here had better build his house next to the fire station."

He didn't act like a man who was the major suspect in a murder. Apparently Marshal Jacobi hadn't mentioned it to him.

"Is there any macaroni left from last night?" she asked them. "Bacon isn't necessary this morning."

The other two stared at her and then burst out laughing.

"There's bread left and some of that cheese and pickled vegetables," Mary Kate said. "Not proper breakfast fare."

"It sounds fine," Emily said. "We can make some into a sandwich for Robert to take to school. Or has he already left?"

"Haven't heard him yet, ma'am." Mary Kate gave the dishcloth one last flap and closed the door.

"I'll go wake him," Emily said. "Although how he could sleep through this, I can't imagine. John, I'll be needing you today."

"Yes ma'am," John said. "Shall I go for the horses?"

"Not yet. Have your breakfast and help Mary Kate clear up, please," Emily told him. "Then we need to discuss several matters before I go into town."

"What shall I do about dinner?" Mary Kate asked forlornly.

"I hope to have another cook by then," Emily said. "At least, as long as word hasn't gone out that the house is cursed."

Robert was still in bed with pillows propped up to block his ears.

"Wake up, slugabed!" Emily tickled the back of his neck.

Robert grunted and tried to burrow farther into the covers.

"None of that, young man," she grabbed his hair and tugged gently. "You'll be late for school."

Slowly he rolled over and opened one eye.

"I'm too tired, Mother," he whined. "Let me skip the morning session today."

"Well, I suppose." Emily was puzzled. "Are you coming down with something, darling?"

"No, yes. Don't think so." He turned back on his side. "Just wanna sleep."

"Very well," she said. "I suppose you wouldn't learn much anyway, unable to stay awake. I'll come up to check on you later."

"Mmmmphff," Robert answered.

Emily left him in peace. As she went out she wiped her hand across her forehead and caught a whiff of something familiar.

How strange, she thought. *It must be the smoke from the bacon fire, but I could swear that I smell opium.*

John was waiting for her in the carriage house.

"Have I done anything wrong?" he asked at once. "I know there isn't much call for the carriage, but I can do other things. I can fix most anything that breaks and paint and chop wood and—"

"Put out kitchen fires," Emily finished. "Yes, I know. I'm very happy with your work. I was hoping you'd be willing to take on the care of our horses here, as well as driving and maintaining the carriage."

"Oh, that would be magnificent!" he answered happily. "It seems fair lonely sleeping in a stable with no horses in it. The pair Captain Stratton bought for you are well matched, both to color and gait, but they could use more training. It'll be grand to have the job."

"Good," Emily said. "I'm sure you'll do it well."

She paused, unsure how to ask the next question.

"Is that all, ma'am?"

"No, John, not quite," Emily squirmed. "I need to ask you about your friend, Mr. Smith."

"Sure," John seemed relaxed. "I don't know who'd want to kill him, though. Jacobi already asked me."

"Did he also ask you why Mr. Smith was in the house at all?"

"Jacobi seemed to think he already knew." John's face showed his opinion of that. "Dan wasn't a housebreaker. I'm thinking he might have come here to warn you of something and there was someone who didn't want you warned."

"I had the same thought myself," Emily said. "Did you tell that to Marshal Jacobi?"

"No, I didn't want him asking why Dan'd be warning you." He looked away from her. "Maybe I should have?"

Emily felt she was being weighed in the balance.

"I don't think it would have made any difference," she said, remembering Jacobi's complaint about lack of funds for an investigation. "But I have to know. I thought Dan had already left town. He was going to try ranching, he said."

"Never said a word about it to me." John scratched his head. "He has been acting oddly the past few weeks, I'll admit. Hiding out in the carriage house just for a start."

"How long have you known him?" Emily couldn't think of a way to ask if John had been part of Horace's plotting.

John smiled. "The first day I landed here, I met Dan. I was fresh up from

California along with a hundred others who'd gone to make their fortunes in the gold mines. I had a brogue so thick that someone asked me if I was talking German. All I wanted was to earn enough to buy a stake in the Idaho mines."

He shook his head at his foolishness.

"Dan needed some men to unload a shipment," John went on. "When he saw I had only the clothes I was standing in and no place to stay, he gave me a blanket, a bowl of stew, and a job. When I'd got back on my feet and learned to talk more like a Westerner, he introduced me to Hogan. I was a groom at a hotel in Mayo before I emigrated. Dan knew I would be happiest only if I could work with horses again."

"Yes," Emily concluded. "For all his rough exterior, I had a sense that he had a soft heart. Why else would he have bothered to tell me about . . . well, never mind. He certainly doesn't sound like a man who breaks into houses. But did he ever talk about what he was doing? Did he ever ask you to help with something not quite, uh, within the law?"

John didn't seem offended by the question. "If you mean helping to shift some goods that might not have come in with customs tags, once in a while, yes," he shrugged. "But not since the war ended."

"Do you know what was in the boxes?" Emily asked.

"Well, they didn't slosh, so it wasn't whiskey." John thought. "The writing on them was all in Chinese, so I couldn't tell you more."

Emily nodded. Opium, most likely.

"Was there anything else Mr. Smith asked of you? Did he ever need . . . someone convinced to keep quiet or warned not to interfere?"

"No, ma'am," John was adamant. "I wouldn't sign up to be anyone's bully boy. I saw enough of that in Mayo. Anyway, Dan didn't do work that needed noses broken. At least, if he did, I never heard of it."

Of course not, Emily thought. *It would have been too easy if this had been a simple act of revenge.*

"Did he ever mention anything about the railroad or a Mr. Holladay?" she continued.

John shook his head. "I know there's a lot of clishmaclaver about what side of the river they're putting the line on, but I don't think Dan was part of it. Did he say something to you?"

"Only that he and my husband might have tried to make some money from the controversy," Emily hedged.

"Must have been something he didn't think I'd be a part of," John said. "I'm sorry I can't be of more help."

"Thank you, John. I appreciate your honesty." Emily rose to leave. "Get whatever you need to take care of the horses. Tell the shopkeepers that they should send the bills to me. Can you have the stables ready by this afternoon?"

"If the snow stops," he said. "Most of the tack is here already. I just need to get some straw and feed, maybe a couple of other things."

"Good," Emily said. "If the weather permits, I'll need to go out about two, I'd say. Will that be all right?"

"Yes, ma'am," John almost saluted. "I'll have the carriage waiting out front."

She went back to the house, passing through the burnt bacon smoke without noticing. All she had learned from John was that he was either innocent or a magnificent actor.

Emily tried to think of someone else who could give her information. It was so aggravating not to know the town and the people well enough to understand what was going on. Once again she wished she hadn't found Horace's note about Mr. Carmichael. The man had seemed so sane and sensible. She felt that he would have been able to help her sort out the information and suggest a new plan of attack. But if Carmichael had been involved enough in her husband's affairs to know too much, then she couldn't rely on him for the truth.

She wondered if she dare approach Ah Ning again. The merchant had obviously not wanted anyone to know she had consulted him, but he had promised to find out more about Ah Sung. Perhaps Dr. See would be willing to arrange another meeting.

She made a mental list of the tasks for the day. Number one, find a cook. Perhaps Alice's servant, Ah Ling, knew of someone. Would Wa Kee extract a punishment if a Chinese worker was hired without going through him? From their single meeting, she wasn't hopeful that the broker would find someone competent for her.

Number two: ask Dr. See when she could meet with Ah Ning again.

Number three: learn more about the history behind the battle between the Eastsiders and Westsiders for the railway rights from Portland to California. Perhaps the lending library or the newspaper office would have back copies of the papers discussing it. She might also ask Mr. Ladd or Mr. Reed. They were both important in the West Side contingent. If she had met anybody involved with the Eastsiders, they hadn't divulged the fact.

Another thought struck her. Had Daniel Smith told her the truth about the money Horace was given to bribe state congressmen? She couldn't see her late husband approaching legislators to buy their votes. It was a job that required more subtlety and patience than he possessed. But it was well within his system of ethics to take the money, do nothing, and come up with an excuse if the representatives didn't vote as promised. Still, it might not be true. Smith could have made up the story, or Horace could have told it to him to cover up what they were really doing.

But how to find out? She could hardly go down to the state capitol at Salem and knock on every congressman's door asking if he'd taken any graft lately.

And it might not have anything to do with the deaths of Dan Smith and Ah Sung.

Or, she reflected, it might have everything to do with them.

She sighed. There was no point in doing more than the first two today. If she managed that much, it would be a miracle. Emily's head was aching again. She pinched the space between her eyebrows. Dr. See must have a remedy for headaches. That could at least give her a reason for visiting him again so soon.

The clock chimed ten. There had still been no sound of activity from Robert's room. Emily went in to wake him again. She did hope he wasn't getting ill; the poor boy had probably spent too much time poring over his books. She'd have to see that he got out more and had fun.

Emily opened the door and saw only his tousled head above the covers. He looked so sweet, just as he had when he was little. She didn't have the heart to wake him. Dear boy! What would she do without him?

———

In his office, Matthew King was trying to decide if he should tell anyone about Andrews's disappearance. It might be better to put out that a sudden business matter had compelled Andrews to leave for a time. When he didn't return, King could seem to send out inquiries. With no information, people could imagine him frozen in the mountains or set upon by brigands. If he turned up later, it wouldn't matter. By that time everyone would have become used to King running things alone. Andrews would approve, King told himself; he certainly wouldn't have wanted to start a panic.

King brooded a while on what to tell their silent partner, if anything. He'd want to know the nature of the business emergency. That wouldn't be good. Perhaps it would be better to say that Andrews left for his health. That was closer to the truth. His note had indicated a seriously troubled mind. The way the man had reacted to a simple case of food poisoning was not sane. He was probably on the edge of a breakdown.

Good riddance to him.

Now, if he could just get rid of Emily Stratton, there would be nothing more to worry about. That damned woman was far too interested in company records. What business was it of hers where the money came from? He wasn't cheating her.

Andrews's pathetic note was still in his pocket. King took it out and laid it on his desk. After a moment's reflection, he rolled up the paper and, lifting the glass on the gaslight, lit one end of it. He used it to light his cigar. Then he let it burn down in his hand, almost to the point of searing his fingers. The ashes fluttered onto the carpet.

See Fan's herbal shop was full of men when Emily came in. Their discussions ceased at once as they all stared at her. Thankful for once for her widow's bonnet, Emily put down the veil. "Good day to you, respected gentlemen," she said in broken Cantonese as she bowed.

There was a stunned silence and then someone snorted. All the men began to laugh. Emily had no idea of what she had done. Had she mispronounced something? Her father had often used the wrong intonation and made ridiculous sentences that either infuriated or amused his listeners.

Someone in the back began to chant, "Big nose, big feet, big skirts, you're no Chinese woman!" The laughter grew.

Emily hoped that the veil hid the tears. She tried to force them back but a trickle ran down the side of her "big nose." This was the sort of chant she'd been greeted with in her first days in school.

"Ignorant peasants!" Dr. See spoke softly but with great force. "How dare you insult a patient in my place of business? Mrs. Stratton." He bowed. "I regret to tell you that the medicine you require is not yet ready. If you return tonight at the hour of the rooster, I shall have it for you."

The laughter had stopped as a flame cut off by a sudden wind. The men all became very interested in the grain of the floor or the knobs on the drawers of medicine.

Emily collected herself. Five o'clock. Since she had no order in, she hoped that Dr. See was telling her that it was a better time for a meeting.

"Thank you," she told him. "I shall be here at the hour of the rooster. Good day."

Safely outside the building, Emily wiped her eyes with her gloved hand. John brought up the carriage at once. He climbed down to open the door and let her in.

"Is everything all right?" he asked. "Those heathens didn't hurt you, did they?"

"I'm fine," she sniffed. "Dr. See was too occupied for me to ask about the cook. I suppose we'll have to go to Mrs. Bracewell's house. Their cook may know of someone."

Alice was out when Emily arrived but her daughter, Felicity, was home with a cold. She seemed happy to see her aunt when the maid brought her into the parlor.

"Please come in, Aunt Emily," she begged. "It's so dull here with Mama and Papa gone for the day and Sarah at school. I'm really not at all ill. It's just that my parents fret every time I cough. They think I'm delicate because my back is crooked, isn't that silly?"

All this came out in a rush. Emily was happy to spend a few minutes with the girl. She chided herself for not making the effort to get to know Horace's nieces, especially after George had been so kind to Robert.

"You should be pleased to have parents who are so careful of your health," she said. "Oh, dear, that sounds dreadfully preachy! I'm sorry."

Felicity laughed. "You're quite right. I really don't mind. They've been so good about giving me extra things, like my music lessons. They even hired someone to read to me for the hour each day when I have to lie in my brace."

"Still, it was rude of me to lecture you," Emily said. "Actually, I came today to speak with Ah Ling. Our cook has left us, and I was hoping he knew someone who would be interested in working for us."

"Oh, yes, I heard about the burglar found killed in your house," Felicity said. "I'm so sorry. I was going to have some tea made for you anyway. I'll ask Lewis to have Ah Ling bring it himself."

She rang for the butler and gave the order. A few moments later a maid returned, carrying a tray and followed by Ah Ling.

The cook bowed to Emily. "I am very pleased to see you again, Mrs. Stratton. I understand that you are again in need of a cook."

"I'm afraid so," Emily said. "Do you know of a good cook who is brave enough to work for me?"

Ah Ling smiled. "It doesn't require as much courage as you think. As it happens, I do have a friend who has been doing menial work grading for the railroad. He is an excellent cook. His English is acceptable. I believe he would be happy to come."

"That's wonderful!" Emily said. "Thank you so much. Could he start at once?"

"I believe so," Ah Ling said. "Miss Felicity, may I leave for a few minutes to find my friend and ask him?"

"Of course," Felicity said. "Do you want to bring him back here?" she asked Emily.

"I'd prefer it if he could meet me at my house at, say, three o'clock," Emily said. "If that's possible."

"I'm sure that will be fine." Ah Ling bowed again. "His name is Lun Ho."

"Thank you very much," Emily said. "I look forward to meeting him."

Ah Ling left at once. Emily finished her tea quickly.

"I hate to run," she told Felicity. "But I have another errand to do before I meet Lun Ho. Please give your parents my regards. And get some rest. You may not be as delicate as your parents think, but a cold can turn into pleurisy and even pneumonia if not attended to."

Felicity promised and Emily left feeling greatly satisfied with the success of her visit.

She still had time to stop at the library. The snow had stopped, although the clouds hung low over the town. All the tree stumps and piles of refuse were hidden beneath a clean white layer, and through it the crocuses continued to bloom. Emily was enchanted with the beauty. She wished she had clothes appropriate for walking. Along the road other, less fashionable women were out working in the farmyards wearing heavy men's boots and jackets. Alice would probably not approve if Emily imitated them.

The steps to the library were slick. Emily gripped the handrail as she slowly climbed. She pushed the door open. The librarian looked up with a smile.

"Mrs. Stratton, isn't it?" he asked. "And what can I find for you today?"

"I'd like anything to do with the companies proposing to build a railroad here in Oregon," she said.

"Why, Mrs. Stratton, how civic-minded of you." Another voice spoke up.

Emily hadn't noticed the man seated in the corner, reading a newspaper. "I'd be happy to give you any information I can. I've been following the debate with interest."

Emily's heart sank. The man so eager to help her was, of course, Mr. Carmichael.

CHAPTER TWENTY-TWO

We the undersigned incorporators of the "Oregon Central Railroad Company" hereby appoint J. Gaston of Salem, Oregon, secretary of the board of incorporators, and authorize and designate him as one of the incorporators of said company, to prepare and open the stock books of said company. . . .

—INCORPORATION ARTICLES FOR THE OREGON CENTRAL RAILROAD COMPANY
(WESTSIDERS)

It is not proposed to discuss the importance of this railroad enterprise to the people of the state, or to urge the importance of aiding it at this time. . . . The names of the incorporators above are a sufficient guarantee that whatever is done will be done in good faith, and for the best interests of the enterprise, and that it will be perseveringly pushed forward to a final success.

—JOSEPH GASTON, *PROSPECTUS OF THE OREGON CENTRAL RAILROAD COMPANY*, 1868

It's quite all right," Emily told Mr. Carmichael nervously. "I don't wish to bother you. I wanted to read some of the newspaper articles about the railroad. I remember that you said you supported the West Side."

"And you prefer an objective view." He smiled. "I'm afraid you won't find it in any of the papers, but at least you will read every possible opinion on the subject."

"Does that include accusations of illegal activities?" she asked, despite her resolve not to trust him.

"Most definitely," he replied. "Everything from bribery to murder."

"Really?" She looked at him with doubt. "Is any of it true?"

He shrugged. "I admit I haven't read anything that convinced me, but, in my experience, if the stakes are high enough, men will do almost anything."

Emily stared at him. It might just be the effect of Horace's note, but Mr. Carmichael seemed harder, more worldly, than before. He put down his newspaper.

"This is something more than a desire to know more about Portland politics, isn't it?" he asked.

"A man was murdered in my home," she answered, looking directly into his eyes. "I want to know why."

"Understandable," he said. "I was shocked to hear about it but what could it possibly have to do with the railroad?"

"I don't know," she answered sharply. "I'm trying to find out."

He closed his eyes and rubbed his forehead. "I beg your pardon, Mrs. Stratton. Of course it's none of my business. Between the upcoming city election and the fight over the railroad, I've come to feel that everything must involve politics. I hope that you haven't been similarly affected. I'm sure that Dan's death was the result of some private dispute. I'm afraid he had some unsavory acquaintances."

"Have you given their names to Marshal Jacobi?" Emily snapped.

Carmichael took a step back, apparently honestly bewildered by her behavior.

"I don't know any names," he said. "I only know that he spent a lot of time in the saloons and his friends were the sort one meets there. Mrs. Stratton, what have I done to offend you?"

He looked so hurt that she felt terribly guilty.

"Nothing, Mr. Carmichael." She tried to control her irritation. "You have shown me nothing but kindness. It's the recent events that have made me somewhat on edge. I beg your pardon for seeming to be unfriendly."

"But I'm an annoying old man who is bothering you with his attentions." He bent to pick up his hat and coat. "I promise that I shan't bother you with them further."

He took his coat from the hook by the door. "Good day, Mrs. Stratton,"

He paused in the doorway. Emily felt the urge to call him back. What if Horace had been wrong? If only she dared ask. Instead she stood mutely as he shut the door and descended to the street.

"Ma'am?"

Emily jumped. She had completely forgotten about the librarian. He had discreetly busied himself at the other side of the room during the conversation. Now he stood in front of her, his arms laden with a stack of papers, some bound, some in thin folders.

"This is all I could find on the various reports from the Oregon Central Railroad companies," he explained.

"Companies?"

"They both have the same name. That's why we call them 'East Side' and 'West Side.'"

"Thank you." Emily held out her arms for the papers. She glanced at the wall clock; half past eleven. If she skipped luncheon, she might be able to get through half of them by the time she was supposed to interview the cook.

"Would you mind going down and telling my driver to come back for me at two thirty?" she asked.

"I'd be happy to," he said. "John Mahoney, isn't it?"

"Yes," she answered, surprised.

He laughed. "I'd heard he'd got a private job with Horace Stratton's widow. Portland is a very small town. You'll get used to it."

If the town is so small, she thought, *then why can't anyone tell me who killed Daniel Smith in my kitchen?*

Three hours later, Emily was forced to agree with Mr. Carmichael. Her only conclusion was that everyone involved with the railroad was a scoundrel.

She was able to extract a few facts from the mass of words, however. The real money wasn't in the building of the line, but from the land on either side of it that the government promised to the company who was the first to finish. Therefore, the side that got the contract would win a fortune and the other go bankrupt. There was no second prize.

Yes, there was enough at stake here to murder for.

But was it the reason Daniel Smith was killed? Had someone found out about the bribes that he and Horace had embezzled from Ben Holladay? Smith was supposed to have been on his way to Eastern Oregon. Had he delayed long enough to try to warn her and lost his life in the attempt? If that was so, then Emily felt even more strongly that she couldn't let the matter rest.

Very well. Mr. Ladd had told her that he was one of the major partners in the West Side Oregon Central Railroad. The others were Mr. Reed, who went to the Unitarian Church, and a Mr. Thompson, whom Emily didn't think she had ever met. There was also a Mr. Gaston, who lived in Jacksonville, almost on the border with California. She wasn't going to worry about him for the moment.

Now, the East Side Oregon Central had to have someone local in charge, even if a large part of the money came from elsewhere. Would this have been the person who had given Horace the money to buy the legislators? She went back to the mound of papers in search of a name.

Here, a notice in one of the newspapers: a Simon G. Elliot had filed for incorporation a few months after the West Side company was registered. He claimed that the other railroad company had not filed properly. The arguments on this made Emily's head swim. It seemed that Elliot was supported by a number of prominent businessmen of Portland, including, she noted, Dr. Hawthorne, who ran the insane asylum on the east side of the river. Simon Elliot also had the support of the governor and a number of legislators.

Had someone else paid them or was their support genuine? Did that make any difference to her quest? The legislature was way up the river, in Salem, more than a day's journey. Of course, that would be no trouble for a determined man, even at this time of the year. Could Daniel Smith have seen someone in Portland who shouldn't have been here, someone who wanted to silence him?

The papers on the table before her had no answer to that.

Emily put her head in her hands. She wasn't sure where to look next. If only there were someone she could discuss all this with, someone who could help her ferret out the truth!

She shook herself and sat up straight. There wasn't anyone, she reminded herself, so it was no use moaning about it. She must get used to making decisions on her own.

And, of course, the next thing she had to decide was if Ah Ling's friend would be acceptable as their next cook.

Lun Ho was waiting by the kitchen door when the carriage pulled up. He appeared to be about thirty years old and was tall for a Chinese, five foot seven or eight, taller than Emily by a good five inches, at least.

John let him into the house and stayed with him while Emily took off her wraps.

"Good afternoon, Mr. Lun," she started. "Mr. Ah at the Bracewells' recommended you. Do you speak English?"

"I do," he replied. "But not well. I am endeavoring to improve, however."

"And how much experience do you have as a cook?" she asked.

"I worked in a mining camp in Southern Oregon," he told her. "Both for the Chinese and foreign miners. I can only bake biscuits but am willing to learn to make bread. Ah Ling says he will help me."

Emily turned to John. "What do you think?"

"I don't know, ma'am," he answered. "I couldn't understand a word of that gibberish."

Emily paused. She looked at Lun Ho. Suddenly she realized that he hadn't been speaking poor or even pidgin English. They had been conversing in her own dialect of Chinese.

"You're Shanghainese?" She couldn't believe it.

Lun Ho shook his head. "I am from a village not far from Peking, but my father brought me to Shanghai as a boy to work for the foreigners in their godown. I carried parcels and ran errands for a Persian merchant."

"Which one?" Emily was learning to be suspicious.

"Elias Sassoon," Lun Ho said.

Emily gasped. The Sassoons were possibly the wealthiest foreigners in Shanghai.

"I did learn some cooking there," Lun Ho said. "But not the kind people like here. I was very surprised when I arrived in America to learn that not all foreigners keep kosher."

"I don't think John or Mary Kate would stay if they couldn't have their bacon," Emily admitted. "But I'm quite fond of Persian food."

"I am quite fond of pork, too," Lun Ho said. "Will you hire me? I would be grateful. I have no clan here in Portland."

Emily studied him. His accent was definitely from the north. He might be telling the truth about his past. But it was strange that he would come to a place where he had neither family nor others from his region. He must speak some Cantonese but, even so, he wouldn't be accepted by the Tong, the benevolent society of the local Chinese.

"Hello, Mother." They all turned toward the voice. "You shouldn't have let me sleep so long. I've missed the whole day of school."

Robert stood in the doorway, hair still uncombed and eyes puffy. He yawned and peered at Lun Ho.

"Don't I know you?" he asked.

"This is our new cook," Emily said. "He lived in Shanghai for many years. We can talk with him."

"That's nice," Robert yawned again. "Can you make fish noodle soup?" he asked Lun Ho in Chinese.

"It is one of my favorites, young master." The man bowed.

"Hire him, Mother," Robert said. "I'm going to wash up and get dressed."

Emily went over and put a hand to his forehead.

"Are you sure you're quite well, my dear?" she asked. "You may have slept because you were sickening for something. Perhaps you should go back to bed."

Robert continued to stare at Lun Ho. "I'm sure I remember you from somewhere," he said. "Perhaps it was Shanghai, but it's been more than two years since I left. No, Mother, I'm fine. I should go over to Hank's and tell him why I wasn't there today."

"Why don't you bring him back with you?" Emily suggested. "I'd like to meet your friends."

"Not tonight; maybe Friday, if our new cook can also make something Westerners can stomach." He grabbed the dish of cold pickle that Mary Kate had left on the table and headed back upstairs.

"May I be going now, Mrs. Stratton?" John asked. He'd been waiting during the conversation and was growing decidedly bored listening to Chinese.

"Yes, John, I'm sorry to have kept you," Emily said. "But please return a little before five. I have another appointment with Dr. See."

Lun Ho twitched at the mention of the doctor. Emily noted the movement and filed it for future reference. Perhaps she would ask See Fan if he knew anything about her new cook.

"Now," she said. "Sit down and we can go over your duties and salary."

John made his escape. In the courtyard he ran into Mary Kate, coming home with a basket of provisions.

"The missus got another Chinese cook," he told her. "You keep an eye on what sort of meat he puts in the pot."

"Oh dear," Mary Kate sighed. "I may have to start going to early Mass and take breakfast at the rectory after. I don't think I can face another chicken foot in the morning."

By the time he went home to dinner, Matthew King had managed to put it about that his partner, Norton Andrews, had gone up the Columbia to spend a few weeks in the mountains to regain his health. King promised their clients that he could handle all business himself until Andrews returned.

In the meantime, he would make arrangements to have Norton's shares transferred to him. The missing gold wouldn't quite cover the cost of the shares, but it would be worth a short-term loss to have complete control.

Now the only obstacle was that Stratton woman. So far, he hadn't had much luck in discouraging her. Maybe it was time for drastic measures. He silently cursed Andrews for absconding just when he might have been useful.

Alistair Carmichael was also preparing for dinner. In his case it meant cooking the meal himself. His friends at the Arlington Club thought him miserly for not hiring a cook, but he rather enjoyed the job. And it seemed foolish to have someone to prepare food for just one person. He also found that he received a large number of invitations from women who needed an extra man of respectable age and manners to seat opposite a single woman at parties. This was not disagreeable to him at all.

But tonight he was dining at home. That was just as well, for he had a lot to puzzle over since his meeting with Mrs. Stratton that afternoon. Why had she suddenly taken against him? He went over all their conversations for a hint of something he had said or done to upset her.

And then why was she looking up information on the Oregon Central Railroads? He didn't remember old Horace having a finger in that pie. But the late Captain Stratton had been apt to stick his fingers in up to the wrist if he thought a profit could be had.

Had Emily found something he had missed? He thought he had gone through every piece of paper Horace had left. What if the bastard had kept a second set of books somewhere else? What if someone had gotten wind of his investigation? Carmichael had tried to be discreet in his delving into Stratton, Andrews, and King, but, as had been pointed out to Emily, Portland was a small town.

A new thought struck him so forcefully that he missed the pan in flipping his fried bread and sausage. Half his meal landed on the floor. He pushed it aside with his shoe.

What if Horace's widow knew all about what he had been doing? In that case, she could blackmail half the men in town for one thing or another. That would also mean that she was aware of his own investigation. Could that be the reason for the change in her manner toward him?

Or could some busybody have informed her that he really wasn't a Methodist?

All the way to Hank's place, Robert had the feeling that he was being followed. It bothered him, not because he believed there was anyone behind him, but because he knew that it was a common side effect of smoking opium. He wished he'd never let Lily talk him into having a pipe. He shared the view of both the foreigners in China and the Chinese upper class. Opium smoking was for the lowest rung of society. The fact that the

Emperor was rumored to be addicted only confirmed this opinion. It had been over two hundred years since the Manchu had come to power but they were still considered barbarian scum by a great proportion of their subjects.

He also was worried that his mother would notice. He knew that she had gone with his grandfather to preach in the most disgusting opium houses in China where almost all of the men were too far gone to even know they were there. She not only could recognize the odor of the drug but also knew the signs of addiction. Apart from his own horror of turning into one of the pathetic wretches one saw everywhere in Shanghai, Robert couldn't bear to have his mother's faith in him destroyed.

He found Hank behind the barn at his house. Jack was with him, and the two of them were sitting on a felled tree passing a flask back and forth.

"Hullo Stratton!" Hank greeted him cheerfully. "Missed you in school today. That lotus blossom of yours wear you out last night?"

Robert forced himself to grin. "Jealous?" He stretched as if just out of bed. As he raised his arms, he stole a glance over his shoulder. Was that someone moving among the trees?

"Not hardly." Hank took another pull at the flask. "You won't catch me with those Chinee girls. Give me a nice strong German whore you can ride for hours, right Jack?"

Jack took the offered drink but made no comment.

Robert sat down next to them. Jack handed him the whiskey. Robert took a sip and passed it on.

"I think I might stay in this evening," he said casually. "I don't want my mother to suspect anything. When Andrews caught me climbing in the other night, I thought it was all up with me. I was sure he'd wake her up and tell her what I'd been doing. He still might decide to."

"Haven't you heard?" Jack said. "Andrews left town today. No one knows when he'll be back. My father thinks it's funny, him leaving so suddenly. But my mother says it makes sense. He needed a rest cure."

Robert grunted. "He needed something. The way he kept going on about people being out to kill him, you'd think he'd been. . . ."

"What?" Hank nudged him.

"Nothing," Robert answered. "I think I'll stay in tonight just the same. I'll see you tomorrow, right?"

The others agreed.

Robert walked home in the soft, melting snow. Andrews's behavior was starting to make sense. He wondered how long Mr. Andrews had been sampling the merchandise and if his father had known that his partner had succumbed to the dreamworld of opium.

He resolutely refused to turn around to see if anyone followed him home.

CHAPTER TWENTY-THREE

Some of the men are very bad, and call the Chinese "moon eyes" and worse. But the China-man doesn't care. He can get good money. It doesn't cost much to live here, and when we go home to China, we can bring much money. . . . We live here because we love money. There are bad rains now, but sometimes there is no rain. Don't you come here; there are too many Chinese already.

—LETTER FROM AH NING TO A RELATIVE, TRANSLATED AND PRINTED IN THE *OREGONIAN,* MARCH 25, 1861

At the hour of the rooster, about five in the afternoon, Emily presented herself at See Fan's office. This time it was empty. She heard rustling behind the curtain and Dr. See came out to greet her.

"I apologize for the behavior of my patients this morning," he said at once. "They have not been treated well, but that is no excuse for taunting you."

"It's no different from the reception my parents and I received when we ventured out of the International Sector of Shanghai," Emily sighed.

"Fortunately, we also had many good friends among the Chinese. They reminded us that every nation has both cruel and kind people."

"That is so." Dr. See ushered her into the private room in the back. "I shall try to remember that when the boys of this town throw garbage at me."

The merchant Ah Ning was waiting for them.

"Thank you for agreeing to see me again," Emily said once the formal greetings had been exchanged. "Have you found anything more about Ah Sung?"

"I have." Ah Ning took the dish of tea from the tray that Dr. See offered. "It is very disquieting. It appears that Ah Sung was not sent to your house by Wa Kee. He went on his own. We have no idea who told him that you needed a cook."

"Then he must have been sent there to spy on me." Emily was angry with herself for feeling so hurt. She had liked Ah Sung. But she had suspected him almost from the beginning. She would like it if, just once, her misgivings were not proved correct.

Ah Ning wasn't so sure her conclusion was accurate. "He may have overheard someone saying that you needed a cook and decided to see you on his own. It's possible that his only mistake was to go to you directly so that he wouldn't need to pay a part of his wages to Wa Kee."

"That is so." Emily nodded over her dish of tea. "But it is also possible that he was paid by someone else to search my house."

"And I am sorry to say that I have not discovered who that could be." Ah Ning paused to give more drama to his next statement. "However, several of my informants have independently told me that Ah Sung was seen more than once with a Daniel Smith."

"What?" Emily spilt her tea. "Oh, I apologize for my clumsiness, Dr. See. Please excuse me."

The doctor refilled her dish. Emily took it in both hands in an effort to stop the trembling.

"Are you quite sure?" she quavered. She thought a word that would have horrified her parents. "The men in America look so much alike, with their horrible whiskers. . . ."

"There is no doubt of it, Mrs. Stratton," Ah Ning said gently. "It may have been a quite innocent connection. However, considering that both men are now deceased, one must consider that they had together become involved in something extremely dangerous."

Emily nodded, unable to speak. She had believed that Smith was trying to help her. Even now, looking back, it seemed impossible that he hadn't been. He had told her he was afraid of that railroad man. What if he had felt the danger but not realized the source?

"Perhaps they both trusted the wrong person," Ah Ning suggested.

Emily thought about that. A phrase of her father's came to mind.

"Satan has a fair face," she said.

"If evil were ugly, everyone would avoid it," Ah Ning agreed. "It may be that both Ah Sung and Daniel Smith were tricked."

Emily's ride home was all too short to absorb the information Ah Ning had given her. She did remember to ask him about Lun Ho. Both men confirmed the cook's story. He had been known in Shanghai and had made a good income working for the Sassoons, but the lure of the Gold Mountain had been too strong for him and he had given up his position with the Sassoon family to come to the gold mines of California. Like so many others, he had then come up to Portland to earn enough to get a stake for the northern mines. He had tried the Jewish families first, but the Germans had not needed a Chinese Persian Kosher cook. Since he didn't speak the same language as most of the other Chinese, he was kept an outsider in that community also.

Emily thought he would fit in to her family quite well.

That evening Lun Ho prepared something with chicken, rice, dried apricots and an assortment of spices. Emily had never tasted anything like it before, but it made her resolve to protect Lun Ho with her life and pay him anything he asked.

Even Mary Kate had been induced by the aroma to try the dish.

"I think my mouth has just had a preview of heaven!" she sighed. "Mr. Lun, did you leave a wife behind in China?"

"Mary Kate!" John was shocked.

"John Patrick Mahoney," Mary Kate said. "A man who can cook like that could have any woman he wanted. I just wanted to know if he'd found one."

Lun Ho hadn't followed the conversation completely, but he had understood Mary Kate's question. "No wife," he said sadly. "She die."

Mary Kate was instantly repentant. "You just ignore my talk, Mr. Lun," she said. "My mother always told me my tongue would get me in trouble, and she was a good, truthful woman."

"As if he'd even want a woman with big clumping feet like yours," John teased.

Mary Kate tossed her head. "They won't fit into those Chinese-lady baby shoes that the missus has in her trunk, but I've been told my feet are quite dainty."

She took off her slipper and showed it to him as proof.

Lun Ho was totally confused. There was only one thing for him to do. "More?" he asked.

Emily couldn't sleep at all that night. She kept imagining Daniel Smith going unsuspecting to his death at the hands of someone he had thought a friend. Mr. Carmichael kept appearing in the role of the villain. He had admitted that he had known Smith. Had he also been the one who contacted Ah Sung? Of course, Mr. King was also likely. Smith had worked for his company.

On the whole, Emily preferred King or Andrews to have killed Mr. Smith. Perhaps Mr. Andrews wasn't as feeble as he appeared. What if he had gone on his trip to avoid being arrested for murder? He might not know that the city wouldn't pay for an investigation. And Mr. King could be in much better shape than he looked, certainly well able to swing a meat grinder.

All she needed was proof.

In his room, Robert was also sleepless. Having spent most of the day in bed, he was full of energy and wondering if Lily was taken for the evening. Ned always said he saved her especially for him, but Robert was no country Reuben. He knew the girl would be sold to anyone who came around with cash. Anyway, it was better not to seem too eager. He didn't want to have any more opium forced on him, either.

But the Hellhole wasn't the only saloon in town. And Lily wasn't the only entertainment. Quietly, he got out of bed and rummaged in his stocking drawer for the bag of dollar gold pieces he had filched one by one from his mother's purse. It would be enough for a stake at a poker table. If he won, good. If he lost, he'd go home when the money was gone.

Robert wasn't obsessed with gambling, or whiskey, or even women, although they could be more compelling than the other two. He was disgusted with men who were. It never occurred to him that the need to experience any vice going was an obsession in itself. Still, he felt that his nightly excursions were a necessary part of life. On their trip together to Boston, his father had encouraged him to sample various pleasures. The only rule that was ever impressed upon him was, "Don't let your mother know." That had become a sacred commandment.

The other thing that his father had taught him was never to lose control of himself. Horace would have been furious about the opium. Alcohol had never really affected him. Robert admired the fact that his father could drink a bottle of rum and still walk a deck in a full gale. But he refused to even try drugs. "Got to keep your wits about you, boy," he'd said. "Or else the bastards will rob you blind."

Horace had been larger than life. When he gave a command, his men jumped to obey. They respected him. Robert knew his father was not always kind to his mother, but he meant to be. Of course he did. Strong men had rough edges. You had to learn to accept that. He feared that his poor mother never had.

The night was cold and blustery. The snow was melting, but a cold rain had replaced it. Robert was halfway down the trellis by his window before he thought of what it would be like to have to climb back up in this weather. He decided he'd face that when he had to. Perhaps the night would suddenly turn balmy.

He went to a saloon near the gasworks. It had no name and was nothing more than a shed leaning against a more respectable building. Inside there was always a poker game going on. The owner usually had a barrel of beer he'd bought from Henry Weinhard, a German brewer who had set up shop down the street.

Robert went in and took an empty seat.

"Deal me in the next hand," he said.

One of men looked at him and sneered. "You can't play here; kid, you don't even shave."

"Neither do you," Robert shot back. "Or bathe, but I don't mind. I'll take any man's money."

"You little . . ." The man started to rise.

"Hey, Sam." The owner tapped him on the shoulder hard enough to keep him in his chair. He leaned over and whispered a few words.

Sam's expression changed. "You don't say!" He looked at Robert with a kind of awe. "So you're Horace's boy. I shoulda known. Well, that being the case, I say, deal him in."

That was the kind of respect Robert wanted to earn for himself.

The wind was blowing the rain sideways by the time Robert decided he had won enough and cashed in. He bought a round for the house, now down to five people, before he bid them all a good night. Two steps into the storm brought him to complete sobriety. He should have worn a rain slicker instead of his greatcoat. By the time he reached his house, he was drenched to the skin. The trellis shook in the wind. He couldn't even see the top of it.

He had his house key, of course. But the front door creaked, as did the stairs. And even worse, Cerberus was now roaming the house, protecting them at night. His bark would wake not only his mother but half the town. How could he explain it when he became the first burglar the dog caught?

Robert circled the house with the thought of trying the kitchen door. Lun Ho would be asleep in the room next to it, but a good Chinese servant wouldn't dream of questioning his employer's behavior, however odd. That still left the problem of the dog.

As he came around the corner of the house, he noticed a light in the room above the carriage house. John was still awake! He could stay in the stable the rest of the night, dry out his clothes and then come upstairs in the morning as if he'd just been out for an early walk.

He let himself in and began to take off his wet things, throwing them onto the seats of the carriage. He noticed a sound coming from above, a sort of rhythmic grunting. Robert smirked. His mother would be horrified if she knew that John had brought a woman up to his room. That could be useful. He wondered what she looked like. He took off his boots and tip-toed up the steps.

The lamplight in the room was soft. The bed in the corner lay in shadow. As Robert peered over the opening, John gave a long moan and rolled off his partner. Both of them sat up. Robert's eyes bugged out. This was something he hadn't tried, yet.

He must have made a noise for John turned suddenly.

"Who's there?" he called.

Robert tried to escape but the men were on him at once. They dragged him the rest of the way up the stairs and threw him on the floor. He looked from one naked man to the other.

He said the first thing that came into his mind. "Mary Kate is going to be so disappointed when she learns about this,"

"She isn't going to," John told him. "Nor is your mother, or she'll learn quick enough about all your midnight expeditions."

"She wouldn't believe you," Robert shot back.

"There's enough other people who'd swear to my side," John answered. "Alec, here, for one."

Robert had already recognized the other man. He was a clerk at one of the drugstores in town. Robert hadn't bothered to hide his activities from anyone but Emily, so he knew he was at a disadvantage. He'd bet no one knew about what these two were up to.

"I'm not going to say anything," he told John and Alec. "I know all about your sort. Father told me that the mandarins had little boys as concu-bines. If I was bad, he said he'd sell me to them."

"We aren't interested in little boys," John said. "Your father was a . . . Well, never mind what. Just forget you ever saw us here."

"That's not going to be easy." Robert shook his head. "But if you let me dry off in the stable and wake me as soon as it's light, I'll keep my mouth shut."

"Deal." John held out his hand. Robert looked at it nervously. He got to his feet.

"Deal," he repeated. "I'll just go down now and hang up my coat to dry. Is there an extra blanket?"

"New horse blankets in the stalls," John said. "Never used and warm enough, I'm sure."

"Fine. Thanks," Robert carefully backed down the stairs, his eyes fixed on Alec and John.

There was a whispered argument above him as Robert made up a bed for himself in the fresh straw. A few minutes later, Alec, now fully dressed, came down the stairs and let himself out. Although Robert lay tensely awake the rest of the night, John didn't leave his room.

These adventures of his were becoming less and less worth the effort.

"Darling, what are you doing up so early on a Saturday?" Emily exclaimed when she came down and found Robert just coming into the kitchen from outside.

"I woke up and thought I'd go out to help John get the stables ready," Robert smiled. "Right, John?"

"Yes, and a grand helper he is." John reached out to pat Robert's head.

"That was thoughtful of you, dear." Emily looked at him fondly. "Lun Ho has made noodle soup for us *and* bacon and eggs for Mary Kate and John."

"Could I have some of everything?" Robert sat down and prepared to attack anything he could reach with a fork and spoon.

"Will you be able to bring the horses home today?" Emily asked John.

"Thanks to young Mr. Robert here, everything is set." John was shoveling food down almost as quickly as Robert.

Emily watched in amazement as the food vanished.

"You must have both worked very hard," she commented.

Robert sprayed soup across the table.

"Sorry, Mother, Mary Kate, sorry," he said. "Something must have gone down wrong."

"That's all right, dear." Emily wiped soup off her cheek. "John, if you could bring the carriage around at one, I need to pay calls today."

"Certainly, ma'am."

"Since you have so much energy today, Robert," Emily suggested, "why don't you take Cerberus for a run?"

All he wanted was a hot bath and a warm bed, but Robert smiled and said that sounded like jolly fun.

Robert had never bothered with the religion of his grandparents. But this morning, he had the distinct feeling that Someone was teaching him a lesson.

Emily dutifully made the rounds of those who had paid visits to her or left their cards. She brought a Chinese embroidered silk shawl to Dr. Thompson to thank her for attending to Mrs. Bechner. She sipped tea with Mrs. Ladd, the only woman she had ever met who had a ship named after her. Horace would never have thought of naming even a rowboat the *Emily*. She listened politely to Alice's recital of the doings of her friends and the peccadilloes of her enemies and then listened with pleasure to a piano recital from Felicity. At each home she would casually ask about the railroad controversy.

Everyone knew about it and all had opinions but no real information.

At last she arrived at the Eliots' home.

Etta welcomed her warmly.

"Do come in!" she said. "Tell your driver to go to the kitchen and Molly will give him some hot cider."

"I'm sure he'd appreciate it." Emily signaled to John to go to the back. "Am I interrupting you?"

"Not at all." Etta led her into the parlor. "Mrs. Burrell has taken Willie for the day. Tom is hard at work on his sermon. I have nothing to do but laze about until someone comes to amuse me."

She laughed as Emily spotted the sewing basket and the pile of mended baby clothes.

"I confess that the art of proper lazing has always eluded me," Etta admitted. "Now, please sit down and tell me how you are doing. I take it that they still don't know who killed that man in your home?"

Emily removed her gloves and took her fifth cup of tea that afternoon. "I'm afraid not. Marshal Jacobi came by to tell me that he wasn't giving up, though. He was thinking of asking the sheriff to help him. I don't actually know the difference."

"One is for the city, the other the county," Etta explained. "But in

Portland they are about the same thing. Marshal Jacobi tends to matters on this side of the river and Sheriff Siletz handles the unincorporated areas, mostly on the east side."

That reminded Emily of the railroad dispute.

"So the East Side Railroad Company is putting their tracks in a place not under city jurisdiction?" she asked. She didn't know if that made any difference, but it was worth considering.

"I honestly don't know," Etta said. "Are you particularly interested in the railroad?"

"I've been hearing about it everywhere," Emily answered. "But I can't understand the issues involved at all. I even went to the lending library to read up on it."

Etta glanced over to the closed door on her right. She thought a moment.

"I should ask Tom first," she said. "But I don't see how he could mind. Mr. and Mrs. Reed are lunching here tomorrow, between the services. We'd be happy to have you join us. Then you could ask Mr. Reed all about it. He's chairman of the Westsiders."

Emily wasn't sure that would be of much use, but she accepted with thanks.

Someone must have a clue as to what was going on. She had to find out. The next attack might well be aimed at her. Or her precious Robert.

CHAPTER TWENTY-FOUR

Mar. 15, 1868 Father says that they will have a railroad out there in about four years and when they do he will go up there and take breakfast there with you.

—LETTER TO TOM ELIOT FROM HIS BROTHER, EDWARD

W as that Emily Stratton who just left?" Matthew King had seen the carriage from his bedroom window and run down just in time to catch sight of the door closing on a black-garbed figure.

"Yes. She didn't stay long," Dorothea told him. "It was just a duty call. I'm afraid she and I really have nothing in common."

"Well, you'd better find something." He looked at his wife with contempt. "At the moment she controls over half my company. I just found out that idiot Andrews sold part of his share to Stratton before he died. It gives his widow fifty-three percent. I just hope to God she hasn't added it up yet, but the way that woman studies the books, she might well be planning even now to take charge."

"Gracious!" Dorothea reached for her smelling salts. "What would happen then?"

"I don't know." His expression was grim. "But from the things she's said already, she'd get rid of our most lucrative trade. Hell, she might give it all to the damn Methodists. So you plan on staying on her good side, if you don't want to end up drinking your tea on a packing box on Second Street."

His wife drew herself up sharply. "I'll do my job, just as I always do, Matthew. But you had better take care of Emily Stratton. I've no intention of becoming a pauper because of someone like that."

"Oh, I intend to, my dear." His tone left no doubt. "I intend to."

The question was, how? It had to look like an accident. Perhaps not even a fatal one, as long as she finally understood that he was determined to keep her from ruining his life's work. The worst of it was that he could just see Horace looking up and laughing at the predicament he'd left for his partner to get out of.

"Don't worry, 'old friend,'" he muttered as he went back to his den upstairs. "I'll take care of your uppity widow and, when I'm done, that boy of yours won't have so much as a pot to piss in."

Robert needed time to think about what he had seen the night before. This wasn't the sort of thing he wanted to confide to Jack and Hank. They wouldn't understand. He was fairly certain that any adult he told would see to it that John was fired at once and Alec, too. That didn't seem right to Robert. He figured that if he could whore, drink, gamble, and smoke opium, others should have a right to their own roads to perdition. But the memory of those two bodies made him squirm inside.

It was too wet to go hiking in the woods. He couldn't stay at home. He didn't want to see his friends.

So he did something that would have astonished his father. He went down to the gymnasium of the Young Men's Christian Association.

He signed in and paid, and the attendant assigned him a shelf to put his things and showed him where the medicine balls and other exercise equipment were kept.

"We have a bowling alley, too," he told Robert proudly. "But you'll have to rent special shoes for that."

Robert was surprised at how many boys from school were there. Several of them were tossing a medicine ball around. He joined them.

The first time the ball came to him, it knocked him over.

The others laughed.

"Hey, Stratton!" John Borver, a lanky boy his age jeered. "You don't ever lift anything heavier than a glass. You've gone soft!"

"You shouldn't be in here anyway," Oliver Harvey added. "This is a temperance group."

Robert struggled up. One of his best talents was never to give in to anger.

"I thought I'd hop on the water wagon for baseball season," he grinned at them. "Would you turn away a poor repentant sinner?"

He made a show of straining to lift the ball, then threw it as hard as he could at Oliver, who caught it easily.

"I guess we should help you get in shape," Oliver decided. "What do the rest of you think?"

"Sure, but I can't see you playing second base even if you exercise from now until June," said John, who was the star player at the Academy.

The rest of the boys followed their lead, and Robert spent half an hour tossing the ball back and forth. He had to admit that they were right. His arms felt on fire. At school in Boston he had played all kinds of sports: baseball, rugby, foot racing, skating. He hadn't done anything like that for months. First there was the long trip to San Francisco, then weeks of sorting out his father's papers, then the journey to Portland. He couldn't believe that he had become so weak in that time.

After a while, he decided to go watch the bowlers. He had played a few times at school, but he'd never been any good at it. Still, it was fun to watch.

He picked a corner where he could see but be out of the way. Soon he was on his feet, cheering as a man knocked down the widely spaced pins his partner had left. When he sat down, he realized that someone had joined him. It was Alec.

Robert moved a bit farther down the bench.

"You needn't worry," Alec said. "I just want to talk to you."

"I told John I wouldn't say anything," Robert said. "What else is there to talk about?"

Alec sighed. "I suppose I just wanted to explain. But I can't give you an explanation that you could understand. The only one I ever received was that God had cursed me. I've tried to break the curse, but there doesn't seem to be anything I can do about it. John says that at least we can go to Hell together."

Robert had a clear vision of himself traveling that road just behind them. But, no, his vices were normal ones. Right. And he could give them up any time.

"I don't know anything about that sort of thing," he told Alec. "I'll keep my word, though, as long as you don't try anything with me."

"Of course not!" Alec seemed horrified at the idea. "Why should I? But, since you've promised not to tell on us, there's something you might want to know. It's about Mr. King."

Robert gulped. "Is he one of you, too?"

"No," Alec laughed. "At least, I don't think so. No, it's about the drugstore where I work. I know that Mr. Andrews keeps insisting to anyone who will listen that the oysters didn't make him sick."

"I was there," Robert shuddered. "It smelled like bad oysters to me."

"Maybe," Alec said. "But I think it strange that the day before he was taken sick, Mr. King came in to the shop and bought an unusually large amount of emetic."

That brought Robert up short.

"Just thought you and your mother would like to know," Alec added. "Seeing as Mr. Andrews has vanished and King has told people that your mother is sticking her nose into things that weren't any woman's business."

"You think he might hurt my mother!"

"Look, I may be completely mistaken," Alec said, trying to calm him. "But it's better to be forewarned, don't you think?"

"Yes," Robert said. "Thank you."

"And you'll keep your promise?" Alec's tone was a cross between a plea and a threat.

"Yes, you needn't worry." Robert was trying to digest this new information. He barely noticed when Alec left.

It couldn't be true. He had no fondness for King, but no one could be such a swine as to want to harm his mother. She was the most inoffensive of people. He couldn't ever remember her yelling at him, or switching him. She had given him complete love for his whole life. It embarrassed him to remember it, but he had cried himself to sleep the first weeks at boarding school because he missed her so.

Could this have anything to do with the break-ins at the house, or the murder? Why hadn't he realized it before? He had thought that Daniel Smith had been killed because of a personal feud, maybe someone else who wanted to rob them. The fact was he hadn't tried to think it out at all.

The champion bowler scored again. Robert had lost interest.

He went back to where the other boys were now lifting weights and doing laps around the gym. He sighed and joined them again.

If his mother was in danger, he had to be strong enough to protect her.

Emily at that moment was feeling quite secure and content. Talking with Etta Eliot had that effect on her. The younger woman seemed so fundamentally happy with her life that it just spilled over onto those around her. Added to that, Emily could expect a decent dinner for a change at home and the chance at luncheon tomorrow to query Mr. Reed about the railroad issues.

She had also completed all the calls that duty called upon her to pay. For the moment all was right with the world.

When they rolled into the courtyard, John proudly took the horses into their refurbished stalls. Emily went with him to admire them.

"Excellent, John," she told him. "They should do fine here. Let me know if anything else is needed."

As she walked to the house, Emily had the feeling that something was wrong, but what? She paused and looked around. Then it hit her. Cerberus hadn't barked when they came in. He certainly had been making a racket when they left. Had Mary Kate brought him into the house for some reason? He was supposed to come in only when they all went to bed.

She went to the kitchen, where she found Lun Ho chopping vegetables while Mary Kate sat and watched him in admiration.

"To think you can do all that just with carrots and cabbage," she was saying. "I can't wait to see what you cook when the garden comes up."

"Mary Kate, is Cerberus in the house?" Emily interrupted.

The maid stood at once. "No, ma'am. Isn't he in his pen?"

"I didn't look. I just assumed he was in here." Emily went back to the fenced-in area where Cerberus spent his days. She didn't see him. There was a lean-to against one side and she peered in, but it was empty, too. He couldn't have jumped out. The fence was much too high. She went back to the gate. Had Robert left the latch up when he put the dog in that morning? Whatever had happened, Cerberus was definitely gone.

In spite of her alarm, Emily felt a grim satisfaction. She finally had a case that Marshal Jacobi would be paid to handle.

Robert was sure he had latched the gate that morning. "I even shook it to be sure, Mother," he insisted. "Someone must have let him out."

Neither he nor Emily said what they had thought of first. Cerberus had been set free so that the house would be vulnerable again. Robert shivered. This made Alec's information all the more plausible.

"It's still light," he said. "Why don't John and I ride over and see if he went back to Hank's uncle's place?"

"I suppose you should," Emily said slowly. "But just go there and back. No stopping to look someplace else."

"Very well." Robert hugged her. "I'm sure he just decided to go visit his old home."

Emily hoped that was true. But all the evidence pointed to the conclusion that they were being told, over and over, in a dozen different ways, that they should abandon Portland and go back to China where they belonged.

Mary Kate had just finished lighting the gas lamps when John and Robert returned.

"He didn't go home," Robert announced. "Hank's uncle says he'll bring him back to us if Cerberus shows up there."

"With all that's happened around the place," John added, "I think I should keep watch tonight in the entry. Do you have a pistol?"

"Yes," Emily said. "Horace kept one in his den. But I don't like to ask it of you. You weren't hired to be a guard."

"Just part of the service." He put one foot out and bowed like a courtier.

"Tomorrow, if Cerberus can't be found, we'll get another dog," Emily promised.

"We should be doing that," Mary Kate added, nodding at John with a grin. "Of the two of you, I trust the dog more."

At that moment, Lun Ho began ringing the little gong that announced dinner. Mary Kate smoothed her apron.

"There now," she told Emily. "You and Master Robert go sit yourselves down. The table is ready, and I'll bring in whatever strange thing we're eating for supper. I tell you it won't matter. That man could cook a slug so that I'd eat it and smack my lips."

Only Lun Ho slept that night. Every gust of wind or cracking tree branch brought Emily upright listening for footsteps. Robert went to bed and then got up every fifteen minutes to check all the windows and make sure John was still awake. In her room, Mary Kate said a novena to prepare herself for whatever disaster might befall them next.

Sunday dawned peacefully.

Emily dragged herself out of bed and prepared for church. She looked out the window. Cold and rainy, what a surprise. She couldn't ask John to drive her when he had been up all night. She'd just have to bundle up and take the umbrella. Third and Taylor wasn't that far away.

It was all she could do to keep from yawning through the sermon. She hoped no one quizzed her on it. As soon as the service was over, she slipped out and hurried home to change for luncheon with the Eliots.

She held the umbrella in front of her face to block the wind and thus she couldn't see much, but she became aware that there was a pair of long, trousered legs keeping pace with her. She stopped and tilted the umbrella back.

"May I see you to your house, Mrs. Stratton?" Mr. Carmichael was wearing the oilskin suit of a New England fisherman. Rain rolled off it and harmlessly to the ground. Emily was jealous of the warmth and impermeability of his garb. Why didn't anyone design something like that for women? "I know I said I wouldn't bother you, but I don't like to see anyone fighting this weather without a guide."

"Thank you, Mr. Carmichael," she said. "But I wouldn't ask anyone to stay out in this a minute more than necessary."

"Oh, I'm quite comfortable." He offered her his arm. "I rather enjoy days like this. It sets the blood racing, don't you think?"

She didn't see any way out of it. Fortunately the weather made conversation difficult. They continued in silence. All the while Emily was think-ing, *Did you wear that to let my dog out? What do you know too much about? Why do you want to drive me away from here?*

During a lull in the wind, she took a peek around the edge of the um-brella. He smiled at her, his blue eyes guileless. The tip of his nose was red from the cold. She went back into hiding. He seemed so sweet and innocu-ous. If only she knew that there was no hidden wickedness lurking behind that pleasant exterior.

At one o'clock, Emily presented herself at the Eliot's door. In her hand was a jar of pickled beets that Mrs. Bechner had put up before her hasty depar-ture. She handed this to the maid, Molly, as soon as she opened the door.

"I hope the Eliots are expecting me," she said.

"Of course they are." Molly took her wraps. "And looking forward to it ever so much." She helped Emily off with her overshoes and led her into the parlor.

The Reeds had already arrived. Both men stood when she came in.

"Mrs. Stratton, delighted that you could come." Tom took her hand and showed her to a chair.

Amanda Reed was seated with Willie on her lap. She nodded to Emily happily as she waved a plush duck at the baby.

"I'm sorry I haven't come by," she told Emily. "Sim and I went down to San Francisco to see about the furnishings for the house we're building. And Sim had some business to do, too."

"About the proposed railroad?" Emily asked.

He regarded her in surprise. "As a matter of fact, I did do some order-ing," Reed answered. "Equipment of various kinds. Are you interested in railroad construction, Mrs. Stratton?"

"More in the financing of it," she answered with what she hoped was a businesslike manner. "I've been going over my late husband's accounts. He seems to have settled our money almost entirely in the import and export trade. I think I should diversify. Everyone says the railroad is the way of the future."

"Oh, I agree," Reed said heartily. "Especially here in the west. Ship-ping will take a beating once the cross-continental link is finished. Think of how much time and money will be saved by not having to go around the horn or put goods on the train across the Isthmus of Panama. And wouldn't it be wonderful to be able to take a train all the way down to San Francisco, instead of risking the stage or a steamship down the coast?"

Emily clapped her hands. "You've quite convinced me, Mr. Reed! I shall certainly invest at once." She paused. "But I understand that there are two railroad companies proposing to construct the Portland-to-California line. I don't know which one to choose."

"Mrs. Stratton, there is really only one choice," Reed said earnestly. "Our company is the only legitimate one. The future is with the West Side Oregon Central Railroad."

"I don't really understand it," Emily replied. "I've heard and read so much conflicting information. For instance, some people say that it would be better to support the east side because it is being funded by a California man who has almost unlimited resources to spend on it. Is that so?"

Reed's manner chilled suddenly. "I presume you are referring to Ben Holladay. I have done business with him, and I never met a more unprincipled man. There are rumors that he is interested in buying out the East-siders, but I have no proof of that. However, either way, they are a bad investment. If Holladay does come in, then your money is in the hands of a scoundrel and profligate. If he doesn't, the Eastsiders run out of cash and won't be able to finish the twenty miles of track in time to get the government land grant."

"I see," Emily said slowly. "But isn't there also some legal question about which company is properly incorporated?"

"You have been doing your homework," Reed said. "Yes, the matter is before the state legislature. But I am confident that they will decide in our favor. Our documents are all in order. There can be no question that we are in the right."

Unless, Emily thought, *someone were to pay key representatives to vote for the other side.*

"I appreciate your explaining all this to me," she told him. "And to the rest of you for taking up your time. The responsibility of providing for myself and my son weighs heavily on me at the moment. It's very important that we have enough to remain comfortable."

"From what I understand of the state of Stratton, Andrews, and King," Reed said, having thawed again, "you need have no fears on that account."

Emily gave Etta Eliot a sideways glance; Etta nodded encouragingly.

"Actually . . ." She took a deep breath. "I was thinking of selling my shares in the company. The China trade no longer appeals to me. There are aspects of it that may be legal but, to my mind, are not moral."

"Bravo!" Amanda Reed had been silent up until now. "More investors should believe as you do, Mrs. Stratton."

"Emily has also expressed an interest in the Ladies Aid Society," Etta told her. "I was intending to propose her for membership at the next meeting."

"You can be sure I shall second it." Mrs. Reed beamed at Emily from behind her wire-rimmed glasses.

"Well, if we've finished our serious discussions," Tom Eliot said, "I believe Molly is waiting to serve our luncheon."

The meal was lovely, and Emily stayed out of politeness to accompany the others to the church to hear Reverend Eliot's afternoon sermon, on human nature. She wasn't surprised to learn that he had a hopeful view of it.

The warm glow engendered by the good food and company lasted all the way home. As her carriage came up the drive, though, she saw that someone had come calling. She wished she had arrived ten minutes later.

Standing at her front door were Matthew and Dorothea King.

CHAPTER TWENTY-FIVE

Feel as if I could never write again

—THOMAS LAMB ELIOT, DIARY, SUNDAY, MARCH 15, 1868

The Kings both turned at the sound of her carriage. Emily knew there was no way to avoid inviting them in, although for a second she considered calling to John to race off as quickly as the horses could gallop.

Reluctantly she descended.

"Good afternoon!" She plastered on a smile. "How kind of you to pay me a visit on such a dreary day! I'm just returning from calls, myself. Please come in. I'm sure Mary Kate has built a fire in the parlor. And you must try some of Lun Ho's Chinese hors d'oeuvres. He is a most exceptional cook."

She knew she was babbling but couldn't stop. The door opened as she was fumbling with it.

"Hullo, Mother." Robert held out his hands for her bag and keys. "Mr. and Mrs. King, I believe we met at church a while ago. How nice to see you again."

"My dear, I didn't know you'd be home so soon." Emily hugged him.

"Could you call Mary Kate to hang up our damp coats in the kitchen and tell Lun Ho to make tea and some of those little *shao mai* he does so well?"

The Kings looked a bit nervous at the prospect of food with an Oriental name. However, their coats, hats, and scarves were taken from them and their overshoes set by the parlor fire, so they had no recourse except to carry on.

Soon they were all seated, sipping black tea with sugar and cream, a great relief to Dorothea King. She looked at the steamed bits of pastry on the tray. Would it be better to know what was in them or just close her mouth and swallow? Next to her, Matthew was chewing one with every appearance of enjoyment. Emily and her son were also devouring the things. Hesitantly, she took a bite.

"Why, it's delicious!" she exclaimed.

"Isn't it?" Emily said. "Lun Ho is a marvel with chicken gizzards."

Dorothea relaxed. "I normally just chop the gizzards to put in gravy," she said. "I never thought there was anything else to be made from them. Do you think he'd give me the recipe?"

"I don't know," Emily said. "I'll ask him."

She poured another cup of tea all around, feeling much less tense. It seemed that her nervousness was groundless.

Mr. King put down his cup and cleared his throat.

"I'm glad that Robert is here today," he began portentously. "There are important matters that we need to discuss and they concern him, too."

Immediately, Emily was again on her guard.

"Really, don't you think it would be better to do this at your office?" she begged. "And, if it has to do with the company, we should wait for Mr. Andrews to return."

"I'm afraid that Andrews isn't returning," King stated. "He didn't go for a health cure. He has absconded, taking a great deal of money with him."

Emily gasped. "Then we must search for him," she demanded. "We can telegraph to San Francisco or Chicago for the police there to be on the lookout for him."

"I already have," King lied. "But he could have gone to ground in any one of a hundred places. He may already be out of the country for all we know. We need to rally together to keep our investors from losing faith."

"What should we do?" Robert asked.

"Well." King took out a small notebook and consulted it. "By my reckoning, he got over ten thousand dollars in gold. If we each put in five thousand of our own funds, no one will be the wiser."

"Does that mean that Robert and I would then own half of Mr. Andrews's shares?" Emily wanted to know.

Curse the woman! He had hoped she wouldn't figure that out.

"This is beyond his shares, which really didn't amount to much, as I discovered." He shook his head sadly. "He had been selling them off for some time, perhaps in preparation for this move."

"I think I would rather buy back those shares than put more money in at the moment." Emily folded her hands as if closing the subject.

"I don't think you understand." Dorothea tried to help. "The shares are just pieces of paper that represent the ships and stock. Matthew needs cash to pay bills that are due now."

"Yes, Mrs. King, but if mother buys more shares then you will have the cash, don't you see?" It was clear enough to Robert.

"Yes, I'll be happy to buy another five thousand in shares for now," Emily said. "At least until Mr. Andrews is found. You may draw up the papers the first thing tomorrow and bring them to me to sign."

This was not going the way King had intended. She already owned more than half the company. He was terrified that she would soon discover it. If she started checking on how much Andrews had left, it wouldn't take long for her to realize that she was the major shareholder.

"That's all very well," he explained quickly. "But first we'd have to find someone willing to sell. By the time we had done that, all the bills would be past due, don't you see?"

Emily thought. "Well, I could give the company a personal loan, instead," she offered. "I'll ask one of the attorneys in town to draw up a letter of indebiture."

King stood up so suddenly that he knocked the tea tray on the floor.

"I have never been so insulted in my life," he roared. "Horace would be ashamed of you for being so petty when the company he founded is at stake. Have you no sense of honor?"

Robert and Emily both bent to pick up the tea things. Emily sopped the spilled milk off the carpet with her napkin. She was grateful for the distraction. If she spoke now, she was sure to accuse King of being as venal as Andrews. That would only infuriate him more.

Robert looked up. "There's someone at the door, Mother. Shall I see who it is?"

"Oh, yes!" Emily said fervently.

She filled in the time by ringing for Mary Kate.

"Mrs. Stratton." King had recovered his temper somewhat. "I'm sure that when you look at this rationally, you'll see that this is our only recourse. I apologize for becoming annoyed. A woman in your position should not be expected to understand the intricacies of trade."

"All the more reason why I should learn." Emily couldn't hold back the retort. Unbidden, she remembered Mr. Carmichael's passionate argument for just that.

"Emily dear, I hope you don't mind our dropping by so late." Alice breezed into the room, followed by George.

Emily had never been so glad to see them.

"Matthew, Dorothea, how lovely!" Alice gushed. "What a pleasant surprise!"

"I heard from Sam Tyler that your dog ran off," George said to Robert. "If he doesn't turn up soon, why don't we go over the river to Linnton and see if we can get you another?"

"Thank you, Uncle," Robert said. "Although I hope he'll turn up soon. Cerberus wasn't here long enough to know it was his home, I guess. I'll remember to keep the next one tied up until he understands."

"George," Emily said after Mary Kate had brought in tea and cups. "Mr. King has been trying to explain a problem with the company to me, but I don't seem to be able to grasp it. Perhaps you could help."

"That's really not appropriate," King jumped in. "George isn't a member of the firm."

"But he is family," Emily told him. "I should have gone to him for advice in any case."

"Don't know how much help I'll be, but I'll give it a shot." George seemed pleased to be asked.

King started to speak, but Emily interrupted. "As I see it," she said, "Stratton, Andrews, and King has a cash flow problem due to Mr. Andrews's sudden absence. Mr. King proposes that we each put five thousand dollars into the company. However, he feels I'm being churlish to want a promissory note in exchange. Isn't that the normal procedure?"

Her brother-in-law laughed and slapped his thigh. "No flies on you, Emily! I can tell you that Horace never let a cent out of his paws without a receipt of some sort."

Matthew King spoke through tight lips. "There is such a thing as an agreement between gentlemen, especially partners," he pointed out.

"Yes, but don't you see, *she's* no gentleman!" George was immoderately amused by his own wit. Emily wondered if he had been imbibing.

King stood and took his wife's arm.

"Obviously, my proposal will get no serious consideration today," he said. "I shall find some way to pay our debts without alarming the shareholders. And I trust that this conversation will go no farther."

"Certainly." George was still tickled by his joke. "I'm a gentleman, at any rate, and I don't see why Emily and Robert would want to jeopardize their income."

"Thank you for that, at least. Come, Dorothea." And with what dignity he could muster, Matthew King departed.

"I can't imagine why old Horace ever took up with a stiff poker like that," George observed. "Now, Alice, you didn't tell Emily and Robert why we came tonight."

"I didn't exactly have the opportunity," Alice said. "We were hoping that you two would like to accompany us tomorrow evening to a recital that Felicity is giving."

"We'd be delighted!" Emily said. "She's very talented. It would be a pleasure, wouldn't it, Robert?"

"Oh, yes. Mother has told me of Felicity's skill," Robert said dryly, "I can't think of anything I'd enjoy more."

Alice and George left soon after, in time for Emily and Robert to have dinner. Afterward, Robert excused himself to do schoolwork.

He dashed off an essay at his desk, studied a few pages of Greek, and whittled his initials in the arm of his chair while waiting for Emily to come up to bid him good night.

"Don't stay up too late, now," she warned. "You need good marks, of course, but your health is more important."

"I promise, Mother." He kissed her. "I'll stop working on this pretty soon."

He waited half an hour or so, until the house quieted down. Then he slipped into the buckskin pants his uncle had given him and put on a calico shirt, his oldest shoes, and a worn coat. He left his watch and took only enough money for the evening. Despite his scare the Friday before, it seemed a shame not to take advantage of the dog not being around. Lily must be thinking that he had found someone better.

The customers at the Hellhole didn't seem to know it was Sunday. A ship had just arrived, and the place was packed with sailors and dock workers. Robert's heart sank. Ned wouldn't have saved Lily on the chance that he might show up.

He went up to the bar and ordered a beer.

Ned Chambreau gave him a wink. "Sorry, son, she's out of commission tonight. Woman stuff, you know. Don't know if I can fix you up with anyone else. You can see there's a line already."

"That's all right, Ned." Robert took a gulp of beer. "Is it allowed just to go up and chat with Lily?"

"Well, for you she might not mind," Ned said. "Of course, you'll pay the same rate as usual. After all, her mouth is working fine, and you may want it to do more than chat."

He went upstairs to check. When he came back, he motioned to Robert that he could go up.

Lily was sitting on her bed, dressed in a long blue robe. When he opened the door she smiled at him, but for a second, Robert saw another look, one of total despair.

"Mr. Ned, he say you want me lickee you," she said. "You want lip rouge or no?"

She got on her knees and started unbuttoning his pants.

"No!" Robert pushed her away.

"What I do?" She cringed as if expecting a blow.

"Nothing, Lily," Robert told her. "Ned got it wrong, that's all. I just need to talk."

"OK, Mr. Robert, I can listen good," Lily sat back on her bed and patted the space beside her.

He sat next to her without touching. For a while they both just stared at the floor. Finally Robert gave a deep sigh.

"I just don't understand America," he said. "I miss China."

"You know China?" She didn't believe him.

"Didn't anyone tell you? I thought my history was known to everyone in town," he said. "I was born in Shanghai. My father was a merchant and a sea captain. And a lot of other things."

"Mr. Ned, he say I be good to you, because you Captain Stratton's son, but I think you born here." Lily took a chance. "I speak Shanghai."

"You do?" Robert's face lit as he switched to Chinese. "Where did you live? We had a house on Bubbling Well Road. Do you know it?"

"Yes, sometimes we were taken there to walk on Sundays," she answered. Her whole manner changed with the language. Her face had more dignity, and a great deal more sadness. "But I lived on Foochow Road."

"Mother and I sometimes went to the theater there," Robert told her. "Did you?"

That led to a discussion of a traditional play they had both seen.

So they talked, and talked, and talked. Robert told her his fears for his mother and how he really didn't want to go to Harvard and study law. Lily explained how she had come to Shangahi. Her family was starving during the wars that led to the suppression of the Taiping rebellion. So they sold her when she was twelve to an agent who said she would become a domestic servant for a rich family. Instead, he took her to Shanghai, where she was dressed royally and feted at a banquet, at the end of which her virginity went to the highest bidder. After a few months of pampering, she was moved to a lower level of prostitution, and then another, until by the time she was fourteen, she was in a brothel on Foochow Road.

"I wasn't talented enough to become a rich courtesan. My feet had never been bound. So I knew that one day I would be thrown into the streets, good for nothing more than the barbarian sailors." She told her story in a matter-of-fact tone.

Robert had seen these women in Frenchtown. He wouldn't have gone near them.

"So, when Captain Stratton offered to buy me and take me to America—"

"What did you say?" Robert's blood froze. "You can't mean my father?"

"Yes," she said. "I thought you knew that. The other girls were jealous. We all knew that Chinese men went to the Golden Mountain to get rich. There were many men there with much money and no wife. They told me I would soon get a husband and have many sons and grandsons. But it has not happened," she ended wistfully.

Robert was still trying to digest this new facet of his father's trade. He had always believed that he was very much a Stratton, his father's son through and through. Now he realized that his mother had shaped him, as well. He felt sick with shame. Perhaps he wouldn't have been so shocked if it hadn't been a girl he knew.

"Lily," he asked, his mouth gone dry. "Did Captain Stratton ever . . . ever . . . ?"

"Oh, yes." She tried to repress a shudder. "But not like you. He liked . . . different things."

Robert closed his eyes. He wished he could also close his mind. It disgusted him to think of his father using Lily in any way. It disgusted him to know that he had used her with the same lack of concern. The girl sitting beside him was all at once more real than the one who always smiled and seemed eager to have him in her bed.

Lily put her hand on his knee. "I never thought to ask. Do you own me now? Mr. Ned, he is the one who tells me what to do, but maybe Captain Stratton was his master, too."

Robert's head was spinning. This was one too many revelations for him to absorb. Shakily, he stood.

"Are you angry with me?" She reached for him in fear. "I will do anything you tell me, even if you don't own me. You are a nice man."

"No, I'm not angry, not with you." He put on his coat. His hands couldn't manage the buttons. "I need to get home. I have school tomorrow."

"You won't tell Mr. Ned that we talked, will you?" she begged. "I'm not supposed to talk, just work."

"I won't say anything," Robert promised. "Good night, Lily."

After the door shut behind him, Lily buried her face in the pillow and sobbed. Speaking with Robert had brought China too close. She remembered all her stupid dreams for somehow escaping this life. No one would marry her and take her home. She would die in this hard land.

Robert ran home, tripping in the dark once and falling flat on his face. He wasn't thinking. He couldn't. The memory of his father was shattering like a kaleidoscope and reforming in hideous distortion. His climbed the tree to his window, oblivious of branches slapping him or the grating of his hands by the bark. Once in, he threw himself on the bed, willing sleep to bring escape from the images in his head.

Of course he knew that his father hadn't been celibate when away from home. The boys at his school in Boston had taken it for granted that their fathers bought companions from time to time. But he had somehow imagined these women as older, more worldly. They were businesswomen, and everyone enjoyed the business.

Talking with Lily had opened up a window in his head. Through it he saw himself and his father in a much poorer light than ever before.

It was hours before his wish for sleep was granted, and even then, the ache of shame weighed too heavily for him to get any rest.

Chapter Twenty-six

According to the books I made seven thousand dollars for my share the first year, but as I was so far behind when I came to Portland, it took all this sum to pay my debts, pay for my childrens [sic] schooling (I had two of them at Boarding school) to go to housekeeping and get us some good close [sic] all around. I ran this place until the fall of 1868, when my wife prevailed upon me to quit it.

—Autobiography of Ned Chambreau, on his time at the Hellhole

Monday, March 16, 1868

School was a welcome distraction for Robert. His Greek professor was pleasantly surprised by how diligently the Stratton boy followed the lesson that day. Perhaps the lad would make a scholar yet.

"Hey, Stratton!" Hank called to him as they were leaving that afternoon. "Coming with us tonight?"

"I can't," Robert answered. "I said I'd go hear my cousin's recital."

"Too bad." Hank moved closer to him to whisper. "Jack says there's a new dancer in the back room at Charlie L's who can wrap one leg around her neck. Don't you want to see that?"

"Some other time." Robert never thought he'd be grateful to spend an evening listening to piano students slaughtering their recital pieces.

The question kept racing around in his mind: did he, or rather his mother, own a house of prostitution? Did they take a share every time Lily "entertained" a man?

Now he understood why it was so important to Emily to be informed about the businesses they had inherited. What other enterprises had his father been a part of? Was his mother even now investigating them?

A horrible thought hit him. What if she already knew? Oh, Lord! She couldn't. The mere idea of his mother in connection with a place like the Hellhole made his stomach rise.

He raised his hand and begged to be excused. The professor nodded, and Robert rushed from the room. He barely made it to the outhouse in time to throw up his pickles and sandwich.

Emily was also pondering financial matters, but not so dramatically. She knew she could no longer live on the misery and vices of others. But she was also afraid of impoverishing herself and her son. Hating her own hypocrisy, she took out the big account books again, along with all the notes and bits of paper Horace had left. There must be some honestly earned money somewhere!

After a day of poring over pages of squalid but, apparently, legal transactions, it was a refreshing change to go to the basement of the Presbyterian church to listen to Felicity and her fellow music students perform.

George and Alice had saved front-row seats for them. Emily noticed that they were only four.

"Isn't Sarah coming to hear her sister play?" she asked.

"Sarah is indisposed," Alice said, her tone not inviting any questions.

George snorted. He leaned over and murmured to Emily, "Sarah says that she's had to endure three thousand repetitions of the piece; one more would drive her into gibbering madness."

Robert laughed. Alice turned her head to remind him of his manners, but just then the music teacher waved his arms for silence.

"We shall commence our little entertainment," he announced, "with a performance from one of our youngest and most promising pupils, Miss Tara Joy Martin."

A girl of about eight skipped onto the stage and allowed the teacher to help her onto the piano bench. She was dressed like a fairy princess, in blue and gold. Even Robert was enchanted by her innocent poise.

But neither Emily nor Robert was able to concentrate on the music, although Tara Joy's piece was lively and well played. Emily passed the time calculating and recalculating what it would take to allow them to stay in their home and if it could be provided through rents on land Horace had bought in Portland years before along with a much reduced Oriental trade. She was rapidly coming to the conclusion that they would have to sell the house and live in something much smaller. She thought she could endure it. She had lived in poor circumstances before. But Robert never had. He had always had everything he wanted immediately. Would he understand why this was necessary?

She squeezed his hand, reassuring him about a danger he didn't know existed.

Robert barely noticed. He kept looking around the room, wondering how many of the men had visited Lily and if his bank account was the greater for it. He wondered how he could find out if the Strattons were the real owners of the Hellhole. It would explain why Ned always gave him such an enthusiastic welcome. The barkeep probably thought it hilarious to take money from his unknowing boss.

They applauded mightily at the end. Emily noticed Felicity's delight at the praise for her playing and how hard the girl tried to stand with her back straight during the ovation. But when invited for hot chocolate after the performance, both Emily and Robert declined.

When they were snug inside the carriage and sharing a lap robe, Robert took a deep breath and plunged into one of the questions that had been tormenting him.

"Mother, I know you've been studying Father's business records," he began. "Do you happen to know if he had any property here in town, other than our house?"

"Yes," Emily answered carefully. "There are several lots recorded, some of which must have buildings on them for he notes receiving a quarterly rent. Why?"

"I was just wondering." His voice sounded too casual, even to himself. "It seems that land speculation is popular in Portland, and I thought Father may have done some of it. Do you know where the land is?"

"Not really," she admitted. "I have to go to the courthouse and match the plat descriptions to a map. I haven't taken the time, yet. But I intend to, quite soon."

"I could do that for you." Robert now sounded overly eager. "I can go after school tomorrow, if you give me the information."

"Well, of course. I'm delighted that you want to help." Emily patted his cheek. "But why the sudden interest?"

Robert shrugged. "Some of the fellows at school keep bragging about how much of the town their fathers own. I wanted to know if we had a share, too."

In the darkness, Emily sounded concerned. "I hope you don't intend to boast to others about possessions!"

"Of course not, Mother," he said. "I was just curious."

"That's natural, I suppose," she said. "Yes, I'd be grateful if you searched the land records for me. As a matter of fact, I've been thinking of selling off much of the import export business and investing more in local enterprise. What do you think?"

"Oh, Mother!" He kissed her. "I think that would be wonderful!"

"Good." She sounded puzzled. "That's very good, darling." She couldn't imagine why this would make him so happy, but it cheered her to think that he was becoming attached to the town that she had decided to make their home. But was it power and prestige that appealed to him or the place? The prospect of making him give up so much broke her heart.

The next morning, she was copying out the land information for Robert when Mary Kate interrupted to tell her that Marshal Jacobi was waiting in the parlor.

"Did he say what he wanted?" Emily asked.

"Just to see you, ma'am. He'd hardly be telling me police business now, would he?"

Emily had to acknowledge the truth of that.

The marshal was bent over, examining the design on one of her porcelain vases when she came in. He straightened at once, causing the vase to rock on its stand. Emily reached out with a cry. Jacobi caught it as it started to tip.

"I beg your pardon, Mrs. Stratton," he said. "It a beautiful piece of work."

"Thank you," she said. "It's quite old. At least, that's what I was told."

He moved away from it with exaggerated care.

"Please sit down," she offered. "Have you discovered anything more about the death of Mr. Smith?"

He perched on the edge of an overstuffed sofa covered in thick green satin. "It's more that I'm learning a lot about his life," he told her. "It seems that Daniel had some interesting friends. One of them was a man named Tom Ager."

"The name is familiar, but I don't know from where." Emily sat across from him.

"Well." He shifted in embarrassment. "You may have read it in the newspaper. Tom had a problem with . . . uh . . . with . . ."

"Oh, now I remember," she said. "I did read about that. The man who stood by the roadside exposing his privates."

"Uh, yes." Marshal Jacobi was clearly shocked. "That wasn't his only peccadillo. He also seems to have been part of a group that pilfered goods from the docks. A box here and there, the sort of thing that could easily be blamed on a miscount on a lading bill or even on customs men."

"And Mr. Smith was the one who checked off the shipments as they were unloaded," Emily concluded. "Did Mr. Ager tell you all this?"

"No, we guessed that something was going on, but it wasn't until Smith died that the process was revealed." Jacobi paused. "The fact is that Ager is also dead. We found a body in a ravine west of town a few days ago. It was badly decomposed, but we are fairly certain that it was he."

"Do you know how he died?" Emily's stomach began to tighten beneath her corset.

"He was shot," Jacobi told her bluntly. "About the same time your cook was killed."

Emily looked at him, trying to absorb what he was saying.

"You've finally realized that Ah Sung wasn't murdered by another Chinese," she concluded.

"I wouldn't go that far," he said. "But I'm looking into a possible connection. I need more information, though. Is there anything you can add to what you gave us about this man?"

The missing Bible leapt to her mind. But what could that have to do with Ah Sung's death? And yet, someone thought it worth stealing.

"There is something, isn't there?" he asked.

Emily capitulated. "It may be nothing." She explained how she found the Bible and how it vanished.

"Would one of your other servants have taken it?" he asked.

"I don't see why," she told him. "It was in Chinese. And at the time, Mary Kate was the only servant I had. She wouldn't even think of doing such a thing."

His expression was doubtful, but he accepted her statement for the time being.

"Well, I can't see how a Chinese Bible could be of any use to anyone here," he said. "But I'll keep it in mind. Was there anything written in it, other than religious comments?"

"I don't know," Emily answered. "I had put it aside to read, but it was taken before I could go through it."

He considered. "He might have written something that would incriminate Smith or someone else. If it turns up, will you examine it for any additions?"

"Of course." She rose. "I'm grateful to you for telling me all of this. And for continuing to work on the investigation."

"It's part of my job," he stated. "Even if I'm not given enough to do it properly. That reminds me. No one has spotted your dog, yet, but my men all know what he looks like, if he should cross our paths."

Emily felt much better knowing that someone else cared about what had happened. She had felt so helpless in the face of an unknown killer. Marshal Jacobi made her feel that she was no longer completely vulnerable to attack.

Now she could concentrate on turning Stratton, Andrews, and King into an honest company, or at least extricating herself from the worst of the business.

Emily had always thought she had nothing of the missionary zeal of her parents. But the idea of leaving King to continue in his wicked ways made her righteously angry.

A thought struck her. Mr. King had said that Mr. Andrews had absconded. Why had she simply accepted that? He had done nothing to convince her of his truthfulness. What if the man were dead? He had continually insisted that someone wanted to kill him. Could he have been right? It might well have something to do with the deaths of Ah Sung and Daniel Smith.

Once again her thoughts were chasing each other around like mice in the wainscoting. This wouldn't do. She sat down and finished copying the information for Robert, forcing herself to concentrate totally on the task at hand.

The clock was just striking one when she put the papers in an envelope for him to take to the land records office. The smell of soup rose to meet her as she descended the stairs. Lun Ho had used copious amounts of ginger and anise with a fish broth. She hadn't realized she was hungry until then.

Mary Kate had set a place for her in the dining room. Emily sat down. Before she had even lifted her napkin, Lun Ho came in with the soup on a tray. There were big chunks of haddock in the bottom of a dish. He poured the broth over them and then scattered onions and sesame seeds over the top.

"This looks wonderful," she said. "Is Mary Kate having this?"

The cook laughed. "She tried it but told me that it wasn't a meal for an Irish girl, especially on Saint Paddy's day. What is that?"

"I have no idea," Emily answered. "Some Catholic festival?"

Mary Kate came in a few minutes later to enlighten her.

"I'd like the rest of the afternoon off, please." She was already tying on her scarf. "It's the feast of the holy saint Patrick, who brought the Christian religion to Ireland and threw out the snakes, and I want to go to Mass and pray he comes back to throw out the English."

Emily nearly choked on her soup. "Of course, Mary Kate. Does John want the afternoon off, too?"

"I'd say he does, but not to pray to the saint," Mary Kate warned her. "He'll be down at the pubs drinking the beer and toasting the Molly Maguires."

"I suppose we all pray in different ways," Emily said.

Mary Kate gave her a puzzled look. "That's an odd thing for a missionary to say. I thought they all taught there was only one way to Heaven."

"Only my parents were missionaries, Mary Kate," Emily reminded her. "I'm just the widow of a heathen sea captain. Please try to be back before dark."

"Yes, ma'am." Mary Kate curtsied. Mrs. Stratton was a dear and no mistaking that, but she sometimes said things Mary Kate could find no sense in.

When Lun Ho came to collect the dishes Emily filled him in on Mary Kate's explanation of the day. He found it as bewildering as she did.

"But I'm sure they find our festivals as strange," he said philosophically. "On the New Year, someone asked me if we were going to have a human sacrifice. He seemed very sorry when I said no."

The rain seemed to be ebbing, so, after lunch, Emily told John he could also observe the day. He had put on a flowing green cravat and looked quite handsome.

"I'm going down to the shops," she said. "If I buy anything heavy, I'll tell them to hold it and you can get it tomorrow."

"That'll be fine, ma'am." He gave an impish grin. "I suppose that herself told you I'd be heading down to the wharf to drink myself numb."

"Uh . . ." Emily began.

"I think I'll be stopping in at the church, just to see her eyes bulge out," he decided. "I may tip a few later, but I promise I'll be fit for work in the morning."

"Thank you," Emily said. "You know I don't approve of spirituous drink."

"That I do, missus, and you're a grand charitable woman to allow me my night out."

There seemed to be a lot more Irish in Portland than she had thought, Emily realized as she left the house and entered the street. Many of the men she passed on her way downtown were wearing green neckties. Quite a few appeared to have already visited more than one of the saloons. Once again, Emily was glad of the widow's cap and veil. It seemed to make her invisible to the lurching groups of men. Still, all too often, she had to step aside quickly to avoid being run into.

She was so busy dodging the revelers that she didn't notice Mr. Carmichael approaching until they were almost face to face. She sighed. This was a meeting she would rather have avoided.

They were on the corner of Second and Yamhill, where the street was paved and the boarded sidewalk in place. Mr. Carmichael tipped his hat. Emily nodded and wished him good afternoon. At first she thought he would continue on his way. Then he hesitated, as if gathering up his courage.

She didn't have the heart to snub him. While he made up his mind, she waited, looking over the display in the window of the dry goods store.

"Mrs. Stratton, I realize that I must have offended you in some way," he said at last. "And for that I am most profoundly sorry. I do not wish to intrude upon you or presume to occupy myself in your affairs, but I have been trying to meet with Mr. King for several days, to no effect. The matter I wish to discuss with him involves information that I can't help feeling you should be apprised of."

This was not what she had expected. "If that is the case, Mr. Carmichael, perhaps you could call on me this afternoon. I shall be in after three."

She finished her shopping in a frenzy, picking up a pair of woolen stockings for Robert in a mustard color he would never wear and getting the wrong sort of hairpins. "Carmichael knows too much," she remembered. Why had she automatically been put on guard by that cryptic sentence scribbled in Horace's notes? What if Mr. Carmichael had discovered the illegal sources of her husband's money? Wasn't that what she was searching for? Was it possible that he might be an ally after all?

It would be nice to believe that Carmichael had information that would exonerate Horace, but Emily had little hope on that score. She wasn't sure that she really wanted him cleared of wrongdoing. She had spent so many years in steadily growing loathing of her husband that it would be terribly upsetting to find out he was capable of doing something decent.

Emily was glad her mother wasn't around to see how unchristian she had become.

Robert came home from school, ate a huge plate of noodles that Lun Ho had prepared, and hurried off to the records office.

A few moments later Mr. Carmichael appeared.

"Thank you for inviting me," he said when he had been settled in a comfortable chair near the fire and given tea and biscuits.

"It's my pleasure," she answered automatically.

"I hardly think so," he answered. "Mrs. Stratton, please tell me how I managed to fall in your esteem?"

"You haven't, Mr. Carmichael," she insisted. "I apologize for giving you that impression. There have been many things occupying me recently, the death of Mr. Smith, for one thing. Please forgive me if I was rude to you."

He didn't seem completely satisfied with her answer, but he accepted it.

"I'm afraid that my reason for wanting to see you will only add to your burden." He looked so sorry that Emily wanted to pat his balding head and tell him everything would be fine.

"It's possible that what you have to say will only confirm something I already suspected," she said gently.

"I don't wish to besmirch the memory of your husband," he added.

It was all Emily could do not to tell him that would be impossible. "I appreciate the truth," she told him. *And I do wish you'd get on with it!*

"Very well." He drew himself up, as if to deliver an oration. "A few days before his death, Daniel Smith called at my home."

Emily hadn't been expecting that. Her face must have showed her surprise.

"I was one of the early lawyers in town," Carmichael explained. "He'd had recourse to my services more than once before. I explained to him that I was no longer practicing and suggested he go to Mr. Mulkey. He thanked me and left. I thought no more about it until a few days ago when my housekeeper showed me a letter pouch she had found behind the sofa. It was filled with documents. Mr. Smith must have left them for me. Perhaps he intended to come back for them."

"Yes?" Emily had no time for a dramatic pause.

"I'm sorry, Mrs. Stratton, but the contents are proof that Captain Stratton was working with Ben Holladay to prevent the West Side railroad line from ever being built. This seems to have included bribery of officials, destruction of property, and intimidation of workers. All of them very serious offenses. I haven't gone through all the papers, but what I've read leads me to only one conclusion." He paused. "I'm afraid, Mrs. Stratton, that your late husband was a crook."

Emily almost laughed at his expression. "You have proof?" she asked. He nodded.

"That's wonderful," she exhaled in relief. "Now we can get to work."

CHAPTER TWENTY-SEVEN

To the mayor & common council; Gentlemen, your petitioner would respectfully represent that Mr. Jacoby the City marshal has placed a quantity of manure against my fence on the west end of the lot on which he now resides it has broken down my fence and falls into my back yard and and [sic] has become a nuisance. I have requested him to remove the same but he has neglected to do it. I therefore ask your hounourable [sic] body to cause the same to be removed or adopt such other measures as you may deam [sic] proper B.F. Risley.

—CITIZEN'S COMPLAINT, 1868

TUESDAY, MARCH 17, 1868

Carmichael's face was a study in consternation.

"Are you sure you understand what this means?" he asked.

"My husband was operating outside the law," she answered. "I had already come to that conclusion. Horace can hardly be sent to prison. Could I be punished in his stead?"

"Of course not!" He seemed horrified by the idea. "You had no knowledge of his actions."

"None at all," she answered the tinge of doubt in his voice. "I still don't completely understand the issues involved. Perhaps I should make restitution for the loss of property?"

"I don't think you could be forced to," Carmichael considered. "And doing so might constitute an admission of guilt on your part."

"I'd be grateful if you'd look into it for me," Emily said. "Presently I am trying to gather together all the information concerning my late husband's business dealings. I'm planning on making considerable changes."

"Are you now?" He looked at her with new curiosity. "You may not have known about the crooked schemes Captain Stratton was part of, but you don't seem surprised by them."

"That is true." Emily was becoming annoyed. "Over the years of my marriage to Horace, his true character became obvious to me. I'm ashamed not to have done something long ago. I was a coward not to face facts."

To her astonishment, Carmichael suddenly leapt from his chair and came over to her, taking one of her hands in both his own. He looked down on her with infinite pity.

"I am so very sorry," he said softly. "I have greatly misunderstood your situation. Please forgive me."

Emily felt tears sting her eyes.

"There is nothing to forgive," she assured him. "In your years as an attorney you must have learned how important it is to people to hide the realities of their lives. Also"—she smiled—"Mr. Smith had already told me something of his share in these activities. He did have a conscience. I only hope it didn't get him killed."

She tugged gently to release her hand from his, although the feeling wasn't at all unpleasant.

Mr. Carmichael seemed to realize that he had overstepped the line of propriety for he returned to his seat at once. He lifted his teacup and sipped it, although the liquid was by now stone cold. He appeared more flustered than Emily had ever seen him.

"Do you have any advice on how I should handle the situation?" she asked to cover his discomposure.

"I confess that I had originally tried to contact Mr. King about this," he said. "But, as I mentioned, with no success. He wouldn't see me. What bothers me the most about this is that the papers indicate that someone else is actually orchestrating, not only the sabotage of the railway, but other nefarious goings-on. The names of King and Andrews are not mentioned, but one of them might be the mastermind all the same. Or they might both be completely ignorant of the situation."

"You mean Horace was working for someone else?" Emily was incredulous. "That doesn't sound like him."

"Perhaps not working for, but in partnership with someone," Carmichael pursed his lips. Emily was struck again with the fact that he was one of the few men in town not covered in whiskers. He had a nice, strong chin.

She brought herself back to the topic. "Mr. Andrews, perhaps?"

"Possibly." Mr. Carmichael was skeptical. "He never struck me as a ringleader, but I won't discount him."

"Thank you for trusting me with this information," Emily said. "But I still don't know what I should do. I have no idea who this silent partner may have been, if it wasn't one of Horace's usual associates."

Carmichael turned to watch the fire, now down to white coals. He picked up the poker and stabbed at it, then took a scoop from the coal scuttle and threw it on. At last he faced Emily.

"I seem to be doing nothing but begging your pardon today," he said.

"You still have no reason to," Emily said with understanding. "I had my doubts about you. I found a notation in one of Horace's books. He was worried about how much you knew."

"He needn't have been." Carmichael replaced the scoop and shut the door of the stove. "Until I read Dan's papers, I knew very little. I had nothing but a suspicion that something underhanded was going on in the struggle for the railroad."

But Emily could tell from his tone that there were other things he did know about. She didn't want to hear them. Any more revelations and she would feel herself obliged to give away everything she owned in order to atone and throw herself upon the charity of the Bracewells. That was more than she could contemplate.

"If I find any more information regarding the railroad, I'll let you know at once," she promised.

"That would be excellent." He stood again as she rang for Mary Kate to bring his wraps. "One more thing, the most important, really. Whoever this man is, he is very dangerous. It's likely that Dan Smith was killed because of what he told us. You must be on your guard every minute."

"We already lock the house every night," she assured him. "And Robert is seeing about getting another watchdog. What more can I do, short of running away?"

Her face told him that wasn't an option.

"Perhaps you could be sure not to go out alone until this is over," he said earnestly. "Your son, as well. I should be very upset if anything happened to either of you."

His expression was of such tender concern that Emily was relieved when Mary Kate appeared. She wasn't accustomed to anyone being worried about her safety, not since her parents had died.

For a long time after he left she sat in the parlor, staring at the glowing coals. The heat they gave out was minuscule compared to the warmth of knowing that someone cared.

Robert had to ask Mr. Hoffman, the city recorder, to help him make sense of the legal descriptions of the property.

"Your father seems to have had bits and pieces all over town," Hoffman commented. "I think he bought a lot at foreclosure sales. Let me see."

Robert was astonished at all the property they had. There was their house, of course, but also several unimproved lots and some that were either leased or rented out. He supposed there was an agent to collect the money. There were a few buildings on Front Street, especially near the wharf. He'd have to go see what they were. At least none were in the region of the Hellhole. He gave a sigh of relief. He didn't profit from Lily's work.

He was still curious.

"Mr. Hoffman, is it possible to find out who owns a specific piece of land?" he asked.

"In principle, yes." Hoffman was also an attorney and didn't like to be pushed for a definite answer. "If you have the plat number and section, I can look it up."

Robert studied the plat map and made his best guess as to the section the Hellhole stood on.

"Hmmm," the recorder said a few minutes later. "This is confusing. The property is between one owned by Jim Lappeus and one of the Failing buildings. But it doesn't seem to belong to either of them. It's a small parcel, divided many times. Let me do some more research on it." He glanced at the wall clock. "Too late today. If you come back tomorrow, I should have it for you."

"If you don't mind." Robert didn't want to seem overly inquisitive. "It's not important; I just wondered."

"Maybe not, but worth following, in any case." Mr. Hoffman shut the record book. "Looks to me as if the owner didn't want his name on anything. Makes me wonder too. The tax rolls might say, but not this afternoon. My wife is expecting me home early to take our daughter to some birthday party or other. Come back tomorrow."

With that Robert had to be content.

After his interview with Emily, Carmichael felt fairly confident that she had no part in Horace Stratton's schemes. He also felt a complete fool. He hadn't been so tongue-tied since he was eighteen. Perhaps he was becoming senile. Fifty-two was a bit young to lose one's wits, but it seemed the only explanation for the way he felt around Mrs. Stratton.

The whole idea was preposterous. It couldn't be allowed to get in the way of the work he had set himself. Even if he had to allow her to be hurt financially, he owed it to the other railroad investors to see to it that these dastardly plots be foiled.

He shook his head worriedly. Now he was even thinking like one of those dime novels.

It would still be light for an hour or so. What he needed was some good hard work in the garden. Digging up a vegetable bed and hauling manure would bring him back to reality.

She seemed so frail in that heavy black gown. So very, very vulnerable.

Carmichael increased his pace. He set his mind firmly on remembering where he had stored the spade.

Matthew King was just locking up his office when he spotted Robert leaving the city recorder's. It was such an unexpected place for the boy to be that he waited until Robert had turned the corner and then went in to investigate.

"Hoffman, was that Horace Stratton's son in here?" he asked.

"Yes, his mother sent him to find out what they owned in town." Mr. Hoffman was busy closing things up for the day and hoped that King would take the hint.

"Was that all?"

"Oh, he was also asking who owned one of those hole-in-the-wall saloons on Second Street," Hoffman said. "Probably ran up a gambling debt and wanted to plead his case with the man in charge. I couldn't find it for him. Now, if there was nothing else?"

He stared pointedly at the clock.

King thanked him and went on home. He made one stop on the way. It was probably nothing, but it was better to be safe than sorry.

Emily was delighted at the extent of their holdings.

"We could sell some of them off and live quite comfortably," she told Robert. "Did you notice when your father first bought the land?"

"I think he picked up parcels of it over a long stretch." Robert explained how his father had purchased the lots cheaply.

Emily's heart sank. Even the land had been acquired through misery. Of course, it wasn't as if Horace had foreclosed on the land. He had simply benefited from the fact that others had not been able to pay their debts. The distinction didn't sit well with her, but for now, she ignored her qualms.

"Mother," Robert asked. "Why should we sell any of it? Uncle George says that land is the best investment one can make."

"I just want to know our exact financial situation," Emily said. "Perhaps tomorrow I'll go out and walk through town to find out just what is built on our property."

"Wait until Saturday and I'll accompany you," Robert offered.

"That is extremely tempting." She gazed on him fondly. "But if it's fine tomorrow, I'll go alone. I've been told that anytime there is a clear day here, one should take advantage of it."

She knew that Mr. Carmichael had said she should always have someone with her, but in broad daylight in the center of town, Emily thought she would be perfectly safe.

Robert went up to do schoolwork before dinner. He was relieved that his mother's stroll wouldn't take her anywhere near the Hellhole. But knowing who did own it wouldn't be a bad thing. He wasn't going back there until he found out.

The next morning at breakfast, Emily took one look at John and knew that she'd be safer on foot. He had tipped more than a few glasses in honor of Saint Patrick. The sky framed in the window showed broken clouds patched with blue. Here and there the sunlight came through in long golden arrows. A good day to take some exercise. Perhaps she would also call on Etta or Mrs. Reed.

Robert seemed unusually pensive as he kissed her good-bye.

"Are you feeling well, my dear?" she asked.

"Oh, fine, Mother." He hefted his book bag. "Just going over Greek verbs. I may be a little late this afternoon. Don't worry, I'll be home for dinner."

"I should hope so," Emily said. "Lun Ho is making a Persian lamb stew."

The air outside was mild, with a deep scent of fir needles and damp earth. Sometime in the past few days jonquils had erupted from the ground and bloomed. Emily felt like a blot of black ink in this colorful landscape.

She followed the directions Robert had written out for her to make a circuit of their property. There was a large section in the southwest part of town that was nothing but forest. She took that on faith. The other parcels showed great variety, from single homes to large boarding houses. There was a stretch along Washington Street that included Dr. See's office and a hotchpotch along Front Street that was mostly Chinese laundries with living space above.

She determined that these would be her first concern. All over town she saw the laundrymen trotting along in their traditional clothing, with caps and queues, carrying the fresh laundry wrapped in baskets swinging from the ends of long poles. Sometimes dogs snapped at the baskets as if the motion were a game for them. Did they pay rent to her? If so, how much? How did they live? Would they return to their families if she offered them the chance?

The Chinese property wasn't part of the corporation of Stratton, Andrews, and King. Who was collecting the rents now? It maddened her that she knew so little. Perhaps that had been among the jobs that Daniel Smith had done for Horace. Somewhere there must be records.

She tried asking at one of the laundries, but no one spoke her dialect. The only English they had was chiefly concerned with washing and ironing.

She returned home feeling that she had accomplished something at least. She could hardly wait to share it with Robert. But the time for his return came and went.

Emily went in search of Mary Kate. She found the maid in the pantry, teaching Lun Ho the English words for foodstuffs. The kitchen smelled of cinnamon and lamb. It made Emily's mouth water.

"Potatoes," Mary Kate said slowly. "Very important. I call them spuds."

"Potatoes," he repeated with Mary Kate's exact intonation.

Emily was momentarily distracted by the image of Lun Ho announcing dinner with an accent from the west of Ireland.

"Robert said he'd be late today," she told them. "But I had the idea it would be sooner. I'm getting a bit concerned. If he's not home by dark, John will have to recover enough to look for him. Would you tell him?"

"With pleasure." She gave a wicked grin. "But the lad'll be home when he gets hungry. Boys usually are."

Emily took this as received wisdom. She went to her room to lie down. It had been a long time since she had walked so far.

Robert hadn't bothered to come in the house after school. He stashed his bag and lunch pail in the carriage house, calling up to John to let his mother know he'd be back in a bit. A growl told him the message had been heard.

He hurried down to the records office. Mr. Hoffman was waiting for him.

"I'm glad you came back," he greeted Robert. "I was just about to close up. I'm taking my wife down to Eugene City for couple of weeks to see her parents. It would have been a shame to wait to tell you."

"You found it?" Robert nearly cheered.

Mr. Hoffman took out his keys and unlocked a desk drawer. "You wouldn't believe the trouble it took to find out the real owner of the Hellhole. Don't look so surprised. I know what's on every square foot of this town. I was suspicious of your motives until I found the answer. How did you guess? I couldn't believe it."

"Oh, just a hint here and there," Robert said casually, wishing he had an inkling of the truth. "Is there something in writing that I can take with me? I want my mother to see the proof."

"I thought you might." The recorder took a folded piece of paper from the drawer and handed it to him. "I copied the relevant passages. It's up to your mother to decide what to do about it, of course, but I think it's appalling that her trust should be abused in that way."

"Thank you. Thank you very much." Robert hid the paper inside his coat pocket. "You won't come to any trouble from this, will you?"

"These are public documents," Mr. Hoffman replied. "You might have found the information completely on your own."

"I understand." Robert shook the recorder's hand and hurried out.

The paper was burning a hole in his pocket, but he didn't dare take it out and read it on the street. What could Mr. Hoffman have meant? Who had betrayed his mother? He'd bet it was that old Carmichael, always looking at her, pretending to run into her by chance. It was disgusting in a man his age.

Robert couldn't wait any longer. He slid under one of the piers that lined the river. Most of the shops overhung the water to take on shipments and drop off garbage. He and other boys often hid in the boats docked there to smoke cigars cadged from their fathers' humidors. Today it was empty.

He looked around but saw no one. Carefully, he drew the paper from his pocket and opened it.

The contents were full of legal descriptions of property, numbers, and dates of transactions. Robert skimmed these until he saw a name.

"No," he said. "Father, how could you?"

He read it over again and again, but the contents were clear. His father had not only bought Lily, he had sold her. And it sickened him to realize who the buyer had been.

Despite the nausea he felt at this new revelation, there was at least hope. There was a chance to free Lily, but he needed help. Who could he turn to? His mother was the only person he had complete faith in. However, this definitely came under the cardinal rule of his childhood. Mother couldn't know.

He sat on the wet rocks until the moisture seeped into his woolen school trousers.

Finally, he decided to go to the one person he could talk to. When he told her what he had found out, Lily might have some ideas of her own about what to do next.

The Hellhole wasn't busy at this time of day. A few local men stood at the bar, reading their future in the dregs of their beer. Ned didn't seem happy to see him.

"You can't have Lily today," he barked. "She's busy."

"I can wait," Robert said. "There isn't a line."

"Why don't you go home and come back later?" Ned almost seemed to be begging him.

"I won't take long," Robert insisted. "I just want to talk."

"Right," Ned smirked. "Like last time. Three hours of 'talking.'"

"Please, Ned," Robert said. "It's really important."

Ned polished glasses furiously for a few minutes, then gave up and nodded.

"She'll be a while," he warned. "Why don't you sit over in the corner there and I'll bring you a drink on the house."

Robert winced. Now that he knew whose house it was, he wasn't sure he wanted to accept it. He went to the little table Ned had indicated. At least from here he could see the stairs.

When the drink came, Robert felt churlish refusing it, especially since Ned seemed so eager to oblige. He thanked him and took a sip. His eyes widened. This was the good stuff. He took another sip.

The minutes passed. No one came down the staircase. Ned left another drink in front of Robert. The men at the bar wandered out. Ned washed more glasses. He left another drink.

The room was unnaturally warm. Robert yawned. His eyes wouldn't stay open.

Slowly his head fell back against the wall. Ned watched him sink into sleep. When he was certain that Robert was unconscious, he pulled a lever under the bar. A panel in the wall opened; the chair tipped back.

When it came up again, Robert had vanished.

CHAPTER TWENTY-EIGHT

"Sweeping, universal truths are as convenient as they are rare. The evils result-ing from excess in drinking are so enormous and so terrible, that it would be a relief to know that alcoholic liquors are in themselves evil, and always to be avoided."

—JAMES PARTON, *ATLANTIC MONTHLY*, JULY 1898

WEDNESDAY, MARCH 18, 1868

Emily stared at the lunch pail and bag. "But why wouldn't he come into the house to tell me where he was going? That's not like my son."

John had brought her the things early that evening when he had finally wakened. He shook his head in puzzlement. Then a blurry memory sur-faced. "Wait. He yelled something at me. I didn't hear it well being still in my bed. I think it was just that he wouldn't be long."

"Try to remember if he said where, John," she pleaded. "Otherwise we'll have to start with his friends and work our way across town looking for him. It could take hours."

"I'm sorry, Mrs. Stratton." The coachman looked truly miserable. "It's a curse on me for celebrating the saint's day too much. I'll go at once. I'll ask at the place where we got the dog."

Emily tried to stay calm. Perhaps Robert had told her something that morning and she hadn't been listening. She had misunderstood once before. He was probably with one of his friends. He'd be home soon and wonder what all the fuss was about.

Mary Kate made enough tea for a regiment and Emily drank it mechanically, all the while listening for John's return.

It was long past midnight before they heard the clop of the horse in the drive. Emily knew by the silence that John hadn't found her son.

"No one's seen hide nor hair of him," the coachman reported. "I woke up one house after another. I even stopped Constable Brannen and asked. I've wracked my poor sad brain trying to think if he told me where he was going, but nothing will come. I swear, I'm taking the pledge tomorrow."

"Go get some sleep, John," was all Emily could say. "You've done all you can tonight. Mary Kate, Lun Ho, you go to bed, too."

"I'll not budge unless you come up too," Mary Kate said. "You'll not be left sitting down here all alone. I'll get you into your nightdress and bring up some warm milk. You won't be doing the poor boy any good by making yourself sick with worry."

"How can I not?" Emily spoke like a small, tired child. "I want to run out into the dark and call his name until he finds me. But I know there's no sense in that. So all I can do is worry."

"You can pray," Mary Kate offered. "I'll say a rosary for him this very night. Why don't you light one of those smelly sticks? If it gives you comfort, I'll not say a word to the priest or anyone else."

Emily sniffed and then smiled. "Thank you, Mary Kate. I'll do that. But come get me at first light. If he isn't home by dawn, I'm calling Marshal Jacobi to organize a search. I can't bear the idea that he's lying somewhere, perhaps with a broken leg, with bear and wildcats prowling near him."

"Then don't think such a thing," Mary Kate said. "Especially when he's probably safe asleep somewhere John didn't look. Now, come on up and let me get you out of those hoops and lacings."

When Mary Kate had finished and gone to her bed, Emily knelt in her nightgown and cap and lit the candle and incense before the goddess of mercy.

"I beg you, Kwan Yin," she whispered. "Bring my boy home safe."

When her knees were stiff and the candle burnt down, Emily went to bed, where she stared at the ceiling until dawn.

George and Alice arrived as soon as they got the message.

"Now, don't get in a panic, Emily," George said. "All boys do this from time to time. He's likely gone off on an adventure and not thought of what it would do to you. We'll find him soon enough."

"Robert isn't like that," Emily insisted. "Something's happened to him."

"There, there." Alice sat down next to her. "George is right. It isn't like in the early days here, when Indians came down and kidnapped children or bears dragged them off."

"That's enough, Alice," George spoke sharply. "I don't recall either of those things ever happening around here. As soon as the school opens, I'll go over and ask Professor Gatch if he'll address the students. One of them is sure to know where he went."

"Thank you, George," Emily said.

Alice suddenly looked closely at Emily. When she came in, she had been too upset to notice.

"What are you wearing? George, go in the other room," she ordered. "Emily is so beside herself that she forgot to get dressed."

Emily looked down. She had got up this morning and put on her Chinese trousers and long tunic, as she always did in Shanghai. It felt so natural that she hadn't given it another thought. She wondered if some part of her believed that it would turn back the clock and her little boy would be safe at home in his bed.

"I'm sorry, Alice." She got up. "I'll go upstairs and dress. Have you breakfasted yet? Lun Ho has mastered griddle cakes wonderfully."

Alice insisted on going up with her and fussing while she put on the layers of clothing necessary to be a respectable woman.

"George is right, of course, about Robert," she said as she examined all the bottles on the dressing table. "Horace was always going off, sometimes for days when he was a boy. He'd come back with some wild story of tracking panthers or being caught in a blizzard on the mountain. It made my mother wild but he never came to any harm."

"Robert isn't like that," Emily insisted.

"He's been away from you at school for two years," Alice reminded her. "Boys change so much at that age. Who knows what friends he made or what influences he came under? I'm so glad I have girls."

She kept up a stream of chatter in that vein until Emily was fully dressed, even to her jewelry. Unable to endure more, she twisted her hair up into a bun and covered it with her cap.

When they came down, Marshal Jacobi was waiting in the hallway. Upon seeing him, Emily stumbled on the step. Alice caught her arm and guided her the rest of the way down.

"Here now!" he exclaimed at the shock on her pale face. "I came by to report on the Smith investigation, and Mr. Bracewell told me about your boy. We can call out the fire department to help hunt for him."

Emily breathed again. "That would be very kind. When I saw you, I thought . . . I'm sorry, have you found something new about Mr. Smith?"

"Not exactly." Jacobi looked sideways at Alice and George.

"We'll be leaving now," George said at once. "I'll go to the Academy first and then ask around town. Maybe someone saw him yesterday."

"And I'll be back later to support you in your hour of need," Alice threatened.

When they had left, Jacobi opened up his leather satchel and took out a book.

"Is this the one that belonged to your cook?" he asked.

Emily took it. The tracts were still stuck in the pages of the Bible. "Yes, I'm sure of it. Where did you find it?"

"Under a loose floorboard in Smith's room," the marshal told her. "Any idea why he would have taken it?"

"None." Emily turned the pages. "He never gave any sign of being able to read Chinese."

"I hate to ask you, with you being so worried about your son," he said. "But if you could go through it for me for any clues, I'd be most grateful."

"Yes, of course. It will give me the illusion that I'm doing something useful," she said.

"Maybe more than you think." He took out a piece of paper. "It seems that it was Daniel Smith who hired Ah Sung and sent him to work for you."

"So he *was* here to spy on us!" Emily exclaimed. "Do you . . . do you think Robert's disappearance has anything to do with this?"

"I don't know, Mrs. Stratton." He looked at her with sympathy. "There's no reason to think so, but I won't rule it out. I have a son almost the same age as yours. He can be a torment at times and gets into things I'd like to horsewhip him for. I'd be crazy with fear if he went missing. I'll get a search organized at once."

In the kitchen, Mary Kate was dripping tears onto the noodle pastry she was rolling out under Lun Ho's direction. On the other side of the table, John was finishing his bacon and eggs.

"What do you think really happened to the lad?" he asked her.

"The way that one was taking on, he could be sleeping it off under a bush somewhere, or lying in a ditch with a knife in his chest." Mary Kate looked around quickly to be sure Emily hadn't come in.

John shook his head. "I don't see him dead. He isn't the type to get into a fight. Mostly, anyone taunts him, he just laughs and buys them a drink. I've seen him at it. He's a charmer, that one."

"Too much a one for his own good, I'm thinking," Mary Kate retorted. "He believes he can laugh his way out of anything. Poor Mrs. Stratton! If he's not found, it'll break her heart."

With this, John was forced to agree.

Emily sat in the parlor, her hands cold despite the red-hot fire. She set the Bible on her sewing table and stared at it a long time without opening it.

It was only the hope that she might find a clue to what had happened to Robert that made her finally start going through the Bible.

From the wear on the edges of the pages, she could tell that Ah Sung had spent most of his time reading the story of David and the Song of Songs. That was normal for those who read the book for the stories rather than religious inspiration.

She opened to the page marked by one of the tracts. Kings: the story of Jezebel. That was another popular one. It didn't seem that there was anything special about the Bible. She picked up the tract and noticed that there was handwriting on the blank side. It was in English, a series of chapters and verses, mostly from Proverbs. Some minister's notes for a sermon? The first one was from Isaiah. Emily didn't need to look it up. "Your country is desolate; your cities are burned with fire: your land, strangers devour it in your presence and it is desolate, as overthrown by strangers."

Emily shuddered. It was easy to see how this would resonate with Ah Sung. This was the China she had grown up in, where the ships and soldiers of the English, French, and even Americans invaded and the army of the Manchu Emperors fought first the barbarian foreigners and then the Taiping rebels.

She went through the list: Proverbs 16, verses 25 and 27, and chapter 17, verse 11; Jeremiah 12, verses 4 and 7. They almost told a story. "There is a way that seems right to a man, but in the end it is the way of death. An ungodly man digs up evil and his lips are like burning fire. The land is devastated; crops and cattle die because of the wickedness of the people. But one person remains righteous. 'I have forsaken my house. I have left my heritage' . . ." Finally, in large black letters, the writer had listed Psalm 41, verse 5. "Mine enemies speak evil of me. When shall he die and his name perish?"

Seeing the verses put together like this, Emily realized how the Taiping beliefs could have spread so quickly. The Hebrews' experience mirrored that of the Chinese, especially those in the south. She could think of a hundred other chapters that would have spoken to them.

But this seemed to tell of a personal journey. If it was Ah Sung who had written these, it almost appeared that he had come to America to find and silence an enemy. Or, she thought suddenly, had the Bible been sent to him as a warning?

Who was Ah Sung? Had his death been the result of something that had happened in China? Was he an evil man, or had he come to track one down and been discovered and eliminated?

Was evil still stalking them?

What has happened to my son?

The book gave no answers.

Mary Kate found her slumped over on the sofa, having cried herself to sleep. She covered her with a blanket and told callers that the only one who could disturb her was Master Robert.

It was pitch dark when Robert came to. He was lying on what felt like a pile of shoes. His hands and feet were tied and a gag smelling of fish was in his mouth. For the first time in his life he was afraid. He tried to wiggle free. Shoes rumbled down around him. A few seconds later his eyes were blasted by lantern light.

"You woke up too soon, pretty boy," a gravelly voice said.

Robert barely had time to see the cudgel before it hit him and he passed out once more.

Emily woke to disappointment. No one had seen Robert. Professor Gatch had asked the entire school to aid in the search, and Marshal Jacobi still had volunteers out combing the woods. None of Robert's friends had seen him after school. He hadn't mentioned going anywhere. Someone thought he had noticed a boy of about the right age down on First Street, but that had been about four in the afternoon.

Mr. Carmichael had come by to offer his services. Emily thanked him and explained that everything that could be done was being done. Carmichael wasn't so sure.

He went to pay a call on Robert's uncle.

George received him in his study, out of range of feminine ears. He offered Carmichael a cheroot.

It wasn't until both men were comfortably puffing that Carmichael came to the point.

"I understand that the search for young Stratton is concentrating on the West Hills and north of town, up by Couch's Lake," he said.

"That's right," George said. "We thought it likely that he went out again to look for his dog."

"What about down by the waterfront?" Carmichael tapped the end of the cheroot on the edge of a dish. "That's where he was last seen, I understand."

"If he were down there, he would have been found hours ago," George explained. "He's not exactly unknown in those establishments."

"Ah, so you are aware of Robert's nocturnal activities." Carmichael re-laxed. "Of course, I couldn't broach the subject to his mother, but it would have been remiss of me not to suggest another possibility."

George sighed heavily. "I know what my nephew's been up to. His fa-ther was just the same. I hoped that Robert, at least, would sow his wild oats and settle down."

"Horace never did," Carmichael observed sourly.

"No, but at least he sowed most of them far from home," George pointed out. "Alice and the girls never knew about his escapades."

Carmichael leaned back in the soft leather chair. He rolled the cheroot in his fingers.

"Some might say that Stratton's 'escapades' simply matured with him," he ventured.

"What's that?" George got up and went to the drinks tantalus and unlocked it. "What do you mean? Like a whiskey and water?"

"No, thank you," Carmichael answered. He waited while George made one for himself. Then he explained.

"When your brother-in-law was home last year, I became aware of some irregularities in his business practices. A neighbor of mine felt that he had been cheated and asked me to look into it."

"That sort of thing goes on all the time." George waved it away with the smoke. "People have been fighting in the courts over the Lownsdale properties for years, for example."

"This was a somewhat more delicate matter," Carmichael said. "My neighbor's complaint was about a transaction not entirely legal. I had to ex-plain to him that those who go outside the law can't expect its protection."

"Well, then," George yawned. "Don't see what I can do about it. Sorry. I was up early hunting for Robert."

"Yes, of course." Carmichael put out his cheroot and stood. "I apologize for intruding. I just wanted to be sure that all possibilities as to Robert's dis-appearance were being considered."

"Good of you to do so." George held out his hand. "And I can see why you wouldn't want to bring it up with Emily. She dotes on the boy. Won't hear a word against him."

"As would any mother," Carmichael said. "And this may well be nothing more than a prank gone awry. He could have stowed away on the boat for Oregon City, just for a lark, or be off with a friend we know nothing about."

"Exactly." George smiled. "Best to put a good face on it and hope for the best."

Mr. Carmichael took his leave. But he was not as sanguine about finding Robert as he pretended.

It was no use burdening Emily with his suspicions. He hoped to God he was wrong. But he was not going to rest until he made sure of it.

He thought of the boy and their conversation in the library. There had already been rumors that young Master Stratton liked high living in low places. But he also remembered the tenderness on Robert's face when he looked at Emily. There was good in the boy, he concluded. He deserved a second chance.

Carmichael was determined that he should live to have it.

CHAPTER TWENTY-NINE

Thursday night, . . . George Townsend, night watchman, entered the press room, and while standing near the engine, put his hand upon some part of the little machine with the remark that he would stop it. Quicker that wink [sic] one of his fingers was caught and cut off clean, near the first joint. The accident was not, however, serious enough to keep George indoors and he was patrolling his beat as usual last night.

—*Oregonian* Saturday March 21 1868

SUNDAY, MARCH 22, 1868

I'm sorry, Mrs. Stratton," Marshal Jacobi said early on Sunday morning. "We can't spare any more time in searching. We've asked pretty much everyone in town, covered the woods halfway into the Tuality Valley. There's no sign of your boy."

"You can't give up!" Emily pleaded.

He shrugged helplessly. "I don't know what else to do."

Emily knew that. Half the town had gone out, tramping through the thorny undergrowth, sliding down the ravines, climbing over enormous fallen logs and poking in the cavities in case Robert had crawled into one and been unable to get out. But there was no indication that he had even gone into the forest.

Marshal Jacobi looked at her with pity. "Believe me, I know how I'd feel if it were one of mine. But, frankly, Mrs. Stratton, I don't think your son is still in Portland."

That seemed to be the opinion of most of the town. Boys of sixteen ran off, some to escape a tyrannical parent, some just for adventure. It happened all the time. It was too bad that he hadn't at least left a note for his mother, but that's the way young people were these days.

Emily remembered poor Mrs. Peterson, wandering Portland with the tintype of her son and being brushed aside. She had insisted her Alex wouldn't have gone off without telling her. No one had believed her. No one but Emily. She wondered what had happened to Mrs. Peterson and if Alex had found his way home.

The doctor prescribed laudanum for Emily but she refused to take it.

"I have work to do," she insisted. "And I can't do it in an opium fog."

"How can you think of working with your son missing?" Alice was appalled.

"The task before me is to find him," Emily answered. "Everyone else has given up. Now please let me get to it."

Alice backed away. Emily's grief had obviously affected her mind. She was far too controlled, too distant. Dr. Thompson said this was a natural reaction to a tragedy, but Alice saw nothing natural about it.

"We haven't given up," George said, with a warning glance at Alice. "Robert's a capable boy. He'll turn up yet."

"Yes, I'm sure he will," Alice echoed. "Why don't you just take a spoonful or two of the laudanum? Just enough to let you sleep. You'll make yourself ill at this rate."

Emily shook her head decidedly.

The Bracewells gave up. "We need to get back to the girls," Alice told her. "But if you need anything, send for us, day or night."

"Thank you both," Emily said. "I do appreciate all the time you've spent with me these past few days. Give Sarah and Felicity hugs from me."

Alone at last, she sat with her hands in her lap, her mind empty of all but longing. The day dimmed and Mary Kate came in to light the lamps.

"Oh, ma'am!" she exclaimed. "You gave me a start. Have you been sitting here all alone this afternoon? I thought you were resting in your room."

Emily roused herself enough to respond.

"It's all right, Mary Kate," she said. "I needed to be alone. I've had someone with me ever since Robert disappeared. I haven't had a moment to think."

"Well, you can think in your bed," Mary Kate decided. "You go on up and I'll bring you a tray. Mr. Lun has made some of that soup with the little noodle and meat packets. I'm getting quite a taste for that food. And the meat is pork. I bought it myself and watched him make it."

"Yes, that would be good." Emily stood up. Her body felt as if it had been through a mangle.

Mary Kate fussed over her, helping her into her nightgown as if she were a child, tucking her in and staying to be sure she ate all her soup. Emily wished she wouldn't. The kindness made her want to cry.

She settled into the clean sheets and soft pillows, hating the idea of being comfortable when Robert might be out in the cold and wet. Where was he sleeping tonight? She felt a sob rise in her throat.

She cried herself to sleep and didn't wake until the sun rose enough to shine in directly on her face.

Monday morning she took the message in the Bible to the marshal. She should have done it at once, but in her anxiety about Robert, she had forgotten. However, he didn't find her theory at all compelling.

"This group of verses could mean anything or nothing," he said. "I can't see what it could have to do with Dan's death. And what are these Taipings you keep talking about?"

It hadn't occurred to Emily that everyone hadn't heard of the rebellion.

"They were a group of Chinese Christians," she explained. "Well, sort of Christians. Their leader was a man who believed himself to be Jesus's younger brother, come to save the Chinese from both the Manchu dynasty and the foreigners. He attracted a large following that took over much of central China. Their headquarters was in Nanking, but the rebellion was brutally put down a few years ago."

"But what could old Dan Smith have had to do with them?" Jacobi was having nothing of that. "He was never in China."

"Mr. Smith must have learned something from Ah Sung," Emily said. "Ah Sung may have fled to America when the Taiping were defeated. Perhaps he was a part of a Taiping group here."

"Yes, but it still doesn't sound like anything to do with Dan." Jacobi looked at the Bible. "Anything else written in it?"

"I haven't checked all of it." She riffled the pages again. "But there don't seem to be any more notes in the margins."

"The fact that Dan took it from your house shows there was something between him and the cook," Jacobi observed. "But I can't find out what the two of them were up to. I'll keep trying."

He didn't give her any false hope, though. She could tell he didn't believe the killer would ever be discovered. He didn't think Robert would ever be found, either.

She wasn't going to accept that.

That afternoon she sat down and wrote an account of what she knew, drawing lines where there seemed to be a connection and a lot of question marks for things she had to find out.

The Bible and the death of Ah Sung suggested that something that happened in China had followed them to Portland. Knowing that the most profitable part of the trade done by Stratton, Andrews, and King was in opium and coolies, that was reasonable.

On the other hand, Mr. Smith had told her that he and Horace had agreed to bribe legislators to support the east side railroaders. That would have infuriated the Westsiders, if they found out. Since Horace and Smith had embezzled the bribe money, the man who gave it to them might also be unhappy. If Horace and Smith had been active in trying to thwart the success of the Westsiders, they could well have antagonized some of the most powerful and wealthy men in Portland.

Mr. Reed and Mr. Carmichael were the only supporters of the west side group that she had met. Neither of them struck her as inclined to violence, but people did strange things when money was at stake.

And where did Mr. Andrews and Mr. King fit in all of this? Mr. and Mrs. King hadn't come by once since Robert went missing. Was that because he was angry with her or because he knew what had happened to her son? Where was Andrews really? Could they have kidnapped Robert to force her to turn over her shares of the company? Perhaps King was waiting until she had been reduced by despair to apathy. She could easily imagine him offering to relieve her of the responsibility of finances.

Daniel Smith had worked for Stratton, Andrews, and King. He might have found out about King's plans and been coming to warn her. King followed him and attacked before he could reach her.

But why kill Ah Sung? And why did Smith have his Bible?

She studied her notes a long time. She might be able to prove that Ah Sung knew of a crime that the firm had been part of in China and that he had gone to Daniel Smith for help in accusing Andrews and King.

No, that didn't work. Why would Smith help him?

Maybe Mr. Smith had lured Ah Sung out to a meeting that resulted in his murder. Then he came back for the Bible, believing that it could implicate him. Mr. King had decided to get rid of a witness and killed him.

Emily exhaled, blowing a loose curl from her forehead.

It almost fit. But not perfectly. And there was still the problem of proving it. She didn't even know where King was when Smith was bludgeoned to death. If he had been in a meeting or at his club with a dozen other men, that would destroy her lovely theory completely.

How could she find out?

The Eliots came first to mind. Tom Eliot seemed to pay calls on half the town every week. He would know when the meetings were and who had attended. And Etta was eager to help her. She had been one of the first to come see Emily when the news about Robert had come out, showing great delicacy by not bringing Willie. Her anguish at Emily's situation had been obvious.

It was tempting to ask them, but it wasn't fair. They were almost as new in town as she. Added to that, there was strong prejudice among some, like Alice, against Unitarians. Emily didn't want them further branded as snoops.

She briefly considered her brother-in-law, but George was too likely to tell Alice why Emily wanted to know, and Alice would tell the rest of

Portland. Also, he was a friend of King's and might take offense at her suspicions.

That only left Mr. Carmichael.

He was a respected longtime resident. Despite being a lawyer, he seemed to have few, if any, enemies. He already had his own misgivings about King's business practices. No one would think it odd if he were to ask where King had been the afternoon of March eleventh.

Goodness! That was less than two weeks ago! It seemed like a century.

Despite his being the perfect candidate, Emily hesitated about asking Carmichael. She told herself that she didn't want to involve him in her search for a murderer and kidnapper. It might be dangerous. If the Eliots asked personal questions, it would be blamed on their youth and unorthodox religion. Mr. Carmichael might attract the wrong sort of attention to himself.

But that wasn't the only reason, Emily had to admit. There was still Horace's warning against Carmichael. Even though the man had explained what he had been doing, Emily still wasn't sure she could trust him. The problem was that she wanted so much to.

Carmichael was someone she needed to have faith in. His calm demeanor and air of acceptance made him easy to talk to. He would listen to her and consider her opinions. He appeared to be sensible, intelligent, and honest.

Even more, he had made her laugh.

Why was she so reluctant to ask for his help?

Maybe because he was too good to be real. No man could be that understanding. She had never known anyone she was that comfortable around. Talking to him was so easy. She never wondered if she had embarrassed herself or offended him.

Emily knew deep down that, if she let herself believe in Mr. Carmichael and he disappointed her, she could never trust anyone again.

The person she loved most in the world was missing. The loss was too sharp against her heart to risk being hurt any more.

She looked at her notes again, drawing more lines, putting in more question marks. At last she threw down the pen, spattering black ink on her black dress.

She would have to place her trust in someone. There was no way she could find all the answers herself. If she made the wrong decision, it might cost her son's life. But if she did nothing, no one else would try to save him.

Having made up her mind at last, Emily sat down, wiped up the ink, refilled the pen, and wrote a short note for John to take to Mr. Carmichael.

Sometime after noon Lily opened her eyes. She swallowed hard in disappointment. The room was still the same: chair, bed, dressing table, clothes hooks, a sliding peephole in the door, which she knew was bolted from the outside. It wasn't a nightmare. This was her life.

The only bright spot in it had been the visits from Robert. But he hadn't come back since the night when they had just talked. Why not? What had she said wrong? If he didn't come back, she thought her heart would wither like a dry leaf and blow away.

A little later Ned came to open the door and let her out to empty the chamber pot and come downstairs for breakfast. She dawdled at the table until the other two girls had gone up to prepare for the night's work.

"This coffee good, Ned." She held out her cup for more. "I startee likee."

Ned gave a broad smile. "That's a good girl," he said. "I told the boss you'd come round soon."

She smiled back. "I learn talkee Merican."

He coughed. "Yes, you talk real good. Of course, the words you're learning won't get you far outside of the profession, you understand."

She forced down the coffee, trying to seem casual. "Mr. Robert, I not see him four five days now. He findee other girl?"

Ned stopped his puttering and gave her a sharp look. "Don't you concern yourself with Mr. Robert. He's left town. Gone on a long trip."

"Oh, okay, Mr. Ned. I go get clothes on now." She got up from the table, willing her legs not to wobble. Ned Chambreau thought he was being so clever, but Lily knew what it meant. All the girls knew what to do when farm boys or young prospectors came in. They'd get them drunk on Ned's special whiskey. Then, when they passed out, they were taken—or thrown—down to the tunnels. From the tunnels they went to ships ready to sail. The captains would pay as much as fifty dollars for an able-bodied man. By the time the men woke up, they were far out to sea.

She didn't know what happened to them after that, but she had never heard of one who came back home.

But Robert wasn't a poor farmer's son or a stranger in town. His mother was a rich lady. He had a big house. Ned had told her to be especially nice to him. The boss, a figure Lily had never seen but imagined as a cross between a mandarin and a dragon, must have been very angry at Robert to take such a chance.

She had to do something to help him.

Mr. Carmichael came as soon as he got her message. He had shaved hurriedly and had missed wiping off a blob of cream under one ear. For some reason, it made him seem much more trustworthy.

"I am at your service, Mrs. Stratton." He bowed. "Command me and I obey."

"I would rather you gave me your honest opinion, rather than unquestioning obedience," she said seriously.

His eyes opened wide. "You constantly surprise me," he said, shaking his head. "I apologize for my assumptions."

"I accept your apology, and ask your pardon for my rudeness," she answered. "But I have a great favor to ask of you, and I don't want you to undertake it unless you agree with me."

She explained her dilemma.

"I have no proof," she concluded. "And before I continue, I want to be sure that Mr. King can't be placed somewhere else at the time of Mr. Smith's death."

Mr. Carmichael rose even higher in her opinion by giving her theory serious consideration.

"Your logic is fine, as far as it goes," he said. "But, as you are aware, there are several areas that are only conjecture. Those have to be solidified with proof before you make any accusation."

"I know that." She tried not to be annoyed. He sounded very much like a prosecuting attorney. "But you must understand that I don't care if we have absolute proof. All I want is enough to get him to tell us what he's done with my son!"

"Of course." He rubbed the back of his neck. "Forgive me again, please. I'll do anything necessary to get Robert back. Right now I agree that Matthew King is the most likely one to have abducted him. I'll try to find out if he had the opportunity to waylay Dan Smith as well. But I'd like you to consider that there may be another explanation."

"I'll consider anything that will bring my son home!" She fought down hysteria.

"Good." He saw that this wasn't the time for revelations about Robert's behavior. "Then you'll permit me to investigate beyond the movements of Matthew King?"

"I don't know what you're talking about." Emily gave him such a look of suffering that he almost forgot himself.

"Sorry, I was thinking like a lawyer." He avoided looking in her eyes. If he did he would say too much, and this was most definitely not that time. "The first thing is to either prove King responsible or rule him out. After that, we can decide what needs to be done."

That seemed to satisfy her.

"You'll begin at once?"

"This very minute," he promised. "I'm going over to the Arlington Club this afternoon. The men King is most likely to have had meetings with will be there. I can find out from them without anyone getting the wind up."

It was all she could do not to hug him. "And you'll report back, whatever the result?"

"I swear." He held his hand up as if in court.

"Thank you," she choked, "I'm sorry to be so emotional. It's only that I've felt so alone."

She held out her hand.

He took it.

"You won't be from now on," he said, holding her hand tightly in both his own. "I'll stay with you to see this to the end."

Realizing that he had already said too much, Carmichael quickly took his leave.

He set out at once for the Arlington Club, the blob of shaving cream dissolving in the heat of his fervor to accomplish the quest she had set him.

———

Emily was beginning to realize that, even if she wouldn't use laudanum, she needed something to calm her enough to be able to continue in her search. She looked at her watch. It was not yet four. She could go down to Dr. See's for a consultation. He would know the best combination of medicines for her condition.

She went up to change into a walking skirt. As she passed the door to Robert's room, she thought she heard a noise from inside.

Her breath caught. She pushed the door open.

"Robert, darling," she called. "Where have you—oh! Who are you? What are you doing in my son's room?"

Standing by the open window was a small form wrapped in a coat and hood designed for a person twice its size. It gave a squeak when Emily appeared, then the coat was flung down to reveal a young Chinese girl in an ill-made dress. She threw herself to the floor in a kowtow.

"Forgive me, most excellent mother of Robert," she begged. "I had to come to you. I didn't know what else to do."

CHAPTER THIRTY

The Act in question [to tax Chinese businesses $15.00 a month] in my judg-ment, is pernicious in every sense. It is in violation of the Constitution of the State and in violation of the Constitution and treaties of the United States, and if allowed to become law would be a system of legalized robbery.

—GOVERNOR WOODS'S VETO OF A BILL TO IMPOSE A TAX
ONLY ON CHINESE, 1867

MONDAY AFTERNOON, MARCH 23, 1868

Emily stared at the apparition. This couldn't be real. Anxiety had af-fected her mind. Chinese girls did not materialize in second-story bedrooms in Portland. But the sound of Robert's name in that accented Shanghai dialect made her step toward it all the same.

The girl didn't move, not even to look up, as Emily approached. She flinched as Emily bent and touched her shoulder, but she didn't try to flee.

"Who are you?" Emily whispered. "What are you doing here in my house?"

"*Wo zhen dubuqi!*" the girl apologized. "My name is Wu Li-An." She spoke into the carpet. "But here they call me Lily. I work . . . by the river."

Emily had already figured that out.

"You know something about what happened to my son?" she asked. "Did someone send you to tell me?"

"Nobody sent me." She still wouldn't look at Emily. "I ran away when Mr. Ned's back was turned. I stole a coat. He'll beat me when he finds me."

Emily knelt and pulled Lily up, gripping both her arms firmly.

"Look at me, Li-An," she ordered. "I won't let anyone beat you. Now tell me, where is Robert?"

"Far, far away," she said sadly. "They put him on a boat, like they did me. He's been sold to the sea captain to work across the ocean."

"Oh, dear God, thank you," Emily breathed. "That means that at least he's still alive."

She sank down on to the floor weeping with relief. He wasn't lying in the forest being gnawed at by wild beasts. He hadn't drowned and been washed down the river. He hadn't been robbed and shot. He'd been shang-haied. To many mothers that would be just as bad. But Emily had been a sea captain's wife.

Lily gingerly crept closer to Emily. She didn't know what to do to help Robert's mother. Slowly, Emily got to her feet. She wiped her face with her sleeve. Then she drew Lily up.

"I want you to tell me everything you know about Robert," she said. "But first you are going to have a hot bath and a hot bowl of *ji-tang.*"

Lily suddenly understood why Robert cared so deeply for his mother.

Carmichael cursed himself soundly as he strode down the street. Why hadn't he had the courage to tell Emily that her son was a wastrel and a profligate who quite probably had come to a bad end? Well, perhaps not in those exact words, but she had to learn sometime. That didn't mean that her conjectures about King weren't possible. If the bastard wanted to hurt her, Robert's behavior just made it easier for him to do it.

The trouble with Emily's reasoning was that King wasn't the sort of person to risk killing a man face to face. He was portly and rarely exercised. Even if he had hit Daniel from behind, the blow might not have done much. Then Smith would have easily knocked him flat. No, if King was responsible, then he had paid someone else to do the deed.

It was the same with young Robert's fate. He couldn't see Matthew imprisoning the boy and then holding him hostage for Emily's share of the company. But he might arrange it so that Robert was removed from the picture long enough to distract Emily from noticing any financial chicanery.

Still, Carmichael wasn't going to renege on his promise. He stopped at the Arlington Club and made some general inquiries that included where Matthew King had been on the Tuesday in question. No one remembered. That didn't surprise him. It was hard enough to keep track of one's own schedule. He did ascertain that there hadn't been any meetings that afternoon at which King might have been expected to be present.

On his way home he stopped in at Wasserman's tobacco shop on Front Street for cigars. Phil Wasserman had just returned from Bavaria with a wife half his age who was already expecting their first child, so he might not be in. But if he were, he'd be full of information. And since, being Jewish, he wasn't a member of the Arlington, he might know something they didn't.

He was in luck. There was a young clerk at the counter, but Phil came out as soon as he heard Carmichael's voice.

"Alistair, good to see you again." He shook Carmichael's hand. "I have some excellent cigars just in, hand rolled in New York. Here, smell this." He held the cigar up to Carmichael's nose.

"Mmmmm! I'll take five dozen."

"I thought this blend would suit you," Wasserman said in satisfaction. "*Jacob, macht ein Gepäck für Herr Carmichael,*" he added to the clerk.

"Why don't we try one now?" Carmichael suggested.

Wasserman thought that a fine idea, and soon the two men were sitting in the back discussing local politics, in which Wasserman was much involved. Slowly, Carmichael nudged the conversation to Matthew King and the missing Norton Andrews.

"King has been losing partners rapidly," Wasserman said. "First Horace dying unexpectedly in San Francisco last year and now Andrews leaving so suddenly. It makes me wonder if the company isn't in financial trouble."

"Not that I've heard," Carmichael equivocated. "I'd understood that

Horace's widow was planning on taking an active part in running the business but now, with her son missing, she may not feel up to it."

"Yes, it's very sad about that," Wasserman said as he puffed. "Of course, the way he was going, I'm not surprised. After all, look at the father. I'm going to see that my sons have a better example."

"So you think young Stratton ran afoul of some thugs in one of the saloons?" Carmichael asked casually.

"I think that Ned Chambreau sent him out the Shanghai tunnel," Wasserman stated. "Jacob saw him go into the Hellhole the night he vanished."

"He did? Why didn't he tell anyone?"

"Jacob's English isn't very good," Wasserman explained. "By the time he told me, it was three or four days after. And we can't say for sure that the boy didn't come out and go to another saloon. I don't want to make any accusations. And I'm sure Daniel Jacobi has already looked into it."

Carmichael didn't agree. "He might not have thought of it. Ned knows better than to try to abduct local men. I can't see him letting Robert be taken. He knows whose son the boy is."

"He'd do it if someone else told him to," Wasserman observed.

"For instance?"

"Matthew King, for one. But I didn't tell you that." Wasserman stubbed out his smoke. "Anyway, I'm not sure if he's the master builder of this."

"Sorry?" Carmichael didn't catch the reference.

Wasserman looked at his friend appraisingly. "You know that I have supported the East Side Railroad Company," he said. "I believe that the route they plan will be better for trade. But since I returned from Europe, I've felt that there have been changes in the control of the enterprise."

"Everyone says Ben Holladay is trying to buy it," Carmichael said.

"So they do," Wasserman agreed. "But I suspect that it's someone local who is pulling the strings."

"King?" Carmichael guessed.

Wasserman shrugged. "I don't know. Whoever it is has gone to much trouble to keep his name in the dark."

"Well, someone's gone to a lot of trouble to destroy Emily Stratton's life," Carmichael said grimly. "I think it's time they were brought into the light."

Phillip Wasserman lifted his eyebrows. "Why, Alistair, I never knew you could feel so passionately about something. We'll make a politician of you yet."

Mary Kate didn't bother to ask where Lily had come from. As soon as she saw the girl's bruised body, she went for the arnica.

"I'll give her a good wash, head to toe," she told Emily. "And then I'll wrap her up nice and warm like I'd be doing to my own little sister at home. The things that men get up to! They're as bad as the British. Come along, my dove. No one will hurt you here."

Lily didn't understand the words, but she responded to the tone and went with Mary Kate.

Emily went down to the kitchen to ask Lun Ho to reheat the soup from dinner. But all the time her heart was singing, *He's alive! He's alive!* On a ship, perhaps being worked hard, but alive. She could get him back.

A short time later, Mary Kate brought Lily down to the kitchen. She had dressed her in some of Emily's Chinese clothes. The trousers were too long, but otherwise, they fit her perfectly.

Lily kept running her fingers over the embroidered silk. "I never wore such beautiful clothes except on the night I was deflowered," she stated.

Lun Ho dropped his ladle.

"Have some soup, Li-An," Emily said. "You and I will talk later."

That night she heard Lily's story. It wasn't a new one to her. She had seen the sad little girls in Shanghai. Her mother and some of the other missionary women had tried to help them but with no success. Prostitution was too much a part of society. Looking back, Emily wondered why they imagined they could end it in China when they couldn't in their own countries.

Her jaw tightened when Lily haltingly explained Horace's part in her life. The girl couldn't bring herself to tell Emily about Robert. It was clear that Emily was upset enough.

"I am so sorry, Li-An," Emily wept. "So very sorry. I stopped him going to the servant girls, but I could do nothing outside the house. Perhaps I didn't try hard enough."

Lily gently touched Emily's cheek. "I think he hurt you worse than he did me."

"No." Emily brushed the girl's hair back from her face. "But we both have suffered. I won't send you back to that place, Li-An. If you want to, you may stay here, or I shall pay so that you can go home to your family."

Lily was overwhelmed. She clung to Emily until she fell asleep. All through the night Emily held her. She knew that this broken flower had been sent to her as a test. She would not fail. Lily was at least one sin of her husband's that she could atone for.

The next morning, Mary Kate went out to call John to breakfast. Before they went in, she told him about Lily.

"The missus is planning on keeping her for now," she said. "And I don't want you thinking she's your private concubine."

"Mary Kate Kyne! What are you saying?" He drew himself up indignantly. "Do you think I'd be abusing a poor mite like that, who's already been hurt so much?"

He seemed so genuinely shocked that she should have such a low opinion of him that Mary Kate was immediately ashamed.

"I ask your pardon, John Mahoney," she said. "You never gave me cause to think you were anything but a gentleman. It's angry I am at all men this morning, for what they did to that little girl."

"Well, I wasn't one of them," he stated. "That I'll swear to."

Carmichael hurried to Emily's house at the earliest suitable hour.

"I think I know what happened to your son," he announced, once he had caught his breath.

"Yes, I know," she said. "He was impressed as a sailor on some ship that was here last week."

"Exactly," he answered, deflated. "How did you find out, and why do you look so happy about it?"

"There was a witness," Emily explained. "And I'm happy because I was imagining so many worse horrors. Now we can find out which ship he was taken to and send someone after him. Half the sailors on Horace's ship had been shanghaied at one time or other. I worry about how he'll be treated, especially if they find out whose son he is, but he's alive, Mr. Carmichael. And there's something I can do to save him. That makes all the difference."

Carmichael had never seen anyone relieved to know their son had been kidnapped and sent to sea, but he could see how it was preferable to believing him dead. If this was what she needed to continue her own life, then he wasn't about to mention the horrid living conditions, disease, floggings, and the chances of a boy Robert's age becoming a catamite for the rest of the crew.

"Yes, of course," he murmured. "Then my great news is rather an anticlimax."

"Not at all." Emily took his hat and handed it to Mary Kate. "You must come in, have some coffee and tell me what else you've learned. Mary Kate, would you bring coffee to the dining room, please? Mr. Carmichael, have you breakfasted yet?"

"No, but . . ."

"Then ask Lun Ho to make up a plate for Mr. Carmichael, as well," she added to Mary Kate.

"Now, what have you learned about Mr. King?" she asked when they were settled. "Can we bring him to justice yet?"

"I'm afraid not." Carmichael poured cream into his coffee. The door to the kitchen swung open and Lily appeared, carefully holding a plate of eggs, bacon, fried mushrooms, and griddle cakes in both hands.

"Goodness me! Who is this?" he exclaimed.

"My redemption," Emily said. "At least part of it, I hope."

After the girl had returned to the kitchen, Emily told him Lily's story.

He shook his head sadly. "So many things we close our eyes to. I knew that the few Chinese women in town were mostly brought in to service the Chinese workmen, but if I thought of them at all, I imagined older women, tougher." He sighed.

"The prostitutes in China are mostly girls of twelve or so," Emily said. "By the time they are twenty, they are either wealthy concubines or living in the meanest circumstances and riddled with disease."

"Mrs. Stratton!"

"I'm sorry," she said. "I thought you knew. It's very sad. But I think it's worse for them here. In San Francisco, I saw a girl, younger than Lily, standing naked on a block to be auctioned off to the brothel owners. She would never have been so publicly shamed in Shanghai."

"And we just spent four years and thousands of lives to free the slaves in our country, only to do this," Carmichael said sadly. "It seems we lost the war after all."

"Just a battle," Emily answered. "And I'm finally learning how to fight. If you could find out for me what ship Robert was likely to have been put on, we can start working to get him home."

Carmichael stared at her, his breakfast forgotten. "And to think I felt you needed protection from the harshness of the world. You have seen things I can't even imagine."

Emily looked away from his honest blue eyes. "I wish I hadn't," she whispered. "I wish I were one of those women who never knew ugliness or cruelty. But I can't change what happened, or what it did to me. I'm sorry."

"Sorry?" Carmichael rose so quickly that he knocked his plate onto the floor, eggs spattering on the carpet. "I'm sorry, sorry that you or any human has to suffer. I think that you are the bravest, most remarkable woman I have ever met."

"Me?" Emily shook her head, bewildered. He seemed sincere. He had so forgotten himself that his napkin was still stuck in his belt, like an embroidered apron. The naked emotion in his face frightened her. And it thrilled her in a way that she had no words for.

She made herself look down at the table until her breathing was quite normal again. Mr. Carmichael became very busy bent beside his chair, scooping up the spilled eggs and mushrooms.

"Thank you," Emily said softly. "That is the nicest compliment I have ever received. Now, we have much to do, if you are willing to help me."

When she dared to meet his eyes, she found that he had composed himself again and was smiling at her. His expression was amused and somehow proud. Emily wasn't ready to investigate all the implications of the past five minutes.

"If you have finished eating," she said, looking at the mess on his plate, "perhaps we could arrange to meet this afternoon and discuss the return of my son. For the present, I intend to go down to town and make sure Lily never returns to that horrible place."

She was oddly honored that Mr. Carmichael didn't even suggest that he go instead.

Dr. See was not pleased when Emily came into his apothecary shop.

"You have brought a lot of trouble to us," he stated. "I won't help you anymore."

"Yes, you will." Emily was in no mood for manners. "The trouble was here long before I arrived. I need to know who I have to pay to free Wu Li-An from the brothel run by Ned Chambreau."

"That's not a Chinese establishment," the doctor said. "I know nothing about it."

"Then I shall go ask Ah Ning." She turned to leave. "And I'll also ask him who it was that Ah Sung came from China to kill and why."

"Wait." He held up his hands in resignation. "Ah Ning will be here soon for our weekly Mah-Jongg game. He'll tell you as much as we know."

He ushered her into the back room and left. A moment later he returned with a cup of herbal tea.

"Don't worry," he said, seeing her expression. "It is a simple blend to clear the blood at the end of winter. I'll have that cup and pour you another."

"No, thank you; this will be fine." Emily took a sip to prove good faith.

A curtain at the other side of the room rustled and Ah Ning appeared. He started when he saw Emily.

"Mrs. Stratton has come to ask for information," Dr. See explained. "It seems she has already deduced much of the truth."

Emily stared at Ah Ning. "You came through the tunnels, didn't you? The ones they used to steal my son with no one seeing. How far do they reach?"

"There is a network running through most of downtown near the wharfs," Ah Ning said. "They were built to take goods to stores without having to go out in the rain and snow. Many Chinese use them to avoid the eyes of the Westerners."

Emily looked down at the floor. Underneath it was another Portland, one she never knew existed. People going to and fro on innocent or wicked errands, moving cargo from ships to shops or disposing of bodies like that of Ah Sung. This was how unsuspecting men were drugged and stowed aboard outbound ships.

Why didn't anyone stop it?

The answer came to her at once: because powerful men found the trafficking too profitable to allow it to be stopped.

"Ah Sung came here to exact revenge." She looked straight at Ah Ning. "It was written in his Bible. He told me he wasn't part of the Heavenly Kingdom, but that his family had suffered from it. Who was he looking for? Was it my husband?"

"No, Mrs. Stratton," Ah Ning said. "If so, he could have been taken care of in Shanghai."

"But Captain Stratton was part of the crime that had to be avenged," she persisted. "What was it?"

Ah Ning exchanged a glance with See Fan, who nodded.

"Your husband was one of many," the merchant continued. "But we knew that there was someone who was sitting safely far away in Portland and causing infinite misery to our families. This man sold American guns to the Taiping rebels. Then, for the return trip to America he bought Chinese people to work in the mines, on the railroads, and in the brothels. They believed they would work off the passage soon with the money they would make. You have seen the truth of that."

"Ah Sung lost his family in the rebellion." Dr. See continued the story. "They were small shopkeepers just outside Nanking. The Taiping shot them. Ah Sung learned of the man who had supplied the weapons that continued the fighting. On his own, he decided to eliminate him. He was very well educated and, as you guessed, he spoke good English. He tracked the man to Portland, entered his service, and, in an ironic turn of events, was told to work in your home and spy on you."

"I can understand why he did this, but he could have come to me," Emily said. "I would have helped him."

"How was he to know that?" Ah Ning asked. "After a few days he began to think you might help. He was impressed by you. He told us you were not like your husband. Otherwise, we wouldn't have agreed to speak with you at all."

"But he failed in his quest, didn't he?" Emily concluded sadly.

"Yes. We don't know if he gave himself away or if someone betrayed him. He went to meet with his master one night. Of the rest, you know as much as we do." Ah Ning bowed his head.

"This man is very skillful at covering his tracks," See Fan added. "Ah Sung wasn't sure of his name until the night he died. He never had time to tell us."

Emily pressed her lips together. "I know who it is," she said. "Even if we haven't found solid proof yet."

She stood and bowed to the two men.

"I promise you, honorable sirs, that I will see that he pays for what he did. Ah Sung's ghost shall have revenge."

CHAPTER THIRTY-ONE

Robert, when he was a child,
At his play about my knee,
If I looked at him and smiled,
Often came and said to me:
"When I get to be a man,
I will love no one but you."
And I answered, "If you can,
Make your promise good and true."

—EBEN B. REXFORD, "CHILD AND MAN," *PETERSON'S MAGAZINE,*
JUNE 1868

TUESDAY, MARCH 24, 1868

Carmichael would have preferred to question the Chinese doctor himself rather than let Emily go alone. But he saw the wisdom in her plan. After all, she spoke the language. All the same, his task seemed like something she had invented to make him feel useful.

He had no trouble getting the names of the three ships that had left Portland with international cargoes in the time when Robert might have been put aboard. There was no way to know which one the boy had sailed in. Carmichael looked at his pocket watch. It was only one o'clock, and he wasn't to meet Emily again until four.

There must be something more to do. He walked down Front Street, oblivious to the traffic around him, automatically dodging the wide skirts of the women doing their shopping and the stacks of barrels next to the breweries.

His steps slowed as he neared a narrow building, nothing more than a two-story shack wedged in between two more prosperous establishments. He'd always known it was there but had thought no more than to avoid it. Now he stopped and glared at its shabby exterior. No sign over the door gave the name of the place, but every reprobate in town knew his way to the Hellhole.

That was the place that let sixteen-year-old boys copulate with fourteen-year-old prostitutes, a place where young men were lured to their doom.

Something in Carmichael broke. He squared his shoulders and pushed open the door.

A few men were sitting at the table having the free lunch with their beer. They looked up in mild curiosity as Carmichael entered.

He marched up to the bar, where Ned gave him a cheerful grin.

"Lawyer Carmichael!" he cried. "I never thought I'd see you in here. What's your pleasure?"

"To see you and the fiend you work for behind bars," Carmichael said quietly. "I've come to tell you that Miss Lily Wu has left your employ and she's not coming back. If your boss objects, have him come see me."

Ned roared at this. "Well, who'd'a thought your tastes ran in that direction. Though I've seen senators and ministers sneaking up those stairs."

"You are a foul, disgusting person," Carmichael told him. "And the man who owns this place is even worse. Give him this for me."

He hit Ned in the jaw with a punch that had thirty years of suppressed anger behind it. The man fell without making a sound.

Carmichael straightened his cravat. He looked at the men at the table as if inviting them to have a swing at him. They looked back in astonishment. None of them had ever seen a fiftyish man in a frock coat and top hat come into the Hellhole and deck the bartender. It was better than a show at the Oro Fino.

By the time he was back on the street, Carmichael was feeling rather ashamed of letting his emotions overcome his common sense. He wondered if Ned would press charges. The man certainly had a right to. He must have looked a fool, stomping in there and blowing up like that.

Still, he walked a bit more jauntily up the road to Emily's house, his long legs striding easily over the rough terrain. Hotheaded it might have been, but all the same, he admitted in his heart, it had felt damn good.

Emily was making good time going home, too. What she wanted most was to confront Matthew King and unmask him before the world as the miserable hypocrite that he was. An image flashed into her mind from one of the ladies' magazines of an undaunted heroine reducing the villain to a quivering jelly by the force of her moral courage.

She couldn't see Mr. King responding so readily.

They had to have a plan. If they marched into his office with their accusation, he would laugh in their faces. There must be a way to get more proof.

She didn't even notice that she had slipped into the plural in her thinking.

Mr. Carmichael was waiting on her doorstep. As she started up the drive, he was rubbing the knuckles of his right hand as if they hurt him. When he spotted her, he stopped at once.

"What did you find out?" they spoke together.

They exchanged information over pots of tea.

"We can send messengers after each of the ships with orders to send Robert home at once," Emily said. "I shall offer a reward."

She seemed content with that, as if she would have him back in his own bed by nightfall. Carmichael saw no need to point out possible complications. He returned to the closer problem.

"We should call in the marshal," he was forced to suggest. "King is obviously a very dangerous man. You believe that Ah Sung came all the way from China just to kill him. And yet, King was able to get wind of the plan and get him first. Dan Smith was used to a rough-and-tumble life, but King or one of his minions killed him too. This is not someone who will confess and repent if we confront him."

Emily wondered how he had come up with the same scene as she had. He had also realized that the whole story was the stuff of melodrama.

"I told Marshal Jacobi what I found in the Bible; he didn't think it was enough to arrest anyone."

"I'm afraid he was right," Carmichael sighed, partly in longing for a nice glass of port. He had come up with some of his best defenses while savoring port. What could be imagined out of a teapot?

"What about Mr. Andrews?" Emily asked suddenly.

"Andrews? But he's nowhere to be found," Carmichael reminded her. "He may even be dead."

"I know," she said. "But he departed in such a hurry. Isn't it possible that something was left behind, some document or piece of evidence that could incriminate both him and Mr. King?"

"Possibly." He wished he had a cigar to go with the port. That made ratiocination so much easier. "But it's just as likely that he took or destroyed everything, or that King scoured the rooms after he had gone."

"But there's a chance, isn't there?" she persisted.

"A chance," he gave in. "No more. And how do you propose to search for this hypothetical evidence?"

She was prepared for the question.

"Do you know there are tunnels running all over the business district of town?"

"Oh, yes," he said. "They're used all the time for transporting merchandise."

"Like Robert," she reminded him.

"Yes," he apologized. "What about them?"

"I think there must be a doorway from them into the main office of Stratton, Andrews, and King," she said. "And from there I know there is a staircase leading up to Mr. Andrews's rooms. The panel hiding it was part-way opened when I came in one morning. They seated me with my back to it and thought I hadn't noticed."

Carmichael's jaw dropped.

"My dear young woman!" He couldn't believe it. "You are not proposing to break into King's office?"

"No," she said calmly. "I'm proposing that we sneak in. You forget, it's my office now, too. I have keys. You can't break and enter your own property. It would be quite legal. But it would be better to go after hours. I don't think it would be of any use to us to search it with Mr. King standing there."

"Just when I thought you couldn't surprise me again!" He put his hand to his heart in mock horror.

"Do you know of a way to get into the tunnels?" she asked.

"Yes," he nodded. "Several, in fact. There's one not far from the office. It shouldn't be much used after dark. But you can't be thinking of going down there."

"Why not?" she bristled.

"For one thing, your hoops wouldn't fit." He measured the width of her skirt with his eyes. "For another, that train would pick up every piece of muck from the ground. There aren't floors in most places, only boards set in the earth."

Emily's expression was that of a naughty child caught with a hand in the biscuit tin.

"As usual, Mr. Carmichael, you are quite right," she leaned forward to whisper to him. "As it happens, I have a very nice pair of trousers."

"Mary Kate, I'm going out this evening," Emily announced at dinner. "Mr. Carmichael is bringing his trap for me at eight. We're going to the theater."

"Yes, ma'am." Mary Kate tried to hide her astonishment. That Mr. Carmichael had been in the house most of the afternoon. The way he was looking at her wasn't proper for an older gentleman to look at a rich young widow.

But Emily didn't act like a woman being courted. She didn't primp in her dressing. In fact, she seemed to be trying to look plain. Instead of curling her hair, she wove it into one long dark braid and wrapped it about her head. She didn't put on any of her jewelry and begged Mary Kate to leave her corset as loose as possible.

Perhaps she was trying to discourage him in a ladylike way. Mary Kate had no idea her mistress could be so devious. She was quite impressed. Emily was even carrying her large reticule, big enough for a picnic lunch, instead of her beaded evening bag. She looked as dowdy as old Mrs. Melette on her way home from market.

"Mary Kate, I want you and John to keep a close watch on Li-An for me," Emily said as she left. "I don't think the men from the brothel will come looking for her, but just in case, bolt all the doors. I know that means you'll have to sit up, but I'll try not to be too late."

"It's no trouble to sit up here by a warm fire and Mary Kate to keep me company," John teased.

Mary Kate tossed her head. "I'll be sitting upstairs, helping Lily with her English. She's a quick one. She'll be speaking as good as anybody before you know it."

"Better than you, I've no doubt," John said.

Emily left them happily bickering.

"Are you sure you want to go through with this?" Carmichael asked as he handed her into the trap.

"It was my idea, wasn't it?" she answered.

They drove through town in silence. Carmichael left the trap at Hogan's, telling the ostler he'd return by midnight. Then he and Emily started walking in the direction of the Oro Fino. A block away, they turned west and doubled back along the alley between the shops. They stopped behind the chandlery. Carmichael drew a key from his pocket and opened the door.

"How did you get a key?" she asked.

"The same way you have yours," he answered. "I'm part owner."

He pointed to a curtained corner. "You can change there and leave your hoops until we come back," he said. "You can get into them unaided?"

"I'll have to," she said.

How she wished she could leave them behind forever! The black silk trousers slipped on so easily. The only difficult part was stepping from behind the curtain and letting Mr. Carmichael see that she had legs. She left on the top of the dress, although she wished she could have dispensed with the corsets, too. A short, hooded cloak would hide her western clothing as well as her face, if necessary.

"Douse the candle before you come out," he said softly. "The light from the streetlamp will be enough to find your way across the room. The entrance is a trapdoor. I'm standing halfway in. I won't risk a light until we're both down."

In the darkness she found the courage to cross the room. His hand reached out to guide her to the ladder.

"I'll go down first," he said. "Then feel your way on the ladder. Can you lower the door as you go?"

"Yes," she answered.

She had not reached the bottom rung when the trapdoor clicked shut. The darkness was absolute.

"I'm right here beside you," Mr. Carmichael's voice was almost in her ear. "I'm lighting the lamp now."

There was a rasp and a flare that hurt her eyes, and then the lantern glowed more gently as he lowered the shade.

"Which way from here?" she whispered. "I'm turned around."

He didn't answer at once. She followed his gaze down.

"Uh, yes." He looked up with embarrassment and quickly collected himself. "That way. The tunnels twist but it isn't far. There should be a mark on the door. Nothing was intended to be hidden on this side."

She followed him so closely that she bumped several times against his back. The parallel boards in the center of the floor were set apart to accommodate wheelbarrows. They hadn't been intended for a stroll by dark lantern.

When she came to a full stop, she landed against him so hard that she had to grab his waist to keep from falling.

"I am so sorry!" she said.

"Think nothing of it," he answered. "Perhaps if you took my arm?"

The flicker of the lantern shaped faces in the crude walls of the tunnel. Emily felt that she was being watched from every angle. Stacks of barrels and boxes became monsters ready to rise and grab her. Emily scolded herself for cowardice.

Suddenly she realized that theirs wasn't the only light in the tunnel. Someone was coming toward them! Quickly, she pulled the hood of her cloak over her head so that it hid her face. Carmichael turned and gave her a nod of approval.

Around a twist of the path came two Chinese men, carrying a collection of packages hung from a pole, the ends balanced on their shoulders. When they saw Carmichael, they started so sharply that the bundles swung in wild arcs, nearly smashing against the wall.

"Good evening," Carmichael said blandly. "I didn't mean to startle you. Carry on with your business."

The two men collected themselves and moved past Emily and Carmichael, muttering angrily.

"What were they saying?" Carmichael asked when they had vanished into the dark.

"Nothing." Emily was glad he couldn't see her flaming cheeks. "They thought I was a Chinese girl you had purchased. They don't like white men using their women."

.Carmichael was silent a moment. "Well, better my reputation ruined than yours," he said at last. "I imagine that your translation was more polite than their actual words."

Emily didn't answer.

Perhaps the encounter had unsettled her, but for the rest of the journey, she had the distinct feeling that someone was following them.

The way up to the office of Stratton, Andrews, and King was not as difficult. A narrow staircase led up to a door, which swung open. Emily had to stifle a laugh. They had come out behind that enormous painting of Horace. No wonder Mr. King hadn't removed it.

"Where shall we start looking?" she asked.

"Why don't you try the office and I'll go on up to Andrews's rooms?" Carmichael suggested.

"There's only one lamp," she pointed out.

"Oh, right. A flaw in my preparations. Sorry."

"Actually, I'd rather not split up," she said. "Now, the desk is too obvious a hiding place unless there are secret drawers."

She began fiddling with it while he tapped on tables and tilted books on the shelves.

"These haven't been dusted in some time," he commented as particles drifted through the air. All at once he gave a trumpeting sneeze.

They both froze.

A moment passed and there was no sound of police whistles. They began to breathe again.

They looked in, over, and under everything in the office. Both of them were smudged with dust, and Emily's braid had come loose and fallen down her back.

"There's nothing here," Carmichael declared. "Let's try upstairs."

Carefully they climbed to Andrews's rooms.

"Either Mr. Andrews is a very untidy man or someone has been here before us," Emily said when they reached the top.

Drawers had been turned upside down and the contents left in heaps on the floor. The shelves had been emptied. A Dresden figurine lay smashed by the bookcase.

"It doesn't look like we'll have any luck here," Carmichael said.

"We can't give up." Emily knelt in the mess. "Mr. King may have missed something."

Carmichael glanced at his watch. "We have about half an hour before we should start back. Let's see how much we can get through."

The task looked hopeless. The cheap furniture held no secret compartments. The clothes hooks were firmly fixed to the wall. The mirror did not swing back to reveal a safe. Carmichael tried them all, feeling immensely foolish.

Emily sorted through the mound of books and papers tossed on the floor. Most of the books were from the lending library. Andrews's taste ran to popular fiction. Emily wouldn't have thought it of him.

There was a little book for personal accounts. This yielded nothing more interesting than that he bought a lot of sleeve buttons in January and seemed to live on cheese and dried beef. There were doodles on some of the pages, sketches of animals and faces. A caricature of Tom Eliot as a schoolboy with a hoop was really quite well done.

Amid the February expenditures there was another drawing, not at all cheerful. Andrews's pencil had torn the paper in places with the force of his emotions. It was of a man with a long beard, dressed in a long greatcoat and holding a cigar. He seemed a proper gentleman of affairs except for his long nose and expression of malevolent glee. And the horns growing out of his head, of course.

Emily stared at the picture. She crawled over to the dark lantern on the floor to see it more closely. Now she noticed two little figures by the man's feet. They were crudely done, naked men tied on a rack. One was rather portly, the other gaunt.

Despite the distortion of the features, the face of Satan was one she knew.

"Mr. Carmichael," she said. "Ah Sung came to America because the man he was looking for never visited China. Mr. King and Mr. Andrews have both been there. You said that you felt there was a silent partner directing the most unsavory business that Horace was part of. I think this could be the man."

She handed him the book.

"You see it, don't you?" she asked. "I've been terribly, terribly wrong."

"I can't believe it." Carmichael took out a pair of reading glasses to examine it better. "He had us all fooled."

"It wasn't Ben Holladay that Daniel Smith was afraid of," Emily said sadly. "Why didn't he tell me?"

"Fear," Carmichael said. "Of him and of your disbelief. It seems poor Dan overcame it too late."

"It doesn't matter who he is; he must be brought to justice." Emily's voice was icy. "He is responsible for more death than you know."

"He will be," Carmichael swore. "Now that we know who, it will be easier to find evidence. There must be records that look harmless but that when put together will form a pattern. I know how."

"You're sure?" She rested her hands on his arm. "It matters more to me than you know."

"Absolutely," he answered. "Even Daniel Jacobi will be able to unravel this one. He may even be able to find a witness."

"A witness," Emily said. She looked up at him in sudden panic. "Lily! Mr. Carmichael, we have to get home at once!"

CHAPTER THIRTY-TWO

"The prevention of crime and disease is much less expensive and more produc-tive of good to the public than their cure."

—"The Nurseries of Randall's Island," W. H. Davenport, *Harper's New Monthly Magazine,* December 1867

HALF AN HOUR LATER

Mary Kate's eye's bugged out at the state of Emily's clothing, espe-cially the skirt hastily put back on and misbuttoned.

"Where is Lily?" Emily asked as she and Carmichael rushed in. "Is she all right?"

"She's sound asleep upstairs, ma'am," Mary Kate answered. "And I told him that she wasn't going anywhere, at least not tonight. I don't care who he is, ma'am. You can't let him take that poor mite."

"Him?"

"She means me, Emily."

Standing in the doorway to the parlor was George Bracewell. He gave a laugh and swayed. Emily realized he had been drinking.

"Well, what the devil have you two been up to?" he leered. "Just goes to show that you can't judge a book by its cover."

"Quite true, George," Carmichael spoke. "We should have remembered that the devil wears many disguises."

Emily was too stunned to move. She had thought she would have time to gather together her evidence as well as her wits before she had to face her brother-in-law.

"What are you doing here?" she demanded.

"Alice heard that you had rescued a soiled dove from one of the establishments downtown," he chuckled. "She sent me over with some clean clothes for the girl and also the offer to take her into our home. She gave the impression that she didn't think your house was the best place to give her a good Christian upbringing. From what I see, she was right."

"You . . ." Carmichael began to take off his coat.

George laughed again.

"Mary Kate, get John at once!" Emily ordered. "Tell him to go for the police."

"The police?" George still found the situation amusing. "I don't need a constable to protect me from him," he said, laughing at Carmichael. "I can take him without working up a sweat."

Emily leapt at Carmichael, catching his arm as he swung back. She felt like a Pekinese trying to stop a mastiff.

"Don't! Please don't!" she cried. "Can't you see that he's baiting you?"

Carmichael looked down at her. Reluctantly, he lowered his arm.

"You're right," he said. "His crimes are so many that I wouldn't cloud them by giving him a reason to lay a charge against me."

"My crimes?" George looked from Emily to Carmichael and back. "That's rich, coming from a pair of flagrant fornicators."

Carmichael didn't react to the taunt.

"You are guilty of the murder of Ah Sung and Daniel Smith," he said. "Of owning a brothel that employs young women as slaves, of participating in the abduction of men to work on sailing vessels against their will, and of any number of other illegal business practices."

"That's fine lawyer talk." George's air of humor was thinning. "But you can't prove a word of it. The Chinese man was crazed with opium. He came at me with a knife. I shot him in self-defense. I have witnesses. And as for Dan Smith, the man had so many enemies you'd have to make a list to keep track of them. Emily, I don't know what this man has told you, but it's all nonsense."

Emily stared at him quietly.

"I trusted you with my son," she said. "And you stole him from me."

"No, I'd never do that!" George snapped. "I was trying to save him. The boy was a dissolute libertine, just like his father. He needed a strong hand, not a woman's indulgence. If he was shanghaied it's because you weren't willing to see the truth and keep him out of places like the Hellhole."

Carmichael looked at Emily. Her lips were white. He would have cheerfully run George through for shattering her faith in her son.

"That isn't all you did," Emily went on as if he hadn't spoken. "You killed Ah Sung's family along with thousands of others, including my parents."

Now both men stared at her.

"That's just madness," George stated. "You go about saying things like that and I'll have you in the asylum before you can blink."

Emily stepped toward him, trembling with fury. "You sold guns to the Taiping rebels at Nanking."

"What if I did?" He was becoming impatient now. "Your husband was as much a part of it as I was. More. It was his company that arranged matters, I only provided funds. You and your precious son did well enough from it. It had nothing to do with your parents."

"You don't know anything about it," she said, focusing on him completely. "If it hadn't been for Christian missionaries, poor deluded Hong would never have confused his visions with revelation. He believed he was God's second son, the younger brother of Jesus. He preached just like the apostles all over southern China and thousands followed him.

"His army took Nanking and they set up a 'perfect' Heavenly kingdom. My father, my poor saintly father, who never learned to speak Chinese properly, thought that if he could just point out the flaws in their doctrine, he could convert all the Taiping to the faith and make a city of God in China."

George yawned. "It's getting late, Emily, and we've been standing here for some time. It sounds as though your father was as mad as you."

Emily went on as though he hadn't spoken.

"He took my mother and they tried to enter the city. They were challenged at the gates and brought before the Taiping leaders. They couldn't explain their mission and were denounced as spies and imprisoned. A friend came to Shanghai and told me. I went to Nanking, tried to explain, to plead for their lives, but it was too late. They had been shot."

"Oh, my dear child!" Carmichael breathed.

George Bracewell yawned. "They were fools who would have died anyway, in a much more unpleasant fashion." He felt his pockets. "I don't know about the rest of you but I could use a cigar."

"You really don't care, do you?" Emily couldn't stop now. "Putting down the rebellion you armed took millions of lives. I saw it; villages burned, women raped and mutilated, children slaughtered or left to die of starvation. People reduced to nothing more than wild dogs fighting over a scrap of food."

"That's very sad," George said. "But nothing that didn't happen during our late war. We could discuss the morality of weapons for days but it still wouldn't change anything. Your accusations are totally unfounded. If you continue to make them, I shall most certainly call Dr. Hawthorne and have you committed—both of you, if need be. I can't have my good name slandered in such a fashion."

He seemed to think the interview was over.

The back door slammed. Emily turned in relief.

"We'll let the marshal decide how innocent you are," she announced. "We're in here, Marshal Jacobi!"

But instead of Daniel Jacobi, Norton Andrews came through the door.

He was more gaunt than ever, his clothes filthy, his beard hanging with cobwebs and chunks of food. It was a second before Emily realized that he was holding a gun.

"Norton!" George recovered first. "That trip of yours doesn't seem to have improved your health. But I'm glad to see you. Just keep that revolver leveled on Mrs. Stratton. She's likely to become violent at any moment. How did you get here, by the way?"

"You've been hiding in the tunnels," Carmichael said. "Why?"

Andrews didn't answer directly. "I saw you two. You went through my things. You didn't find anything, did you? I hid it all. But you wouldn't believe me, would you, George? You didn't trust me, so you tried to poison me."

"Oh, Christ! You're all stark staring insane," George shouted. "Carmichael, you can't believe any of this."

"Actually, I believe more now than I did when we found this." Carmichael held up the little accounts book. "Now that I know you sold guns to the Chinese, I realize why you were so afraid of it being known. You also provided weapons to the Union army, or at least you took the contract. What would your position in town be if it were known that our boys died because you sent arms to China instead?"

"What the . . . Andrews, you ass! How could you have kept records of that? Whatever you wrote in there, you'll only incriminate yourself!" George made a lunge for the book.

"No, you don't!" Andrews reached for it too.

There was a deafening explosion.

George Bracewell stopped in midair, his mouth open in astonishment. Then his body collapsed heavily onto the carpet.

Andrews stood over him, the gun still smoking.

"Too good for you, you bastard," he said.

Carmichael gently took the gun from his hand.

When Marshal Jacobi finally arrived, he knew immediately that this case, at least, would require no further investigation.

The next morning, Emily told Lily that no one would try to take her back to the Hellhole.

"You are free to do whatever you want," she explained to the girl. "I can send you back to your family with enough money to provide a dowry for you and your sisters."

Lily thought about that. "I don't know. I think I would always be afraid that my father or my husband would sell me again, if there was a famine or more war. I'd like to send something to my family, though."

"You want to stay in America?" Emily was surprised. "What would you do here?"

"I would learn to read and write and speak English," she said. "Perhaps I could get a job doing embroidery or as a servant. Maybe one day I could start a shop. Chinese people have shops here."

"For now, would you like to stay here, with me?" Emily asked. "I used to teach English at the mission school in Shanghai. I could help you."

Lily wasn't sure. "Every day in the street I would see men who had visited me. It would be nicer to go where no one knows what I did and no one would ask me to do it again."

In the end, Emily and Lily agreed that she would go to a boarding school in Corvallis, south of Portland. It was far enough to be removed from her previous life but close enough that Emily could visit now and then.

"I would even like to see Robert, when he comes home," Lily confessed. "If you would permit it."

"If I could only have him back home, I'd permit anything," Emily answered. "If it weren't for you, I wouldn't have known how to find him."

The next morning, Emily was brought out of a deep sleep by a high-pitched howling just under her window.

"Is it a fire?" She stumbled out of bed.

In the hallway she met Mary Kate, coming up to fetch her.

"You won't believe it, ma'am," the maid told her. "That poor dog has come back to us! Half starved, he was, and tied up by the look of it. That horrid Mr. Bracewell must have been keeping him someplace. It looks like the dog chewed through the rope and escaped. There's a raw place on his neck."

"Cerberus came back to us?" Emily was astonished. The dog had only been with them a few days.

Mary Kate nodded. "I'm thinking he came back looking for Master Robert," she said.

Tears filled Emily's eyes. "Cerberus made his way home. My Robert shall, too."

The trial of Norton Andrews seemed to be constantly delayed.

"The *Oregonian* is saying that Mr. Andrews killed George in a fit of insanity," Emily told Mr. Carmichael some days later. "They are making it seem that George was a pillar of the community, almost a saint."

"Would you rather have your nieces spend their lives with the shame of their father's wickedness?" he asked her gently. "Would you want them to know he was a traitor?"

She folded the paper. "I don't know. I hate the lies. If I had known the truth about Robert, I might have been able to save him. He would be here with me now. If I had had the courage to face the truth about Horace, I might have taken my son out of his father's influence."

She stared out into the garden, where early roses were starting to bloom. Carmichael didn't answer. He had no answers.

"What will happen to Mr. Andrews?" she asked.

"They are still debating whether to commit him or hang him," Carmichael said. "The opinion is leading toward the latter. If he's put away, the state will have to pay for his upkeep."

"It always comes down to money, doesn't it?" Emily said bitterly.

"Not always," he said. Honesty compelled him to add, "But very often."

"And Mr. King is still with us, richer than ever, since none of the profits he paid to George were ever reported. We can't even prove that he was part of the sale of guns."

"He won't last long in town," Carmichael promised. "How is your sister-in-law?"

"Fairy distracted, I'm afraid. She's taken to her bed." Emily grimaced. "Unfortunately, my experience of widowhood doesn't give me the understanding I should have. Sarah and Felicity are coping beautifully, though. Sarah is running the household like an adult. It's only for their sake that I'll keep silent on their father's true nature."

"They are nice girls. They'll need you to guide them in better ways than their mother can." Carmichael was watching how Emily's hands moved nervously in her lap.

"And what about you?" he dared to ask. "How are you?"

She gave him a sad smile. "I'll not be complete until I know that

Robert is safe. But I was talking with Etta Eliot the other day. She spent the late war in Missouri, you know. She reminded me how many mothers know for sure that their sons will never return to them, that they'll never marry or have children of their own. I think of the people like Ah Sung, who lost everything." She laughed. "It doesn't make me feel any better, just ashamed of myself for grieving so much."

"I wish I could help," he said.

It flashed through Emily's mind that what she wanted most was to curl up in his arms and cry until all the pain was gone. However . . .

"You've done so much already," she said. "I don't know how to begin to thank you."

"I can think of one way," he stood.

Emily waited, fearful and hopeful at the same time.

"Would you do me the honor of . . ." He paused. "Allowing me the pleasure of walking you home from church next Sunday?"

Emily caught the laughter in his eyes. She smiled and held out her hand.

"I shall be looking forward to it," she said. "By the way, I don't mind that you aren't a Methodist."

It was his turn to blush.

The day after Easter, Emily was out in the garden, enjoying the riot of flowers before the rain started again. It was amazing what had suddenly appeared in beds she had thought were nothing but mud: bright jonquils, shy lily of the valley, gaudy tulips. All these had been hiding through the winter, just waiting to bloom.

Emily knew exactly how they felt.

She was spinning daydreams in the air when Mary Kate came out to announce a visitor.

"It's a stranger," she told her. "Says he has a letter for you."

"For me? How odd. Ask him to come back here."

The man Mary Kate brought back seemed vaguely familiar. He was tall and lean with blond hair bleached almost white by the sun and skin weathered by the elements.

"Mrs. Stratton," he said. "My name is Alex Peterson. I have a letter for you from your son."

Emily swayed as if she might fall. Robert! Wordlessly, she held out her hand. He gave it to her. She stared at it in disbelief. But there it was, her name and address on the envelope in Robert's schoolboy scrawl.

"Did you see him?" she asked. "Where? When? How did he look? Is he all right? Come, sit down and tell me everything."

"There's not much to tell, ma'am." Peterson sat next to her on the garden bench. "I met him in Hong Kong about three weeks ago. His ship had just arrived, and he was looking for someone going back to San Francisco who would post a letter for him."

"And he was in good health," Emily prodded.

"As far as I know." Alex turned shy. "He was in high spirits when we met, it being a tavern and he having just come ashore." Hastily, he added, "He seemed in fine health, ma'am."

"I see." Emily couldn't take her eyes from the letter. "Do you mind?" she asked Alex.

"Of course not." He took the glass of lemonade Mary Kate brought out to him.

Tenderly, Emily slid the letter out of the envelope.

It was in Chinese.

"Dearest honorable mother," he began.

I know you must be frantic for word from me, but this is the first time they let me off the ship. I didn't join the crew willingly, but I'd spent enough time sailing with father to make myself useful. When the captain learned I could read and write Chinese as well as English I went to the head of the class. I'm staying on for a while to work for a shipping company here and then I'm going back to Shanghai before I return home to you. Here is an address to write me, only send it to Robert Saunders. Father has quite a reputation among sailors and it's not one I wish to answer for.

I've learned a lot these past few weeks. I'm so sorry for the things I did, many of which you know nothing about. Please forgive me. I'm going to make as much of it right as I can.

One thing I must tell you. I was going to do it the night they took me away. I shouldn't have stopped at the Hellhole first. When I was looking up the property we owned, I discovered that Uncle George is not to be

trusted. Promise me that you won't let him handle any financial matters.
I'll explain everything when I see you again.

With all my love, your son, Robert

Emily sat looking at it for a long time. Alex sat patiently beside her. Suddenly, she remembered where she had seen his face before: on a faded tintype carried by a worried and despairing woman.

"Alex, have you been home, yet?" she asked.

"No, ma'am. I came here first."

"Then you hurry there at once, young man. Your mother is waiting for you."

AUTHOR'S NOTE

The Shanghai Tunnels really exist under the streets of downtown Portland. Many of them are boarded up or have been destroyed in civic
renovations, but a number have been found and can be toured. Even though
I grew up in Portland, I knew nothing about them or about the seamier side
of city history until a few years ago. I thought it was time I took a break
from European archives and learned more of the history of my own back-
yard.

Most of the people and places in this book really existed. Some of
them I found in census records and city directories or old newspapers. Others have left records behind: letters, date books, diaries, and lawsuits. Very
few of them became famous, even in town, and so I have created personalities for them. Of the ones about whom I have more information, I have
tried to reflect the personalities they showed in their work. My absolute
favorite people are Unitarian minister Thomas Lamb Eliot and his wife,
Henrietta Mack Eliot. They were a moving force behind almost every phil-
anthropic establishment in Portland for more than fifty years. Even more,
they seemed to have shared a lifetime of love, adventure, and humor. They
deserve to be better known.

The treatment of Chinese immigrants on the West Coast is well documented. Many, including the Chinese themselves, spoke out against repressive laws and persecution. As of 1868, little headway had been made.

Emily's story is, of course, complete fiction, but the world she lived in is as close to real as I could make it. I hope you enjoy exploring it.